USA TODAY bestselling author **Natalie Anderson** writes emotional contemporary romance full of sparkling banter, sizzling heat and uplifting endings—perfect for readers who love to escape with empowered heroines and arrogant alphas who are too sexy for their own good. When not writing, you'll find her wrangling her four children, three cats, two goldfish and one dog…and snuggled in a heap on the sofa with her husband at the end of the day. Follow her at natalie-anderson.com.

Clare Connelly was raised in small-town Australia among a family of avid readers. She spent much of her childhood up a tree, Mills & Boon book in hand. Clare is married to her own real-life hero, and they live in a bungalow near the sea with their two children. She is frequently found staring into space—a surefire sign that she's in the world of her characters. She has a penchant for French food and ice-cold champagne, and Mills & Boon novels continue to be her favourite ever books. Writing for Modern is a long-held dream. Clare can be contacted via clareconnelly.com or at her Facebook page.

IMPOSSIBLE HEIR FOR THE KING

NATALIE ANDERSON

THE BOSS'S FORBIDDEN ASSISTANT

CLARE CONNELLY

MILLS & BOON

First published in Great Britain 2023
by Mills & Boon, an imprint of HarperCollins*Publishers* Ltd,
1 London Bridge Street, London, SE1 9GF

www.harpercollins.co.uk

HarperCollins*Publishers*, Macken House, 39/40 Mayor Street Upper,
Dublin 1, D01 C9W8, Ireland

Impossible Heir for the King © 2023 Natalie Anderson

The Boss's Forbidden Assistant © 2023 Clare Connelly

ISBN: 978-0-263-30685-9

IMPOSSIBLE HEIR FOR THE KING

NATALIE ANDERSON

MILLS & BOON

For the incomparable Louise—
we might have polar opposite processes,
but what giggles, support and inspiration we do share!
I cannot thank you enough.
Here's to all the joy.

PROLOGUE

'How was it possible for such a mistake to be made?' Niko Ture, King of the North Pacific nation of Piri-nu, stared at his most trusted soldier waiting for an explanation he knew could never be satisfactory. 'The level of incompetence is beyond comprehension.'

'Agreed,' Captain Pax Williams answered.

Niko—far more emotional—reeled as a raft of possible appalling consequences struck him. 'Was it an accident or was this deliberate?'

'The investigation is underway. I only found out through a security contact at the clinic who spotted the anomaly.' Pax bent his head. 'But—'

'We need to bring that woman here now,' Niko interrupted sharply. 'I need to know. Where is she? *Who* is she?'

Wordlessly his captain handed him a slim file. Irritated, Niko flicked it open and skimmed the sparse text, frowning at the highlighted points.

'I've tracked the vessel she's aboard,' Pax said. 'With your permission I'll lead an extraction team at 0400. We'll have her at the palace before dawn.'

Niko stared at the photo of the young woman, still thunderstruck at the information he'd just learned. Nondescript, frankly dull-looking in those loose black clothes, he ordinarily wouldn't give her a second glance. But this was no ordinary situation. Apparently—*impossibly*—this plain woman might be the mother of his unborn baby. 'I'm going with you.'

He knew Pax was about to argue and he lifted his head and stopped him with a look. 'I'm boarding that boat. You would too, if you were me.'

Pax stared back for a split second before inclining his head. 'Of course, sir.'

Niko looked again at the face of the young woman who was somehow caught up in a palace intrigue of epic proportions. Was she innocent or was she guilty?

There was only one way to find out.

CHAPTER ONE

MAIA FLYNN FASTENED the scarf holding her hair out of the way and sighed at the bane of her life. The coffee machine's regular temperamental performance issues were always worse when someone else had tried to use the thing. Late last night someone clearly had, given grounds were scattered over the galley. They'd left the resulting chaos for her to clean. Nothing new there except today that stale coffee smell was particularly nauseating. Yet it was a shame she didn't drink the stuff. She could do with a caffeine kick because even though she'd slept through the midnight coffee-making mess, once more she hadn't had enough sleep. She felt constantly tired from the pressure of too many guests, too much stress and no end in sight. She ought to be used to it, but in the last few weeks her baseline fatigue level had only worsened.

Ignoring her father's miserly 'not for the crew' rules, she poured a little glass of the premium pineapple juice reserved for their wealthy—invariably rude—guests. Then she pulled her favourite whittling knife from her pocket and the small wood block she'd been shaping in her limited spare seconds. She needed a moment of mindfulness before dealing with the destruction caused by the spilled coffee. But as she focused on the blade a muffled thud sounded from an upper deck. She paused warily. The guests shouldn't wake for a couple of hours yet, which meant it might be her father, the captain of this 'luxury' yacht. Though generally he didn't surface this early either. Holding her breath, she listened intently but after a few seconds there was nothing more. She sipped some juice and turned back to the wood. This was her favourite part of the day—pre-dawn—when the sky gently lightened before the slow emergence of the sun. It mattered little that she could see it only from the small porthole in the galley. It was the only time she had to herself, it was peaceful and she always felt a hit of optimism—*today might be different*.

In reality she knew she faced a relentlessly long day prepping food for the guests and the crew. She rarely left the boat that had been her home her entire life and while she yearned to escape, it wasn't possible yet. Not when she had nowhere else to go, no money to get there with and no formal qualifications to 'prove' her skills and get another job. It wasn't like her bully of a father would ever give her a reference. He'd be too furious that she'd dared walk out. But she needed to find a solution soon both for her independence and her health. She wished she'd been able to consult the doctor when they were last on shore but her father had phoned in the middle of her appointment and she'd had to leave before getting the results of the few tests they'd been able to complete—

There it was again. Another sound out of place, so soft she almost didn't notice it. But a sixth sense struck, shooting sensation down her spine. She whirled to face the doorway, knocking the glass of juice as she did. She suspected it might be a still-drunk guest from last night coming for something to eat.

It wasn't.

For a split second she stared at him—stunned and ignoring the smash of the glass and splash of the juice at her feet. Tall, lean, clad entirely in black—from the close-fitting skullcap to the mask covering his mouth—he even had some kind of stuff smudged on his skin to obscure what little of his face remained visible. Horror hit. He looked like a mercenary. But for an infinite second his brown eyes bored into hers— as rich as the coffee grounds, only far warmer. They locked on her and a lightning strike of *something* hit.

She couldn't speak. Couldn't scream. Then she remembered what she held and lifted her knife, amazed her hand wasn't shaking.

'Don't. Don't be scared,' he whispered, holding his hands wide in surrender. He didn't move a step nearer. 'It's okay.'

It wasn't *okay*. But she froze, trying to understand why he was here, why he was hesitant—why he almost looked *worried*. Maia lifted her chin and pretended her little knife was so much more than it was. She'd get to her cabin. She'd lock the door and hide. They could take whatever they wanted then. For a second she even felt she had a chance because he, despite his size, seemed so oddly wary.

She stepped backwards. He still didn't move but his gaze was intent upon her. Emboldened, she moved faster but the spilled juice proved treacherous. Her foot slid out from beneath her and despite her sudden lurch she couldn't recover. She whacked her wrist on the bench as she flung out her arms to stop her fall. The knife clattered as it hit the floor. But *she* didn't. Because in the swiftest move she'd ever seen a man make he caught her.

'Easy, *easy*. I've got you.' He lifted her effortlessly. Lifted her close. So close.

She grabbed hold of him—tightly—instinctively relieved she'd not fallen. Instinctively reaching for *strength*. His hands gently, swiftly moved over her back, both pressing her into his chest and checking she was still all in one piece. It was oddly—*crazily*—comforting.

'Okay?' he muttered.

She could smell the sea, mixed with something spiced—something her senses decided was *interesting*. She closed her eyes and tried not to breathe—not to notice the appalling, raw appeal of him as he pulled her more tightly against him. This was the closest she'd been to another human being in a very long time and it was freaking her out in all *kinds* of ways. Struggling to process what was happening, she froze when she heard a low murmur from behind her and then felt an answering vibration in his chest. He was talking to someone else and she was too stunned to even understand the words. But she understood that there was more than one of them. Which meant this was a raid. Probably for the cash they suspected they carried on board. The perils of a gambling cruise alone in the northern Pacific Ocean. Her father had a gun and wasn't afraid to use it, but somehow they'd snuck aboard unseen. Which meant they had *skills*.

Panic finally fired adrenalin through her. She had to fight for her life. She wriggled and managed to lift her head and stare up into his eyes.

'No,' she muttered and drew breath to scream.

But he was swift again. He clamped his hand over her mouth. She twisted her chin and locked her teeth on the flesh she found. She bit. Hard.

He flinched but didn't release her. He merely pulled her back into his body.

'Please, don't,' that deep voice roughly whispered into her ear. 'I'm not here to hurt you, Maia. I'm so sorry, but there's no choice. We're leaving. Now.'

He knew her name?

She was so shocked that her body slackened—releasing her jaw she collapsed against him so completely that he had to widen his stance to stop them stumbling. Now both his arms were around her again and it felt so shockingly secure that she didn't even think to scream. She sensed rapid movement around her. In seconds someone from behind her taped something over her mouth and dropped a dark cloth over her head, blackening everything while the first man still held her. She felt him draw a deep breath and mentally willed herself to become a dead weight that would be impossible to lift. Only he hoisted her in his arms like she weighed little more than a small seashell. He didn't toss her over his shoulder in the classic firefighters hold but cradled her against his chest— as if she were something delicate and precious. It should be cumbersome yet they were moving. Fast. Up the stairs and outside—she felt the lightest breeze before they moved down again almost immediately. They were leaving the boat. He held her tighter still as the world lurched and heaven help her, she curled frightened fingers into his top and burrowed her head against him, seeking the stability she sensed within him.

After what felt like an age of chaotic movement, he finally sat while still cocooning her in his arms. He rested one arm heavily over her legs while the other was a steel band clamping her against his chest. In the silence she heard his heartbeat steadying and his calm, determined breathing. He was measuring his own response. Suddenly she felt oddly *safe*.

She'd lost it mentally, surely. She had her mouth covered and was blindfolded. She had no idea who he was or where he was taking her. To have Stockholm syndrome in less than twenty seconds had to be some kind of record. Just because he smelt good and had meltingly deep brown eyes, solid, warm muscles and had offered an apologetic whisper… Her suddenly sensual response was dreadfully inappropriate. She forced herself to focus beyond her personal sensations.

She heard the quiet splashes of an oar in the water. Yes,

there was definitely more than one of them and she was definitely in danger. She shivered, shrinking inwardly.

His arms tightened fractionally. 'I promise I'm not going to hurt you, Maia.'

That really was a hint of regret in that rough whisper.

Who was he? She didn't recognise his voice. She didn't think he was ex-crew or a previous guest. What did he want with her?

This had been perfectly planned and executed. But why? She didn't think anyone much knew who she even was. So, either there'd been some kind of mistake or she'd been cased as an easy target for trafficking. Yet that wasn't an issue in these parts. Maybe she was to be the first.

Sure, she already was a slave of a sort for her father but she wasn't in physical danger with him—that threat was more emotional. But *this* man? She grew even more hyper-aware of his hard-packed muscles and the all-encapsulating size of him and that faint scent sea-spray and mouth-watering spice. That sensuality resurged. She shrank further in on herself to try to stop it. And all that resulted from her doing that was that he held her closer still as if he were wordlessly wrapping comfort around her. And then he offered the words too—as if he could read her mind.

'You're safe,' he said huskily. 'I promise you're safe.'

She didn't know how long it was before he lifted her too easily again. She was only a few inches shy of six feet—taller than many men so this was a weird feeling of weightlessness and a complete loss of control. There was only a moment of rocking, uncertain movement before he sat again, keeping her locked in his arms the entire time. She heard an engine roar to life and knew she was now aboard a bigger boat. Sure enough, she could feel the hull of the speedboat smacking against the water as it raced forwards. Wind penetrated the hood on her head. The man who held her remained utterly silent this time.

Then whispers. Orders. Movement around her. She was carried again—heard not just his footsteps but several people's. Car doors. Motion at speed. Still silence.

She briefly felt the sun on her arms before it went cold. Then they'd entered a building. Maia was exhausted but he'd held her all this time—surely he must be exhausted too? Then she heard only his footsteps. He set her down on something soft and finally released her. She stiffened—stupidly scared by losing the reassurance of his embrace. What was going to happen now?

'Wait here, Maia.'

His footsteps receded. A door closed.

Her hands were free but Maia remained frozen, desperately listening to determine if she was truly alone. At last, she lifted the hood from her head and blinked rapidly, adjusting her eyes to the bright light of day. She winced as she peeled the tape from her mouth and then stared, shocked. This was no grimy basement. There were no chains or ropes or anything of nightmarish horror awaiting her. This room was resplendent. She wasn't on a bed but a plush sofa and other sumptuous lounge seats faced her. Was this some fancy hotel?

I'm not going to hurt you, Maia.

That rough promise rang in her ears but she'd been afraid to believe it. But this room threw her off balance. Ornate wooden carvings decorated the doorways—she knew the skill with which they'd been carved and while the furniture she sat on was modern and comfortable, there were antiques in the corners and art on the walls that weren't hotel standard. They were national gallery–worthy. A film of sweat slicked across her skin. She was so far out of her league. There were three doors she could try but she figured they were probably

locked or guarded or both. She edged towards the wide window to see what she could from there instead.

Maia was used to pristine views of Pacific beauty. It was
the clues on the land that made her jaw drop and there was
one very big clue right in the middle of the immaculate gardens below her. A tall pole with the flag of Piri-nu barely
fluttering in the still warmth.

The wealthy nation was situated in the Pacific Ocean between Hawai'i and Marquesas. They were the islands Maia
would most likely call home although she really considered
herself to be stateless—she wasn't sure she even had a birth
certificate. But her father liked to work near Piri-nu because
of the extreme wealth of its visitors. The nation was prosperous not just from agriculture, nor tourism because of its natural beauty, but also as an aerospace technology hub. One of
the world's largest telescopes was situated here together with
a massive space rocket launch infrastructure that attracted
billionaires and geniuses from around the world.

Any remaining fear faded in the face of pure confusion.
This was laughable. Why would anyone want to kidnap *her*
and bring her to the palace of the playboy king?

CHAPTER TWO

MAIA HEARD VOICES at one of the doors and backed against the window to keep as far as possible from whoever was about to walk in. Her pulse lifted as the door opened. Would it be her captor with the muscles and salty-spice scent?

The man who walked in was powerful, self-assured, stunning. Her hard-pumping heart made blood pound in her ears. He was as tall. He was as strong. But this was the king— Niko Ture himself!

As he closed the door she couldn't stop herself staring, snared in the deep, dark, coffee-coloured eyes that gleamed like the water at sunset. Even though she didn't have a smart phone she'd seen his image often enough on the old television in the crew room where they sometimes watched the news so she recognised those sculpted features now—the angular jaw, the distinctive high cheekbones. The stunning symmetry of his bone structure almost made her swallow her tongue. But she'd not been able to see the jaw of her kidnapper because of that mask. So she studied this man more intently—unable to quite believe the direction of her thoughts. He kept one hand in his trouser pocket, giving him a louche look, and that snow-white shirt was a touch too perfect, lovingly skimming that lean muscled chest. He didn't usually look this serious on that screen. He was usually smiling.

'Maia,' he said. 'I'm Niko, King of Piri-nu.'

'I'm aware,' she gritted.

Was she supposed to curtsey? Because that wasn't going to happen. Every muscle had gone into shock and she couldn't actually move a millimetre. The impossibly handsome, popular royal was her total opposite. Had *he* summoned her to be brought before him? Surely not. How would he have even *heard* of her? Her poor heart pumped even harder.

'You may call me Niko.'

Why would she call him by his first name? There was no reason for her to have that privilege.

He casually strolled closer with the assured, panther-like grace of a man well used to the effect he had on ordinary people. Especially women. And yes, that included her.

'I apologise for your unexpected journey,' he added smoothly. 'I understand it was a little rough.'

He 'understood'? As he neared she could only stare like a stunned fool at his beauty. His face gleamed with vitality. Well, except for *one* patch of his skin just above his jaw which seemed slightly muddied. Maia blinked as her suspicions—now confirmed—stalled her breath. She breathed a little deeper and caught the slight scent—

The *arrogance*!

Her brain fuzzed. He *was* the one who'd pressed her so tightly to his body! He was the one who'd whispered those reassurances in her ear. He was the one who'd carried her so easily. But suddenly his looks didn't have the same 'stunned mullet' effect on her. Sure, she was growing hotter by the second but now it was anger, not latent lust. Did he think he could get away with anything if he suavely offered some minimal, meaningless apology?

Probably. No doubt he'd been doing it his whole life— doing whatever he wanted. But right now he was *lying* to her because he knew exactly how *unexpected* her journey had been. Exactly how rough. Because he'd been right there all along.

'You've not quite cleaned all your war paint off.' She bristled, pointing to a spot on her cheek, mirroring where the smear of black was still stuck on him.

His gaze sharpened and his mouth twitched as he leisurely lifted his hand and rubbed the mark away.

But Maia glared pointedly at the hand he'd kept in his pocket all this time. 'Did I break your skin with my bite or merely leave a bruise?'

'Did you know it was me all along or only just work it out now?' That smile broadened to genuine amusement. He wasn't at all ashamed that she'd caught him out.

Maia was stunned into stillness all over again. She shouldn't feel anything but outrage but her body decided to do its own thing. Her breasts tightened and her breathing shortened and she was shocked to realise the tension she now felt was fully sensual in nature. She obviously hadn't been around any attractive men recently, so her body had decided to flare up in front of the first one she saw. But it was unacceptable. This entire situation was unacceptable.

'It seems you need to practice your abduction skills,' she snapped.

'Perhaps I do.' He gave another flash of that unrepentant smile.

But this king had no need to abduct anyone. He was a wildly popular playboy who'd ascended to the throne five years ago after the death of his grandfather—the crown skipping a generation because of the tragic death of Niko's father when Niko was in his teens.

'Forgive me for being stunned that you've run out of suitable women to sleep with and must now resort to stealing perfect strangers from their homes in the middle of the night,' she said.

'I'll forgive you anything.' He lazily nodded. 'And you are indeed a perfect stranger. But the truth is I have no need to abduct women to sleep with me. That's not why you're here.'

Of course it wasn't.

Humiliation slithered from the cesspit of queasiness roiling in her lower belly and spread across her skin in a heated blaze. He probably wanted her to be a maid—to make his coffee and fresh pastry and bring it to him and his lover-of-the-day in bed.

But that didn't explain why'd he brought her here under the cover of darkness. Why he'd not just asked her, nor told anyone else on the boat his intentions. But maybe he'd ensured no one had seen her journey and her arrival at the palace because she wasn't *worthy* to be seen here. She glanced down, deeply aware of her dishevelment. Shame sloshed. She felt hot and clumsy and ugly in her worn galley clothing. She was nothing like the beautiful women Niko was always photographed with when he was abroad. And she was not Piri-nu society worthy.

She was the illegitimate child of a waitress and a gambler. Her mother had run off before Maia had turned four, unable to fight her father's controlling nature anymore. Unfortunately, she'd left with a man who'd turned out to be even more controlling and he'd not wanted another man's child. He'd made her mother cut contact with Maia completely. Most of the time Maia didn't think about it, but right now she was alone and afraid. And her father would never try to rescue her from this, he'd be far more likely to try to extract something for himself. Such as money.

So she would face this obvious mistake down and she would survive all by herself. She was good at that.

'Why *am* I here?' Maia pushed through the mortification and asked.

His smile had faded and his razor-like cheekbones made him look starkly sombre. 'Because I'm afraid you might be pregnant with my baby.'

She stared at him, nonplussed. 'You *what*?'

'I think you're pregnant. With my child.'

The man was mad. Certifiable. Maia laughed. Except it veered dangerously close to hysterics in a nanosecond. She gasped, biting the emotion back. She refused to fall apart in front of *anyone* and certainly not this entitled, arrogant piece of work.

'You know, it doesn't surprise me that you can't recall who you've slept with,' she said, masking fear with sarcastic fury. 'I understand there are multitudes of women who've had the dubious honour of being in your bed but *I* am not one of them and I never will be.'

'I'm aware that we haven't slept together.' He regarded her steadily, apparently unmoved by her snark about his hyperactive sex life. 'And I agree that such an event is extremely unlikely.'

She paused, cut by his quick, harsh reply. But of course it was true. He'd never want to sleep with her when he had his pick...

She glanced again at her black capri pants and plain T-shirt, work-stained and worn. Usually she didn't serve the clients. Her father preferred his nubile stewards do that. Maia remained out of sight and she liked it that way—or at least in that particular environment she did. She plaited her hair, coiled it into a bun and secured a scarf over the top. It was hot in the galley and the last thing she wanted was a loose strand falling into her food. But she'd never felt as unattractive as she did this second. No make-up. No pretty nails. Her style was best summed up as brutal utilitarianism. By necessity, not choice. Her father didn't think she needed a clothing allowance and as she rarely left the boat she didn't need anything that was too delicate to work in.

King Niko was watching her intently. 'Eleven weeks ago you went to the Coral Shore Women's Clinic. You were a walk-in who benefitted from a last-minute cancellation.'

Maia watched seriousness mute the gleam of his brown eyes.

'You were there because you had some personal concerns but you didn't get the chance to talk through them with the doctor,' he said. 'Instead you had an initial physical examination with a nurse practitioner. Or you thought that's what was happening. A routine smear test of some sort.'

'How do you know this?' She was beyond humiliated that the king knew such private details about her.

'But after that physical, the clinician left the room and for some reason you didn't stay to see the doctor. You left, telling the receptionist you couldn't wait any longer. Your boat left port only a half hour later and you've not returned to land since.'

Her heart raced. 'I live on board my father's charter vessel. I'm part of the crew.'

'Is the rest of the crew unpaid as well?'

The earth rolled beneath her feet. How did he know *that*? *Why* did he know that? And how could he possibly think she might be *pregnant*?

She felt the walls closing in as he advanced upon her. Was that a flicker of regret in his eyes? If so, it was swiftly obliterated by steely determination and he didn't stop talking. He didn't stop saying this crazy stuff in that too clinical tone as he stepped too close for her comfort.

'What you didn't know was that there had been a miscommunication within the medical centre staff. The clinician who entered your room wasn't aware the other appointment had been cancelled. That appointment was for an insemination. You were wearing a mask and you are not dissimilar in appearance to the woman who'd been meant to be there.'

'Not dissimilar?' Maia's heart lodged in her throat. 'An insemination?' He couldn't possibly mean what... He couldn't possibly be serious. 'Why would they have a sample of your...' She hesitated.

She might be inexperienced but she'd grown up surrounded by salty seafarers, many of whom called elements by their most base name possible. But not, perhaps, in front of a king.

'Traditionally a prince couldn't be proclaimed the immediate heir without first proving his virility,' he said. 'By providing the *next* heir. This was to preserve the lineage and keep the crown within the family. Usually this wasn't a problem as any heir was generally married and had procreated long before the elder king passed on. But I was pretty young when I became crown prince and had no intention of marrying and fathering a child at that point in my life. Fortunately I was able to prove my virility by more modern means.'

She was so appalled any decision to mind her mouth was forgotten. 'You mean they studied your spunk like you're a stallion or something?'

His eyebrows shot up. 'You're asking if they treated me literally like a stud? Then yes, that's exactly what happened.'

She was both appalled and fascinated. What a weird world the man lived in. 'But all of that must have been ages ago.'

She didn't know exactly when his father had died, only that it had been sudden. A second tragedy since his mother had died in an accident a couple of years before. 'Why would they have kept that sample?'

'Apparently, it was considered too precious and they wouldn't dream of just discarding it.'

'As if it was some sort of sacred artefact?' She gaped, her mind boggled.

He suddenly laughed. 'You disagree with that assessment?'

But this was no time to be laughing. And he 'discarded' it all the time, did he not? With all those stars and models and socialites that he seduced when he was overseas. 'You didn't know they'd kept it?'

As his smile faded Maia tried to understand the outrageous complexity of what he'd told her. An awful thought stuck her. Had he a partner that no one knew anything about? Was he trying for a child with someone who would be feeling so hurt and betrayed right now? Yet why would that be necessary—wouldn't they just try for a baby the usual way? Unless there were problems, which just made everything worse. And the man wasn't even engaged to anyone—or was he? And was she really having all kinds of *wrong* reactions to someone else's lover?

'How was it possible for such a mistake to be made?' She asked desperately, trying not to consider the implications of what he'd said.

'My question exactly.'

'*Why* would they have taken your sample? It's—'

'Being investigated and those found responsible will feel the consequences,' he interrupted stiffly. 'What has occurred is unforgivable. I can only apologise that you've been caught up in it.'

'But why had they decided to use it?' She frowned. 'Do you think it was deliberate?'

'That's not your concern. Rest assured there was only the one sample so this can never happen again, but we must deal with the situation before us now.' The stark expression in his eyes sent a shaft of foreboding through her. 'I brought you here to do a pregnancy test so we can be sure this error hasn't resulted in a more permanent complication,' he said grimly.

Maia didn't move. She was unable to believe that what she'd

thought was a routine smear test had actually been a syringe full of the king's semen. And now she might… She might…

No. It was beyond mortifying that she'd not even *known* what that clinician had actually been doing. But it had been her first ever smear test and she'd not exactly been watching. She'd been so embarrassed to be exposed like that to someone she didn't know she'd stared the other way. She'd not asked the woman any questions because she'd been too shy. She'd been building up the courage to do that with the doctor. But when the woman had left the room Maia's father had called to demand she return to the boat immediately as they'd had an unexpected booking. He'd been furious she'd left in the first place. She'd fled—assuming she'd get notified of any abnormal results. But she certainly hadn't expected something like *this*.

'It's not possible,' she muttered. Surely she would know? But she hadn't known *anything*. She was more than naive, she was ignorant and never had it hurt more that her mother had abandoned her. She'd never had the sex talk. She'd never been told anything—she'd had to figure it out herself and frankly, her sporadic internet searches had been somewhat unreliable. 'There's no way I would have gotten pregnant from that…'

'It is very, very unlikely, but it *is* possible,' Niko said. 'So we simply need to rule it out. Get that negative test and I'll ensure you're back on your boat within the hour.'

She went very still. 'But if it isn't negative…?'

There was a brief hesitation before he brought back that beautiful smile. 'If that happens, we'll work that out then. But it is unlikely.'

But Maia wasn't overly reassured because now she thought about the fatigue that had been bothering her the last few weeks. The stench of the coffee grounds. The irregularity of her monthly cycle was nothing new but what if…? And she'd thought the slight tightness of her trousers was from sampling too many of her pastries recently. Because she'd craved the croissants more and more. Just plain. And what about the unusual bout of seasickness she'd experienced only last week when she was more likely to get land-sick than seasick?

She felt terribly ill right now.

'I have a doctor waiting,' Niko added firmly. 'You simply need to provide a sample.'

She stared at him blankly.

'You'll understand that this is of the utmost concern. I am the *king*, Maia.'

She heard the edge as he underlined that word. His power. And he assumed she was his subject, didn't he? But she was Maia Flynn and she lived beyond the borders of anyone's world—half shadowed, not participating wholly anywhere. They skated into international waters while her father ran his not-quite-legal business dealings and high-stakes gambling cruises.

Maia had become skilled to secure her own safety—learning to cook from the grizzled French chef who'd been her best friend and better guardian to her than any other. But in doing so she'd cemented her own imprisonment because her father hadn't allowed her to leave the boat since. She created the things his clients liked for free. Chef Stefan had lost his job and she still felt guilty for being the reason when he'd only ever been kind to her.

'There's a restroom through that door,' Niko added crisply. 'Everything you need is in there.'

She had no choice to comply. And there was far more than she needed in the bathroom—it was full of unopened luxury toiletries that would delight even the most demanding guest. The lone medical sample container on the counter was incongruous. And terrifying. When she emerged a few minutes later an impassive man wearing a white coat was waiting for her.

Awkwardly she gave him the container and he immediately fussed over a small side table where King Niko now stood.

The doctor turned to explain the process. 'Two lines will appear on a positive result—'

'Doctor, please leave us.' Niko abruptly dismissed him.

Maia turned. The beautiful man now looked every inch the ruthless mercenary who'd kidnapped her in the first place. His wild displeasure was menacing.

She darted a glance behind him and saw the white plastic stick on the table. Lines had already appeared in that little window. *Two* lines. Devastation barrelled into her. She was pregnant.

'It can't be right,' she mumbled hopelessly. 'It just *can't* be right.'

The doctor passed her and she thought she saw compassion briefly flicker in his face before he melted from the room.

'Amongst other things a DNA test will now have to be performed.'

She stared, all the more confused. '*Why?*'

'To ensure that the baby is mine, not some other man's.'

Her jaw dropped. For a long moment their gazes meshed. His eyes narrowed and she heard his sharp intake of breath. She made herself glance away, more humiliated than ever. She was horribly aware of heat scorching her whole body. There'd been no man. *Ever.* But some instinct warned her not to reveal that to him. She needed to act as if she had some sort of street cred. And she needed to scrape together some kind of control in this rapidly deteriorating situation.

'Of course,' she muttered belatedly. 'I will agree to that.'

Incredulity flared in his eyes at her reply. 'You will? I'm so glad.' He studied her for another moment. 'The doctor will do a full physical examination and talk with you. We need to ensure this is something you can safely manage.'

'Safely?'

'You should not suffer adversely because of this incident. Your health…'

She realised he had concerns because she'd gone to the doctor in the first place. 'It should be fine,' she mumbled, embarrassment burning her skin hotter still. 'It was just painful.'

'Sex?'

She gritted her teeth, her humiliation now total. 'No. My cycle. My periods. They're irregular and painful.'

'Oh, okay.' He frowned. 'Please be frank with the doctor. We will take every possible care of your health.'

Maia didn't know how to answer. It wasn't that she'd feared a pregnancy might be unsafe—she'd feared she might not get pregnant at all what with how irregular everything was. Yet now she was apparently pregnant and she hadn't slept with anyone!

He waited, clearly wanting something from her, but she didn't know what it was. His gaze on her intensified. 'I would like you to have this baby, Maia.'

The thought that she wouldn't hadn't even occurred to her. That reply came instantly to her lips. But she bit it back. She needed to understand more. While what he'd just said *sounded* conciliatory—a *request* not an order—she suspected that was somewhat foreign to him. Sweat slid down her spine. She was pregnant with a king's baby. What would he want from her? How did he see this moving? She needed to ascertain how far he would take his control and power over her. Because the *last* thing she wanted was for her life to be controlled by another man. She'd lived too long like that already. So she gestured around the room's palatial splendour. 'Do I really have a choice?'

His jaw tightened. 'If you don't wish to have a relationship with the child once they are born, that is your decision.'

The sweat slicked over her skin turned to ice in an instant. It was like she was suffering from the instant onset of a tropical fever—running hot one second but chilled to the bone the next. And now the world pitched beneath her feet. She reached out for something to balance. The worst sea swells were nothing on this sudden rockiness.

'Maia?' he snapped.

His arms were around her again and it was such a relief that she collapsed, leaning in and letting him take her weight.

'Maia?' A gentler question this time. More like the promise he'd made to her early this morning when she'd not known who he was.

She'd missed this feeling of being safe in his embrace. As if she'd found safe harbour. Yet it was madness because she knew it was a lie. The last thing she was here was *safe*. Anger surged—raw and unstoppable—and the words spilled before she could think to stop them.

'This child is *mine*. I am its mother and I will be raising it.'

Her mother had left her and she would never, ever do that to her own child. So she lifted her head and furiously flung her position in his face. 'You want this child, you get me too.'

'Fine,' he snapped right back at her. 'But if this child is mine then you get *me* too.'

He glared right into her eyes. Only inches apart that faint scent of the sea and that disturbingly good spice seduced her. She felt his biceps flex and the awful thing was that with his body pressed against hers she felt even more faint. All she wanted was to stay leaning against him. Heat surged, chasing off the chill that had weakened her only moments before. Everything slowed—her pulse, her breath, time itself. For a long, long moment she gazed back into those beautiful brown eyes, watching as his long lashes half lowered as his focus fell to her mouth. She felt the attention like it were touch. He was closer. Her lips tingled, parted. Deep in her belly she felt the drive to press her hips against his. Her nipples tightened and as she breathed she felt them rub oh so slightly against his hard chest. Desire ignited.

Kiss me.

She gasped, suddenly mortified that she might've muttered the shockingly inappropriate wish aloud.

He blinked, his expression shuttering. 'Are you okay now?'

'Yes,' she mumbled, desperately pushing herself away from him. 'I guess I don't have my land legs yet.'

Anything to excuse that mortifying moment of weakness. Anything to get away from him and be eternally grateful that she'd only said that in her head.

But he made sure she was entirely steady before releasing her.

As he walked to stare out the window, Maia gave herself a mental slap—*pull it together.*

Niko hadn't thought anything fanciful in that moment— he just hadn't wanted her to faint. His concern was wholly on her health and she was making a colossal fool of herself thinking she'd seen otherwise. But the tightness of his hold and the intensity of his gaze upon her had made her senses reel and there *had* been a moment in which he'd leaned closer, breaching polite distance into intimacy. She *hadn't* imagined it. But perhaps it was simply so normal for him he couldn't help himself. He was so practiced at seduction it was second nature and he didn't even realise he was doing it.

'We're in agreement, then,' he said, finally turning back to face her. 'You will stay here. We're forced together through circumstance.'

She hadn't said she would stay here. He had so much more power than she did and she knew too well what it was like to be at the mercy of someone not just bigger and stronger but with connections and money and all of the control. And they were only *forced* together because he was insisting on it.

'What was with the dawn raid?' she challenged him. 'Why couldn't you just phone ahead and then board like normal?'

'We weren't sure of your knowledge of the situation, plus your vessel has evaded authorities in the past,' he answered. 'We expected the operation to be very quick.'

She was an 'operation'. A problem, not a person. And what did he mean by her 'knowledge' of the situation? Had he thought she might be complicit in this catastrophe in some way? How could she have been?

'Obviously now things will change,' he added grimly. 'Your father will be informed of your whereabouts.'

'Don't tell him about the baby.' Agitated by the thought she stepped towards him. 'I don't want you to tell him.'

Her father would not be an ally. He would want to take what *he* could get from this. He wouldn't get it—but the shame of it would be too awful. She had to handle King Niko herself.

'Of course I won't if you don't wish me to,' Niko assured her calmly. 'Frankly I'd prefer that we keep this quiet while we ascertain paternity and then make the necessary arrangements.'

And just what were those necessary arrangements to be?

He watched her keenly. 'If the child is mine, then I am sure we can come to an agreement where you'll be better off than you have been until now.'

That soft, patronising assumption angered her. It wouldn't be an 'agreement' but an order. How could her life be better when she still had little choice in what she did? Now she had less chance of getting her freedom. And as for her poor child?

Bitterness flooded her, forcing a sarcastic snap. 'Wow, you make it sound as if I've won a lottery of some kind and I should be all "hashtag, grateful"!'

CHAPTER THREE

NIKO RUBBED HIS temple and tried to remind himself that the woman before him was still in a state of shock and he needed to be patient. But it was an unusually difficult task. Nobody, but nobody, spoke to him the way she had—repeatedly—in the five minutes since he'd walked into the room. That she'd challenged him about his sex life, her voice vibrating with judgement, had been enough to irritate him, but for her to be so clearly appalled by the generous assurance he was now trying to offer? It was unreasonable. This situation was bad enough without her creating unnecessary drama. It wasn't as if he were thrilled either. Despite being almost thirty he'd had zero intention of marrying any woman anytime soon. He'd have to eventually, but he'd not planned to for a decade more at least. Children would have been minimal. An heir and a spare at most. Having seen his parents' struggles a love match was utterly out of the question and so, as distasteful to him as it was, he'd been preparing for the lesser of two horrors—a passionless arrangement similar to that of his grandparents.

He'd intended to select someone able to handle the challenges of public life, someone who had the upbringing, education and experience to perform the job. Someone from a nearby nation perhaps, but one definitely from a similar level in society as him. That certainly wasn't some young

Cinderella who'd spent almost all of her twenty-three years below deck on her father's grimy illegal gambling boat. She was the worst possible option.

So yeah, he wanted to snap back at her and he swerved close to it. But he took a breath and saw how sallow and tired she looked. Like any cornered creature she was lashing out to defend herself. He'd seen Pax's bare bones report—she was virtually a slave for her own father, so he understood why she'd be prickly. He would rise above her aggravation. If he was the father of her baby, he would execute an understanding tolerable to them both. They wouldn't actually have to have much to do with each *other* at all in this.

A muscle in his eyelid twitched and he struggled to stand still. The urge to step forward and fold her into his arms again almost overpowered him. It was flat-out crazy. But she wasn't anything like he'd expected. He'd locked eyes on her just before dawn this morning and seen everything that *hadn't* been visible in the long-range-lens photo in Pax's file. She had midnight eyes, big beautiful orbs that were unfathomably deep and mysterious—the sort a man could lose himself in for aeons and honestly, he had. He'd lost sense of everything for a moment, his purpose—hell, his own name. He'd gazed endlessly, absorbing the height of her, the narrowness of her shoulders, the length of her neck, the fullness of her lips. All her features added up to a beauty that had shaken him. And those hypnotic eyes had simply tempted him.

Now he tried to suppress the empty ache but the contentment he'd felt while holding her for the duration of that journey had been *weird* and worse, he missed it. He'd refused to relinquish her, ignoring the querying looks from Pax. But she was his responsibility and he'd *felt* her fear. It had been imperative that he try to reassure her somehow, even slightly.

He had the desire to do that again now. Problem was that desire was being diluted by another even stronger one.

No. It was probably just the uncertainty of the situation pushing him to literally take charge of her. Basic instincts often generated physical actions, right? Like lust. He would ignore it. She needed reassurance only, not unbridled seduction.

'Perhaps you should be grateful,' he said quietly. 'After all, you might not have known the truth of your condition for some time and that could've brought complications for you. At the very least you'll now get the medical attention you need.'

It's your job to look after her. His father's words echoed in his mind and he tensed. He would not fail this time.

'And whether the child you carry is mine or not, I promise you'll continue to receive the care you need throughout this pregnancy and beyond.' He stepped closer, unable to resist that urge to be nearer, needing to impress upon her his uncompromising position. 'But let me also promise that *my* firstborn will be the heir to my throne, regardless of their gender. My firstborn will have everything that is rightfully theirs. *Everything.* Honour. Riches. Protection. And my name.'

Despite his distaste for marriage he would ensure the legitimacy of this child. Secrets and shame had destroyed too much of his family already. It was never happening again.

She swallowed. 'Your name?'

'We'll marry as soon as the paternity is confirmed.' He saw panic swoop into her eyes. 'In name only,' he added swiftly. 'While you're pregnant.'

'But then?' She stared at him in consternation. 'No king of Piri-nu has ever divorced.'

He hesitated. It was bitterly unfortunate and of course he

dreaded condemning someone to palace life for good but he had no choice.

His aunt Lani had been illegitimate—the firstborn offspring of his philandering grandfather. She'd been reared within the palace walls but her lineage not just unacknowledged, but hidden. She'd worked as a maid and had unknowingly served her own blood relatives. The devastation that had ensued when the truth came out was something Niko had never forgiven himself for. And he would never allow anything like it to happen again.

He would do better for this child. Maybe he would even allow them to make their own decision regarding claiming the crown eventually. Maia could have choices too. Initially they would be limited but beyond the birth, he would assist her however he could.

'There will be support and more freedom than you think,' he said.

She was pretty and with new clothes she might be stunning. And while she had zero society training, that could be provided. Except even with all that, Niko knew how hard someone could find palace life. Somehow he had to come up with something satisfactory. He just didn't know what it was yet.

Divorce would only be a last resort.

'Are you saying I have to marry you and finish growing your baby but then I'll be free to live my life however I please?' she pushed him.

'There will be certain limitations.'

'Such as?'

The defiance in her eyes set his teeth on edge. 'We're getting ahead of ourselves,' he gritted out, barely reining in his temper. 'Perhaps we need to wait for the paternity results before finalising our marriage details.'

She stared at him in horror all over again. 'How long will it take to get those?'

'I'll get the doctor. I believe he brought the necessary equipment.' He saw her flinch and felt a flash of compunction. 'You'll be okay, Maia. I promise you he is our best.'

He didn't return to the room with the doctor. Maia needed privacy and he needed time to think. But he paced right outside, oddly anxious as he waited for the examination to be completed. He needed to know she was well enough to withstand this pregnancy. He'd asked the doctor to make very sure of that. Because right now she didn't *look* it and she'd had that near fainting spell. But then he remembered the fight in her body when he'd grabbed her this morning—her lithe agility and defiance. She had spirit and strength when she needed it. And if she had proper support then they might get through this.

He whirled when the door opened. 'Everything okay?'

'I'm going to do an ultrasound scan to check the foetus,' the doctor said. 'I wondered if you would like to observe.'

Niko hesitated. When Pax had first come to him with concern in his face and told him about a possible mix-up at the medical centre, Niko had thought he was pranking him. It was the most preposterous thing he'd ever heard. He, like Maia, had laughed. It was a catalogue of coincidences impossible to believe.

Pax was tracking down information about who'd been scheduled for the insemination and how it was that his sample had been used. He didn't yet know if there were sinister implications but in all this he'd never believed that such a random procedure would have been successful. The doctor had added false reassurance too. After all, it would have had to have been the right time for Maia. Apparently it had been and he might just have to step up and become a father. The one thing he'd never wanted to do, alongside a woman he didn't know at all and who wasn't the right kind of woman destined to be his bride.

Unless, of course, she was already pregnant by another man and this baby wasn't *his* at all. Yet oddly, that prospect made him unaccountably angrier and yes, he realised he would like to observe the scan. He wanted to see Maia's face.

'Thank you.' He nodded.

Back in the lounge Maia was reclined on the sofa. Her trousers were loosened and tugged down only enough to reveal her belly. He averted his gaze from the paler skin and gentle curve. She'd turned her face away and didn't acknowledge his arrival. He suppressed the sudden urge to cup her cheek and gently turn her back to him. Her avoidance bothered him not because it was a blatant disregard of protocol, but because it felt more personal. He felt she disliked him. Oddly—because it really shouldn't matter—he disliked *that* realisation intensely.

He glanced down and saw she'd balled her hand into a fist. He saw the purpling patch on her wrist from when she'd hit it as she'd almost slipped in trying to get away from him. Shame licked his insides. Plus her lips were puffier and redder because of the tape they'd sealed across her mouth. He'd noticed it when she'd had that dizzy spell just before—that pout had been appallingly tempting. Regret filled him. Whether this was his baby or not, this woman needed better care.

He focused on the portable monitor as the doctor slid a wand over Maia's stomach. For a moment it was all grey swirls. Then it was there. A blob. Then identifiable parts— head, limbs, *life*. The heartbeat sounded like galloping ponies.

'That's fast.' He glanced at the doctor in concern. 'Is that—'

'Perfectly normal, Your Highness,' the doctor calmly replied without taking his assessing gaze from the screen. 'Everything is looking very well. The measurements look appropriate for the time of the original appointment and the foetus is developing well.'

So it was the right size, right stage of development to be *his*. He glanced back at Maia's face. She'd been looking at the screen as well and now she looked at him and he saw the truth in her eyes. This was *his* child. Even as she lifted her chin in slight defiance. He was suddenly certain there was no boyfriend. His possible bride was not promiscuous. Her disapproval of his sexual mores echoed in his ears. Yet he'd also seen the flare in her eyes when he'd held her close through that dizziness. And he'd felt her response. It hadn't been fear. It hadn't been distaste. It had been heat. Temptation curled. Niko Ture was used to being well regarded and if he had to win over his reluctant bride he knew one way to do it.

No. This wasn't about proving a point or about personal *pleasure*. No doubt that was what she expected of him and he was filled with the desire to behave contrary to her disapproving expectations. They were going to have to get along for a lifetime which meant instead of seducing her, he might have to make her his friend. But Niko had few true friends. He didn't trust many people and the likelihood of him trusting her?

He sighed. She would be a business partner at best. Ideally a distant acquaintance. The palace was large enough for them to reside in effectively separate households. But that didn't get around the fact that his people were going to demand much that she didn't yet understand.

What had happened at that clinic was a mistake, maybe. A miracle, definitely. It was the most appalling complication of his adult life.

He ushered the doctor out, speaking with him briefly in the

corridor to arrange a full debrief later. And to get something he needed now. When he returned she'd tidied her clothing and was awkwardly perched on the edge of the sofa. He drew up a small footstool and sat before her, smiling to himself when her eyes widened.

He squeezed ointment from the tube he'd gotten from the doctor.

'What are you doing?' she asked.

He held his hand out for her to put hers in. 'May I?'

Maia stared, confused by his gesture and intention and that soft smile. Confused because she'd just seen proof of a tiny life growing within her on that screen. Confused because she had no idea what she should do next. There was too much to process—that she was pregnant was truly a miracle she couldn't yet believe. For so long she'd secretly feared that would be impossible—not just because she'd thought she might never have her freedom to find a partner but that she might not have the physical capacity for pregnancy even if she did. But now there was absolute contrariness—amazement and incredulity and *wonder...*

All her weak body wanted was to tip back into this *stranger's* arms and cry—both scared tears and happy tears. But Maia never cried and she wasn't about to start now.

'Your wrist.' He nodded simply. 'It's bruised.'

'But you don't need to—'

'Please. It's herbal, it won't harm the baby.'

She was stunned he was thinking of the child's well-being so efficiently already. But as she stared, she absorbed his calmness and slowly that half smile compelled her. Suppressing her embarrassment she put her hand in his. She knew to him it meant nothing. He was used to touch. But *she* wasn't and it took everything in her not to shiver when he carefully clasped her hand.

He rubbed the ointment onto her wrist with soft strokes. Maia stared at his long fingers as he rhythmically soothed the grazed skin and she tensed, desperate not to tremble in response. He was more gentle than she'd ever have expected and the sensations stirring within her were too intimate.

'I'm sorry you were hurt,' he said huskily after a few moments. 'It was the last thing I wanted to happen.'

'That was my best knife,' she muttered awkwardly. 'But I can get it when I go back.'

He glanced up briefly before focusing on her wrist again. The starkness of this situation became clear.

Was she *ever* going to go back? Her lungs tightened. No more staying below deck on her feet for hours, making snacks for gambling guests. But she would be stuck *here* instead. With this man. As his bride.

His touch suddenly sizzled and she swiftly pulled her hand free.

He sat still, silent, apparently all understanding and patience.

She had to do better. Thinking quickly, she quelled the tremble in her hands enough to lift the uncapped tube he'd placed beside her on the sofa and took a dab of ointment. Then she held her hand out for his.

She heard him catch his breath but she didn't lift her gaze to meet his eyes. She had no hope of compelling him with a look the way he had her. If she looked at him she would lose courage and she needed to show her equality to him in this. Here and now at least.

His hesitation was momentary before he put his hand in hers. It was so much bigger and she rested it in her lap. She lightly stroked the fleshy base of his thumb, smearing the fresh-smelling ointment over the part where her teeth had left a faint mark.

'I meant to hurt you,' she admitted softly.

'I know,' he said. 'I don't blame you. I would have done the same.'

She stared at the strong hand that dwarfed both of hers, seeing the smooth copper tone of his skin, the neatly trimmed nails. It was beautiful hand—like the rest of him. And it was heavy. It held such power.

'I understand why you did what you did.' She finally glanced up and braved those brown eyes that saw so much. 'Still think you could have just called ahead.'

'Would that really have been wise?'

She couldn't stand the hint of sympathy in his expression. He thought he knew things about her. But he knew nothing.

His hand was warm on her lap. But this tenderness wasn't real and the instinct to reject its blossoming facade burned. But before she could say anything more he lifted his fingers and touched her lower lip ever so gently, tripling the sense of intimacy.

'I'm sorry about this too,' he muttered.

Her lips throbbed at his touch and sent a searing shot of desire all the way to her belly. But she kept looking into his eyes. 'You silenced me.'

'Yes.' His hand dropped. 'I had no choice.'

No choice but to take away *her* choices. And he was going to do it again, wasn't he? Sorry or not, he was still going to do it.

'There are always choices,' she argued. 'Can't you just make a proclamation of some kind? To make the baby your heir without us having to... You're the *king*.'

Didn't he have all the power?

'And not even a king can change some things,' he said. 'There can be no question of my child's validity. Their rights. What's happened is not this baby's fault and they'll not suffer anything adverse because of it. I'll do whatever it takes to protect them from any possible harm.'

Would he protect them even from their own mother if he considered her to be a threat? Maia felt his conviction and understood. She could be within his circle. Or she could be on the outside. That was the only 'choice' that was hers. He held all the cards. The child would be born here and be the new heir to Piri-nu.

But Maia had protective instincts of her own. This was a child she'd not been sure she'd ever be able to have. So she too would do whatever was required to protect her or him from any possible harm.

Being separated from a mother caused harm.

Having one's life completely controlled caused harm.

So she needed to buy time to think everything through. To make her own plans.

'Well.' She attempted a small, pacifying smile. 'I suppose we need to wait for the results of the paternity test before making all the decisions anyway.'

He blinked.

'I'd like to rest now,' she added. 'I'm very tired.'

'Of course.' But he looked at her searchingly for a moment. 'Would you like a tray sent up? Some pineapple juice perhaps?'

She'd spilled her juice when he'd appeared. He'd remembered the sort. Which meant he noticed things. Small things. Maybe *all* things. Which made her even more wary. If she'd thought it impossible to escape her father, Niko would be even harder.

'No, thank you,' she muttered.

'Well, if you think of anything all you have to do is push this button and someone will come to attend to you.' He pointed out the small call button.

'It's like a five-star hotel,' she joked wanly. 'I can order room service.'

'You can order anything you want.'

Anything. She heard a hint of huskiness and something rippled deep inside. But she refused to let her mind wander into that dangerous territory and reminded herself that she was the one usually answering such summonses—waking up to make fresh brioche for roaringly drunk, starving guests at two in the morning. Now she could make someone else do that for her if she wished. It was the last thing she'd do.

'Anything except my freedom,' she said softly.

'Yes.' He nodded. 'Except that.'

She regarded him sombrely. 'Thank you for your generosity.'

She meant it. But her freedom—and that of her baby—was the one thing she was going to fight for.

CHAPTER FOUR

IT WAS A relief when he left. Her brain—annoyingly sluggish in his presence—came back online. She didn't have time to indulge in self-pity—she had her escape to plan. She needed every ounce of energy to *think*. Because no way was she marrying that man. Not *any* man. Well, not for the next five years at least. She'd dreamed of her freedom for too long. She wanted to explore, to study, to carve out a career that she chose for *herself*.

She wasn't being tied to a future held within someone else's control. And a king was used to being in complete control of his whole world. He said he wanted her to have choices but that was a polite platitude. She knew exactly what it was like to live with a dictator and she wasn't about to swap one for another.

But she was pregnant. She'd just *seen* that baby in black and white on the screen. It was impossible to believe. But it was also *amazing*.

And of course the child should know its world, its heritage, its father. But Maia didn't need to *marry* him in order for that to happen. Niko's view was insanely old-fashioned and of course understandable because he was king. But he needed to learn he couldn't control her. She wasn't going to agree to everything he decreed the second he spoke. And he expected that.

If she didn't stand up to him, if she didn't get some strength here, she would be in a worse position than ever before. So she needed to make her stand now. She needed to get space and time so he understood that she too would have some power in her position.

Then there was the mortifying fact she was sexually attracted to him. Had discovering she was carrying his baby heightened her awareness of his sensuality? Was it some basic instinct to want him—some gut drive to protect the unexpected child within her?

Except it had happened in that first moment when she'd turned and seen him standing there. He'd been completely unrecognisable yet she'd felt an instant passion tug within—

Surely it wasn't that. Surely she was mistaking the adrenalin surge of fear for attraction. She was confused, that was all.

But there'd been so many moments since then. Every time he got within two feet of her she felt her arousal rising. It was awful and she needed to get a grip.

She moved. One door led to the bathroom, one to the corridor, but she'd yet to investigate that third. She opened it and glanced in. The bed was the first thing she saw. Clad in luxuriously soft-looking white linen, it was huge. She quickly shut the door again, her heart thumping. She'd never slept on a bed like that. She'd never *seen* a bed like that. And it was most definitely big enough for two. Hell, for three or four or more…was that what he was used to? Heat washed over her face.

She scurried back to the sofa and curled up on it, trying to figure out what she could do. Trying to figure out how on earth any of this could have happened. Had someone planned to impregnate themselves with him as the father? The ramifications were appalling—that someone might want to use that against him was frightening because he was a powerful man. It didn't seem likely anyone would be so bold. But he was right, that part wasn't her problem. It was his. She had enough to deal with. The air was still scented with that herbal ointment and it was surprisingly soothing. As she sat—failing to formulate any kind of plan at all—the last of that adrenalin drained out and the fatigue that had plagued her these last few weeks hit again. At least now she knew the reason for it. Her eyelids felt heavy. She closed them. She was not going to cry. Not ever.

She had no idea what time it was when she woke. Truthfully she could sleep hours longer but that wasn't an option. She had work to do. She needed to go on a reconnaissance mission and figure out whether any escape was even remotely possible. But she had some hope because Piri-nu was prosperous and its population was content and proud of its king. She'd never known of any civil unrest here, so fingers crossed palace security wasn't as tight as it might be in other places. Maybe those guards might be a little complacent. Only then she remembered the efficiency with which they'd extracted her from her father's boat. Still, she had to try. She opened the door that Niko had used. She quickly walked the length of the wide corridor but when she turned the corner she encountered a severe-looking guard coming her way. She froze. He was beef-cake muscles enormous and scary and the aviator sunglasses didn't hide the fact he was glaring at her and could probably see straight through to all her guilty plans.

'Is there something you need, ma'am?' he asked.

She hesitated, thrown by being called ma'am. 'Is it okay if I go for a short walk in the gardens?'

He paused for a second as if waiting on someone else's response. 'Would you like me to escort you?'

She shook her head. 'No, thank you, they're just down those stairs?'

He inclined his head and she walked past, faking confidence. He hadn't actually refused her.

At the bottom of the stairs she passed another soldier who didn't so much as blink as she walked past. But she saw the earpiece he wore. So perhaps that first guy had radioed him to let him know it was okay.

Outside she realised it was later in the day than she'd thought. The gardens were lush but the air was heavy and hot.

'You have your land legs back now?' a sardonic query came from behind her.

Her pulse picked up. So he'd been summoned. Was it the guard in the corridor or were there cameras that were too well hidden for her to have spotted? It had to be the guard. The king had better things to do than watch a security feed all day.

'Apparently so,' she mumbled, turning to him. 'I seem to have slept almost all day, I needed to stretch out a little and test them.'

They weren't the only things she was testing. She'd glanced at the high fences and the ornately carved gates at the nearest part of the palace perimeter and seen that the carvings would make good footholds. Maia was good at scrambling up and down narrow ladders and spaces. Now she just had to keep her brain on track while in Niko's presence.

'What about food—have you had anything to eat since you woke?' Niko paused and cocked his head. 'Will you dine with me tonight?'

There was a commanding thread that undermined the 'optional' element of his invitation. Maia braced. 'If you don't mind, I'd like to retire to my room and have a small tray there. I've got a lot to process.'

Niko stared, then slowly nodded. 'Of course, I understand. Another time.'

'Thank you.' She swallowed.

She'd thought he wouldn't be used to anyone turning him down about anything and his almost immediate acceptance seemed a little off. But then it dawned on her—he probably didn't desire to dine with her at all. He'd been making an effort that he was happy to be saved from. After all they had *nothing* in common and their paths never would have crossed if it weren't for this crazy mix-up.

Heat flushed through her all over again and she was glad of the darkening sky.

'But please allow me to accompany you around the garden before you go in,' he said.

She was still wary of his too agreeable, too innocent tone. But it would be too rude to refuse him something that ought to be innocuous. She could still scope out all she needed to under the guise of awed enthusiasm. 'Of course.'

'The gates were hand-carved more than a century ago.' He glanced at her as she startled. 'You seemed interested in them.'

'The whole palace is very beautiful,' she hurriedly gushed. 'The whole island.'

'Indeed. All of them. The whole country in fact,' he replied mockingly.

She gritted her teeth.

In this season dusk barely lasted before full darkness fell and it was often heralded by brief intense storms that blew through, cleansing the stifling humidity with a downpour of rain. But today's storm hadn't yet happened and the heaviness in the air pressed upon her skin. Tension built both inside and out of her—making it impossible to breathe or to think properly. The heat was too much.

He suddenly led her diagonally across the springy lawn and stopped by a small side door that she'd not noticed. 'If you go through here and up those stairs it will take you straight to your corridor. It's faster and you'll avoid the weather that's about to hit.'

She stared at the door. It was small and unobtrusive and perfect and she couldn't believe he'd shown her exactly what she needed. 'Thank you.'

But Niko didn't step aside to let her pass, instead he looked down at her. She was at a disadvantage, not only in stature and strength, power and money, but now in illumination. Because while the interior lights shone through onto her face, he had his back to them and thus remained in shadow. So his expression was impossible to read in the sinking darkness while her face was visible. She felt that heat inside wanting to burst. She stared at him almost fixedly, determined to mask her inner turmoil. She would not fall beneath his sensual spell again.

'Good night, Maia. Please eat and then sleep well. I have the feeling we're going to have lots to settle tomorrow. But I hope we'll be able to agree on the things that matter most.'

Her throat clogged unexpectedly. Perhaps he was trying to do the right thing, but it wasn't enough for her. She made herself nod, unable to answer verbally. Because tomorrow she wasn't going to be here.

Twenty minutes later Niko stood beside Pax and studied the screen. 'What did she order to eat?'

'Salad. Fish.'

Niko smiled at Pax's sparse reply and watched her sitting on that sofa again. He regretted the fear he'd made her feel first thing this morning but there'd been no other way given the secrecy this situation required. *Delicate* wasn't the only word. There was *danger* here too. If people had planned to take advantage of the sample that had been stored at that clinic, then they must be aware of her existence now. That meant she might be at risk. The child might be at risk. He didn't want to scare her any more than she had been but she was *safest* here at the palace. With him.

He'd spoken with the doctor at length and now he shifted, needing to pace, as angry energy rippled. What the man had told him added layers of complication to the mess they already faced. And made his care of her all the more crucial.

But *she* wasn't pacing, wasn't crying. She'd done neither of those things all day. She was still, deep in contemplation. Not taking advantage of any of the entertainments available in the room—neither the books nor the screens with several streaming services. Not the offer of a massage or any kind of relaxation treatments. She just sat.

Pax glanced at another of the security feeds. 'She slept for eleven hours solid.'

'Yeah.' More anger rippled through Niko. She'd curled up on the sofa, too exhausted to bother making it to the bedroom. She'd been so still it had been unnerving. He'd found himself checking on her, here in Pax's office, far too many times through the day. Just to make sure she was actually still breathing. To make sure she was still there. There weren't cameras in the bathroom or bedroom of course. There was no need given there was no way to escape from either of those rooms without coming through the small lounge where she now sat. When she'd finally woken she'd disappeared into the bathroom for a while, returning having clearly showered. He'd felt a ridiculous speck of disappointment that he'd still been unable to see her hair. While the fabric covering had gone, she'd swept her still-wet hair back into a bun at the nape of her neck so it was still impossible to determine anything much about it, including length and colour. She was still in those black trousers and that worn shirt. He should have arranged a wardrobe for her but he'd been so preoccupied processing the consequences of her pregnancy he'd not thought of it until late this afternoon. An assistant was on the job now. Tomorrow he would start over with her. Or so he'd intended—until he'd seen her just before.

'She's not going to stay,' Niko muttered grimly. 'She's going to run.'

'You're sure?' Pax asked. 'She said something?'

Niko shook his head with a jerky movement, unable to explain how he knew, just that he did. His sixth sense screamed certainty. When they were outside Maia Flynn had stared him down. There'd been no coy look, no flirtation, not even a demure lowering of her lashes. No subservient mark of respect for her king. That wasn't how she saw him at all. But it was as if he'd momentarily seen into her mind. He just *knew* she was going to attempt an escape. So he'd given her information that would help. Just to see.

For once Pax removed his sunglasses and bent nearer to glare at the screen. 'I'll go—'

'No.' Niko felt that primitive rush of responsibility. She was *his* problem. 'I'll follow her if she leaves the palace. I want to see how she plays this. Don't let anyone interfere with her progress.' He watched her gaze flicker to the window. To that view of the water. 'I think she'll go to what she knows,' he mused quietly. 'She'll go to the dock. She'll try to get on a boat. She'll go before dawn. Allow it.'

Pax nodded slowly. 'I'll ensure we have people there. We'll make sure she's okay. We won't lose her.'

'I know we won't,' Niko said grimly. There would be no repetition of history here. No emotional, desperate journeys. Accidents happened when emotions were heightened—it was what had happened to his aunt after all. And his mother.

But he needed to know how far Maia would go. It piqued him, that she would lie and plot. That she was so appalled at the prospect of staying here with him that she would put herself at risk made his hackles rise. What did she expect? That he would allow a possible heir to the throne to just leave? *He* was trying his best in what was an appalling situation for them both. That she'd consider running away was unacceptable. But, a little voice whispered within, wasn't it *understandable*?

No. There was too much at risk. Too much that was important.

He would give her a little rope and if she ran, then he'd tie her all the more tightly. That was in the best interests of all of them. He could not see another in his family suffer by being outcast from the palace circle.

Yet still he felt for her—she didn't want this life with him and she didn't even have the motivation his mother had had when she'd married his father—and that hadn't worked. Even love was not enough.

'Here's the knife she dropped.' Pax suddenly turned to him and almost smiled. 'I retrieved it while you were in the midst of that scuffle.'

Niko ignored the rare tease from Pax and regarded the small knife thoughtfully. It was smaller than he'd realised, more like a fruit parer. But while the blade was small, it was sharp. And apparently it was her favourite. For what, and why?

'Thank you for that. Good.' He took it and weighed it in his palm.

Pax jerked his chin at the little bruise on Niko's hand. 'Not like you to hesitate and get caught.'

'It's not like me to jump innocent women,' Niko growled back grimly.

But in truth that hesitation had been more than the distaste of the situation. She'd had her back to him, bending over that knife, but when she'd turned he'd seen the shine in her midnight eyes and there'd been that moment, a jolt of recognition—not of name, or status, but something far more elemental.

The shock of it had rendered him immobile. But in a flash *she'd* been all limbs, all fury as she tried to get away. As she'd slipped. He *still* couldn't forget the sensation of holding her in his arms as he'd stopped her fall. Of locking her between his legs, feeling her lithe lusciousness. Of knowing her in a way he'd never expected to. He should not have felt aroused in any way given how inappropriate and extreme those measures had been. Yet he had been. When he'd then held her close on the journey it wasn't for control, but for her comfort. For his own comfort too. He'd wanted her to understand that she was safe. When he'd finally felt her body relax into his it had brought him a satisfaction unlike any other.

He pocketed the knife and turned back to the screen as thunder hit. She didn't so much as flinch. She was too focused on whatever it was she was thinking. Niko also ignored the rain drumming noisily on the roof. He was going to find out what she had planned, no matter what.

Exhilaration rose at the prospect of duelling with her again. Because she *was* going to challenge him and he was so ready for it.

CHAPTER FIVE

THE DOCK WAS eerily quiet—not even the song and swoop of birdlife disturbed it. It was as if the birds too were holding their breath in solidarity with Maia. She walked quickly, used to being unobtrusive and unnoticed. She'd covered her hair and kept her head down. Given that her freedom depended on this, her adrenalin was stratospheric for the second time in twenty-four hours. She had to succeed because it wasn't only her life on the line. It was her child's as well. Nothing mattered more than ensuring her baby's liberty.

Escaping the palace had been surprisingly easy. There'd been no guard on her door and none on that side door through which she'd gotten into the garden. The carved wooden gate was small and, again, both unlocked and unguarded—or at least able to be opened from the inside. It had taken less than two minutes in that time just before dawn—when the sky was lightening but the world still—to get onto the street and disappear around the corner. It had to be because no one would dream of hurting the king, right? The man was too popular and the city too safe for them to need round-the-clock guards with guns.

She felt a flicker of guilt at abusing the trust he'd bestowed upon her by not having literally locked her away. She believed him when he said he didn't mean to harm her and that he wanted to do what was best. But he also thought *he* knew best and that she would simply agree to everything *he* wanted. But Maia could never sign her life over to him. Her mother had gone from one controlling man to another and she wasn't making the same mistake. In order for things to move forward she needed to reclaim something to negotiate with and honestly the only power she could think of was that of her own placement—literally *where* she was. If she was out of reach, then she had some chance.

The walk to the dock took forever but the sky was barely lightening by the time she got there. The exhilaration from her palace escape faded as the most challenging bit lay ahead. A number of fishermen were preparing their boats to depart for the daily catch. She only needed one to say yes. Her heart thudded.

Take it easy, act like this is normal.

Because it was. It was how most islanders moved around islands outside of ferry hours.

'Any chance of a lift to the next island?' she asked the older man at the first boat.

'Not stopping there, sorry.' He glanced at her for a moment. 'Try Tai further on the dock. White stripe. He's heading to Mica first.'

'Thanks.'

Mica was only two islands up the Piri-nu archipelago but it was a start. She took a steadying breath feeling more vulnerable than she'd ever felt in her life but she straightened her shoulders. No one knew her—or the secret she carried. She was still dressed like a worker. Which was exactly what she was.

'Tai?' She addressed the man with his back to her.

He turned and she blinked. He was younger than she'd expected. But she saw the glint of a wedding band and the distinct—usual—lack of interest in his gaze. 'Any chance I can get a lift to your first stop?'

If she could get to one island, she could then get another boat and could hop her way through. The sooner she got to the first, the better chance she had. No one knew she was missing yet and she was sure King Niko wouldn't want a scandal given he'd gone to such lengths to ensure her arrival at the palace was unknown.

'It's a ninety-minute run,' Tai said bluntly. 'Do you get seasick?'

She stiffened. 'Not usually.'

'Can you help with the ropes at the stern?'

'Of course.'

'Then step on board.'

She studied the boat as she did. It was old but well maintained. Safe enough in this weather. She headed to the front of the boat, eager to help them get moving before her disappearance was discovered. Hopefully she had a couple hours yet before one of those maids appeared with a dining tray.

The boat rocked as she moved forward but she felt the ripple of freedom. She released the line then coiled the rope neatly. The boat manoeuvred away from the dock. It seemed the young fisherman was keen to get underway too. She remained at the stern, looking towards the sea as the engine chugged, getting them out of the inner harbour and hoping the next phase would go as smoothly. She was finally enacting the desperate escape scenario she'd imagined from her father's boat for years but never had the courage to attempt before now. Ultimately she would aim for somewhere as far as New Zealand or Australia. Once she was there she'd try to get a job in a cafe. If she could find someone to give her a chance she was sure she could prove herself. It wouldn't be for that long of course. She had no intention of hiding from Niko forever. She just needed time and space to figure out how to manage *him*.

'Where is it we're going, Maia?'

She closed her eyes, rooted to the spot.

Of course it was too good to be true. Of course it had been too easy.

She heard a splash and reluctantly turned, opening her eyes in time to see Tai—if that was even his name—swimming to shore. Leaving her alone with her captor king looking at her with condemnation in his deep brown eyes.

Well, she wasn't going to cower before him and apologise. It was his own fault for assuming so much yesterday. As if she *ever* wanted to be his queen? As if she ever could do as she was ordered for the rest of her life? As if she could let her child *see* her do that?

'How did you know which boat I was going to choose?' she asked.

'I didn't. I had a man on all of them.'

Her stomach knotted. 'You followed me from the palace.'

'You even used the door I showed you.'

So he'd predicted her every move, and the barely leashed fury in his eyes revealed the temper that could explode at any moment. And wasn't he justified in that? Could she really blame him?

She'd thought she'd been so brilliant but all she'd done was poke the bear and now things would only be worse. 'Are we not turning round immediately?'

'We are not,' he said. 'You've just proven that I cannot trust you, Maia. So now we change the plan.'

She chilled. 'You've sent the fisherman away.'

'The *soldier* away, yes. But you can trust me. I can steer this boat.'

'So can I.' She suddenly lifted her chin in brave—possibly foolish—defiance. 'So if you happened to go overboard in the middle of the ocean I could journey on and find my freedom forever.'

'Are you threatening the king?' He laughed briefly—bitterly—before stepping close. 'Would you want such an accident to befall the father of your child?'

She stared back up at him, provoked into pushing him back however she could. 'What makes you certain you're the father all of a sudden? I thought you weren't getting the test results—'

'I know you're a virgin, Maia.'

The statement stunned her. She stared up at him awash with shock, then anger, then such overwhelming embarrassment that she couldn't speak.

His expression changed. 'The doctor examined you yesterday, remember?' he asked—his voice slightly more gentle, slightly husky.

'But that was for—' The horror of her total humiliation hit. She hadn't realised that the doctor would have been able to tell or that he would have even considered to look for such a thing. She'd thought that physical exam had been to assess the pregnancy, not her personal *status*...

It was such a horrible violation of her privacy. And she was so stupidly naive and clueless on all these things. She burned, blinking rapidly even though her eyes were dry. Her mother flashed into her mind and Maia's fury bloomed brighter still. She wasn't only hurt that her mother had abandoned her but angry because Maia had been left so ignorant as a result. And for that doctor to have told the king something that was so personal, so private, so awkward—

'You've really been enjoying yourself at my expense, haven't you?' She gasped.

'Not at all,' Niko answered directly, his unapologetic gaze fixed upon her. 'It was a tangential discovery, Maia. He wasn't deliberately investigating that aspect of your... life.' For a moment he actually looked awkward. 'Given that discovery though, he opted not to perform the DNA test. Especially because he said you'd suffered abnormal pain for a long time. He said that was why you sought treatment that day.' He paused. 'But you'd not tried to get help for it earlier.'

He paused again but Maia simply couldn't speak. It hadn't been easy when she lived on the boat so much. That appointment had been a cancellation. She'd thought she'd been *lucky*.

'While the DNA test will still be done at some point, we both already know the result. He and I agree there is no need to subject you to further testing at this stage.'

Was she supposed to be *grateful* for that? Because she wasn't. She just wanted to curl into a ball and hide.

'The doctor considers it vital that you get rest for this stage of your pregnancy,' he added.

'And the doctor didn't consider telling any of this personal information to me directly?' she asked acidly.

'He would have today if you hadn't run away.'

She gritted her teeth in annoyance. 'But he had no scruples about breaking patient confidentiality and telling *you* already.'

'Because I am the king and these are *exceptional* circumstances. I want only what's best for both you and the baby.' He drew a sharp breath. 'Stress is not what's best.' He looked at her. 'Running away is not what's best.' He turned and went to the wheel.

'And only you know what is best?' She followed him furiously. 'Only you can decide?'

He lifted his chin in a mirror of her defiance. 'Am I such an ogre, Maia?'

She honestly didn't know. But she couldn't cede all power so soon. 'I feel uncomfortable about how much you seem to know about me. I feel like you've had people pry into my personal life.'

'That's not entirely true. My most trusted security man

is the only one to have made inquiries. Then it is only the medical centre and the doctor. I am trying to protect your privacy as best I can. That is why I removed you from the boat in the way that I did.'

'It leaves me feeling violated. Nothing is mine.'

'Your thoughts are your own.' His eyes flashed. 'Your body too.'

'Is that so?' She stared at him mutinously. 'You're saying I can go anywhere and do anything?'

His jaw clamped. 'I meant in an intimate capacity. You don't need to fear anything from me. I know you think I'm some kind of player but—'

'I get it.' Her petulant ego didn't need to hear yet another time about how little he was attracted to her. She was safe from any sexual attention from him. Fine. Great.

'Right, so you seem to think you know a lot about me too, correct?' he said. 'People pry into my personal life all the time. I'm saying I understand the discomfort of that sensation.'

'You're the king, it comes with the job.'

'Yes,' he said soberly. 'It does. This isn't what *either* of us wanted. You need time to process the situation. You need rest. You need to be safe.'

Safe from *what* exactly?

'So now you're taking me where—to some kind of prison?' she asked sarcastically.

His jaw tensed. Why succeeding in angering him gave her small satisfaction she didn't know. She'd never been this shrewish before. But then she'd never been impossibly pregnant and kidnapped by a king before either.

All Niko wanted was to do the right thing but it seemed no matter what he did or how he framed it, she found fault and flared up. And in turn, well, he was rapidly heading towards nuclear. Both the failure to soothe her and his response was unusual. He'd seen Pax's report so he hadn't been going into this situation completely blind and yet he'd still managed to blow it. Since when was he so lacking in charm? He convinced people to do his bidding all the damned time without having to actually order them.

Maia Flynn had lived all her life on a vessel that could sink at any time. Like some low-level casino cruise, they voyaged around the Pacific, taking passengers into international waters for illegal high-stakes gambling. Her father had been investigated several times but never charged. Certainly never convicted. Maia worked in the galley not just full-time, but literally every hour she was awake.

Didn't she realise she never had to work again if she didn't want to? That she would have all the riches of the world—that she could live a refined, relaxed life in the palace? Wasn't that better than what she'd endured all her life so far?

So why had the thought of staying with him been so repellent that she'd felt forced to run away first thing this morning?

He'd never intended to throw the fact of her virginity in her face. He'd not even been going to bring it up. It was too personal. But inexplicably he'd gotten so mad at the mere sight of her, he'd snapped. There was no denying the veracity of the doctor's finding—her immediate expression had confirmed it all. But he wasn't about to tell her the other things the doctor had told him at the time. That he was 'fine to sleep with her'—just to 'be gentle and take it slow.' Niko had furiously changed the topic. He did not need guidance on bedroom performance from a doctor. Besides which it was irrelevant because he was never going to be intimate with Maia Flynn. He would install her on his private holiday island with his most loyal servant in safety and she would want for nothing. Ever. He would make it so damn heavenly she'd never want to leave.

His long-dormant protective instincts had surged. He'd not realised they were so strong. This wasn't only about the baby, this was about her. She had medical issues that hadn't been diagnosed properly, and she'd not had the care she should have had. All that was going to change. Rest. No stress. Nutritious food. These things he could supply. He could make life more than good for her. This wouldn't be anything like what had happened to his aunt. He could do a better job than his grandfather ever had. And he would damn well do a better job of looking after her than he had looked after his mother.

So seducing Maia wasn't on that list. But awareness crackled and a wicked whisper constantly suggested he get closer. She was the one woman he shouldn't touch. But for some unknown reason she was the one he wanted more than his next breath. It was such a cliché to want something simply because it wasn't allowed. That's all this was, right? The temptation of forbidden fruit.

Well, he would resist and dismiss that temptation. He would keep his distance and encourage her to accept what was going to happen. They would have a marriage of convenience, not intimacy, and she could have all the freedom she wanted out here. She would be alone while their names were still joined. But beyond that—

'We need to press on,' he said abruptly. 'We have quite a way to go.'

As he put the boat into full power he saw a sparkle illuminate her midnight eyes. She clearly loved the water despite the lack of freedom on her father's boat. Being out here in the sunlight, chasing the light winds, moving towards his favourite island, he too felt his mood and energy lift. So he stayed silent, unwilling to debate pointlessly with her about a future that was already settled.

As the sun rose higher she moved around the boat, first

tidying the ropes into neater coils, then polishing with a soft cloth she'd found somewhere. As if she couldn't rest. As if she didn't know she didn't have to work anymore.

'You work on deck on your father's boat?' he couldn't resist asking.

'Only sometimes, when we don't have guests. I'm not the best but I know the basics.'

'And of course you have your sea-legs.' He gave in to the temptation to tease. Just a little.

It was a mistake. She shot him a look and despite the distance between them on deck the atmosphere thickened and he felt her challenge as if it were an actual arm wrestle. In seconds he was so close to snatching her into his arms again. When she finally turned away he gritted his teeth and summoned every ounce of restraint he could.

Three hours later Maia stood at the stern keenly seeking more glimpses of the large wooden mansion through the lush palm trees. The sand was pale gold and powdery and in the blue depths below them she could see beautiful coral, colourful fish and her favourites, the turtles.

Her heart pounded as she realised a terrifying—tantalising—truth. 'This is your private island.'

It was small and isolated. They would be alone and there would be no escape from *him*. And already there'd been that moment when he'd simply looked at her and she'd all but combusted on the spot. A wild feeling swept over her. She needed to get away not just from him but the dangerous direction of her own thoughts—the feeling that she would so easily succumb to the attraction that was so stupid. So inevitable.

'Yes,' he said.

She was glad he'd not berated her more and simply pushed on in silence. He'd surprised her with his boating skills. He knew what he was doing, where he was going. But of course this was literally his world. He'd radioed a couple of times and she'd no doubt they were being tracked. She'd grown hotter and hotter not from the sun but the more time she spent in his company.

'I often swim from here,' he added. 'But I'll get the inflatable for—'

'I can swim,' she snapped. 'I'll see you there.'

Before he could answer—or move—she stretched her arms wide and dived straight in. When she surfaced she heard a long string of cursing from the boat behind her but the instant hit of happiness at being in the ocean was too strong to be squished and she simply laughed. The journey had wrought a tension within that she could no longer stand. She adored the water. She was strong in it. And *free*. Now she swam like it was a race for gold—anticipation making adrenalin surge again. She was almost at the shore when she felt a tug on her leg. She recognised the firm grip. She'd been expecting it. Frankly she was pleased it had taken him as long as it had to catch her. She kicked out and put her feet down. This near to the beach the water was just above waist deep on her but on him—

She stared as he surfaced right beside her. He was barechested. He was also furious. But as that wasn't uncommon it was the bare-chested bit that floored her.

'There are rocks you could have hit when you dived in,' he shouted. '*Why* must you always challenge me, Maia?'

She was too busy absorbing the fact that he'd taken the time to strip to his briefs and still caught up to her to answer immediately. Then she was unable to do anything but stare at the swathes of smooth, copper-toned skin and the sharply defined muscles. She gazed at the stunning circular tattoo across his shoulder while another slid down his ribs to the side of his heart.

'I don't know,' she breathed. But she felt more alive than she had in days, months, hell—*years*. Restless energy fired through her so powerfully that she was desperate to release it.

'Don't you?'

The water lapped and the smallest of waves impacted on her like a tsunami. She stumbled and fell against him.

'Then let me show you,' he growled, his hands instantly going to her waist. He lifted her right off her feet. Maia looped her hands over his shoulders and clasped them together at the nape of his neck. For balance, right? But the action allowed her to be pressed more intimately against his bare chest. He was hot and hard and strong as he pressed her closer until they were plastered together from chest through stomach, hips, thighs. And then mouths.

Mouths most of all.

His lips locked on hers. His tongue flickered into her mouth and entwined with hers. He kissed her increasingly intimately, plundering her mouth with luscious thrusts the way he'd fill that other, aching, empty part inside her. The part that had slickened and heated and that she couldn't help rubbing against him. With power and passion and relentless depth he commanded her response and she gave it all. While her innards went weak, her arms remained strong. Energy flowed through her and she clung to him like a limpet. Mind lost, only instinct remained. And the *hunger*. That all-consuming hunger simply grew. She was not releasing him. She was not ever ending this searing kiss. Pleasure shot through her entirety. She arched her feet, half kicking to keep afloat, to keep every inch sealed to him. Her clothes were sopping and as her shirt was already old and thin it now might as well not exist. She could feel more than her own reaction. She could feel *his* ferocity of passion. It made her quake. She heard his low growl and felt the vibration from his chest through hers as his hand swept down her back and pressed, driving her hips harder against his. She shook even more then as his fierce erection jutted against her. She parted her legs to let him fit better, nearer to where she wanted his touch most. His hand tightened on her hip, grinding her on him.

Another wave knocked them. This time he lost his footing and she slipped from his hold, her lips torn from his, the seal—the flare of insanity—severed.

She staggered and straightened at the same time as he. It wasn't fast, it was confused. And then three feet separated them. Breathless she glanced down and saw her nipples were diamond hard. So were his. So was something else of his.

Shocked she slowly stared up his straining body. He too was breathless and she tried not to stare at the way his gorgeous chest was rising and falling, and his defined abs rippling. Instinctively she lifted her hand to her mouth, automatically moving—too late—to hide the swollen sensitivity of her lips and their blatant, desperate ache for more. Finally she dragged her hungry gaze all the way up and she looked him in the eye.

His expression was burnished with arrogant defiance and his lips were curled into a saturnine smile. 'You more than met me halfway, Maia.'

'I stumbled—'

'You wanted it and you *liked* it.' He turned away.

She didn't like that he turned his back to her. She felt instantly cold.

'Aron,' he said gruffly.

'Your Highness.'

Stunned, Maia swivelled towards the beach. There was an ancient man walking towards them on the fine white sand, impassively holding white towels and studiously not looking her in the eyes.

How long had he been there watching them? The awful thing was she'd been so lost to passion that they could have been in front of a *stadium* full of people staring and she wouldn't have stopped. She wouldn't have given a damn. Because all she'd wanted was more of Niko's touch. That realisation shocked her all over again.

But the elderly manservant didn't bat an eyelid. Apparently he wasn't fazed by a fully clothed, soaking woman being kissed to within an inch of ecstasy in the midday sun.

'Thank you, Aron. This is Maia. Can you please show her around the facilities. I would like her to be accommodated in the coral room.'

'It is already prepared, Your Highness.'

Niko turned to her and an exasperated but amused look entered his eyes. 'Go with Aron, Maia. You'll be perfectly *safe* with him.' He underlined the word edgily, as if mocking her for feeling unsafe with him.

Well, she *wasn't* safe from the very mixed feelings Niko wrought within her. But she didn't move. She refused to jump to his every order in the way he so clearly expected. 'What are you going to do?'

His eyes widened and his already charged body tensed. Yes, he was definitely unused to being questioned. He never had to answer to anyone. But Maia stared at him expectantly and she was determined to wait for an answer.

'Kingly things,' he said stiffly.

'*Kinky* things?' She deliberately misinterpreted what he'd said and allowed tartness to sharpen her tone. 'Well, that makes total sense.'

Yes, it was childish. And yet she was totally satisfied when she saw his jaw drop as she turned her back on him and stalked up the beach.

CHAPTER SIX

NIKO LITERALLY, FIRMLY, rubbed away his rueful smile with his fingers on his lips as he watched Maia march up the beach towards his favourite place on earth. Her stiff spine radiated outrage but even so he couldn't resist appreciating the lush curve of her waist and sensual flare of her hips that he could now finally see because her shapeless clothes were sodden and stuck to her skin. His hand tingled from where he'd gripped her softness only seconds ago. Happily the horrible headscarf had been lost at sea in that frantic swim and her hair had loosened from its knot in all the effort. Now it hung in gleaming black ropes right to the small of her back—the silkiness had whipped his skin when he'd brought her flush against him and he wanted to wind it around his wrists.

As she stalked off like a wilful, dangerous Siren all he wanted was to rip that unsexy outfit from her beautiful body, clutch her close and bury himself deep in her astonishingly fiery hold. Instead he just stared, sluggishly processing what the hell had happened. How had he responded to her touch so ravenously? Why, when once more the way she'd spoken to him had been shocking?

Unvarnished. Honest. Devastating.

'Be gentle and take it slow' had been the unsolicited advice from that damned doctor. Hell. Niko had just ravaged her mouth in full-out beast mode. Explicitly carnal and with extremely uncharacteristic possessiveness, he'd displayed zero finesse nor the patience to seduce her slowly given what he knew about her.

Yet apparently she hadn't needed slow, had she? She'd been as hot as he. Hungrily rubbing those lush breasts against him in a way that made him forget where they were, why they were here and hell, frankly who he even *was*. All that had mattered was capturing the full force of her fire in his arms. Damned if she hadn't burned his brains to ash in an instant. And she hadn't been afraid to throw out an equally inflammatory comment in the aftermath, had she? Though then she'd turned red and fled. That seemed to be a habit of hers. Was she wary of reprisal? Maybe she should be. But maybe one day soon she'd have to face the full consequences of letting her sassy, sweet mouth run amok on him...

But that flush suggested she'd been as surprised by her snap as he was. She was like a skittish kitten testing new-found claws. Maybe it all *was* new to her. Because surely if she'd been like this with any other guy before now, no way would she still be a virgin. Just none. So either she hadn't been playful like this, or some fool had never picked up on her sensual challenging side and encouraged the hell out of it. That aspect of her definitely ought to be developed, and wasn't Niko just the man to help her with that?

No. No, he was not.

Grimly Niko put his rampant lusty thoughts on ice. This wasn't one of his usual offshore weekend flirtations. This was a permanent problem and the whole thing was complex enough without him tossing gunpowder into the mix. For all his security reports, he barely knew her. More importantly she certainly didn't know him, nor what royal life was like or what the expectations on her would be. He had to keep his focus on the basics required. That was an arrangement they could both cope with. One that would be supportive. Discreet. Manageable. *Controllable*. He'd intended to keep things calm this morning, not to let his annoyance about her escape attempt show. He'd been going to make her feel *safe* and confident about staying in Piri-nu with him. That she had nothing to fear from him.

Instead he'd gotten his hands on her the first chance he had and dived into an all-out lust-fest that had backfired completely—

With a frustrated growl he turned his back on the beach so he couldn't stare after her anymore. He'd return to the boat and ensure the damned thing was moored securely. He hadn't had the chance to double-check what with her rash leap overboard. Plus he'd get the electronic gear he'd not been able to bring in the water. He'd not had the mental capacity to explain all that to her when she'd questioned him on his plans. Truthfully his mental capacity had been zilch. And maybe it was rude of him not to take the time to show her to her room, but if he'd taken her in there now he'd have seduced her in seconds. Given what had just happened in the water he knew he could. He'd have taken everything but frankly, given the battle he was still having with an extremely intense arousal, they'd have finished in less than five minutes.

Not happening. *Ever.*

Because while Niko wasn't afraid of having fun with a woman, he did *not* lose control of himself in any situation. Yet just then he almost had and he *still* couldn't stop thinking about the one tiny taste he'd had of her. She'd been ardent and sweet and the answering thrusts of her tongue as her wet body writhed against his were going to haunt him hard. As it was, all he'd wanted for the last twenty-four hours was to have her in his arms again and it had been hotter than he'd ever imagined, so how was he going to cope with this intense attraction while they were stuck together here?

He needed a bloody ice bath.

Maia had to force herself not to press her hands to her lips, which were still tingling from the intense press of his. She desperately suppressed memories of that teasing flick of his tongue, the sheer force of his passion—the sensual guidance of his hands, of his lips, compelling her to open for him—but her body rebelled, still tingling, still aching for more. Steadying her shaken emotions was impossible so she forced herself to focus on what she could *see*. The problem was that what she saw simply made her already erratic pulse skip even more.

It was pure, undiluted paradise—the beach was a sweeping arch of sand that led to lush emerald trees while a dramatic mountain rose up behind. She tried—and failed—not to fall deeper beneath the spell of her location with every step. If she were alone she might have cried at the beauty of it—the *luxury*—but she wasn't alone so she held it together like always as Aron, the elderly servant, pointed out the facilities in a smooth, calming tone that she deeply appreciated.

The stunning mansion was secreted away in the heart of lush green palm trees, and its own focal point was a gorgeous outdoor area. Aron gracefully gestured to the lounge chairs dotted perfectly at the rear of the infinity-edged salt-water pool and spa and to the dining area with elaborate outdoor kitchen and barbecue. Conscious that she was dripping a trail of water behind her, Maia was speechless as Aron showed her through main building—the relaxing living room, the formal dining room, then large gym and den on the lower floor.

'Your suite is this way.' Aron then led her to a separate building connected to the main via a shaded walkway. 'The king's suite is through there.' Fortunately they kept walking. 'It has his study and other personal facilities.'

The bedroom suite Aron took her to was a dream, with polished wooden floors, vast windows and dreamy, luxury linen. It encapsulated peace and space and everything a tired lonely person could long for. Light, neutral drapes created a soothing frame for the most stunning view she'd ever seen. While she loved the water and was so at home there, this was the best slice of land she'd ever seen. This was pristine beach and beautiful trees and it evoked a sense of serenity as well as that beautiful blue of the water—the endless expanse to the horizon was so evocative of the freedom she'd always longed for.

'Are there other staff on the island?' She finally overcame her embarrassment enough to indulge her curiosity.

'Rarely,' Aron replied.

'None at all?' She was amazed. While she didn't want to be rude, Aron seemed awfully old to have to maintain this entire property all by himself.

'The king values the privacy he has here.' He shook his head. 'I served the king's father and his grandfather before him. It is an honour to work for King Niko and this is the most beautiful place in the world.'

She wondered if this was a reward for the elderly loyal staffer. 'You don't get lonely?'

'Since my wife passed on it brings me peace to be here. My children and grandchildren are frequent visitors. King Niko allows them use of all the facilities. He's very generous.'

She felt that embarrassment heat her cheeks again. 'Does the king often stay here?'

Did he bring other women here? Aron hadn't appeared to be phased by that mortifying display on the beach. Perhaps all this was normal for Niko. Yet the thought of other women being here and enjoying this luxury made her unreasonably irritable.

He was frequently photographed with women when he was abroad, but not filmed actually *kissing* any—a hand on the back, perhaps, a gesture that could be construed as chivalrous, not lecherous. But the insinuation of intimacy was there— the stars in the model or actress or socialite's eyes said it all. Every time. With every one of them. But Maia was not jealous. She had no interest in nor claim on him. Except if they *were* to marry—then that would have to be discussed, because she refused to be an unwanted wife whose husband repeatedly cheated on her. She wasn't going to sit around and be humiliated even if the marriage was to last only a short time.

'He stays only occasionally and for a few nights at most,' Aron answered. 'Please let me know if there is anything you need. This room hasn't been used since the refurbishment and I might have forgotten a couple of things in my hurry to get it ready this morning. Do forgive me if that's the case.'

'When was the refurbishment?' she couldn't resist asking.

'Coming up eight years now.'

'No one has stayed in this room in *eight* years?' Maia gazed again at the serene, spacious room with its stunning view. What a waste it seemed. Yet something curled within her—pleasure at being special—that she was allowed to use this precious space when almost no one ever did.

Of course, it dawned on her only a moment later that if Niko did bring women here they probably stayed in *his* suite. *Idiot.*

'I think you've done a beautiful job preparing the suite. Thank you,' she muttered shyly. 'I'm sorry about this puddle I've left...'

Aron's eyes twinkled. 'King Niko likes things to be very relaxed here and it is a beach house, at heart. A little water won't hurt the floors. I will leave you to freshen up now.'

She didn't know what was to be expected. What they were going to do. How she was ever going to get free now. She was grateful for the space to process what had happened. Of course her escape from the palace had been too easy to be real. Perhaps it was part of a plan to subdue her—to seduce her into submission? If so, how she was going to resist him? Part of her simply didn't want to. Maybe he would try everything he could to get what he wanted. But maybe she would do the same.

She peeled off her damp work trousers and hung them over the railing in the hopes they would dry super quickly in the rising heat as the day matured. She wanted to check out that pool and the beach but she wasn't sure of the protocol. Playing it safe she went to the bathroom and rinsed off in the gorgeous shower—trying not to think about that kiss while constantly thinking about nothing else. When she emerged she discovered her clothes were gone from where she'd hung them. Aron had clearly slipped in and out of her suite again as there was now a silk robe on the small chair at the foot of the massive bed.

She pulled it on, almost able to wrap it around herself three times over, and walked out onto the private deck, breathing in the view. A hammock was strung between two trees down by the beach. Beyond that she saw Niko paddling a small boat back from the fishing boat they'd anchored in the bay. She watched as the waves pushed him onto the shore. He hopped out, splashing in the shallows to pull the boat further up onto the sand. Maia's jaw dropped as he did—not because of his display of skill and strength, but because the man was as naked as the day he'd been born.

She *should* look away. But she didn't. She couldn't. She just stared, her mouth still ajar as he secured the small boat and then splashed back into the sea. Once deep enough he lifted his arms in a graceful arc and dived. His movements were powerful and so assured, she knew he'd swum this cove a million times. This was his home and he'd shed the regal persona and the weight of duty—coming here he was free to be himself. She saw the strength and purpose in his stroke. She also saw the joy. Something within her softened towards him and sent a pulse of desire around her body.

She shouldn't be watching him. It was pure voyeurism but she simply couldn't tear her attention away. Eventually she realised a low throbbing sound was growing louder. An incoming helicopter. Niko must have heard it too because he swam back to shore. He walked out of the water onto the beach. Scooping up a towel that he wrapped around his hips, he stood at the shoreline, his back to her, his face lifted to the sky, watching for the machine.

It didn't land. Instead a large pallet was released on a line. She saw a figure in the open hatch, making some sign to Niko. She saw the wide slash of his smile as he moved to un-hook the crate, the movement of his chest as he laughed and made a rude gesture with his hand. The guy in the helicopter made one back. They were friends then. Niko and the scary-looking guard who always wore those reflective sunglasses.

Niko was already unfastening the net securing the crate when Aron emerged from the house wheeling a trolley with him. As the noise from the helicopter faded she could hear their laughter as the Niko stacked the boxes from the crate to the trolley. As he then pulled the trolley towards the house, he glanced up towards her. It was too late to draw back out of sight. She made herself remain still. She wasn't going to apologise for seeing all that she had. If he was going to flaunt himself around the place completely naked, then he was going to be seen.

Five minutes later someone knocked on her door and she was not disappointed to see Aron and not Niko standing there when she opened it.

'Some items have arrived for you, ma'am,' he said. 'The

king was aware you had only the clothes you were wearing and hopes you'll find something acceptable in this selection.'

Stunned, Maia stepped back to let Aron wheel the trolley in. There were three large boxes. That was a lot of clothing.

'Would you like assistance to unbox?' he asked politely.

'No, thank you, Aron,' Maia said softly, mortified that she had to be clothed like some urchin. 'I'm sure you've a lot more important things to do with your time. I can manage.' She didn't want to make more work for the man. 'Where would I find the king if I wanted to thank him?'

'I believe he's gone back into the water.' With a slight bow, Aron closed the door behind him.

Maia turned back to the windows. Sure enough Niko was stretching out in the water with those strong, long strokes again. Probably still not wearing anything. Well, she couldn't lose all time again just by standing there staring at him. She faced the boxes. Part of her wanted to reject everything he offered but she hadn't the confidence to emulate his nudist approach. Finally curiosity won and she opened the first box, and it was like every Christmas she'd never had.

As she unfolded each item she placed it in the large walk-in wardrobe. There were bikinis in bright shades, shorts, loose linen trousers and long cool dresses—some floral, some neutral, all soft and beautifully stitched and gorgeous. These were quality items that she could never afford to buy for herself. The shoes were mules and slides, perfect beach wear where it didn't matter if the size wasn't quite right but as it happened they fit perfectly. There was a box of toiletries with moisturiser and after-sun lotion plus a small make-up kit of sampler-sized products that she hadn't the skill to use.

But she used the comb and coiled her hair into a high bun, hot from the effort of unpacking the embarrassment of riches that had been given to her. Worst of all she loved every item.

She stroked the yellow bikini, drawn to the bright colour. Despite having just showered, she would explore that pool and hopefully avoid him for a while yet.

The temperature of the water was just cool enough to be refreshing in the heat of the afternoon and it was luscious. She floated, feeling guilt bloom for her attempted escape this morning. It worsened because part of her was pleased to be brought to this place. She didn't *deserve* to enjoy it given she'd run away and only made things even more difficult. Wincing with embarrassment, she dived deep to escape her own thoughts.

As she surfaced she spotted Niko walking towards her. Fortunately he had a towel around his waist. Maia meant to keep her eyes on the water but she just stared—hot again even while standing chest deep in water.

'How long do you plan to keep me here?' She went on the defensive.

'As long as it takes to figure out what we're going to do.'

'I thought you'd already decided what we're going to do.'

'Perhaps we need longer to talk things through.'

'You mean you've discovered you need longer to get me to agree to whatever you want?'

He watched her.

'Because you're used to making all the rules. Everyone saying yes, all of the time.'

'You think life is ever that simple?'

'Mostly, for you. You're the king.'

He stared down at her for a long moment and she had the odd feeling he was literally counting beats before answering her. 'You haven't actually given us a chance to talk. You assumed you'd have no voice and no choice, so you ran before even trying,' he said calmly. 'And I don't entirely blame you when—'

'You might think you do, but you don't know anything about me,' she interrupted hotly, uncomfortable because he was right.

'Then why don't you talk to me?' he countered. 'Why not give us a chance to get to know each other and work this out *together*?'

She waded to the opposite side of the pool and climbed out. The thought of being bracketed with him made her restless and her immediate instinct was always to run. Yet he sounded so damned reasonable. How was it that now she felt bad for skipping out when he was the one who'd kidnapped her in the first place in a display of power and might, money and control? How did she end up feeling guilty for not 'giving him a chance'?

And how had she been such a fool as to get out when he was standing right beside her towel and now she was stuck in nothing but a tiny bikini?

'We have to work this out, Maia,' he said quietly. 'And contrary to what you seem to think, I don't have all the answers already. Perhaps you do?' His expression tightened as he stared at her. 'I'm looking forward to hearing what you had planned to do once you'd made it to that next island.' He picked up a towel and walked towards her—stretching out his hand to offer it to her.

Utterly awkward, she stretched to take it, trying to maintain as much distance as possible between them.

His gaze was harder now and she heard him draw a sharp breath. 'I'm going to shower and change for dinner. We'll eat in twenty minutes.'

CHAPTER SEVEN

CHANGE FOR DINNER? Maia scrambled as soon as he'd stalked off. He was displeased. Well, that made two of them.

After another quick shower she left her hair loose, it was almost dry already, and pulled one of the dresses on. It was modest yet sensual at the same time because of its silkiness. She walked out to the patio, unsure whether they were dining in the formal dining room or in that outside area.

She licked her lips, pangs of hunger hitting hard. For the first time since her abduction she felt like eating a full meal. But she paused when she spotted him staring at her from across the patio. She just stared back. He wore linen shorts and a barely buttoned shirt that displayed the very fine physique she well knew he had. He'd shaved so that angular jaw was emphasised together with those impossibly stunning cheekbones.

'Some of the clothing fit you okay.' He cleared his throat almost awkwardly. 'One of my men went to your father's boat to collect some of your things but...'

Shame curled upwards, a constant. 'I only had a few work clothes there.'

'That's what he said.'

She studied the large stone tiles she was standing on. It was worse than that. She only had one pair of shoes to her name and the few clothes she owned bore the boat's logo and were old and stained. 'I don't need much. I—'

'Don't,' Niko said gruffly.

She looked up, startled at his tone. He'd silently moved nearer.

'Don't make excuses for him,' he added quietly.

The anger in his eyes torched something within her. He knew. Because his soldier had seen. And she was horrified.

'What did your soldier tell him?' she asked.

'That the king had heard of your work and wanted to try some. That you'd agreed to come to the palace early in the morning and had been so excited you'd forgotten to leave a note.'

Excited. Maia blinked. 'And he believed that?'

'He wanted to know how much you were being paid. My man was at pains to reassure him that you were being very well taken care of in all areas.'

But her father wouldn't have been bothered about *that.* It was only ever about money for him. She curled her hands into fists but knew them to be useless. 'You must think I'm pathetic.'

'No. Why would you—'

'Because I should have run, right?' she interrupted roughly. 'I should have run away from *him.* From *that* life. But I didn't. Not in all these years'

'How could you? You were stuck in the middle of the ocean most of the time. What were you supposed to do? He didn't pay you. He controlled everything. You had no money. No real options.'

'You know everything.' She stared at him in consternation and pressed her fists to her flaming cheeks.

'I know a few sparse facts. I have no idea about the full picture.' He hesitated. 'Maybe you can talk to me about it sometime,' he added quietly. 'Not now. But maybe when you're ready.'

She appreciated the attempt but he was inviting an intimacy neither of them really wanted or were ready for. She saw the guarded look in his eyes and she felt so sorry.

'I needed time,' she explained softly. 'I know we have to work this out. I wasn't intending to run away forever. I was never going to stop you from...' She sighed. 'I just needed to claim some control of my own. I had no idea what I was going to do. I just needed to prove—to myself more than anything—that I could. I can't be a doormat for the rest of my life. I just can't.'

He looked down and cleared his throat. 'I do have something else for you.'

She closed her eyes in instant rejection. She didn't want anything more from him. She didn't want to be this charity case that he felt sorry for. She didn't want to be this *helpless*.

'Maia.'

She opened her eyes and saw his fist right in front of her but then he unfolded his fingers and she saw her whittling knife resting in his palm.

'Oh!' Her heart leapt. 'You have my knife.'

He nodded.

She rapidly blinked. 'You trust me enough to return it to me?'

'I figure it's not going to do too much damage if you turned it on me.'

'Are you sure about that?' She attempted a weak joke to cover her emotion.

'Not going to go too deep. It's like a paring knife, right? Taking only layers.'

'True.' She cleared her throat. 'But there are some points of a body where damage could be done.'

'Oh?'

'Here.' She pointed to his neck and as the joy of getting

the knife back circulated, she warmed to the topic, suddenly laughing. 'And of course, damage could be done to more intimate places.'

He cocked his head, surprise flashing in his eyes. 'But Maia.' He suddenly smiled wickedly. 'Why would you risk damaging something that might bring you so much pleasure?'

'That might *what*…?' She stiffened. 'Oh *please*…'

He threw back his head and laughed freely. 'The look on your face…' He laughed harder.

That embarrassment of before burned off in the heat of his amusement. 'You're shameless.'

'Yes,' he admitted happily. 'Because sex shouldn't be shameful. It should be fun. Life's too short not to enjoy it fully.'

Life wasn't only too short, it sometimes wasn't fair either—and some circumstances didn't allow for fun.

'Now I know to search you for the knife before we go to bed.'

'*We're* not going to bed,' she growled.

'Hmmm.' He was so close to her, so close but not quite touching. 'I understand that you know how to protect yourself but you're not going to need those skills with me, Maia. Because I'm not going to do anything that you don't want me to. I won't come near you again unless you ask. Or I ask and you say yes.'

Neither of those things were going to happen.

But the flutter of temptation strengthened every second he smiled at her. She wasn't going to be able to hold it back. 'Your playboy reputation is fully deserved then.'

That smile deepened. 'You don't think it's part of a ploy to keep up the international profile of Piri-nu?'

'Please. A virile playboy king as a promotional strategy? Surely you can think of something better than that.'

'People like romance and possibility.'

'Well, you definitely give them plenty of possibility.'

'Oh so judgemental, my sweet.'

'You don't take anything seriously.'

'No,' he corrected her outrageously. 'I haven't taken any *relationship* seriously. Every few months I enjoy spending time with women who would have no intention of fulfilling a duty that isn't theirs and suppressing their own dreams. Women like that are safe choices for me, Maia, and I'm a safe choice for them. It's fun and I'm not going to apologise for occasionally enjoying myself when I work hard the rest of the time. It's not even that often. Yet you seem to resent that I sometimes blow off steam?'

She was shocked by his blunt honesty. And suddenly jealous. 'Maybe I've worked hard my whole damned life. Maybe I want to blow off steam too and I've just never gotten the chance—' She broke off, embarrassed.

'Never? No chance? No cute guest one time?' He stared at her intensely.

She winced. 'My father's guests aren't exactly my type.' She didn't want to talk about this. Didn't want his pity.

'So you have a type?'

'I haven't had a chance to figure that out yet.'

'Because you've never had the chance to meet anyone else.' He paused thoughtfully. 'It's not fair.'

His humanity was worse.

'I'm sorry,' he added. 'This whole situation really isn't fair.'

Not on *either* of them. She was never the bride he'd ever have selected for himself.

'I guess we can't all get whatever we want, whenever we want. Not without repercussions or some kind of price to pay,' she muttered.

'We should get what we want *sometimes* though. Even just some of what we want,' he countered. 'Just as we can't always get everything we want, we also shouldn't have to miss out on everything all of the time. We ought to be able to get some things sometimes, right?' He regarded her steadily.

'There's still a price. There's always a price.' For people like her anyway.

He looked at the little knife he still had in his hand. 'Perhaps you're right.'

Maia couldn't answer him. The thing she wanted to get? Him. Just him. His attention. His touch. And she was angry with herself for being that predictable. That needy.

'Truce, Maia?' He held the knife out to her.

'Okay.' She took it from him. Maybe she would take all she could from him. 'Truce.'

Niko made himself take another deep breath and counted to five while doing so. Anything to try to keep his focus. But he kept failing. Any calm he might have recaptured through his marathon swim session this afternoon had been instantly tossed overboard at the sight of her in that flowing dress that clung in only a couple of very soft-looking places. As for her stunning hair—it was finally loose and visible to him. She had beautiful jet black tresses that were so long, so rich in fullness and colour that all he wanted was to run his hands the length of them and pull her closer. He wanted to feel its silkiness tease his skin as she straddled him and bent her lush mouth to—

He was meant to be providing reassurance and building trust! Not teasing her about them getting it on, and worse, letting his imagination venture into a heated intimacy that he surely didn't actually want!

But curiosity was in control—he was fascinated by her

and desperate to find out more about her. And the realisation
that her inexperience wasn't because she wasn't interested but
that she'd just never had the chance for fun before was stunning. He'd been an idiot not to understand that already. And
he was grateful that she'd not suffered worse at the hands of
any of her father's guests. All of whom were greedy and un-
afraid of skirting the law.

She shifted restlessly. 'We ought to go inside and have
dinner.'

She was running away from the intensity between them
again. 'So soon?'

'I imagine Aron's gone to a lot of trouble and I don't want
to disrespect him by taking so long that his food spoils.'

For a second he was startled. But her consideration made
sense. Had that happened to her?

'People who are spoilt sometimes aren't conscious of the
effort made around them,' she said.

That was possibly true although not, he preferred to think,
of himself though. 'Aron knows me and my timetable here
very well. He prepares cold salads because I'm often late to
dine here.'

'Because you lose track of time while entertaining?'

He suspected the acidic drop in her tone was based more
in jealousy than judgement and he wanted *her* to have some
fun. He wanted not just to *see* that, but wanted to make it
happen for her.

'Because I'm often working late,' he corrected. 'But if I'm
not working I'm off swimming or diving, running or climbing, and no one is here to stop me or to ask other things of
me—'

'And do you always do all those things naked?'

He paused, momentarily thrown. 'You saw?' He suddenly
laughed as she blushed. 'I do apologise if what you saw of-

fended your sensibilities. When you dived overboard I was still fully dressed. I stripped to my briefs but they're uncomfortable for swimming after a while. So when I went back to secure the boat I opted for full freedom over chafing.'

She didn't answer. She just fidgeted with that knife.

'But right here is the one place where I am free to be as naked as I like,' he said quietly, amused. 'My time is wholly my own and Aron understands that.'

She glanced back up at him and he was shocked to see her expression had turned haunted and suddenly he lost himself in those midnight eyes.

'Why aren't you married already?' she asked softly, almost pleadingly. 'What would you have done with me now if you were married?'

He honestly didn't know. 'Fortunately that *isn't* the case.' And he guessed that was one thing to be grateful for. 'We're both single so the solution is simple for us.'

'But marriage isn't simple for anyone. You shouldn't be forced into something you don't want either.'

'I do want this.'

'No you *don't*.' She shrugged. 'Why has it been so complicated, Niko? What's not "safe" about a serious relationship? Why has it been so impossible to consider settling down?'

'I am trying to settle down now, am I not? *You're* the one being obstructive in that plan.'

'Only because you think you have to. Not because you *want* to. Why don't you ever want to?'

She saw that truth and he realised he'd told her too much. Now he was going to have to tell her more.

'I don't think it's fair to burden someone else with this lifestyle,' he said.

Maia glanced around. 'Yes, so terrible to ask someone to share a Pacific paradise with you. All these awful palm trees and coral reefs and the space to swim and dive, run or climb…' she echoed with a little laugh. 'Naked even. It really is just wicked of you.'

'*This* isn't the daily reality of my life.' He chuckled. 'This is the holiday that I get only occasionally. There are limits on what I can do and I know you're not going to believe me but many choices that other people take for granted get taken away.'

'But you also have many choices that other people may never get. Everyone faces sacrifices and limitations in their lives.'

'It's not the same.' He shook his head. 'Your life isn't your own. You have a duty not just to your family, but to all the citizens of the country, and to the country itself. People want to know you. You're expected to uphold the values. To bring prosperity, to maintain peace, to keep the country progressing at the same time.'

But it sounded weak to him. This was a woman who'd intensely experienced not having a life of her own—just in a wholly different way.

'I get that it's a big job but why do you think someone wouldn't want to share it?' she asked. 'Or support you in it? Do you think no one but you could handle it?'

She thought he was arrogant. That he was making more of it than what there was. She was wrong.

'Because the reality is more exhausting and frankly more mundane. It's not all glamour. There are a lot of meetings. Many decisions. Seven days a week. It's relentless.' He sat back.

He'd seen people's health suffer. More than once.

His mother had struggled, the strain of her emotions weakening her as she strived to please everyone. While his grandmother had suppressed every emotion she ever had and become an automaton—barely a human in the end. And his father? He'd lost the love of his life and then totally self-destructed.

'So you have little flings when you're overseas because there's no threat of someone taking them seriously?' Maia asked.

'If I seduced some local society beauty she would offer to sacrifice everything in her life. Her family would expect it of her and they would expect me to ask it of her. I'm never asking anyone to do that.'

'But isn't that what you're asking of me?' She paused. 'Because of the baby?'

But she didn't have much in her life to sacrifice—he could offer her far more than she'd ever had. He gritted his teeth. 'Not everything. Not necessarily forever.'

'How can it not be?' She stared at him hopelessly. 'I can't ever walk away from my child and I get the feeling you won't do that either.'

'No,' he said huskily. 'But I can give you much that you've never had, Maia.'

She looked up, those deep eyes all mystery. All intensity and pain. And rejection.

'We make a *temporary* fix to ensure this child has all they are owed,' he said roughly. 'We can do that at least, can't we, Maia?'

'I'm not saying yes to anything yet,' she said.

That she hadn't instantly said no was oddly enough for now. He didn't want her polite acquiescence. He wanted her to give him some lip again. He wanted that quite literally.

He inwardly groaned. The sudden single-track groove of his mind and the endless ache to pull her into his arms and kiss her was appalling. But the desire didn't spring from any goal to seduce her into saying yes. But to make her simply feel good. He wanted to give her pleasure.

So much for staying away from her. Yet it seemed she couldn't help reacting to their chemistry either. Which meant they might have to deal with it head-on at some point. It just had to be more thought-out and considered. She needed to understand the boundaries and limits of any relationship they embarked upon. So did he. It would solve several problems. Including the believability of their sudden marriage. Beautiful, warm, yearning, sensual. He'd lost his head for her warmth and innate sensuality...

But she was far more vulnerable than he'd realised and he didn't want this destroying her. He couldn't bear to see that happen again.

At least they'd had some moments of laughter in there. Maybe he could build on that instead.

'I'll just get the food Aron has prepared.' He fetched the small trolley Aron had left in the shade and lifted the silver domes that protected the simple salads. Fresh fish rested on ice.

'I use a table top grill to cook the fish,' he said. 'It's very thinly sliced so it only takes moments. Are you hungry?'

'To be honest I'm starving.'

'I'm sorry, I should have considered that sooner.' He gestured to the table. 'Juice? Sparkling water?'

'You don't want a glass of wine?' she asked.

He shook his head. 'You're not—'

'Don't let that stop you from having any.'

'I can cope without pleasurable indulgences for a while, Maia.'

Her startled gaze shot to him. Yeah, she was definitely thinking along the same lines as he was. All the time.

He'd have a whisky when she'd gone to bed and he could

ease the tension in every single muscle. For now he had to just stop bloody staring at her.

'Maybe I'm not the spoilt jerk you want to see me as,' he said.

'You're a little bit spoilt,' she muttered mutinously.

'Yeah, well you're a little bit stubborn.' He sighed. 'Neither of us is perfect, apparently. But we can both try our best, right?'

She nodded.

'I apologise if you were expecting something more Michelin five-star with fancy sauces. We keep things simple here.'

Fresh salads. Fresh caught fish. Fresh sliced fruit.

'Aron seems old to be working still,' she commented as he put the fish on the searingly hot grill.

'Aron suffered great loss in his life,' Niko said quietly. 'He likes to be busy. But a maintenance team comes each week for a day to turn the place over. They leave meals for the week for him too. Chopping a handful of tomatoes and raking a few leaves is the extent of his work, really.'

'You're protective of him.'

'Yes,' Niko said.

'He's worked for you for a long time?'

Aron knew everything. And he was as guilty, as hurt, as Niko was because of what had happened not just to Niko's aunt but his mother as well. Aron had loved them too. He had failed them too. In that Niko and Aron had each other.

Niko sighed. 'He is very loyal. He made a lot of sacrifices.'

Maia lifted a fork to her mouth and tasted a small morsel. Her eyes closed briefly.

'This needs nothing more. It's naturally delicious. Where did you learn to cook fish like this?'

'Here. I learned to catch it and prepare it too.' He stared

at her soft lips, watching the tantalising flick of her tongue, absurdly pleased to see her enjoyment.

'You've been coming to this island since you were little?'

Now he was happy to answer her questions and keep his mind out of dangerous waters. 'We came a lot when I was very young. A lot of long weekends.' His mother had rested on that veranda. He'd not realised that she needed the quiet to restore her fragile emotional energy. He'd not understood how much she needed to convalesce that until he was older— when hearing his father chastised yet again by his grandparents. 'Less in my early teens, I was sent overseas to a boarding school.'

'Why overseas?' She looked surprised.

'It was considered a vital part of my education to mingle with other future leaders and nobility. To learn other languages, history, science and the arts of diplomacy.' He'd made a good friend in particular there. 'I got to see a lot of the world and do things that I might not have had the chance to do otherwise. After my mother died it was a help to be busy there. It wasn't long after I finished that my father then died and I became the heir. I needed to learn much from my grandfather so didn't come here.' He dragged in a breath. 'But after *his* death I came here for a short period of mourning.' He'd just needed to be alone for a few days. 'There'd been a storm and much of the building was damaged. Over the next couple of years I refurbished it.'

'You laid the stonework yourself?' she challenged.

'Some of it, yes. I hadn't the skills for the fine details, but I worked as a labourer for the craftsmen whenever I could. This was a project I put everything I could into.'

He'd worked through his grief. His guilt. Pax had lived on-site and worked alongside him as part of his own rehabilitation. So had Aron.

'Because you love it here.'

'Because I *need* it.' He froze, stunned at his emotional outburst.

To admit that he *needed* anything to anyone was unusual for him and he didn't know why he had. He glanced up. She was gazing at him with those mysterious eyes. If he wasn't careful he'd slip into them and never emerge again. But honestly, right now he wouldn't care if he were lost in them for good.

'What else do you need?' she asked huskily.

He lost all power of speech. His body had the answer. Only the one.

Her eyes darkened. Hardened.

'Don't you need a wife who can provide you with all the usual wifely things a king requires?' She licked her lips. 'Like one who provides more than one heir? Don't you need a woman who will provide support at events and then relaxation for you? Someone who can speak all those other languages with you, one who understands diplomatic nuances…?' She angled her head and hit him where it hurt. 'Shouldn't you have a society beauty of noble birth who's been educated in *all* the arts of keeping her king content?'

The woman she described was *exactly* the kind he should have. And the last one he wanted. Emotion bubbled again but she didn't know how close to the edge he was and she didn't stop.

'Wouldn't your parents have wanted to approve of—'

'My parents were a love match,' he interrupted her harshly. 'My father refused to accept the marriage that was arranged for him. My mother was a local girl he'd met as a teen.'

Maia's eyes widened. And yeah, she knew *nothing*.

'They married in secret so they couldn't be stopped. The formal, public ceremony was a cover-up that took place several weeks later.'

They'd been teen sweethearts who'd vowed to do anything for each other. And had.

'Were they happy?'

He paused and went for the truth. 'They loved each other to the end but no, they weren't happy.'

Maia flinched and suddenly he was compelled to hold nothing back.

'It wasn't a fairy tale, Maia. Love wasn't enough for it to work. My mother was unsuited to palace life and family dynamics were difficult. He tried to protect her but she wouldn't let him sacrifice his duty for her. She tried but it wore her out.'

Look after her.

His father had instructed him every time he left to work and Niko and his mother had come here. Because—soft and empathetic—she was worn out easily simply by loving too much.

'My father loved her and she loved him but she couldn't quite be happy there.' Nor had Niko been able to make her happy—he'd not been able to help her, he'd not been able to stop her from driving away that night. All of that hurt and he couldn't forgive himself for any of it. For his aunt's misery. His mother's. And ultimately, for both their deaths. 'She couldn't cope with his parents' disapproval…'

Maia swallowed. 'What happened?'

'She spent as much time here as she could.'

'They lived separately?'

'No, it was occasional escapes. My grandmother was a rigid, stern woman who thought that everyone should be able to meet her very exacting standards. She did her duty and expected everyone else to do theirs too with no question. Obligation to the crown was everything and she couldn't understand why her new daughter-in-law couldn't handle the sacrifices required.'

But his mother had been a woman who tried to champion everyone and who exhausted herself in the process. Wanting to be the best she could. Never accepting that she was already enough. Never taking the breaks that she needed. Working herself around the clock to try to please his grandparents. The high standards that no one could ever possibly meet. She'd ached for their approval. She'd wanted to please everyone. And that was impossible.

Niko wasn't asking any woman to attempt that on his behalf.

'Your grandmother sounds formidable. Was *hers* a love match?'

'She'd been my grandfather's betrothed since they were very young,' he said, letting all the cynicism colour his tone. 'Arranged marriages don't always work well either.'

Maia looked at him. 'No?'

'My grandfather was not faithful. He was not expected to be. Not even by her. She turned a blind eye to certain infractions. To ensure stability I suppose.' He sat back. 'She dove into being the best queen she could be. But she grew inflexible and bitter.'

Both wives had been failed. But nothing was as bad as what had happened to Aunt Lani, his grandfather's firstborn child. She'd been betrayed—unacknowledged. She'd been *used*.

He looked down at the table. It was his family duty to provide heirs to the nation. But arranged marriages could hopefully be managed. He'd wanted to make his the shortest he could, which was why he'd planned to delay getting married for as long as possible. Then he'd marry someone with her own life. A minor royal from another island nation maybe. His counsellor of state had kept him apprised of possibilities and he hadn't exactly been disappointed when a couple on his list of possibilities had married other men. But a love match would be even worse.

'So you don't want to marry at all,' Maia said.

Somehow she'd had him spilling family stuff he'd never spoken of. Like a mysterious nymph, drawing him into lowering his guard. Yet into danger at the same time. All innocence and confusion and fire.

'I've been delaying it for as long as possible.' He nodded. But now he had no choice and he wasn't going to let her try to convince him otherwise. 'Unlike my grandfather I've always been scrupulous in my use of birth control measures. I've never had a possible incident before now.'

Something flickered in her face. Distaste? Jealousy? It pushed him to provoke her more.

'And just so you know, I've never brought a woman here, Maia. It's too personal a place for me.' He leaned towards her. 'You're my first.'

She stared at him and his pulse thudded at the smokiness clouding those mysteriously deep eyes. 'Am I supposed to feel honoured?'

Feeling finally flowed again. Even if it was a dangerous complication, it was better than the numb emptiness of before. He wanted the tantalising heat and the tempting risk of her explosion. So he dared her again with a drawl of pure intentional arrogance. 'Don't you?'

CHAPTER EIGHT

'I'M UNDER no illusions, Niko. You only brought me here because I tried to run away and it's the one place you could bring me that was secure—other than the palace dungeons. And the dungeons wouldn't do in this day and age. Not for someone in my delicate condition. You'd be universally condemned and that wouldn't do for the popular playboy king, would it?' She lifted her chin. 'So *I* am not honoured at all.'

But that this place was too *personal* for him to bring his lovers intrigued her more than she liked. He didn't like to share certain parts of himself with anyone. She wondered why—his parents' troubles, perhaps. It certainly didn't sound like his childhood at the palace had been blissful.

He came here because he needed time and space to himself. Perhaps he was more of an introvert than his charming facade suggested. Perhaps he needed to recharge and refresh here, where he could soak in the sea and stride to the top of the mountain and feel utterly at peace. At home. Hell, naked if he felt so inclined. She totally understood—and it humanised him too, too much.

A tight smile curved his lips but those angles of his mathematically perfect features sharpened. 'It's getting late. You'll want to go to your room and stay there, Maia. There are sea snakes and other biting creatures that hunt here at night.'

'Maybe I'll bite them back.'

He lifted his hand and showed the mark she'd inflicted had all but disappeared. 'You can't even break skin. Stay inside.'

'What are you going to do?'

He stared at her for a long moment. 'You sure you want the answer to that question?'

She stared right back at him. He didn't intimidate her, he *excited* her. And that was the problem—but it was the one she couldn't resist. 'Yes,' she said. 'If I'm to be stuck with you then I expect to know what you're doing, when you're doing it and who you're doing it with.' She pushed back from the table and took a couple of paces towards the pool to expend some of the energy coiling too tightly within her. 'I'm not going to be quietly content and remain in complete ignorance of my husband's assignations.'

His gaze intensified as he looked up at where she stood in the moonlight. 'So you agree that we'll marry then?'

'I've agreed to nothing. Yet.' Something sparked within her. She didn't believe for a second that he would actually hurt her. Quite the opposite. She had the intuition that he could make her feel something unlike anything or anyone else in the world. 'I'm still considering my terms.'

'Your terms?' He watched her. 'What more do you want?' He shot her a wolfish smile as he listed the bare necessities he'd provided for her. 'You have food, shelter, clothing—'

'Actually, there was one small issue with that delivery.'

'Oh?'

'There was no underwear.'

The way his eyes widened she knew it had been an inadvertent mistake, not a deliberate strategy. '*What?*'

'It's okay.' She smiled blithely at his breathlessness. 'I can use a bikini.'

He blinked.

'But I didn't tonight,' she added.

His gaze tightened. 'Are you telling me you're wearing nothing underneath that flimsy dress?'

'I figured you wouldn't mind if you noticed. I assumed your lovers would be confident, sensual people but you seem to be blushing.' But she was blushing more because he was looking at the dress as if he could tear it away with one movement. Which, to be fair, he probably could.

'Maia.' His bossy king voice emerged. 'Don't provoke me.'

She struggled to keep her gaze on him. 'What do you mean?'

'I mean I'll prove the impact I have on you in the next second if you don't stop trying to make me—' He broke off and suddenly pushed back from the table to stand. 'If you don't want me to retaliate in kind, then I'd advise you to stop right now.'

Maia remained in place as he walked towards her. She wasn't going to run away from him this time. But in truth, every muscle was locked so tight she couldn't have moved even if she'd wanted to.

'Or do you *want* me to retaliate, Maia?' he asked silkily. 'Is that what this is? Because all you have to do is ask. But maybe you can't quite bring yourself to do that yet. So maybe we change the communication. Maybe you just have to say *no*, and I'll stop. But maybe I'm not going to stop until you do.'

She stared up at him in shock as he cupped her jaw and his other hand lightly ran the length of her hair.

He leaned closer. 'Just take, okay? I'll give and you take.'

Was *that* how this was working? But he was right. It was a gift. Lush little kisses. So different to that passionate, out-of-control onslaught in the water this afternoon, but no less powerful. She melted into his strength and he suddenly bent her back, supporting her completely to then kiss her deeply. She moaned, feeling the passion run right through her. But it wasn't enough. She wanted more. So much more that it terrified her.

'Stop,' she muttered desperately. 'I need you to stop.'

He instantly did but even so she pushed him, straightening and turning swiftly away.

'Maia.' He grabbed her arm before she could escape. 'Stop. Speak to me.'

'And say what?' Hurt bubbled up. 'You proved you can make me want you in an instant. Can't you be satisfied with that?'

'That's not—' He drew a harsh breath and suddenly stepped back. 'Go to bed, Maia,' he said huskily. '*Rest.* You need it.'

As if that were ever going to happen now? Her body was wired. How had that become a conflagration of such heat and passion so quickly?

But he'd walked away so easily. He'd not tried to convince her to continue. Which was good, right?

No. It was irritating.

She went to her suite, glad of the open windows and whirring fans. She was too hot, too irritable, thinking too much to sleep. Besides, the bed was too big. Too still. She'd spent her life on the water, feeling the gentle swell of the sea. Sometimes the rough waves. Always in motion. She'd never once had an actual mattress. She felt stupid but it was too soft. And it made her think of things that weren't going to bring any kind of peace to her over-imaginative mind. With a frustrated sigh she wrapped the silk robe more tightly around herself and went from her veranda to the hammock. She would cool down for a while in the light wind and listen to the waves.

It was an immediate comfort to lightly sway and stare up at the stars that were so familiar to her. She identified the constellations as a form of distraction, calming herself by remembering the generations of way-finders who'd traversed this ocean several times over—moving from island to island and finding freedom and prosperity.

She didn't know how long she'd been out there but she heard footsteps approaching and lay still, hoping he wouldn't see her. Of course she had no such luck.

'It doesn't matter how much you try to shrink yourself down, that robe is gleaming like a pearl in the moonlight.' He expelled a frustrated puff as he leaned over to look her in the eyes. 'What are you *doing* out here?'

'I'm not used to sleeping in a bed like that.'

'Like what?' He looked so outraged she was forced to explain.

'So big. And flat. And it doesn't move. It's too still.'

He stared at her. 'You sleep in a hammock on board your father's boat?'

'Yes. In the store.'

His jaw went angular.

'I actually like it,' she added hurriedly, seeing the storm grow even bigger in his eyes. 'I prefer it to having my own cabin. It's away from the others and more private.'

'You've lived in that your whole life?'

'I like the sway of it. And I like listening to the waves,' she continued defiantly, ignoring the appalled judgement in his voice. 'The sound calms me.'

He stared at her for interminable seconds. 'It calms me too,' he said brusquely.

To her astonishment he turned on the spot and left her in a jumble of want and misery and confusion. She pressed hands to her hot cheeks. She was hopelessly attracted to him and she had no idea how to handle it. Ten minutes later she heard heavy footsteps again. They were deliberately heavy—because she knew too well how silently he could move when he wanted to.

'I've put up another hammock on your veranda,' he informed her with a growling edge. 'At least there you'll be sheltered from wind and rain. You can bring down the hatches if you want for additional privacy but as it is now no one will see you other than me. There are some blankets and a pillow too.'

'Niko—'

'I have an outdoor shower area in the garden by my suite,' he interrupted her gruffly. 'So don't go wandering if you don't want to see any more…things.'

With that zinger he stomped off again. Maia lay for another moment purely to catch her breath. Then she went back to her own veranda. He'd left a lantern on and she saw the hammock was one of those silk ones more suited to balmy nights than wild weather. Sure enough there was a pillow, a soft blanket inside. He'd even put a table within reach for that lantern with a glass and a jug of iced water as well. He'd thought of everything.

She clambered in and closed her eyes. But she could hear the flow of running water in the distance and knew he was beneath that shower and her mind decided to torment her with a play-by-play replay of him wading deep into the water in all his naked glory…

And how was she ever supposed to go to sleep *now*?

To her astonishment she did sleep—for hours. Even more amazingly she woke not just feeling refreshed but with an odd amount of energy—more alive than she'd felt in weeks.

She went to the kitchen to ask Aron if there was anything she could do but he wasn't there. She waited, unable to resist peeking into the pantry. And when he didn't show after a while she decided to make herself something delicious. That was one craving she could satisfy for herself. She lost track of time entirely and when Niko walked in and skidded to a halt she startled.

'What are you doing?' he demanded. 'I thought you were sleeping in...'

She whirled, putting her knife and block into the pocket of the apron she'd commandeered. 'I was. Then I woke up.'

'Why are you baking? You don't need to do that here.' He flared angrily. 'I would have gotten Aron to get you some pastry if I'd known you wanted—'

'I know, but I wanted to make them myself.'

'You wanted to stand sweating in the kitchen?' he said sarcastically.

'I felt like doing something. It's not a chore when I *choose* to do it. I didn't think Aron would mind.' She was suddenly worried. 'Will he mind? I haven't seen him at all this morning.'

'Because he's gone to visit his family offshore. We're completely alone here for the next couple of days.'

She stilled. 'Why have you done that?'

'Why do you think I've done that?'

She swallowed and ducked from his gaze.

'But the last thing I want is for you to slave in the kitchen for hours.'

'Well, what am I supposed to do? I can't just sit around...'

'Sit around what?' he prompted.

Staring at him all day. She *needed* distraction. Desperately.

He suddenly smiled. 'You should take the time for yourself, Maia.'

For herself? She wanted him to distract her. 'You don't need to feel sorry for me, Niko,' she flared. 'I don't want your pity. You don't need to spoil me.'

'Why not?' he countered. 'Why shouldn't I feel sorry for you? Why shouldn't I want to spoil you?'

'I'm pregnant. Not useless.'

'I'm not talking about resting just because of the baby,' he muttered. 'Why is it so hard for you to accept a little pampering in your life?'

'I don't need it.'

'Don't you? Doesn't everyone? I sure as hell do.'

Her eyes widened.

'I make no apology for taking breaks. For doing the things I enjoy.'

'Women.'

'Being in the water,' he corrected and then shook his head with a rueful smile. 'You really have a one-track mind, Maia Flynn.'

She felt that heat and suddenly nodded. 'It's a recent thing,' she admitted apologetically. 'Do you think it's the hormones?'

'Maybe.' He leaned against the counter and laughed. 'I'm talking about taking time for myself. Yes, to come here and swim naked all damned day if I want. I like it. Why shouldn't you do whatever brings you joy too? You've worked your whole life. You should be able to have a few moments of peace for yourself.'

'Why can't you believe that I actually was?' She pulled her knife from her pocket. 'I do have a few things like that.'

He was instantly alert. 'Show me?'

For once it was an actual request, not a demand.

'It's just little.' Embarrassed, she pulled the block from her pocket. 'I raided the woodpile, sorry.'

'You can take anything you want.' He studied the partial figurine she'd been whittling. 'You're an artist.'

'Hardly,' she scoffed. 'I'm a hobbyist. It's just something to fill in time.'

'It's more than that.' He held the half-carved miniature sea turtle in the palm of his hand. 'Did someone teach you?'

She nodded. 'Our chef, Stefan. He taught me how to make pastry and he also taught me to whittle. Sometimes there weren't any offcuts or driftwood or anything so we'd just use vegetables. Or coconut shells. Whatever was at hand.'

'You were friends?'

Stefan had been more of a father figure to her than her own father. He'd certainly been more kind. 'His marriage had broken down and he'd lost contact with his own children. I think perhaps with me he had a chance to…' She shrugged. 'He was a good man who'd made some mistakes in the past. He had regrets, you know? He taught me lots of useful stuff— placing orders in each port, haggling in the market, where to find good books in the hostels, diving for shellfish. He helped me with my correspondence school work. I was a distraction for him I guess.'

'I'm sure you were more to him than just a distraction.' Niko glanced into the distance. 'Where is he now?'

Maia plucked the little carving from Niko's palm and put it back in the apron pocket. 'My father can be difficult. He drinks, he's controlling, he's constantly trying to make money, but he's not usually violent. When I was a kid Stefan kept me busy in the galley—out of the way and safe—and he introduced me to something I grew passionate about and that I became good at.' She looked at Niko. 'And that was the problem. I got too good.' She smiled sadly. 'I actually thought Dad might say well done, you know? But all he did was terminate Stefan's contract because I could make croissants just as well as him—which wasn't actually true, by the way. But I'd made him redundant and I had to take over the galley full-time.'

Niko's smile had gone—he was all cheekbones of perfection. 'How old were you?'

'Sixteen.'

'How long had Stefan been with you?'

'Since I was two.' Fourteen *years*. She'd lost her best friend overnight. 'I've not had contact with him since he's left.' She turned back to the pastry that had rested long enough. 'I'm sure he's fine. He would have picked up work easily, he was very talented. I don't know why he put up with my father for as long as he did.'

But she felt heartsick about it. If it hadn't been for her he would still have had that job.

'It wasn't your fault, Maia. Your father took advantage of you both and Stefan would have known that. Maybe you're why he stayed as long as he did.'

She blinked rapidly. 'It's in the past.'

'Doesn't mean it doesn't still hurt, sometimes.'

She glanced at him—his own pain hurt him too.

'That's his knife, right?' Niko asked huskily. 'That's why it's your favourite. It's old. It's been well cared for.'

She nodded. He'd given it to her the day he'd had to leave.

The atmosphere thickened with tension. She felt her emotional control slipping. She did not cry. And she wasn't going to now.

'I need to get this into the oven.' She fussed over the pastry dough that had barely rested long enough.

'Of course.' He cleared his throat. 'I'm going to do some work.'

An hour later Maia finished cleaning up in the kitchen. She tore a piece of fresh croissant but it didn't satisfy the hunger gnawing her insides. Hot and restless she went to her room and changed into the yellow bikini and released her hair. But at the pool she found Niko already in there. He'd been floating on his back but when she walked out he splashed and stood, watching her approach. He didn't smile. He didn't speak.

Somewhat intimidated, Maia glanced around in case she'd missed something but the only thing new was paperwork on the table nearest the water. Well, she wasn't interested in reading any of his private royal documents or anything. She turned back and caught his attention roving over her body. She should've wrapped her towel around herself. His frown deepened the nearer she got to the water.

'What's wrong?' she asked.

'Might be best if you run away again, Maia.'

She stopped at the edge of the pool. 'Why?'

A muttered growl beneath his breath. 'Because I am *trying* to behave but I need some space from you in order to get myself back under control.'

'Space from me?' She glanced down.

He rolled his eyes. 'Yes, Maia. From you. From you and your midnight eyes and bountiful breasts and stunning hair that smells so delicious.'

She gaped, feeling her body respond to the astonishing compliments. But she didn't believe him. 'You're struggling with the loss of your lifestyle.'

His eyebrows shot up.

'It's okay.' She paddled her toe in the water. 'I'm actually *not* judging. I get it. You're young and fit. You weren't ready to settle down and you were living life and having fun. So you're used to indulging your appetite and of course it's going to take some…processing that you now can't.'

'I can't?' he echoed blandly. 'Is that what it is?' He waded closer to her. '*You're* young and fit. But you're *not* living life and having fun. You've *never* indulged your appetite and don't try to tell me you don't have one.'

Her smile twisted. 'I'm not a king though, am I?'

'Are you saying people are only interested in being with me because of my status?'

She laughed. 'Sure. Yeah. That's definitely it.'

He shook his head. 'You can't think of any other reasons why they might want to be with me?'

She shook her head.

'No?' He rested his hands on the edge of the pool and looked up at her, laughter in his smouldering eyes. 'Not any? Cutting me down to size again, Maia?'

'It's impossible. You're too arrogant,' she muttered.

'I might be arrogant, Maia. But I also know when a woman is interested in being with me.'

Her pulse skittered and she stiffened her decidedly shaky legs.

'She might look at me a little too long. Especially when she thinks I'm not watching her. But I am. Because I'm acutely aware of her too. And I'm attuned to her responses.' He levered out of the pool and walked towards her. 'I watch her breathing. Her blush. The beat of her heart. The look in her eyes. So many snippets reveal secrets.'

Maia couldn't move. She also couldn't stop trembling. 'Maybe she's got a fever.'

'Oh, she surely does. The same one as me. Lust is a fever that steals other appetites and becomes the sole focus until it is all you can think about, all of the time.'

'Must make life quite challenging.'

'Unchecked, it absolutely can. It can make concentrating on other things difficult. Which is why it's good to indulge it before it balloons that far out of control.'

'Is that what happens?'

'I don't know. I've never not indulged it. Whereas you never have. So you tell me.'

She felt an odd dizziness sweep over her and a forlorn wish burst from her. 'Don't laugh at me.'

'I'm not.' He looked into her eyes with a frown. 'I would never laugh *at* you, Maia.'

She wanted to believe that about him. But she wasn't sure. She'd heard the laughter of men from overhead so many times. She'd heard the crew joke about no one wanting her. About how easy it would be to seduce her because she was so starved of attention. She'd heard that exact plan from one younger group of guests. So she'd known to resist the fool who'd come downstairs to deliberately flatter her. The assumption she'd be easy pickings.

'Well, don't flatter me to try to get me into bed,' she added distantly. 'I know guys do that.'

He leaned closer. 'They do?'

She nodded angrily. She'd hid her hair beneath a scarf not only to keep it from getting in her face when in the galley. She'd kept her head down and her body shrouded in a large apron even in the heat to hide. Self-preservation. Avoidance. Even when the cute young guys came on board because they sometimes turned out to be less cute and more pushy.

'I'm not experienced. I'm lonely. I'm unattractive. Because I'm always working hard with no one paying nice attention to me. Meeting almost no one. So hit me with a few generic compliments and I'll be an easy lay, right? It won't take anything much to make someone like me feel special.'

He'd frozen. 'Someone said that?'

'I *heard* them making the plan. They didn't know I could hear everything when I was cleaning their stupid cabins.' She scoffed at herself softly. 'And the tragic thing was I'd thought he was actually quite cute.'

'Maia—'

'So I'm not going anywhere because I'm quite sure you can control yourself,' she snapped at his sympathy. 'But if you can't, *you* can leave.'

He stared at her. 'I'm not going anywhere.'

CHAPTER NINE

THE AWFUL, awful thing was she was shaking and he wasn't even touching her. She quickly turned her back on the pool. The view beyond was incredible but she barely saw it because a wall of heat rose within her and it was unstoppable.

'Maia?'

She heard a muttered oath and his hand felt light on her face. 'You're too hot,' he growled. 'You overdid it.'

He pushed her, leading her to the shallow steps of the pool that were currently in the shade. He made her sit so now the water lapped over her feet.

He moved out of her sightline for a moment. Next minute he pressed a cold glass into her hand. 'I knew you shouldn't have spent hours in a hot kitchen.'

She sipped the juice, savouring the sweet yet acid bite of the pineapple. 'It's not that.'

'No?' He took the drink and drained the remainder before setting the glass on the marble tile beside them. 'Then what?'

She shivered and he sat one step up behind her, drawing her back against his chest. 'Lean on me for a minute.'

His strong legs stretched out either side of her. Encircling her. Reminding her of those moments when he'd held her through that boat journey when she'd been blindfolded. When she'd not known who he was. When she'd not even known she was pregnant. When she'd felt absurdly, yet completely, safe. The safest she'd felt in so very long. Now he ran his hands down her hair, sweeping it from her shoulder, exposing her neck—cooling it. Her breathing slowed.

'Better?' A soft query right beside her ear.

She nodded, unable to resist sinking more fully against him and inclining her head so more of her neck was exposed to the delicious, tickling tease of his warm breath on her sensitive skin. He slid his arms around her waist and, giving up her resistance completely, she rested her head on his chest.

'What do you need, Maia?'

She shook her head imperceptibly. Something she shouldn't.

'Maia?'

A question. An admonishment. A prayer. He was so very gentle and she so warm. Yet goose bumps rose on her skin. Being this close to him filled her with the sweetest, sharpest longing. Every cell yearned for contact with him.

'I cannot resist you,' he muttered.

'But you want to.'

'Because it's what's…honourable.'

'Is it honourable to refuse a woman—' She broke off on a sigh as his fingertips glided to her breast.

'Is that what I would be doing?' he asked. 'Then I won't refuse you.'

Her bikini top slipped down so easily—exposing her breasts to the air and her nipples to his hands—to the teasing swirls of his fingertips, to a pinch and a soothing stroke. To his palms as he cupped her. She moaned at the press of his mouth on her neck. He kissed, licked, sucked…*savouring*. And she just heated. Melted.

'You never wanted me before,' she muttered sadly.

His laughter was soft. 'I never met you before.'

'You said this happening was extremely unlikely.'

'I was being rude because at that time I was feeling extremely provoked.' He pressed another kiss on the side of her neck. 'I'm never going to be sorry for this, Maia. Will you be? Because if so, we need to stop now.'

'Don't stop.'

He stroked down her belly with a gentle hand that she couldn't resist. Her breath caught as he hit the band of her bikini bottoms. He had one hand between her legs now but not beneath the stretchy fabric of her bikini bottoms. She whimpered, wanting his touch, aching for him to explore her even more intimately. To be in her. Instead those fingers simply teased. Skating over where she was most sensitive. Where deep inside she was slick and soft for him. Her moans escaped, louder, and she moved restlessly, instinctively seeking more. In the drowsy heat of the afternoon she had to close her eyes and somehow he knew. His hold on her tightened and he encased her in a velvety heat.

'No one but me can see you. No one but me can hear you. There's only us.' The possessive satisfaction in his whisper turned her on even more. 'Trust me, Maia.'

She spread her hands wide on his thighs, savouring the tense muscles beneath, the sensual pleasure of pressing them so he closed his hold more tightly around her. This was what she liked. Being cocooned by him. Not just embraced. But overwhelmed. Overpowered. And yet, she felt such freedom in his hold.

'Let go, Maia,' he commanded. 'I've got you.'

But his hands coaxed. They were so gentle, so relentlessly, devastatingly, frustratingly gentle. She tensed as every muscle locked—strung out in the agony of arousal she was so, so close to breaking.

'Now, darling.' A gravelly whisper.

Her cry was rough and raw as she shuddered and her hands curled like claws into his strong thighs. He pressed them closer still. He was literally her vise. Holding her even as he shattered her. And in the long tumultuous shudders of ecstasy he held her closer still.

Niko wasn't living the rest of his life without touching Maia the way she wanted to be touched. He wasn't saying no to her. *Ever.* He wanted her and he would have her regardless of any damned consequences. Because she wanted him too. He believed in honesty. In taking the good things where and when they could be found. Because life was full of difficulties. For everyone.

'There's nothing wrong with pleasure, Maia,' he said quietly when she'd stilled in his arms and had been silent for a little too long for his comfort.

'I know.' She twisted her head to look at him and there was strength and quiet dignity in her gaze. 'I haven't had it. Not nearly enough of *any* kind of pleasure and honestly, none sexually. Not like that. But I want more. Can you deliver?'

His heart stopped. 'I'll do my best.' But for once his confidence faltered and confusion rose. 'We just need to burn this out,' he said huskily, trying to reassure himself as much as her. 'It's a distraction. We get through it and move forward. Then we can think again.'

She gazed into his eyes, her own slightly dazed. 'It's like that for you too?'

'Yes.' Hell, yes. A round-the-clock fascination from the moment he'd first seen her. But he had to normalise it—minimise it. 'This is chemistry Maia. You've not felt this before?'

She shook her head.

Oh hell. He was screwed. 'It's lust,' he added hoarsely. 'Raw attraction. Nothing more.'

'I didn't think it was anything more,' she growled back at him. 'I don't even particularly like you. You're an autocrat who's completely spoilt and who thinks he can get away with anything.'

He suddenly laughed, deeply aroused. 'And you're a wilful woman determined to get her own way. Neither of us is willing to compromise.'

'It seems not.'

'It's going to be a battle.' And he was going to relish it.

'I don't want to fight. I want you to teach me.'

'Teach you what?'

'How to please you the way you just pleased me.'

He was dumbstruck. His mouth was dry and full of cotton wool or something. So was his brain. Maybe it was the sun but he'd never felt as hot in his life. He kissed her. Couldn't touch enough of her. Couldn't get to everything he wanted. Not soon enough. Not now.

'Teach me,' she breathed again when he released her lips long enough for her to actually speak.

'Just touch me.'

And she did. But too lightly. Not far enough. Not fast enough.

Her hand skimmed over his stomach. 'How many hours do you spend in the gym to keep your body so beautiful?'

'Aren't you glad I do?' he challenged softly, hearing the acidic edge to her question. 'It's turning you on right now.'

Earlier her judgement had scoured—an abrasion he wanted to reject—sliding beneath his armour. But she wanted him not in spite of it but because of it. She liked challenging him on this level. A sensual game in which she wanted to best him. And he would play with her.

'Touch any part of me you want, Maia.' He lay back on the marble, feeling the sun-warmed stone warm his already hot skin. '*Every* part.'

That silenced her. Her eyes went round and suddenly he

felt a qualm. Maybe she *would* best him. He watched the sensual ripple of her body—the pure physical expression of arousal as she braved up and straddled him.

He could only stare. She had such beauty—complex, earthy, unexpected. Her newly unleashed sexuality undid him. He couldn't resist cupping her breasts. Wanting to pleasure her again but wary of pushing for too much, too soon. The flush in her cheeks deepened. He saw that spark again. That challenge.

'Don't try to control this,' she whispered. 'Let me be free.'

He almost swallowed his tongue. He lifted his hands from her in surrender. Allowing her to access any bit of him she wanted. He really hoped she wanted that bit currently acting like a damned flagpole. Dazed, he watched the undulation of her hips as she bent above him and explored him with her hands. Her hair teased him and she traced his tattoos with her fingertips, with her tongue, and he breathed in the uninhibited, natural dance of her desire. This absolute release of self-consciousness, of control was a rare gift. He saw the focused gleam in her eyes and was transfixed, suddenly harder than he'd ever been. He was literally aching for her touch and scared to even move in case she pulled away. His mouth was dry but he was unable to swallow. And the sweetness of her sudden, swift kiss did nothing to sate him. He wanted more. He wanted all of her. He felt the need so desperately in a part so deep he'd not even realised it existed.

Five minutes ago her hands desperately rubbing his thighs had driven him to distraction. Feeling the passion, the fervour in her fevered caresses and her aching need had stunned him. There was such heat there, such longing, so much that she'd hidden from him—from the world—for so long. He wanted to draw her out. He wanted her to be free. But his customary eloquence was gone. His customary control gone.

'Maia.' He was hoarse with want.

He *needed* her to touch him. He needed that soft hand right where he was so hard it hurt. He tensed as she trailed her fingers ever so slowly to the waistband of his board shorts. He gritted his teeth, shaking as she slipped her fingers beneath. And then—he who had infinite experience—suddenly, completely lost everything at first contact.

A guttural roar of pleasure and frustration escaped him as he was tossed into a paroxysm of white-hot ecstasy. He growled again, pumping up into her firm hold, his pleasure spilling far, far too soon. And what pleasure it was—his whole body, even the damned soles of his feet, tingled and he gasped for recovery. He'd been unable to withstand the slightest touch. She'd defeated him with little more than a sigh and a sweet kiss and a tentative tug. He stared up at her, stunned. He'd come at first stroke, mortifyingly quickly, as if *he* were the virgin, barely coping with a singular caress.

She sat back and doubt entered her eyes. 'Is that it?'

He groaned again and then could only laugh helplessly even as he panted, pressing the back of his hands hard on his eyes to try to recover his brain. But she'd utterly overwhelmed him.

'Did I do something wrong?' She sounded shy. 'I didn't expect it to be so quick.'

'Neither did I.' He laughed again. But then he dragged in a breath and his energy surged back. He sat up and wrapped his arms around her so she couldn't slip from his lap. 'You didn't do anything wrong. That was just...'

'Just?' She was watching him like a wary little mouse. All wide eyes and silence.

'Incredible.' He kissed her, then breathed deep again and stood—lifting her with him—loving the way she automatically wrapped her arms around his neck. 'If we stay out here we'll get sunstroke. We need a bed.'

And he needed to get his head together.

But he could only stare at her for a second—clad only in those bikini briefs, her luscious breasts bouncing with their stiff little nipples rubbing against his chest like the little lick-me beacons they were... Yeah, she was a wet dream and he did not deserve this. But he refused to be a better man. He awkwardly snagged a couple of croissants from the kitchen counter on the way through to his bedroom. He put her on the bed and handed her one of the croissants before biting into the other. And moaned. Buttery soft and delicious. Of course it bloody was.

And she just smiled at him cheekily. 'Niko?'

Maia was *pretty* sure she'd pleased him. But his groan had seemed awfully sudden and for a second after when he'd looked at her—he'd seemed shocked.

'Eat,' he ordered gruffly.

'I'm fine.'

'Just eat something,' he advised. 'You're going to need it.'

She almost baulked at the ferocious intensity smoking in his gaze. Heat sparked. She was already too aware of the intimate ache deep inside, the hunger barely at bay. Sensation curled through her, making her restless. Heating and slicking deep in secret parts.

He finished his pastry in two more bites and his wicked smile slowly widened. 'You decimate my expectations every time,' he said. 'I should have known.'

'Is that a good thing?'

'I have a feeling we're about to find out.' He frowned at the pastry still in her hand. 'Do I need to feed it to you myself?'

She was astonishingly aroused at the thought.

His eyes sparkled. 'Oh Maia, we're going to have fun to-gether.'

'That is the plan,' she said, desperately nibbling the edge of the croissant as if she had any control over herself anymore.

Sleeping with him was most likely going to be the biggest mistake of her life. But it was one worth making. She wanted this. To know. To understand. To have him in her arms. En-joying her and giving her the things she'd been denied so long. Attention. Lust. Ecstasy. The delights of sensuality were a side of life she'd shut away for so long. She wanted what other people had and he could give it to her. He already had. It's just that she was greedy and wanted more. And it was so nice not thinking about anything more. Not worrying about the future. There was only this delicious excitement and that she felt no self-consciousness at all amazed her. She felt ut-terly safe with him here like this—to say what she wanted, to do what she wanted.

'You're so beautiful.' He pushed her back onto the bed and knelt over her.

She *almost* believed him this time. And then it didn't mat-ter because he was touching her. Stripping the bikini briefs from her. Kissing her. Tasting her. Every writhing inch. Until at last his hands stroked her nipples while his tongue slid over the secret nub of her sex. Her hands stretched wide on the big bed seeking something to hang on to as she shook with ecstasy almost as quickly as he'd done before. But then he still didn't lie with her the way she wanted him to. He got off the bed.

'Where are you going?' she demanded, ferociously angry. Hungry.

She had what she wanted but she wanted more.

His smile was strained. 'I've never been intimate without protection. I'll just get—'

'I'm already pregnant,' she interrupted. 'I know you won't do me or the baby harm.' She lifted her chin and blurted the truth. 'I don't want anything between us. I don't care. I know—'

She broke off at the smouldering intensity as he suddenly swore pithily.

'Are you sure about all this?' He growled. 'It can't be undone, Maia.'

'I'm not stupid—'

'I know,' he bit back. His hands on his hips, a picture of aroused, edgy male. 'But this will change things.'

'Don't feel you have to—'

'*Stop*.' In less than a second he was back on the bed, straddling her, his big hands taking her wrists. 'Stop doubting how much I want *you*.'

She stared up at him. Her lips felt full, her whole body was humming with the remnants of bliss but with an emptiness that ached like nothing else.

Don't take this too seriously.

This wasn't forever. This was dealing with the chemistry neither of them had anticipated. He kissed her and she moaned. Desperate relief. Desolate yearning. The paradox of having but still wanting. Of not wanting it to be over yet wanting it all *now*. She twisted, unable to contain the battle within.

'Maia.' He sealed over her. Pinning her down until she stilled.

She felt him draw in a deep shuddering breath and then any last little doubt was obliterated in the steamy passion of his next kiss. She could kiss him for all eternity. Lose all time, all sense of self.

He lifted her slightly, pushing her legs further apart with his. 'You're going to be mine, Maia.'

She shook her head and swept her hands over his shoulders, feeling the muscles working in his upper back. 'No. You're mine. Just for now.'

He smiled and slid his hand between her legs, guiding the way for the part she really wanted.

She gasped at his ultimate, absolute thrust of possession.

'Maia?' A guttural groan. 'Am I hurting you?' He asked hoarsely. 'I *really* don't want to hurt you.'

'I'm okay.'

'Not the answer I wanted.' His eyebrows flickered and his smile became strained as he ever-so-gently rocked within her.

But the moment of pain had passed and she drew a breath of pure erotic understanding. He was here. Hers. Caressing her from the very inside.

'I like it,' she breathed huskily. *I like it. I like it. I like it.*

He hauled her closer and she liked that even more, barely aware she was moaning exactly that. He surged a little harder, pushing them both closer to an edge from which were was no return. She understood and indulged the primal need to meet him. To rise. Her body hummed, dancing to the beat he set for her.

'Hell, Maia.' A throaty growl of encouragement and approval beneath which she heard his need sharpen.

'Mmmmm?' She arched higher, harder.

A low, sexy gust of laughter made her smile in response. And he kissed her for it. That this could feel so good stunned her. So, *so* good—that just like that he tossed her into that place of heat and blinding, blinding light.

The place she now liked best of all.

Five minutes later she still hadn't the energy to move but it was the most delightful exhaustion of her life. Warm bliss literally shimmered through her veins and every cell was smiling.

'You're okay?' He was so very gentle.

She couldn't wipe the smile from her face either. 'Hmmm. I think so.'

He laughed again, the ultimate smug sound. 'Have I *finally* pleased you, Maia?'

She thought about it for a moment, watched the gleam darken in his eyes and saw the lift to the edge of his mouth.

'Honestly?' She smiled at him with a teasing rush of freedom. 'No. Not yet.'

CHAPTER TEN

DESPITE HER EXHAUSTION, sleep eluded her. Her mind buzzed—unable to process everything. What she'd done. What he'd done. How it had felt. Everything was new. She'd never actually *slept* with someone before and barely slept in an actual bed let alone one as vast as this. She faced one way. Then rolled. Flipped onto her stomach. Rolled again.

'Maia?' His amusement was annoyingly audible.

'How do people do this?' She sighed irritably. After twenty minutes of trying she decided it was impossible. 'I'm going to the hammock.'

'Just hang on, Ms Impatience.' Niko flicked a couple of buttons and cool air circulated more strongly in the room. 'It's just that you're feeling overly sensitised.'

She was about to argue when he pulled her back against him, pressing her close so she was burrowed right into the curve of his body. He slung a heavy leg over hers and wrapped his arms right around her so she was tightly caged in his embrace. It would take a lot to wriggle free. He was like her personal weighted blanket—not just cocooning her, but anchoring her. It was absolute bliss. Her breathing settled. Even if she didn't sleep it didn't matter because she didn't think she'd ever felt as content as she did right now.

'Better?' he asked.

She nodded quietly. Not wanting to break the magic of his hold on her with even a word.

* * *

Ten hours later Niko was all but climbing out of his skin waiting for her to wake. He'd peeked in on her three times in the last twenty minutes and she'd been a picture of serenity, her glorious tresses smothering the pillow, her curves peeping from the sheet he'd covered her with. He was pleased she was resting well. Her pulse had picked up after they'd finished last night. He'd known it was a sort of over-stimulated anxiety, he'd felt something similar and the only thing he'd thought to do was simply hang on to her, like a life raft, as the inner storm passed. And it had for them both as she'd finally, fully relaxed in his arms.

He poured his second coffee of the day and rolled his shoulders, easing the tension building in there. She'd stunned him, beautiful Maia, with her uninhibited enjoyment of his touch. He just wanted more. Now.

Finally she appeared, wrapped in a silk robe like a present, and shot him a shy smile. 'I slept in.'

'In a bed and everything, well done.'

She shook her head. 'No need to mock.'

He grinned and got the glass of pineapple juice from the fridge that he'd poured in readiness over an hour ago. He watched her drink it and then edged a croissant towards her.

'Thank you.' Her eyes softened.

She was too easy to please.

Him? Not so much. 'Need anything else?' he asked huskily.

She stared up at him, her midnight gaze mysterious, assessing. After a moment she set the half-eaten croissant down.

'Yes,' she breathed. 'You.'

He hoisted her onto the counter and was buried deep in seconds because she was hot and ready and her uninhibited sighs only encouraged him to go faster, harder. He growled, relishing her energy, and then picked her up and took her back to his bed where she belonged.

But hours later he sighed regretfully and disentangled his limbs from hers. 'I need to do some work. It shouldn't take long.'

'Go right ahead,' she said airily. 'I don't need you to entertain me.'

'Really?' he turned and mocked, tugging her close just because he could. 'You don't need me to help you pass the time in a pleasurable way?'

He didn't like to be so summarily dismissed. But the hitch in her breathing gave her away.

It wasn't until the late afternoon that he finally managed to attempt paperwork. She whittled in the shade and he couldn't stop himself watching her. He made it through about ten minutes before tossing the papers to the side and taking her to the pool to lose himself again in their sensual tangle.

He couldn't get enough of her innate playfulness and spirited tease. There was such a lack of deference in her eyes. He relished her frank enjoyment. That she was his match in this was shockingly unexpected. But then she'd not had it before, had she—pleasure. Not much at all of any kind. It was one thing he could give her. Again and again and again until they were finally through it for good. Then they'd be at peace and could parent this child in a simple, rational arrangement.

'How long does it take to get to the top of the hill?' she asked the next morning.

'Too long for you today,' he said. 'We'd need to take supplies.'

'But are there waterfalls?'

'There are and you can explore them another time when you're more...'

'More what?' She faced him. 'I'm not weak. Niko. I get bad period pain. I thought I might struggle to get pregnant. Apparently that's not the case. Yes, I have some bad moments. But most of the time I'm perfectly fine.'

'You get faint,' he pointed out.

'Land legs,' she said.

'Not all the time.'

She stared at him for a second then sighed. 'I get breathless around you. That's what that is.'

Her confession did something funny to his heart and he tried to make light of it. 'Honesty, Maia?'

'I try to be, when I can.' She too assumed an airiness that didn't fool him in the least. 'Are you honest?'

'I try.' He teased but then sobered. 'You want to know how I feel around you?'

She stilled. Yeah, she did.

'Hungry,' he answered simply. 'Constantly, achingly, ravenously hungry.'

'Gosh, how challenging,' she murmured. 'Maybe it's hormones for you too?'

He laughed softly and pulled her onto his lap. 'Some kind of chemistry for sure.'

It was another hour before they dressed. 'If we're going to walk it needs to be now before that weather hits.'

He kept their pace leisurely, not moving too quickly because he suspected she was more tired than she was willing to admit. He kept his eyes on the sand, scooping up stones occasionally to inspect before either pocketing or tossing them back onto the beach.

'It wasn't to your standards?' she teased. 'You only keep the perfect shells?'

'Not shells, pebbles.' He shot her a smile. 'Olivine. The glassy green ones.'

'You collect them,' she said slowly. 'There's that bowl on the table in the lounge.'

'Yeah.' He shook his head sheepishly. 'Old habit. I used to take the best to my mother.' But some days she'd been too washed out to look at them. 'She would get headaches and we'd come here for a few days. Escape the palace!'

Look after your mother.

'Maybe she just got migraines,' Maia said. 'People do, you know. It might not have had anything to do with the palace. She might have gotten them even if she lived a quiet life in a fishing village on one of the outer islands.'

He shot her a sceptical look. 'Yeah, but I don't think the palace helped.'

'I don't think your *grandparents* helped. Sounds like they were disapproving taskmasters who put pressure on both your parents.' She shot him a laughing look. 'I don't blame your mother for protecting you from some of that for as long as she could.'

'Protecting me?' He was startled.

'You don't think that's what she was doing?'

'No. She came here to convalesce.'

'Sure, but she brought you too. Maybe she was using her migraines to advantage you both.'

He suddenly smiled. 'You think?'

His grandparents had always disapproved of his time on the island but his mother had insisted that he needed to re-connect with the land and water. She'd been right.

'What happened to your mother?' he asked. It was only fair, right? He'd answered hard questions without wanting to. Without meaning to.

'She walked out when I was very young,' Maia answered. She glanced over at him and sighed. 'She worked on the boat as a steward. They had an affair. I came along—unplanned and not particularly wanted. She would have left him sooner if it weren't for me, I think. But she escaped with another man who abused her worse than my father ever had. He didn't let her contact me for years.' She scooped up a piece of driftwood and ran her fingers over it. 'I guess sometimes it's better the devil you know, right?'

'She didn't try to take you with her?'

'My father wouldn't have let me go. It's not that he actually cared about me, it's just that he's very controlling. He regards people as possessions and he doesn't like to lose any of his possessions. He only likes to accumulate them.'

'And use them.' He sighed.

'I was probably safer being left with Stefan than if I'd gone with her.'

'And she didn't try to help you in all this time?'

'I don't think she can help herself let alone anyone else,' she said quietly. She gazed out across the water. 'I want to do better for this baby.'

'Yeah.' But Niko's bad feeling grew. Her mother had abandoned her. The one true carer in her life had been sent away when she was in her teens and she blamed herself for that. She blamed herself for her mother staying as long as she had with her father too. She felt unwanted. She'd worked hard and long—quietly keeping herself needed, safe. Barely getting the necessities she actually needed. Like basic medical attention. A cold, cold frustration built within him.

'I'm okay, Niko.' She suddenly smiled at him. 'You don't need to try to fix anything. It is what it is.'

'I only want to ensure the baby and you *both* have all you need.'

Maia didn't deserve the difficulties and demands that came with him. His mother hadn't coped with them. His grandmother had built an emotional wall that nothing and no one could get through. But Maia wouldn't have to participate in public life. He could keep her sheltered here. She wouldn't have to work in the way she'd had to all her life.

'We're too far from the house,' he growled as the rain began to fall in large splots. 'We're going to get drenched.'

She chuckled. 'I don't mind.'

He did. He didn't want her slipping. 'Come on. We'll go in there.'

The small shelter was on a slight rise—poles and a roof and only one side, but it was better than nothing.

But inside there was more than he'd realised. There was a small wooden table with three photo frames and a partially burned candle on top. It was neat and so carefully presented. He'd not realised Aron had set those things here—he wouldn't have come in if he had. It was too personal.

'We shouldn't be in here,' Maia said softly.

But Niko was in here now and he couldn't help walking towards that little shrine. His heart ached.

'Who is she?' Maia asked softly, looking at the central picture that he'd been gazing at for long moments. 'A relative?'

'The likeness is obvious, isn't it?' he muttered.

'The cheekbones.' She nodded. 'The nose.'

'Yes.' But he pointed to the other photos first. 'That's Aron's wife. These are my parents.' His father was gazing at his mother as she smiled directly into the camera lens. It said it all to Niko. And he could hardly stand to look at it. So he returned to the photo in the centre. 'That's Lani. Aron's eldest.'

He saw the confusion flickering in Maia's eyes and yeah, it didn't explain the cheekbones. 'She was my grandfather's firstborn. She was born two years before my father. Three years after my grandfather had already married. He was a cheat. He didn't acknowledge her—his illegitimate daughter. He didn't care for her mother. Aron raised her and she became a maid in the palace. Ultimately she worked as my mother's primary attendant, a nanny to me too. We were all very close.'

Maia turned to face him. 'Did you know who she really was? Did *she*?'

'No. Not for all those years. She was denied her name. She was kept in seclusion, a source of shame. Never acknowledged. But never given her freedom either. She missed out on everything she should have had. She didn't get her own damned life. I mean, Aron was wonderful. He tried. So did his wife. But it didn't make up for the fact that she was basically kept as a playmate and then a servant for my father.'

'So that's why you want this child to be legitimate.'

He nodded. 'I would never do that to a child of my own.'

Maia nodded. 'What happened to her?'

'It was coming up to her birthday. She'd always wondered, I think. She'd mention it to Aron sometimes—about how she didn't look like any of her younger siblings. He said nothing, of course. But he couldn't reassure her enough. I think he wanted to tell her but couldn't. She and my mother were very close and they talked about it when we were here. You can see the mirror-image bone structure with my father. I was home for the holidays, full of facts from my marvellous education. Home DNA kits had just hit the market and I suggested that she could get one if she really wanted to find out. She got all excited. She told Aron. And that was when Aron finally told her. I'd forced him into betraying the king.'

'Maybe she should have been told so much sooner,' Maia said. 'I don't think that's something you ought to feel guilty about.'

Yeah, well. He did. Because it had hurt Aron too. So badly. 'Poor Aron was so loyal. He was doing what was asked of him but I think it tore him up for all those years. He loved Lani, he wanted to protect her. But...' he looked at Maia sadly. 'It shouldn't have happened to her.'

'What happened when Aron told her?'

'Dad was away—he didn't know Aron had said anything. My grandfather was at our house in the hills. Lani wanted to confront him—right away. And my mother offered to go with her.' Of course she'd offered. She'd cared deeply. 'Mum said she'd drive. I asked if she had a headache and she said she didn't, but I could tell. So I should have stopped her. I knew those headaches affected her vision and it was always my job to look after her when she had one.' His father had always told him to. 'I should have stopped them both. They should have waited until the morning. They were both so upset and they left.' He shook his head. 'Mum drove the coastal road. She missed a corner.'

'Oh, Niko.'

Yeah. 'They both died.'

'How did your father cope?'

'He didn't. He stopped caring about anything. Especially himself. I never saw him sober again and he hardly saw me at all. He sent me back to boarding school. He blamed me for her death and he never recovered from it.' He stared at the image of man who'd loved too much to live without his wife. 'He banished Aron. My grandfather was furious but he just clammed up even more. He wouldn't talk about it. Ever. And he expected Dad to be stoic and get on with the job. But Dad just never recovered from losing the love of his life. He was stuck in hellish grief. He made a bunch of poor choices, ended up with high blood pressure, high sugars and only a couple years later had a fatal stroke when he was far too young. My grandfather lost both his children right before each turned forty.'

'I'm so sorry, Niko.'

'Yeah.' He sighed. 'It sucked.'

She stood for a moment, then moved to the table and took a match from the box, lighting the candle that Aron had there.

'You know it wasn't your fault, right? Not any of it.' She turned once the flame had steadied. 'It wasn't fair of him to blame you like that.'

He swallowed hard and tried to smile. 'Life isn't fair though, is it? You know that too.'

She looked up so softly. 'I'm still sorry all that happened.'

He nodded. They stood for a long time, just watching the candle flicker.

'The rain's stopped.' He'd realised eventually. 'We should go back while it holds.'

He blew out the flame and they walked back in silence. Back at the house he felt oddly unsure of what to do with himself. But Maia went into the lounge and came back out to the pool area with something in her hand.

'Want to play poker?' She looked at him with limpid eyes.

He stared, nonplussed. But in the next second vitality warmed his veins and a helpless laugh escaped him. 'Maia…'

She smiled at him. So beautiful, so sweet and she nodded towards the pile on the table where he'd emptied his pockets. 'I'll play for your stones.'

'True treasure. Very wise.' His mood lightened. 'But what are *you* going to put on the table?'

She shot him an arch look. 'My knife.'

'Wow, bold.' He took a seat with a smile. 'You're feeling confident, then.'

She shrugged, then winked. Easiness blossomed and her distraction—he knew it was that—worked. She brought him back to here and now and it was okay. Maybe this whole thing between them could be okay.

She was a card shark of course. There was no way she'd

spent so long on a gambling boat and not learned some tricks. But her pleasure in beating him was a pleasure for him in itself. He watched as she carefully pawed through the little stones, picking out several of a similar size. 'These are going to be perfect,' she muttered.

He shook his head. He hadn't realised she really wanted them. 'You know I would have just given them to you if you'd asked.'

She glanced up at him, surprise sparkling in her beautiful eyes. 'You would?'

He blinked. 'Of course.'

Maia sat with her feet curled beneath her, pointlessly whittling a new-found piece of wood that was rapidly becoming shavings and nothing else. She'd come close to cutting herself accidentally twice in the last two minutes. Something she hadn't done in years. But the man beside her was an appalling distraction. He was sprawled back on the cushions beside the pool, ignoring the papers scattered beside him to feast his eyes on her like a sexually satisfied sultan from centuries ago. But he was more than that. He was a nice guy who'd been so hurt. He'd suffered loss after loss after loss and had guilt piled on him when he didn't deserve it. And here he was trying so hard to do what was right. He didn't want to repeat any mistakes of the past. He wanted his child acknowledged. He wanted to ensure both she and the baby were well cared for because he felt as if he'd failed to do that for others in the past. And that was all so very honourable. But somehow she felt more uncertain about everything.

It was five days since he'd brought her here. Four nights in which she'd slept not just in a bed, but in his arms. Three days of absolute pleasure. But more than that—there'd been laughter. There'd been companionship of a kind she'd never really had. And she didn't quite know how to handle it.

'I'll get you some better wood if you want?' he offered.

'No, that's not the point.' She smiled. 'The joy is in making something out of nothing very much, you know? And it doesn't matter if you muck it up because you can just throw it away because it was just scrap anyway.'

'Is that what you do with them?' He sounded outraged. 'You just throw them away?'

'Well, no,' she admitted sheepishly. 'I leave them in little places. Then look for them if ever I go back.'

'Like a calling card?'

'More like secret graffiti—*Maia was here*—but only I know.' And only she cared really.

'In, like, ports?'

'On beaches mostly.' She bent closer to focus on creating a decent beak for the little bird. But once again she missed. 'Damn.'

His chuckle made her glance up. He had the oddest expression in his eyes.

'What?' she asked, then almost cut herself again.

'No one's going to be surprised to learn you're pregnant.'

'What? Why?' She put her hand to her belly but it seemed as not-quite-flat as it had been the day before.

'Anyone who sees you is going to know how thoroughly you've been…'

She glanced back up at him sharply. 'Been?'

The word was crude but appallingly it turned her on anyway.

'You look like you've spent hours in bed yet not slept a wink,' he elaborated lazily. Leaning close he brushed her hair back over her shoulder. 'Your hair is wild, you have a kiss-swollen mouth, two love bites on your neck and yet your nipples are still screaming at me through that bikini top. You look ravished and ready for more.'

He sat back looking too smug. The flare of lust that had shot through her suddenly iced. Was *that* why he'd slept with her—why he'd been so passionate? So people would take one look at her and know she'd been his sexual plaything?

His gaze narrowed. 'For the record, the look suits you. Very much. You have colour in your cheeks and sparkle in your eyes and you look ten times more alive than you did the morning I took you from that tinpot boat.'

'Gosh. I'm flattered,' she said coldly. 'Isn't that a marvellously convenient side effect of your sexual skills? To make it look convincing to the world that yes, you've seduced this woman and oh look, now she's pregnant,' she groused. 'But I'm so sorry you felt you *had* to do that.'

'Maia.' He gaped at her.

Yes, she was grumpy. She was unaccountably, incredibly grumpy and yes, she was kicking off. But she needed to push this because she'd suddenly realised this isolated lust-fest wasn't necessarily *real*. At least, not for him.

'Did you sleep with me so you can sell your paternity story? Was it all about proving your virility?'

'Are you serious right now?'

Yes, she was. It suddenly all made sense. He'd only bought her to the island to create a narrative about their 'love' story. To have the world believe in them as a couple. It was calculating and she felt so naive. He was probably desperate to get back to his city life and not have to spend all these hours entertaining her. He'd probably been *bored*.

But *she* hadn't been. She'd laughed—she'd loved those long hours in bed when he'd taken so much time with her. But she'd read all of that wrong. He was only doing what he had to do, to get what he wanted. And when would she ever learn that people didn't stick around for her for long?

'You don't want anyone to know the truth about the conception,' she said.

'Well, I don't particularly want our child growing up believing they were a sheer fluke thanks to fate.'

'No one should ever know,' she said.

'Hopefully they won't.'

'But if they did, it shouldn't matter.'

'But it *would*. This child's paternity would be open to question. But that's not really an issue now, is it? Given we *are* lovers, Maia.'

'You seduced me only so you can say that.' This was all a cover for the baby.

'Don't be ridiculous.' He glared at her. 'And maybe we ought to clarify who seduced who, Maia.'

'As if I had any control over you?' she said. 'But now you've gotten that mundane task out of the way, perhaps we can move on.'

'Maia—'

'What? There's no need for us to remain here now you've had me every way you want.'

'I haven't actually,' he purred. 'There are lots of positions we've yet to explore with each other and there is no way I've *taught* you everything you need to know in bed.'

She was not being derailed by that thought. She was calling a halt to it now. 'Tough. We're done.'

'*What?*'

'I want to go back to the city,' she said firmly.

He stared, wariness flickering in his eyes before he stiffened. She knew then that he didn't want her to go there. Not back to the palace. Why did he want to keep her isolated?

Was he afraid she would embarrass him somehow? Her horror simply deepened.

'You can stay here. You're safe and free to do anything you like here.'

'Swim, sleep and have sex? I want more than that.' She was furious that he was trying to block her. She would fight for the lifestyle she'd longed for. 'I've been shut away below deck for most of my life. The last thing I want is to be shut away on a remote, unpopulated island for the next who knows how long. Even if it is a paradise island, it's still a kind of prison. I won't let you hide me away like some shameful secret. I want to do things. See things. I want to *breathe*.'

She wanted independence and liberty. She wanted to go shopping. She'd never been paid. Never had money. She wanted a job. There were so many things she'd never had and never done.

His expression had turned stormy. 'You're saying this isn't enough.'

'No. It's not.' Her nerves tightened but she needed this. It felt good to declare her needs. To put her own desires as her priority—for the first time in her life. Even so, she braced for his explosion.

He regarded her intently. 'Fine. That's fair enough.'

She glanced up, startled that he'd agreed so swiftly.

'We'll return to the city. See if you like palace life better this time round. You're the one who ran away, remember?' He tugged on a T-shirt with jerky movements. 'It's hardly been a walk in the park for me either by the way. Trying to run my country from a remote island. Disappearing and not turning up to events that have been scheduled months in advance.'

'I'm so sorry *your* life has been so inconvenienced,' she said sarcastically. 'But as it happens you're not the only one. I have the ultimate accidental pregnancy going on.'

CHAPTER ELEVEN

NIKO DIDN'T KNOW what to think. Somehow an off-hand remark had caused a combustion of epic proportions. But if Maia wanted more, she would get more. It took nothing to make the arrangements. In less than an hour they'd helicoptered back to the palace—returning to formality, to constraint, to all those rules, too quickly. But he would show exactly how willing he was and far he would go to look after her and keep her happy.

'There's a gala tonight,' he coolly informed her the minute they were left alone in the suite he'd insisted she be accommodated in. The one right alongside his. 'I'd intended to send my apologies but you can come with me instead. I'll never be ashamed to be seen with you, Maia.'

She looked unsure. 'A gala?'

'A variety performance. Singing. Music. I think some dance, I can't remember all the exact details.'

'Like the theatre?'

'Yes, the theatre,' he snapped.

Her eyes suddenly brightened. 'I've never been to the theatre.'

Speechless, he stared, his anger instantly swamped by the desire to see her reaction to such an entertainment. And by bitterness that she'd not been before. Something else brewed deeper. He'd wanted to keep her safe and honestly he still didn't know if there was a direct threat either to him or to her given what had happened at the medical centre. He'd wanted time for Pax to complete his investigation. Only now she'd had enough of the island and he refused to keep her prisoner there.

'I might need to go shopping,' she said apologetically. 'For underwear at least. Will one of the beach dresses do?'

'No,' he muttered. 'I'll come with you.'

'You don't have to,' she said annoyingly quickly. 'I'm not going to try to run away.'

He gritted his teeth but failed to stop the resurgence of his temper. 'I know that.'

'Did you want to vet my choices?' she suddenly flared. 'What if I promise only to get clothing that will show off how thoroughly I've been...*seduced*.'

'That sounds perfect,' he snapped. 'We'll start with evening dresses. Backless and braless.'

'Of course, Your Highness.' She dropped a mocking curtsey. 'Your wish is my command.'

His jaw tightened. She seemed determined to take *everything* the wrong way and he was beyond frustrated that everything seemed to becoming more complicated by the hour. He missed the easy alignment they'd had only yesterday. He'd wanted to see she was safe. And he'd wanted to see her have some *fun*. Instead he'd been provoked into retaliating and she was huffier than ever. He needed to kiss her. Now.

'Your Highness?'

He whirled away from her as an assistant called through the door. An interruption. Of course. That was life in the palace. Constant interruptions. Constant demands when all he wanted was to be alone with her.

So he *would* go with her to those shops. He would snatch any moment he could have with her.

* * *

An hour later Maia tried to keep her chin in the air as she walked out of the dressing room but she was inwardly baulking at how revealing the dress she'd furiously swished off the rack actually was. Ordinarily she never would have picked one like this. Both low and high cut and skin-tight, she wouldn't have the confidence to wear it in *public* in a million years. In a bedroom however? Well, *that* was a possibility. Doing this to aggravate Niko was likely to backfire yet she couldn't seem to stop herself.

Niko took one look at her, whirled on his heel and barked at the hovering assistants. 'Empty the store. Leave. Now. All of you.'

She gaped. 'You can't just—'

He spun back and pulled her against him before she even had the idea to step back. 'I am the king. I can do whatever the hell I want,' he growled.

'Really?'

'Yes.' His lips traversed the edge of the dress, the high crest of her breast. 'And I want to do you.'

It would take only a nudge of the fabric and her nipple would be exposed. But Niko didn't nudge—he slid his hand beneath the skirt and up to where she ached instead.

'Spoilt, Niko,' she hissed, scandalised even as she spread her legs for him. It was appalling to consider how little she truly cared when all she wanted was him to touch her like this—to want her as desperately as she still wanted him. She needed this contact. Her head fell back as he kissed her neck, but as her eyes drifted shut she spotted something and froze. 'There are security cameras.'

'Williams will have the footage deleted,' Niko slurred recklessly and then a gleam entered his eye. 'Or give it to me.'

He kissed her—his tongue circling, his *finger* circling. It was too much, too soon and she was so close to coming apart. She gasped and clasped his shoulders, shivering as she tore her mouth free while pressing her hips nearer to him. '*Niko...*'

She needed to be alone with him. She ached for the release, she wanted the luxury of time and space—for once she longed for an actual bed. *Now.*

He dragged in a sharp breath, stilling momentarily. Then he suddenly dropped his hand. 'You're right,' he said huskily. 'I apologise. I'll leave you to finish choosing your dress for tonight. *Alone.*'

He remained only long enough to ensure she had her balance. She barely did. Because she'd never felt as angry. But he left the shop without a backwards glance.

Captain Williams appeared to accompany her mere seconds later. Scary, silent, stupidly wearing those sunglasses inside. Only once had she caught a glimpse of his eyes—so ice blue they were almost colourless. He had a scar too, so maybe that was why he wore the sunglasses. She felt bad for her mean thought. She couldn't ask him. He wasn't exactly someone she could confide in.

'The king is not used to not getting what he wants,' the taciturn soldier said. 'It's good for him.' He took up position near the door. '*You're* good for him.'

Maia was too surprised to answer. The man never spoke and he certainly shouldn't be commenting on that. Plus he couldn't be more wrong.

It wasn't her job to be 'good' for King Niko. Honestly, they just seemed to bring worse out in each other the more time they spent together.

Niko struggled to stay still while the barber clipped his hair. 'Oh, just leave it,' he snapped irritably, waving the man away from him.

He'd not recovered since returning to the palace over two hours ago. How had he lost all control as to start pawing her in the middle of a *shop*? Why hadn't she returned yet? Why had they left the island? Why had he agreed so swiftly instead of staying calm and convincing her to stay? They could have indulged this bone-deep lust until it was exhausted at last. Whenever the hell that was going to be.

The moment Pax walked in without knocking Niko growled. 'What took so long?'

'Ms Flynn was enjoying herself,' the soldier answered expressionlessly. 'Wasn't that what you wanted?'

Honestly, Niko just wanted her back beside him and he was too annoyed with everything to shoot Pax a quelling look. 'Where is she now?'

'Finishing dressing. She asked me to tell you she won't take long.'

Niko breathed a little more easily. He glanced at the barber hurriedly packing away his tools and regretted his short fuse.

'I apologise.' He never took his temper out on his staff. He never felt this irritable. Ever. 'Forgive me, please. I'm just...' He paused and reached for the right word. '*Nervous*.'

The barber looked startled, then offered a wary smile. 'Of course, Your Highness.'

Niko knew full well the palace gossip machine would be in full swing in two minutes on the basis of that comment. Frankly, it wasn't a lie. He was feeling edgy. And regretful. But now they were running late and they didn't have the time to talk through strategy for the evening. Maybe this way was best. If she were overwhelmed with information she might want to bail. She didn't understand the consequences of being seen out with him in this context. And his admission of nerves just then? That he was taking her to the theatre? It was as good as a declaration nailed to the palace wall.

Ten minutes later he knocked on her door. 'I'm sorry, Maia,' he ground out. 'There's not much time before we're...'

He lost everything except vision as she opened the door. Thank the gods he kept that because the gorgeous coral dress hugged her breasts then fell in a stunning swathe to the floor, skimming the slight curve of her belly without betraying her secret. It was so much more 'palace appropriate' than the revealing number from the shop but it seduced him as swiftly. Reduced him. He was nothing more than a man unbearably aching for the woman in front of him.

He just wanted to rip it off her.

He could make them delay the performance. He could be as late as he liked. But she'd called him selfish once already today and he didn't fancy a repeat of that loss of control. Because she was right and he was ashamed because he'd not been thinking about anything other than how much he wanted to touch her.

'It will only take me a moment to finish,' she said.

Yeah? It would take him less time to finish exactly the way he wanted to.

But he didn't. He could—*would*—resist. This wasn't a test only for her, he realised. It was for him as well.

As he'd suspected the message to the barber had had its intended effect. The entire palace staff were lined up for his departure.

'No wonder you're big-headed,' Maia murmured as they briefly paused at the top of the stair to take in the liveried display. 'Does this happen every time you leave your own house?'

A chuckle escaped him.

'What's so funny?'

He couldn't tell her yet.

The audience stood as they entered the theatre—last of

course. And they stared. He held her hand as they were guided to their seats. It was another wordless declaration and yes, caused a massive murmur to ripple throughout the auditorium. Then a burst of thunderous applause. She glanced at him and he just knew she was wishing she could roll her eyes at his perceived pomposity. He just smiled at her, feeling guilty that she didn't even know their fate was sealed.

'Thank you for singing the anthem so beautifully,' he turned his head to mutter when they finally took their seats.

'Well, I wasn't about to flub it with the whole world watching.' She spoke without moving her lips an impressive skill he personally found very useful. 'Though to be honest I'm amazed I actually knew all the words.'

He laughed, releasing a speck of the tension that had been riding him hard. But then the performance began and another tension consumed him. He tried so hard, but he couldn't stop himself watching her. She wasn't just absorbed in the performances, she was *entranced*. And he?

He was no better than an animal fixated on his next feed. He'd drag her away at half-time if he could—but he couldn't do it to her. She was luminous—loving every moment—while he endured the pleasure and pain of watching her but not touching her.

The minute they were alone he was apologising to her. Then he was kissing her.

He would take all that he could, when he could.

Maia had never felt so self-conscious. There'd been an insane number of people lined up in the palace to see King Niko off, but it was nothing compared to the entire audience staring up at him now. Most had repeatedly glanced up at him throughout the performance instead of watching the action onstage. One woman dressed in blue just a few rows away hadn't taken her eyes off him for the entire time. Of course, Maia didn't blame her. He looked devastating in that crisp white shirt and black trousers. He'd shaved, showing off the cheekbones that gave her palpitations. More handsome, more rakish than ever.

'You enjoyed it?' he asked as he guided her into the small room behind the royal box in the theatre.

'I've never seen anything like it.' And she was relieved to have a moment without everyone watching.

'We're expected to go backstage to meet some of the cast.' He watched her with amusement. 'Would you like that?'

'Of course, if that's what's expected.'

'But would you like it?'

'Yes.' She smiled at him. 'Those singers were amazing. I'd like to tell them how much I enjoyed their performance.'

He nodded and she moved to exit the small room.

'Stop,' he breathed harshly and grabbed her arm. 'Stay a moment.'

She looked up at him, startled.

'I want to apologise,' he muttered. 'I was a jerk to you today. I just wanted to see you having fun. I wanted to be in on it. But of course you should have been free to go just…find what you wanted on your own. I'm sorry I wrecked that for you.'

Her heart thudded. *That* was why he'd wanted to go with her? Why hadn't he said so at the time?

'I wish we hadn't left the island so soon.' He groaned.

In this second so did she. Sexual attraction was a storm— it was like being picked up by gale force winds and carried away with no control, no ability to decide her direction… but she was so glad he seemed to want her equally intensely. 'I'm sorry too.'

'No—'

'Your Highness?' a voice called from beyond the curtain.

Niko released her and smiled. 'Let's go meet the stars.'

He introduced her as his friend. She smiled—knowing enough from the stewards on her father's boat to carry her through. She voiced her appreciation politely but genuinely to each performer. The woman in the blue dress was there with the dignitaries. Still staring.

But Niko had them out of there in record time.

Back at the palace it was as if they'd entered some sci-fi film in which every other human had vanished off the face of the earth.

'I'm astonished there isn't a welcome party waiting for you.' She gazed around the vast emptiness in amazement.

He chuckled. 'I requested that they give us privacy upon our return.'

'Everyone really stares at you all of the time, don't they?'

'Perk of the job.'

She shot him a laughing glance. 'I'm not feeling sorry for you.'

'I never imagined for a second that you were.' He angled his head. 'You enjoyed it tonight?'

'Very much, actually. The concert, that is. Not so much the staring. Did you notice the woman in the blue dress? She didn't stop staring your way the entire night.'

'Blue dress?' He frowned, then suddenly froze as recognition jolted into his eyes. 'Oh.'

'Oh?' She paused, reading awkwardness in his expression.

But then he swallowed and lifted his head. 'She's the partner of the bass player of that international band. We knew each other a few years ago when I was visiting New Zealand.'

She understood immediately. 'You were intimate?'

'Briefly.'

The blue-dress beauty was a former lover and while she might be someone else's partner now, she clearly still had eyes for Niko. Again, Maia didn't blame her.

But the blue-dress beauty was a woman Niko had *chosen*. Maia wasn't. She was literally a vessel. The fertile recipient of a shocking error. Fate had twisted them together in some Machiavellian amusement for reasons unknown. And Maia was wholly unsuitable to be his bride. 'You should have told me earlier.'

'So you could avoid her?'

Maia flicked her hair. 'So I could swap notes.'

A half smile creased his mouth. 'Jealous?'

'No,' she lied.

'To be honest I'd forgotten she might be there. To be completely honest I'd forgotten *her*.'

'Is that supposed to make me think more of you?'

'You're the only woman I'll marry.'

She still wasn't sure about that at all. 'If I do marry you, it will only be because of a mistake.'

'And yet I can't keep my hands off you.' He advanced on her.

'You have a high sex drive. It's nothing to do with me.'

His smile finally faded. 'And what about you? Have you just discovered your own high sex drive? Does that have nothing to do with *me*?' He shook his head. 'This is *us*, Maia. This is only like this between *us*. You and me.'

Her pulse thundered. 'You said we were just burning this out.'

'Yeah, well. Maybe I was wrong.'

'You're the king,' she goaded. Driven—yet again—by that inner demon who lived to provoke him. 'You're never wrong.'

'I'm *human*, Maia. And as you know more than anyone, I don't always perform at my best. Especially around—' He sighed heavily. 'I'm volatile around you.'

'You don't like that.'

'It's unusual,' he clipped.

'I guess this is an unusual set of circumstances.'

'Do you know, I don't actually think it is the circumstances,' he said. 'I think it's just you.'

'Then perhaps I should go.'

His hands landed heavily on her waist. 'You're not bloody going anywhere.'

She tossed her head as the fire ignited. *This* was what she'd wanted. To push him into pulling her closer.

'Nobody has ever driven me crazy the way you do.' He stared at her for a long moment.

She squirmed as he read the hunger she knew she couldn't hide. And sure enough he suddenly smiled.

'You don't have to taunt me into sleeping with you, Maia,' he lazily leaned closer to whisper hot and rough in her ear. 'I will do this with you anytime. Just bat your lashes. Crook your damned little finger. Lick your lips. Anything. I will pleasure you anytime you want. Because I want you incessantly. Endlessly. All the *bloody* time.'

Primal satisfaction surged at his admission of uncontrolled desire and in seconds she melted. They sank where they were, barely beyond the doorway of his suite. He stripped away the soft coral silk and dragged in a stunned breath when he saw the lace underwear she'd enjoyed choosing with him in mind. His reaction was everything she'd wanted. Because in seconds the underwear was gone and he was between her legs, stroking her to searing heights. She liked the danger of him. The strength. The way he moved to hold her as if he would never let her go. As if she could never, ever escape. 'But I like taunting you…'

'Well then, my sweet little vixen, you'd better be prepared for the consequences.'

He flipped her over and lifted her to her knees. She gasped, stunned as he moved behind her. Desire ignited as he touched her in ways she'd never imagined. She was so hot and he was so wicked.

'What are you doing?' she moaned helplessly, so, so close. 'Why have you stopped?'

His smile was pure devilishness.

She batted her lashes. She crooked her little finger. She licked her lips.

And with each invitation he rewarded her—with attention, with kisses, strokes, teases, but never giving her enough to let her have her release.

'Niko!' she gasped in lustful outrage and desperation.

'Ask me nicely,' he dared. 'Just this once.'

Breathless she twisted from his hold and lay back on the floor, inviting him with her spread legs, with the arch of her hips, with the sweep of her hands across her breasts and down her body...in an effort to tempt him into loss of control. In an effort to get what she needed all on her own.

But he swiped her hands away with a devilish laugh. 'Oh no, my darling. That pleasure is for another day. Today you only come on *my* touch.'

She met his playful gaze and conceded everything. 'Then touch me. *Please.*'

He didn't just touch her. He took her—hard. Her orgasm was instant. She cried out—shocked at the intensity. But he kissed her through the comedown, then laced his fingers through hers and slowly built her up again. The connection was intimate and enduring. He rocked into her over and over, somehow pressing closer and closer still. His gaze bored into hers—with soft amusement, such tenderness and savage tension.

'It wasn't so hard, was it?' he choked. 'You're all I can think about.'

He was locked so deeply inside her that she felt the rigidity in every inch of him.

'My beautiful Maia.'

This time she finally believed him. This time she revelled in a release unlike anything ever.

She was so spent he had to carry her to his bed. So spent she couldn't even open her eyes. She'd thought he wouldn't hurt her. And he absolutely wouldn't. Not deliberately. But suddenly she understood how deeply he *could*. He made her believe she was beautiful. He'd made her feel wanted. And now, in the aftermath of such total ecstasy, her heart ached for even more. And suddenly she was restless again, like she'd been that first night, but this time for different—far scarier—reasons.

In the darkness Niko chuckled softly. 'Come here.'

He pulled her tightly into his arms, knowing her too well. And as he stroked her hair, he took her heart deeper into his clutches with every caress.

CHAPTER TWELVE

'MAIA.'

She stirred then came awake swiftly. 'What's wrong?' Maia wrapped the sheet around herself as she sat up.

Niko's jaw was looking particularly angular this morning.

'It seems your father is unhappy,' he said. 'He's been making this known across town. Spreading the news that his daughter has been abducted by the king to be his sex slave.'

She gaped, her cheeks burning. 'You're not serious.'

'I'm going to speak to him,' he said shortly. 'Williams has brought him downstairs.'

'Don't see him,' Maia said quickly. 'I don't care what he says. I don't care what anyone thinks.' She looked at Niko's deepening frown. 'But you do.'

'I am the king, Maia. I must uphold certain standards.'

'But no one is ever going to believe him.' She tried to laugh it off. 'Like *you* need to abduct anyone?'

'I did exactly that though, didn't I?' He stared at her moodily. 'It's one thing to be seen as a playboy. It's quite another to be seen as a sex offender.'

'But you're not.' Her lungs constricted but still she tried to offer another smile. 'I…was willing.'

'Were you?' He didn't smile back at her. 'What choices did I give you really?'

'Every choice that matters.' She lifted her head proudly. 'I slept with you because I wanted to. I could have said no but I didn't want to. In fact I think you're right and I might have started it. And I have no regrets.' She looked at him, her heart quaking. 'Do you?'

He didn't answer. 'I *must* announce our engagement, Maia. It's past time.'

'No.' Maia rejected the idea immediately. After last night there was no way she could marry him. 'No, Niko.'

'To be frank it's already done, Maia. Our going out together last night was as good as any formal engagement announcement. That's why the staff all lined up to see you leave with me. They know their king has selected his bride.'

'*No.*' Her jaw dropped. 'That's not possible.'

'There's a reason you've never seen me on a date here in Piri-nu, Maia.' His lips twisted ruefully. 'The smallest signals are taken very seriously.'

'Being seen in public with a woman doesn't make it imperative that you marry her. That's ridiculous.' She didn't want to marry him. Not like this. Not because of this. 'I don't want to marry you, Niko. It's not necessary.' She swung out of bed and hurriedly tugged on some underwear. 'I'll see my father and tell him to stop. You needn't concern yourself. It's not your job.'

'When it's my name he's slandering?'

'It's mine too and he's *my* father.' Once more her father's interference was impacting on her life. Because of him she was not good enough to be Niko's bride. She would see him now and tell him to leave.

'I'm not letting you face him alone.' Niko folded his arms and watched her tug down the sundress she'd grabbed.

'I don't need protection.' She stilled with the strangest, most sudden certainty.

She felt oddly free from fear of her father. She could— would—hold her ground and she would not let him destroy what she had with Niko. Even if it were only for now. There was nothing he could do to her *personally* now.

'Maybe I want to be there only to make sure your father doesn't instantly die from the daggers in your eyes.' Niko finally smiled. 'It won't be easy but I promise I won't interrupt. But I would like just to be there.' He drew a deep breath. 'But it can be Williams if you prefer.'

She didn't particularly want Niko there but she infinitely preferred him to Captain Scary-silent. 'You can stand at the back. *Quietly.*' She turned. 'I'll see him off now.'

She would get it over with before this rush of confidence left her. But oddly it didn't. She was calmer than she would ever have imagined she could be when facing her father and openly defying him for the first time in her life.

The ruddy-faced man glared at her as she walked in but it wasn't her he addressed.

'You have to marry her. You've ruined her.'

Maia saw the glint of avariciousness in her father's eyes and knew she was nothing but a pawn to him—a possession. A thing to be bartered and to make money from. Because it was always all about money with him. Money and control.

'What century do you think we're living in?' she asked coolly. 'I wanted to leave the boat and King Niko graciously enabled me to do that. He's shown me nothing but kindness and generosity and you're to stop the rubbish interpretation you're spreading around town. It's not true.'

Her father laughed. 'As if you're not warming his bed every night?'

She held her head high with sheer grit. 'I'm a free woman and I've no intention of marrying anyone at this stage of my life.'

'So you're happy to be his whore?'

She saw Niko's involuntary step forward out of the corner of her eye and lifted her hand in a quelling gesture without taking her attention from her father. 'Don't try to slut-shame me. I've done nothing wrong. Certainly nothing *illegal*.' She paused for effect before asking him coolly, 'Can you say the same?'

His eyes narrowed and he walked closer to speak directly to her. 'Are you not going to try to take advantage of this situation, you stupid girl?' he hissed sharply. 'Don't you understand what we could achieve here? I'm trying to *help* you. At the very least you could get money—'

'May I advise you to stay out of Piri-nu waters, Father,' she said firmly, overriding his attempt to convince her. 'I think the stakes in some of your games might exceed the laws here. I'd hate for you to be caught out by that.'

'You wouldn't—'

'And I won't. If you leave right away.' She made herself smile. Made herself believe that this didn't matter.

'You're even more useless than your mother.'

'Goodbye, Dad, I don't expect we'll see each other much in the future.' Maia turned her back on him to walk from the room while she still could.

'Maia!' He yelled her name the same way he'd yelled it her whole life. 'You can't walk away—'

She paused. 'Actually, I can.'

'You'll regret not taking my help,' he sneered. 'He'll tire of you. You have nothing. You are nothing and you'll end up with nothing.'

At that she turned to look at him one last time. 'And you offered me so very much more?' She shrugged. 'I have more than you right now. I have the one thing I'll never let myself lose. My *integrity*.'

The one thing her father had never had in the first place.

She would be true to herself. She walked out of the room, no longer caring who heard, whether Niko was with her or not. She marched straight back to the suite she'd shared with him last night.

Five minutes later the door opened and Niko entered the room.

'Are you okay?' He walked slowly towards her as if wary of her mood.

'Did you threaten him?' she asked.

'No more than you already had,' he replied. 'He wasn't interested in sticking around to talk to me. I think he was surprised by you.'

Because she'd always been so compliant. Because she'd never stood up for herself before. For so long she'd simply accepted her fate.

But it was because of Niko that she now could. Because of this impossible mess that she finally had one element of freedom. Now she would push for everything. *Nothing* mattered more.

She looked at him. 'I'm not going to marry you, Niko.'

His expression hardened. 'I don't think—'

'You can consider me your concubine, but I will never be your bride,' she added.

'My *what*?' He halted, startled.

'Concubine. It's an apt word. Evokes a sort of decadence that's perfect for you.' And *them*—the passion they shared for now at least.

'Maia—'

'You can declare our child your heir without us being married. You're the king. You know you can do this.'

'I don't want to.'

'But you can. There would be no question.'

'Is the thought of marrying me really so distasteful?'

She actually couldn't *bear* the thought of being married to him. She would be his lover—happily, for as long as they were both interested in that element of their relationship. She would always be the mother of his firstborn child. But she should *never* be his wife. She couldn't cope with that.

Because she was so far in love with him it was cruel.

She wasn't good enough. The last twenty minutes had cemented that fact. For a moment there she'd thought she was. Her father had ruined it. But the reminder was a good thing. Everyone would have found out soon enough anyway.

'Thanks to my father the world now knows I share your bed.' She tossed her head. 'They know I'm your lover. Soon enough they'll know I'm going to be the mother of your heir. That is *enough*.'

'You must let me give you the protection of my name. They'll vilify you.'

'I know you care what they will say about me. But you also know they'll only say even more if I were to become your *wife*.' She shook her head. 'It's too permanent, Niko. As your lover I'll be tolerated. Not as your wife. I'm not the right choice. I'm not your equal. Not in any way. And as for my father…my mother…' She shook her head at him. 'You never would have chosen to be with me if it weren't for everything and we both know it.'

He stared at her, an obstinate expression building in his eyes. 'How we met is irrelevant. We must do what is right.'

'But marriage *isn't* right,' she argued all over again. 'If we do it this way, then there won't be any kind of perceived *failure*. No public end of a relationship or the breaking of promises made. There's just been a liaison and an accident. I am your lover. I know there will be no escape for good, Niko. I'll always be near the palace. We'll always be part of each other's lives. We have to be because of this baby. But you and I, this intimacy, will end eventually, you know it will.'

He suddenly paused, whirling to face her. 'Is that why *you* did it?' he questioned sharply. 'Did you give me your virginity so you could cast yourself as a seductress?'

Maia stilled, suddenly hurt. Suddenly scared. He had no idea, did he. Of how she really felt. And perhaps that was for the best. 'I—'

Niko turned at the bloody knock on the door. 'What is it?' he snapped.

But he took one look at Williams' face and walked out of the room to speak with him in the corridor. Frankly he needed the breathing space from Maia's defiance. Her *luminescence*. The quiet dignity in her declaration of her integrity had stunned him. More stunning was her display of power and serenity since. Her sudden stubbornness that he had the sinking feeling he wasn't going to be able to sway. She was rejecting him. And he was suddenly incensed because *she* wouldn't see sense.

'What is it, Pax?' he asked heavily.

'The investigation into the medical facility is complete.'

Niko stiffened. 'And?'

'Genuine mistake,' Pax confirmed. 'It was the same clinician who retrieved the wrong sample and who treated Maia in the rooms. She isn't well herself. Her vision. But she was hiding her declining eyesight because she needed the job.'

'Money?' Niko slumped against the wall and bowed his head.

'Family commitments, yes.'

'Poor woman.' Niko didn't have it in him to be angry with someone other than Maia right now and certainly didn't have the heart for recriminations. 'Is she okay?'

'She's distraught. I've asked that she gets professional support. They're revising their storage processes of course and upgrading the technology. It was an appalling chain of events unlikely ever to be repeated.'

'So it wasn't some kind of threat, no sick sort of succession plot to create an heir?' Niko double-checked.

Pax shook his head. 'I shook the tree hard, but there's nothing.'

'Which means there's no threat to Maia from this?'

'Not from this, now.'

'Any other threats to her?'

'Nothing aside from the interest generated from her appearance with you last night. That's only going to heighten over the coming months.'

Niko gritted his teeth. 'Thanks, you can go.'

Pax said nothing more and walked down the corridor. But Niko didn't go back into the room where Maia was waiting. He paused just outside the door, trying to wrap his head around the confusion of the last twenty-four hours. None of this was as simple as he'd thought it could be.

Last night he'd felt contrarian. Wanting to show her off and hide her away at the same time. It was the zillionth time he'd seen such a performance but the first for her, and seeing her so sweetly transfixed by the show had brought him immense pleasure. Frankly he'd forgotten Athena was going to be there last night. He'd forgotten most of the women he'd been with. He hadn't thought about another woman in days. He'd had his hands too full coping with Maia.

The contradictory feelings were so freaking complicated and he couldn't straighten them out. And the anxiety underlying it all was rising. Niko didn't do anxiety. He did certainty. He was good at it. So this was very weird and very uncomfortable.

But the fact was any danger Maia now might face was purely because of him. She was losing her freedom because of him. Her life would be irrevocably changed because of him.

None of this was what she would have chosen for herself. Ever. And she didn't want it. She was pushing to put herself in the position of his lover. To reduce herself—shrink inwards and accept less than she ought to ever have. Because that was what she was used to.

Meeting her father had sickened him. Worse was the realisation that he wanted the same outcome as that man. To be aligned in any way with that the guy seemed wrong. But they wanted the same thing for vastly different reasons, right?

Her father was a man in power telling her what to do. Telling her he knew best. That he wanted only to 'help' her. Not listening to her at all. Hearing that cruel tone, the coercion, the manipulation had made him realise that he was doing the exact same thing.

He really wasn't as different to Brant Flynn as he'd liked to think. They were both men taking advantage of what authority they had to get what they wanted. All but haggling over her. Not letting her choose.

The levels of control she'd been subjected to her whole life were exhausting. Everyone had things they *had* to do, that was part of life but Maia hadn't had the most basic of freedoms nor the chance to discover things for herself. She'd never had normal *options*. So how could she know what she really wanted when she'd never had the time or space to figure it out for herself?

But one thing she'd made clear was that she didn't want to marry him. He'd been trying to convince her from the start and she wouldn't budge—today she was more vehement, more calm about it, than ever.

And now he felt unsure that the intimacy they'd shared had only happened because she'd felt some innate need to protect herself. That she'd wanted to please him and thus keep herself safe somehow.

She'd said she would still sleep with him but she wouldn't marry him. She didn't want to live in the palace as his wife forever. That was a hard no from her. And if he insisted? She would become disenchanted. She would become resentful.

She would try to run away again. And he didn't think he could stand that.

He'd wanted to do right for the child but also do right for her. To give her as much freedom as he could allow. But there was no real compromise in this situation as it currently stood. There couldn't be. And now he liked her. He even cared about her. Which made it all the more imperative to stop this in its tracks now. He shouldn't have brought her back to the city. He shouldn't have shown her off in public. In doing so he'd put her more at risk than she'd already been. Now there was such speculation and a lot of it was accurate. But if he moved swiftly, decisively, then he could fix this.

He was the king. He could make a proclamation. He could recognise his child. Niko *needed* not just to listen to her but *hear* her.

He leaned against the wall. He really didn't feel good. A selfish part of him didn't want to relinquish his hold on her. But the lust still consuming him would surely fade.

She'd said all along that she wanted her freedom. He'd never realised or understood how and why she so deeply needed it. But she'd had virtually none. She'd had to work almost all of her life—without the recompense anyone should ordinarily get for it. She'd had no chance to explore and find out what she really wanted to do. She hadn't ever had her own choices.

She'd wanted to go shopping on her own and he'd been too selfish to even understand that. He'd wanted to see her joy—as if, what, he could feel *smug* about being the one to provide her with that experience? He'd made it all about him and never really considered her true wishes. He'd never really understood her—or what her motivations were. And she was still trying to accommodate him.

Of course he'd wanted her to have everything. He'd wanted to spoil her. He'd genuinely thought he'd tried. He thought he'd been understanding, patient and generous. He winced at his self-delusion. As if he could save her somehow?

But he knew better than most how one could live in the most beautiful place in the world, and have all the riches in the world. But those things didn't mean *happiness*.

And Maia had also had very little love. She'd had little time for fun and friendships and play. His head ached as he worked through the most unpalatable prospect that perhaps she'd only stepped into his bed *because* of that lack of affection. Perhaps it was exactly as those jerks had tried to do on her boat that time. She liked him purely because he was one of the few people in her life who'd actually been nice to her. He'd made her *feel* good and she'd mistaken that for thinking that *he* was good. And he realised now he was *not* good enough for her. Because he'd wanted to put power and duty first—not a *person*. Which meant he was just like his grandfather after all. Overlooking someone's very existence in order to not disrupt the lineage. Niko had been prepared to overlook her unhappiness. He'd been so arrogant he'd assumed he could make her happy *enough*. But *that* wasn't good enough. And none of this was good for the stability of Piri-nu. He'd been making rash decisions that had only worsened the situation.

But now he knew exactly what he had to do.

'What's happened now?' Maia stared as Niko walked into the room, carefully closing the door behind him.

His unusual pallor instantly raised her concern. She'd never seen him pale.

'Has something else happened?' She swallowed. 'My father—'

'Has gone. It's not him.' He paced to the window.

She watched, her anxiety spiking as he seemed pull his thoughts together.

'I just wanted to clarify your...' He hesitated and cleared his throat. 'Proposal for how we might move forward from here.'

Her mouth dried. 'Oh?'

'You were saying that you're happy to continue being my lover, but that you won't marry me. Is that correct?'

She nodded, unsure about the rapid return to that awkward conversation and the even more awkward way he was summing it up. He was like a robot all of a sudden.

'How long did you think the intimate aspect of our relationship would last?' he asked.

'I...' Now *she* had to clear her throat. 'As long as it was convenient, I guess.'

He nodded thoughtfully. 'And we would remain exclusive for as long as that was convenient too. Is that what you were thinking?'

Her stomach churned. She didn't want to answer that. She didn't want to *contemplate* it.

But Niko didn't give her long to answer anyway. 'What happens when one or other of us wants to change the situation?'

Did he mean when he was tired of her?

'Then I would live somewhere else,' she said mechanically. 'Somewhere nearby. I mean, the palace is *huge*...' She watched him warily. 'Or I could find a small apartment in a building not too far away.'

'But what about work? What would you like to do?'

Honestly, Maia hadn't thought *any* of this through and she didn't know. Why did all that need to be decided now? Couldn't they just stop the marriage pressure and figure other things out as they went along? But there was an implacable set to his features and she felt a qualm. He was still—*only*—fixated on duty. He was only offering marriage because she was pregnant and her father had forced him into moving on that even more quickly. But he was wrong. Of course she wanted what was best of this baby but they could achieve that—better—without being married. Because she now felt a strong, desperate need to ensure *she* too was safe. Last night she'd realised the extent of her feelings and if she were to marry him, it would destroy her. Because he didn't feel the same.

'I don't know,' she admitted softly. 'I could always go back to the island.'

'But you enjoyed last night.' Inexorably he found fault with her suggestion. 'You wanted more in your life than what the island offers. You want to be able to shop or go to the theatre, the movies even, a sports game. All those things.'

'That doesn't matter,' she mumbled.

'What you want doesn't matter?' He looked at her intently. 'That's unacceptable to me, Maia.'

But what she *really* wanted was impossible. Unspeakable.

He folded his arms across his chest. Looking bigger, tougher. Closed off. 'You're going to Australia this afternoon.'

'What?'

'Australia. This afternoon. The tickets are just being arranged right now. We're expediting a passport for you.'

'What?' She couldn't have heard properly. She stared at him as the words sank in. He'd been gone so long and this was what he'd been doing? 'You're sending me away?'

'Yes.'

She stared at him, trying to work out why. Last night had been amazing. She'd felt on top of the world. But there was a catch because it wasn't actually *real*, was it? It was a pretence. A convenience. It meant nothing. And he'd had enough of her. Already. So quickly. The novelty of her had worn off and there was nothing left to interest him. Only she couldn't quite believe that all those moments had been that shallow. She couldn't believe that he felt *nothing*.

'Is this because I won't marry you?' She began to get angry. 'Are you so annoyed that I won't agree to *everything* you want that you're punishing me?' She stepped closer in disbelief. 'Are you that spoilt, Niko?'

'This is not a punishment.' He stared at her. 'That's the opposite of my intention. I want you to have your freedom, Maia.'

Her freedom? She stood very still as a horrible feeling opened up within her. 'Don't tell me you're doing this in my best interests...'

'But this is exactly what's best, Maia.'

'Not if I get no *choice*,' she argued.

'Well, you don't. Not immediately,' he said grimly. 'Initially I need to be sure you're safe. We have a home there that is already serviceable.'

Serviceable. 'And then? What's the long-term plan, Niko?'

'It's best if you go right away.' He didn't answer her actual question. 'I think it will be easier for you to adjust to the change in our relationship.'

She stared, bereft of speech as the horror of the situation grew. 'The...' Fear whispered out. 'You don't want me at all anymore?'

'It's not helping either of us,' he said grimly.

Helping? She couldn't even echo the madness.

Was it normal to have the best night of your life and then have it fall apart? How had she felt something so vastly different to him? How could they be so completely opposite in their assessment of that experience? Was she this naive? This inexperienced in relationships?

'I know you're upset,' he gritted. 'But—'

'Yes. I am. Shall we blame it on pregnancy hormones?' she interrupted, her mouth running off before her brain could stop it. 'Or say it's because I'm inexperienced? But they're both just excuses to dismiss my *feelings* because you're uncomfortable with the fact that you've just hurt me.' She blinked rapidly. 'Because you *have*, Niko.'

She hated that acidic tears were so close. She never cried. But even though she swallowed she couldn't stop the rising emotion. 'You broke your promise.'

'Which is why it's better to do this now before it gets worse.'

'*It?*' She stared at him, humiliated, and yet defiance surged. She would not apologise for having *feelings*. 'You mean how I *feel* about you?'

He glanced away. Apparently looking at her was now too awkward. 'You're confused, Maia.'

Oh, wow. Was he really going to dismiss what she felt and thought and experienced? Did he really think he 'knew better'?

'Then clarify this for me, Niko,' she invited coldly. 'Explain all. Why am I being sent away and how long for?'

'I think we need time and space apart. This is too much for you to have to make decisions on right now.'

She paused. So this was coming from a place of protectiveness? She narrowed her gaze. 'Why the sudden switch when less than an hour ago you were chomping at the bit to announce our engagement?'

'I've had a chance to think more clearly.'

He'd had time away from her. And he was worried about the decisions she'd tried to make—her determination that she would *not* marry him. That had truly bothered him— why? Did he want her to change her mind? Hope—almost destroyed—suddenly fluttered again.

She stood and walked towards him. 'Did last night mean anything for you?' she asked and took all her courage in her hands. 'Because it meant something to me, Niko. And I don't want to go away. I want to stay here with you. We can work this out—'

'No.' He stomped on that flicker of hope. 'This isn't right. It's asking too much of you, Maia.'

Why had he suddenly leapt to that conclusion?

'You think you're the only one capable of handling hard things? I'm just as strong as you. If not stronger.' She gazed at him, trying to understand what he was thinking. 'And I'm not your mother, Niko. I'm tough. I've survived so much more than you'll ever really know.'

'Yeah, and you shouldn't have to survive more. You should just have—' He broke off. 'Whatever you want.'

'Then why not *ask* me what I want instead of making some unilateral decision? Instead of assuming that you know everything? Why not listen to what I'm telling you. I want—'

'You *can't* know what you want!' he fired back in frustration. 'You've never had the chance to even understand all your options.'

She sucked in a breath. 'So no matter what I say, you won't believe that I might *want* to stay with you?'

'It's irrelevant because you *can't*.' He stared at her stonily. 'Because *I* don't want you to.'

And what he wanted happened.

'I only want what is best for you,' he said.

'You only want what's *easy*,' she shot back.

'You think this is easy?' he retorted furiously. 'It would be *much* easier to make you stay here with me, Maia, and you know *exactly* how I could get you to set aside your resistance.'

She stared at him, her heart shattering as he admitted using his skill to seduce her. To manipulate her. But she also knew he was wrong. 'But you can't, can you, Niko? You've realised you can't. You can seduce me to a mindless mess but I'll still say no to marriage. You know I won't change my mind. And you can't cope with that.'

They glared at each other.

'You're right. I don't want you forced into staying here.'

'But I do want to stay. I just don't want to marry you.'

'Why not? Why am I good enough to sleep with and not good enough to marry?' he asked.

His twist of reality all but destroyed her and the truth spilled out. 'Because this isn't going to last. Because you're not in love with me.'

He stared at her. 'You do not need me. You do not need *this*. Go, Maia. You be everything you want to be. Do it all. Discover everything. Please, I want that for you.'

Not *I want you*. But *I want that* for *you*.

She heard the nuance and understood. He really didn't want her.

'You've been fighting for your freedom for all this time and now I want to help you get it and you're suddenly all angry with me?' He threw his hands up. 'I can't win.'

'Because everything's changed.' She stared at him pleadingly. 'Hasn't it?'

He shook his head. 'It's just been an intense few days.'

'No. That's not all.' She stared at him, willing him to admit even just a little to the truth of their connection.

'Don't, Maia.'

'Don't speak the truth?'

'You can't even know what that is,' he said heavily. 'You have no basis for comparison. You've been isolated your whole life. You haven't had the chance to find out what you might want. How can you really understand anything you think you feel?'

So he *was* using her inexperience against her. There was nothing she could say to convince him otherwise. Because he still wasn't listening to her. He wanted her *gone*.

Badly. Because he cared. But not enough about *her*. Not in the way of him actually wanting her. Not enough to try.

'I want you to be free to be who you are.'

'I am with you,' she said. 'I don't hold back with you. I'm not afraid of you. And I'm not afraid to ask for what I want with you.' And she couldn't be afraid now. 'It's just that I want more. Of you.' She drew a deep breath. 'I only want *you*, Niko. That's all.'

She wanted the best for him too.

He flinched. 'You're not staying here, Maia. Do you understand? We're not ever getting married. I will never ask you again.'

She froze. 'But you said—'

'It doesn't matter what I said. I was wrong. It's not in your best interests.'

He was being so patronising. Furious, she glared at him. 'And the baby?'

'Will have my name. Will be my heir. But will be free to make their own choices when they're old enough.'

He wanted what *he* thought was best for her. Because in his way he did care. But not in the way she wanted. She wanted him to care so much that he'd be *unable* to let her go. She'd never been wanted just for herself and she still wasn't. She wanted him to hold her and keep her. Always. And it was *such* a stupid, impossible fantasy, but she couldn't get it out of her head. Because last night had been *so* amazing. 'And that's just it for us? We're over?'

He stiffened.

'Why won't you compromise?' she asked. 'Why isn't this enough?'

Couldn't they make this work just as it was?

'I'm sorry, Maia—'

'I don't want you to feel sorry for me,' she snapped, her voice raw with emotion. 'I want you to *love* me!'

He stared at her. Silenced.

'But you know what? I feel sorry for you. You can't be

honest, can you? You can't admit anything deeply personal. You won't let yourself be vulnerable. Because you've been hurt.' His heart had been broken by his parents. 'All those women you dated? You said yourself they were safe choices. But that was because *you* never had to invest emotionally. You took what you wanted. Fun, frolics. A few laughs. Little more. Your *heart* was never at risk. You literally had nothing to lose. It was shallow and fun. But you could walk away at any time and you did. But you *can't* walk away from me, Niko.' She stared at him. 'And now you can't cope with me. So you're *sending* me away instead.'

'It's not that I can't cope with you.'

'No?' She rose and walked towards him. 'Isn't that exactly what this is?'

'I don't want you to be hurt. You've had enough pain.'

'We've all been hurt, Niko. Everyone gets scared. But you have to be brave to get the good things. They don't just come to you. They don't just happen.'

He shook his head at her.

'I know your mum struggled.' She looked him directly in the eye. 'And I know you feel things deeply. You're a highly sensitive person, Niko.'

He was frozen. Staring at her.

'So *you* don't take personal risks. You said you wanted to protect me. And this baby. But you're really only protecting yourself. This distance you want is like a shield.' She stared up at him. 'You don't want to have to be responsible for someone else's happiness. You don't have to do anything to make me or this baby happy. All you have to do is open up and let me in.'

She paused. Waiting. Hoping.

But he didn't answer.

CHAPTER THIRTEEN

'SHE'S LANDED SAFELY,' Pax informed Niko from the doorway.

Niko nodded, not looking up from the paperwork he'd been struggling to process for the last two hours. 'You have someone watching over her?'

'From a distance, yes. She was adamant she didn't want a minder.'

Niko gritted his teeth. He could just imagine her irritation but he was determined that she would be safe there in the Australian coastal city. She would be able to explore all she wanted, at least for a little, before the baby was born. She could have some freedom while he figured out a better future for her. Distance was the best course of action right now.

It would be hard not to have his child on the islands full-time, but this child needed their mother and Maia wanted to give them everything she'd not had. Niko would not stand in the way of that. He'd had the good fortune of having a mother's love and he wanted his child to know that too. Eventually he'd devise a visitation and an education plan so the child would understand its heritage…he would make this work.

He realised Pax was still standing in the doorway and he glanced up questioningly. Pax's expression was even more impassive than usual.

'What is it?' he asked, suddenly wary. 'Is something wrong?'

After a beat Pax stepped forward and closed the door behind him. 'There is a problem in Monrayne.'

'Monrayne?' Niko stood immediately. 'What is it? Pax?'

'I have to go.' Pax removed the sunglasses from his face, revealing the jagged scar above his left eyelid and his ice blue eyes. 'I realise this is unfortunate timing.'

'No, it isn't.' Niko dismissed Pax's apology and welcomed the rising concern. They'd been there for each other since boarding school and he would do anything he could for his friend. 'Everything is settled here now.'

Pax's gaze turned sardonic but Niko didn't want to talk about Maia anymore. This was exactly what he needed. Something to think of outside of himself. Only Niko knew the secret his security chief had hid for the last decade—Pax Williams wasn't only a soldier. Pax Williams wasn't even his name.

'You must go,' Niko said firmly. 'You must do what is right.'

Pax looked at him steadily. 'As must you.'

Niko stiffened and his resolve hardened. 'Yes. I'll go with you.'

'*No.*' The cloak of obedience fell away and Pax denied him imperiously. 'I'll handle this my way, Niko. You *do* have matters to attend to here,' he added with the implacable authority of the prince he really was. 'Perhaps it's not only about doing what is right, but also doing what you *want.*'

Niko didn't appreciate the unwanted advice. Besides, hadn't Niko been doing only what he *wanted* for years?

He shut down the conversation by bowing to his friend instead. 'If you need anything—'

'I know.' Pax nodded brusquely.

But Niko knew he wouldn't take up the offer because Captain Pax Williams was the long-lost Prince Lucian of the Central European kingdom of Monrayne. And if he was finally ready to reclaim his title, he now needed no one.

Niko stared at the door long after Pax had shut it behind him and desperately determined that he needed no one either.

Not *ever*.

In theory Maia could do anything she wanted. Go anywhere. See anything. She had money, a maid in the rooms next door. She had a driver and a car at her disposal 24/7. For the first time in her life, her time was completely her own. And she had no idea what to do with it.

She'd promised Niko's scary silent soldier friend that she would stay in the city, and she genuinely didn't want to cause any of them any more trouble.

She'd said Niko was a coward. He wasn't. He'd been braver than she had. It was mortifying but he'd been honest in refusing her offer of compromise. He wouldn't take advantage of her any longer. It was her own fault it had happened in the first place. She'd made it so easy for him. She'd launched herself into his bed within twenty-four hours of meeting him. So starved of attention she'd said yes in seconds. She'd behaved exactly how those horrible guests on the boat had once joked she would…

But oddly she couldn't regret it. It had been good. And if it were only a good time then maybe she'd be able to get over it swiftly.

But it hadn't only been a good time. It had been *him*. He'd made her *laugh*. He'd made her feel seen and heard. He'd made her feel strong and beautiful and special. And he was too easy to like—not just to *lust* after but actually like. He was sharp and kind, incisive, amusing, outrageous. And hurt. There was that deeply hurt side hidden in him too.

He'd wanted to do what he believed was right. So he wasn't

all that selfish and spoilt really. He was dutiful and aware of the impact of his world upon others. But he didn't love her. For about five minutes there she'd thought she could have it all. But he didn't want that. Not with her.

Maia needed that. She needed a man who loved her. Someone who was honest and brave.

So she needed to figure out what to do with her new-found *time*. It wasn't enough to not have to worry about her money. She needed purpose and dignity and a passion for herself. That she could put everything into before the baby arrived. And then she would pour all her love into that sweet child.

And she would be okay. She would survive. She had no choice but to.

It was almost two weeks before Niko braved the island but in the end he had no choice. The hellish headache had been building for days. A migraine, he figured. His first. Some small semblance of the sort his mother had suffered. *Stress*.

In the end he took the helicopter. He'd stay just the one night. He'd relax and shake off the relentless throb in his temple. But as he stared moodily across the water and the house came into view he'd honestly never felt more miserable. It was self-indulgent and weak. He dropped his bag in the bedroom. He'd asked Aron to remove the hammocks before he arrived but he still saw them in his mind's eye. Every damned room was haunted by her presence.

He walked out to the pool and saw the small carving on the table Aron had set for one.

'Where did you find it?' he asked the elderly man when he wheeled a silver trolley out.

'It was tucked away in a little corner of her deck. I found it when I took down the hammock as you requested. I'm not sure if it was meant to be found.'

No, she'd have thought she'd stowed it safely. Leaving a little marker of herself hidden away.

He picked up the beautiful sea turtle and studied closely the intricate way she'd inlaid some small stones into its shell. The stones he'd found on the beach. The ones she'd won from him. She'd used a couple of obsidian chips for eyes. A tiny tormenting treasure to remind him not just of her, but of her skill. And her strength in adversity. She created beautiful things out of whatever little scraps she had to hand. So what would she build if she had more resources to play with? Something infinitely beautiful.

Something *priceless*.

He became aware that Aron was scrutinising him equally closely.

'I know what you're thinking,' Niko said.

'I'm sure you do—'

'Stop it. I already know I've screwed up.' He sighed heavily. 'Bring me a bottle of whisky, will you?'

'You might have another headache tomorrow, sir.'

Niko put the sea turtle down. 'I'm quite sure I will.'

But once Aron had fetched the bottle and then left him alone Niko simply stared at the amber liquid. The path of his father when he'd lost his wife. The devastation of losing the love of his life had led him into such poor choices—self-medicating his suffering. Only suffering more. Causing suffering too—to Niko. To Aron. To himself.

Niko would not do the same.

His family weren't fabulous at loving others healthily. His grandfather had failed to love his daughter, Lani. He'd failed to even *acknowledge* her.

He'd seen his father struggle to balance the expectations of his grandfather and the care his wife needed. And her accident had destroyed his father. But his mother had shown him the way forward, hadn't she? She'd striven to teach him balance in their time here. Making him stop to rest and recharge in nature. To count the stones, to fish and appreciate the ocean's bounty, to run in the sands where his ancestors had thrived for centuries.

But it had taken Maia to point that out to him. She had taken her sharp little knife and shaved away the pieces that he preferred to keep in place. She'd peeled away that protective layer with her challenge, her wit and her warmth. She'd left him exposed, revealing the truth of his loneliness. His hurt. His guilt. His fear.

And now he longed for the sweet balm of her body. He could bury himself in her and ignore the world. But that wasn't enough for her. She wanted—and deserved—more. So he'd sent her away. He'd thought he was so honourable. Putting her well-being first. Letting her be 'free.' 'Protecting' her.

But she was right about that too.

He'd been protecting *himself.* Hiding his heart. But she'd tried to fight for him. Only he'd been too blinded by fear to realise it.

But she didn't think good things could just happen for her. She thought she had to work for them somehow—had to put herself on the line, had to be willing to accept *less.*

Why won't you compromise?

Why isn't it enough?

He couldn't agree to her outrageous concubine offer because it had felt *wrong.* Only now did he realise just why.

She shouldn't have had to do that. She should have *everything.* The security and freedom to be found within love. She shouldn't have to *fight* for everything she wanted or needed. She should be given it. She never had though, had she? She'd never had the unconditional, unwavering love every person should have. She should always know just how deeply, how truly and how passionately she was loved. She should never doubt it. *Ever.*

He'd let her down so badly.

But she was strong, a survivor. She would be surviving just fine right now. *He* was the one who wasn't.

He was sensitive. He had been distracting himself with safe affairs. He'd been avoiding the decisions about his future not because he didn't want to hurt someone else, not because he didn't want the emotional responsibility for someone else, but because *he* didn't want to lose any more. *He* was hurt.

She'd thought he wanted her only because of the baby. That couldn't be more wrong. But he'd not been brave enough to be honest with her. But the truth was he'd not gotten his balance back from the moment he'd stepped on board that boat. She'd upended his world. Not the baby. But Maia herself. And baby or not, he wanted Maia. He missed Maia. He loved Maia.

And he wanted her back.

CHAPTER FOURTEEN

IT WAS A good thing Pax had gone to the other side of the world. He'd be apoplectic about the risk he'd consider Niko was currently taking. No bodyguard. Economy class as incognito as he could. Then public transport. He'd have driven himself to the apartment but he'd not slept at all on the flight and knew it would be dangerous to drive. But he got there and it was with a mix of terror and relief that he finally knocked on the door.

There was no answer. He knocked again. Waited. Then let himself in.

'Maia?' he called and checked every room with increasing desperation. He'd wanted to see her so badly and she wasn't here. In the end he sank onto the sofa in the lounge, setting the sea turtle on the small table in front of him. He'd wait. But he'd not slept the whole flight. He'd been planning everything he wanted to say—not daring to imagine her response—so desperate to see her, but he'd not imagined that she wouldn't be here. Now he didn't know where she was and it *sucked*. He pressed his hands to his eyes in a futile attempt to stop the stinging disappointment and sheer desolation.

'Niko?'

Oh great. Now he was hallucinating.

'What are you doing here?'

He dropped his hands and blinked. Yeah, he was definitely hallucinating, because Maia was right in front of him, clad in the gorgeous yellow bikini she'd worn the day he'd made love to her for the first time. He just groaned—helpless, wordless, devastated.

'What's wrong?' The apparition knelt down before him. 'Are you ill?'

He froze as a decidedly real, warm hand softly pressed against his cheek.

Shit. Was she really here? He grabbed her wrist and held her hand to him. 'Maia?'

She immediately stood—her arm now stretched out awkwardly. 'What's happened? Is it Aron? You look…'

'Terrible? I feel terrible.' He reluctantly released her wrist and shook his head. 'I didn't think you were here. I thought you'd gone.'

She looked at him warily. He didn't blame her.

'I was in the pool up on the roof,' she explained. 'What are you doing here?'

'I made a mistake. A big one.' He was suddenly trembling and his brain was doing a very bad job of remembering everything he'd wanted to say.

'You're not supposed to be here.' Maia was struggling to cope with the shock of finding him in the apartment. And he'd brought the small turtle she'd left on her balcony on the island. She'd hidden it there, a secret reminder that Maia was there—*once*—but he'd found it and brought it with him. Now she needed to move because she was about to lose all emotional control and she wasn't doing that in front of him again.

'Maia—'

'No.' She stepped back from him. 'No.'

He suddenly stood, suddenly huge and overpowering, and her barely taped together heart shattered.

'Maia, darling. Please—'

'No.' This time her denial wasn't for him, but for herself.

She was desperate to stop the tears—to stop him seeing. She tried to run but he drew her against him before she could—wrapping his arms right around her so tightly like the morning he'd first met her.

'Maia.' He whispered her name in her hair as he cradled her in such a strong, secure embrace. Holding her so safe that every emotion tore free.

'Please don't do this to me,' she pleaded into his solid frame. 'I can't go through this again. I can't—'

'I'm sorry.' He pressed her closer into his chest, stroking her back, clearly feeling her whole body trembling. 'I'm sorry I didn't tell you everything. I couldn't admit it. But now I'm here and—'

'*Why?*' she cried angrily, pushing back enough to look up at him. 'Why are you here? What do you want?'

'I want...' He drifted off, staring into her eyes for such a long time and heaven help her, Maia just fell for him all over again—lost in the gleaming intensity of his warm brown gaze. Something new flowed through her—settling her pulse, slowing her breathing—*certainty*.

'Wondered if you'd do dinner,' he finally mumbled. 'Maybe a movie. Get married. Make love. Lots. Have this baby. Live a long time. Love each other always. That was pretty much the plan. Figured other details might...might...' He suddenly sighed, a shuddering release of yearning.

She blinked and tears spilled.

'Maia.' He wiped her cheeks gently and rested his forehead on hers, his eyes gleaming with the thing she'd never dared dream of seeing. 'I don't want to compromise. I don't want "just enough." In this I am spoilt. I am selfish. I want *everything* possible.' He drew breath. 'But most of all I want *you* not to have to compromise. *You* should have everything. I just hope that you still might want to have *me*.'

She couldn't move. It was like it had been from the beginning. He stole her breath, made her brain dizzy, made her body melt.

'I'm not asking because I feel like I have to, ought to, should…' he breathed. 'I'm asking only because I want to. So badly. Because I'm so bloody miserable without you, Maia.'

All she could do was lean in close and it was enough. The kiss ignited everything. She clutched him.

'Missed you,' he muttered again and again between kisses. 'Don't go away ever again.'

'Don't *send* me away ever again.'

'Yeah. Never.' His beautiful smile was filled with apology. 'Oh.' He suddenly stiffened. 'I found Stefan.'

'What?'

'I tracked Stefan down. He's spent the last few years moving from job to job. He was glad to hear you're well and that you've left your father's boat.'

'Why did you go looking for him?'

'Because he was nice to you and he was badly treated by your father. Which is the absolute opposite of what should have happened. I wanted to see if he was okay or if he needed anything.'

Niko's thoughtfulness, kindness and honour awed her. 'And did he?'

'I offered him a part-time retirement job on the island. Aron can only make salads and I thought that our children might like a sweet pastry with breakfast.'

'Our *children*?'

'I half hoped you might want more than one? I'd like a big loving family.' He hesitated, his eyes widening. 'But only if you do too. When you do. I mean you haven't had much choice around—'

She put her hand on his mouth. 'I would love a big loving

family. Thank you for finding him for me. For even think-ing of it.'

The bikini was gone in moments. His shirt and trousers were slightly more troublesome but they got there.

'I've never had someone want me,' she whispered. 'Some-one really and truly just want *me*.'

'*I* do. So completely.' He braced above her. 'And I offer you all of *me*.' He tightened his hold. 'My arms to hold you. My ears to listen to anything you want to tell me or even just to tease me. My whole body really, however you want me.'

'Now, I want you now.' She'd missed him so much she was already hot and ready and they both groaned as he pushed home.

'I offer my loyalty. My fidelity. I'll only ever be yours, Maia. Because you have my heart. I didn't want to admit that before because I was scared and I'm sorry about that. But I love you, Maia. And I'm here and I don't ever want to let you go again.'

He thrust deep, pressing closer and closer still—anchor-ing her to him. She wrapped around him and simply hung on. Letting him love her. Letting him take her so fast, so in-tensely, she couldn't even scream. She simply shook—and he just held her closer still, until he groaned with agonising ecstasy.

Maia couldn't move after that cataclysmic release. She felt as if she'd been tossed through every emotion and was utterly wrung out. All that remained was joy.

She lifted her head just enough to catch his eye and smiled. 'Is that all you've got?'

He began to laugh and she too giggled. But suddenly her laughter turned to tears and he swiftly wrapped his arms around her again—so tightly.

'I've got you,' he muttered.

She knew the reassurance was not just for her, but for him too. She hugged him tightly back and as her sobs eased she heard his sigh of aching contentment.

Her longing. Her absolute truth escaped her too. 'I love you, Niko.'

'Thank you,' he whispered.

His fingers rhythmically combed through her hair in a tender touch of love. Of wonder. She closed her eyes. Jewels and thrones and things meant little—what she'd found with him was family and yes, *freedom*. To be herself, to ask for what she wanted—to give and to take. Because there was no freedom more complete than that she'd found in the security of his love.

CHAPTER FIFTEEN

Almost three years later

PRINCESS KAILANI LIKED to splash her father. Repeatedly. King Niko sat in the shallow end of the pool and patiently helped his toddler refill the little bucket—that she would then tip all over him. And giggle. And immediately refill it again.

Niko didn't mind. He loved his daughter, the sunshine, the *time* that he had to do this.

'Mama?' Kailani questioned, staring at him with her big brown eyes.

'Soon. She'll be home soon,' he answered, distracting her with a different water toy.

Honestly, he couldn't wait for Maia to arrive either. She'd had a meeting on a nearby island and frankly he'd expected her to be here already. He'd seen some coverage on his tablet earlier—Maia sitting in a circle of dignitaries discussing ship workers' rights. Sometimes he was so filled with awe of her he didn't know what to do with himself. She'd flourished, his beautiful wife. Popular with his people, down to earth, she had an accessibility and relatability that other royals from nearby nations had told him they wished they could bottle. He got it—she had a quality, a resilience and a generosity, that was rare and that he would never ever take for granted. Often they worked together but sometimes for practical reasons they took on separate engagements. That was what had happened today. But Niko's straightforward plaque unveiling had concluded sooner than anticipated so he'd been able to bring Kailani to the island a little earlier than planned. While Maia's meeting had run late.

Aron shuffled out from where he'd been sitting in the shade. 'The boat is almost here.'

Niko had thought the old man had been dozing—apparently not. Apparently he too was watching for Maia. 'Great.'

'I've just taken the pain au chocolat from the oven.' Stefan appeared in the doorway, looking pleased with the timing.

Yeah, Niko and Kailani definitely weren't the only ones watching for the return of their queen.

Niko lifted his daughter into his arms and carried her down the beach to the water's edge to greet her. It was a glorious day—above and before them the blue expanse stretched to infinity. There was no storm coming, only heat. He could see her sitting in the stern, her glorious long black hair gleaming in the late afternoon sun. Her smile flashed as she watched him encourage their daughter to wave at her.

She waved back and there was such a sparkle in her eyes Niko melted. The entire weekend stretched before them. They scheduled at least two whole weekends here each month to have completely to themselves. It was part of the balance they'd carefully worked to achieve together. Barefoot, Maia jumped into the water, not caring that the hem of her pretty dress was soaked even though she'd hitched it up.

'I'm devastated you're wearing a swimsuit,' she whispered to him tartly, her smoky gaze drinking in his still-damp skin.

'Couldn't scare the staff. Or our daughter—you teasing wretch.' But Niko could kiss her—passionately—loving the equally hot, hungry welcome of her mouth.

Then he laughed as their child wriggled restlessly on his hip and held out her arms to her mama.

'I missed you,' he muttered as he lifted their daughter into Maia's embrace.

'It's been eight hours.' She kissed Kailani's sweet cheek.

'Yeah, and I missed you for all of them.'

She wrinkled her nose. 'Crazy man.'

'Crazy in love.' He slung his arm around her shoulders and drew her close and turned towards their beach home. His happiness right this second simply couldn't be surpassed.

But Maia glanced behind her shoulder and called back, 'Are you guys okay? Do you need help?'

'We're fine, thank you, ma'am.'

Niko had been so busy feasting his eyes on his wife he hadn't even noticed other people disembarking. Now he frowned. He didn't want *work* following them here. That wasn't the plan for this weekend at all.

'What's going on?' he asked Maia.

'I'm pre-empting your over-protectiveness.' Maia smiled at him impishly.

'My what?'

There was an odd light in her eyes now—a sheen that made him stop still right where he was, halfway up the beach with his feet bare and sandy. His plump toddler babbled sweetly, oblivious to the sudden tension filling her father.

'I'm ensuring you'll have all the reassurance *you* need,' she said.

Reassurance? For what? He turned and stared more closely at the cluster of people lifting boxes from the rear of the boat. He recognised one of the men. It was the doctor who'd cared for Maia when she was pregnant with Kailani. So he was here now because…?

Anticipation swept through him like a king tide. 'Maia,' he murmured throatily.

His wife simply smiled even more impishly.

He didn't need to be a rocket scientist to figure this one out. But at the same time it was so *good* he really didn't want to be wrong. He tugged her closer so he could whisper, 'Have you something to tell me?'

She giggled. He loved it when she giggled. When she teased him. When she looked at him like this—with love in her eyes and vitality oozing from every pore. He just gazed back at her. She'd never looked more beautiful.

And now his chest was so tight he couldn't breathe. 'You've already done a test?'

'Just this morning. Then I rang the doctor and asked him to come here.' She nodded. 'He's brought his fancy portable scanning machine with him,' she said. 'I didn't want to confirm it—or see anything—without you and I also knew you wouldn't want to wait. You'll want all the information, immediately.'

Yeah, she was very right about that. But still he was stunned. 'We've only been trying a short—'

'And isn't that just typical of your...*stuff*?' she interrupted him with a laughing look.

He chuckled and pleasure flooded him. 'Stefan's been baking all afternoon in readiness for your arrival. I'm sure Kailani would enjoy a petite pastry with him and Aron while we meet with the specialist?'

Maia nodded. 'I've asked the maid to show him to our private lounge.'

Niko's tension proliferated. He needed to know. Now. Most especially that everything was okay—that *Maia* was okay.

Maia had known Niko would be impatient. Frankly she was too. It had almost been impossible to focus on her meeting today so she'd had to work extra hard and then she'd gotten fully into it and it had actually made time fly all the more quickly.

She set Kailani into her small chair and smiled as Aron and Stefan immediately fussed around the small girl. She rarely heard from her father and while that sometimes saddened her, there was so much more *to* be grateful for. Kailani had two grandfather figures who adored her and taught her so much. Maia too had their love and support. As did Niko.

After a few minutes she took her husband's hand and walked to the small lounge.

The doctor had set up his equipment. Maia smiled to herself as Niko paced about the room while the doctor helped her. She'd never forget the sight of him standing at the beach clad in just his black swim shorts, his bronze skin burnished in the sun, his tattoos drawing her gaze to his rippling muscles, his protective yet playful hold of their child, his smile as he watched her approach. He was stunning and that he was hers still amazed her.

'This is earlier in the pregnancy and we need to do a different scan from the first one we did when you were pregnant with Princess Kailani,' the doctor explained. 'So don't worry that you're going to see less on the screen.' He smiled apologetically at her. 'And unfortunately, it might be a little uncomfortable.'

Niko paced about even more quickly.

'It's okay,' Maia reassured him.

'I'm here for *you*,' he declared. 'You don't need to worry about me.'

'But I can see *you* worrying.' She chuckled.

The scan was a little uncomfortable and seemed to take much longer than the first one. Niko stopped pacing completely and just stood nearby, alternately staring at her, then the screen, then her again while the doctor just focused on the screen.

'Is everything okay?' Niko finally asked through gritted teeth.

'Yes…' the doctor answered slowly. 'But—'

'But what?'

The doctor breathed out. 'There's more than one gestational sac.'

Maia met her husband's startled look.

'Pardon?' Niko muttered hoarsely.

'There are two…' The doctor paused thoughtfully again, his focus still intently fixed on the monitor. 'I'm just checking… Yes. Just the two that I can detect at this stage.'

Just the *two*? And what did he mean by 'at this stage'?

'You mean twins?' Niko clarified urgently. 'You mean we're having twins.'

The doctor finally smiled. 'Yes. Congratulations.'

Maia couldn't believe what she was hearing.

'It's very early and while it's not probable, it's also not impossible that there might be more,' the doctor explained. 'Sometimes little babies like to hide behind their siblings. But there are at least two in there—looking very good.' He glanced at Maia reassuringly. 'Looking just as they should.'

'Not impossible…' Niko echoed. Then he suddenly looked tense. 'Twins. Maybe triplets? Does this make everything more risky for Maia?'

'Of course we'll monitor Queen Maia very carefully all the way through this pregnancy. But she's very healthy and I see no reason why this won't progress perfectly normally.'

Niko puffed out a harsh breath. 'You'll stay within reach of us at *all* times.'

'Of course, Your Highness.'

'Thank you, Doctor.' Maia smiled and spoke more gently. 'You took such great care of me last time and Kailani and I were both fine. I know this will be fine too.'

The doctor flushed slightly. 'Thank you, ma'am.'

'Yeah, thanks…' Niko ruffled his hair, looking shell-shocked. 'Uh, would you mind…'

'Giving you privacy?' Beaming, the doctor bowed and swiftly left the room, closing the door behind him.

Niko dropped to his knees beside her. 'Maia—'

'You have a real talent for over-achieving,' she said dazedly.

His smile was shamelessly smug for a second but then it faded and emotion welled in his eyes. 'No, I'm just unbelievably lucky,' he muttered huskily. 'I've never been more grateful in my life for that screw-up at the clinic that day. The thought of never meeting you otherwise?' He cupped her face in his hands. 'Of you being stuck on that bloody boat? Of us not having all of this together? I can't bear to think about it.'

'I know.' Tears spilled. It was silly because she'd never been as happy and here she was crying. 'Hormones already.' She wiped her cheeks inelegantly. 'Zillions of them, apparently.'

With a laugh he kissed her and she clung to him with desperate need. They had such riches already and such joy to come. The big family they both wanted would be here even quicker than they'd planned and she was so excited.

'Oh.' She pressed her hand to her forehead. 'I'm hot and flustered. I need a shower.'

'Happily, I have the best shower in the world.' He stood and scooped her into his arms.

'I'm still capable of walking,' she teased even as she clung to him delightedly.

'Indulge me in my primeval need to demonstrate my strength and ability to care for my woman,' he growled.

'Oh,' she breathed meekly. 'Okay then.'

And care for her he did. In the lush outdoor shower where thick tropical foliage screened them, he removed her pretty dress with such gentleness and such tease it was a good thing he was there to help her remain standing.

'You were amazing today. Your speech was fantastic.' He carefully soaped, then rinsed, then kissed every inch of her body.

'You watched it?' She sighed dreamily.

'Of course I did.' He scooped her up again and carried her back inside to their bed.

'Twins,' Maia marvelled in wonder as he placed her onto the cool linen. 'Isn't it a good thing we live in a palace with an abundance of bedrooms.'

'You know they'll be banging our door down early in the morning to come crawl into bed with us. Kailani already does that.' Laughter and heat danced in his eyes.

'Then isn't it a good thing we have a big bed.'

'Think we better make the most of it now, actually.' His gaze turned serious. 'I need to love you…'

'*Finally!*' She rubbed against him. 'Come on then…'

His smile returned. 'Those hormones driving you again, huh?'

'No.' She shook her head. She was all seriousness now. 'It's love.'

His kisses were hot, his touches tender as he gently slid down her body and tormented her with such intimate strokes of his tongue. Maia arched and trembled in his hold. She loved it when he gifted her orgasms like this. But she was greedy. She wanted more. She wanted it all.

But Niko paused. 'Are you sure you're okay for—'

'Indulge *me* in *my* primeval need…' she ordered him in a passionate whisper. 'I'm so excited I need…' She wrapped her legs around his waist and pulled him to her in a wild challenge. '*This* is where I need all of your strength. This is where I need all of *you*.'

And she desperately, *desperately* needed him now.

'I didn't think I could feel any happier than I did standing by the water with Kailani watching you come home to us,' Niko said huskily, holding a mere inch above her—so still, so close, so hot. 'But this is just incredible.'

'*Yes!*'

There was no living through this moment without their full surrender to passion. He was everything—sweetly relentless, fiercely demanding. Maia sighed with desperate delight, meeting him with an animal fervour of her own as they pushed to the brink and beyond. She shattered as the exquisite sensations claimed her reason. She loved him as he loved her—with everything she had—*hard*. And then it was so soft, so complete, so intimate…and she was indescribably happy.

Eventually he summoned the strength to roll to his side. He smiled at her, his brown eyes brimming with joy. 'Let's go find Kailani. We need to tell her she's going to be a big sister. What do you think she's going to say? Lord, what are Aron and Stefan going to say?'

Maia giggled at his excitement. She felt it too. And she too felt such gratitude. Their gorgeous daughter was going to have *everything* they longed for her to have—as were their precious babies who'd yet to arrive—parents who were there for them, elders who adored them, a more balanced public life, siblings, security…

And love. Always there would be so much love.

* * * * *

THE BOSS'S
FORBIDDEN
ASSISTANT

CLARE CONNELLY

MILLS & BOON

CHAPTER ONE

'YOU UNDERSTAND WHAT this job involves?'

Salvador da Rocha was staring at Harper Lawson with obvious scepticism, his golden-brown eyes glinting with something like cynicism. She knew enough about the man to have come here expecting his trademark arrogance to be on display, but this was next level. She fought the temptation to remind him that he was hardly in the best bargaining position, given his hard-working personal assistant, who had already done a full handover with Harper, was taking a well-deserved two weeks off, leaving Harper alone. He needed Harper, but it was evident he didn't *want* to need her.

'Yes, sir.'

He steepled his fingers beneath his chin, eyes boring into hers. To unnerve her? She wondered if she should save him the trouble and tell him there was nothing he could throw at her that would get under her skin. She'd worked for too many jackasses in her time to be bothered by Salvador—even if he happened to be the head of the company and one of the wealthiest men in the world.

'Amanda works long days, sometimes seven days straight. If I need to travel, she comes with me at a moment's notice. She organises my life. Every part of it. I rely on her completely.'

Harper didn't bat an eyelid—she knew this much from Amanda herself.

'If you accept this job, for the next two weeks you will exist to serve me. Do you understand that?'

She ignored the strange shiver that ran the length of her spine at his choice of words, his accented voice deep and fascinating.

'In exchange,' he continued after a small pause, 'You will be given a sizeable bonus.'

Harper's stomach turned over and her fingertips tingled. A 'sizeable bonus' was exactly why she'd let Amanda talk her into this. As one of her mother's oldest friends, Amanda was one of the few people in Harper's life who understood her personal situation. In fact, it was Amanda who'd pushed Harper to take the job at da Rocha Industries in Chicago two years ago. Because Harper worked hard—harder than almost anyone she knew; she had to. She needed every cent she could earn to pay down her mother's medical costs, and da Rocha Industries was renowned for its generous remuneration packages.

But this 'bonus' was another matter entirely.

'How sizeable?' she asked bullishly. It was a question that might have embarrassed some, but for Harper she'd long passed the point of having the luxury of decorum when it came to money. She had to be mercenary in order to survive. Her skills were many and marketable, and by trading on them she intended to give her mother the very best, most comfortable life she could. Unfortunately, round-the-clock care didn't come cheap.

Salvador's lips flickered with an emotion she couldn't understand, but she tilted her chin defiantly, refusing to be ashamed for asking.

'I think it's a fair question,' she murmured. 'You're asking me to enslave myself to you for a fortnight and, while

I'm more than willing to do so, I would like to know what my compensation will be.'

He turned to his laptop and clicked a couple of buttons. 'In addition to your regular salary,' he said, leaving her in no doubt he had her personnel file on screen, 'You will receive four months' pay and the associated benefits.'

'Four months,' she repeated, doing the mental calculations on a small exhalation.

He turned back to Harper and another shiver ran the length of her spine.

'That should give you some insight into the level of service I'll expect.'

She arched her brows. 'I'm a very hard worker, Mr da Rocha. Surely you're aware of that?'

'I can see you have excellent references.'

'But you're not sure?'

'I'm never sure of anyone,' he responded immediately. 'My trust is earned.'

'Then we're at an *impasse*,' she pointed out, her own expression neutral, green eyes slightly narrowed as she regarded him. 'You need cover for Amanda, and I'm the best option you have.'

'You're very confident.'

'Yes,' she said with a shrug, the silk of her blouse rippling over her slender body like a waterfall. For a moment, Salvador's eyes dropped lower, and a little flame of heat flickered in the pit of her stomach. It came without warning and caught Harper by surprise. She tamped it down immediately, refusing to acknowledge the effect someone like Salvador could have on a woman. In this moment, she wasn't a woman and he wasn't a man—they would be working together closely for many hours a day, and she'd learned the hard way that it was never a good idea to mix business with pleasure.

'You understand this is a live-in position?'

For a moment, her eyes flickered beyond Salvador to the view of the lush, tropical rainforest behind him, then to the sparkling South Atlantic that glistened all the way to the white sand beaches of Copacabana, just across the strait.

Ilha do Sonhos, the private island from which the reclusive billionaire lived and worked, was one of the most beautiful places Harper had ever been. As the helicopter had come in over the landing pad, she'd enjoyed the panoramic views of the ocean with the seemingly prehistoric land mass of the island, craggy mountains, rugged cliffs, spiked grasses and enormous, windswept trees creating a lush, green jungle across it. It was wild and almost looked uninhabited, except for this home, all timber and glass, with incredible views in all directions.

'Yes.' She brought her gaze back to his and a jolt travelled through her. She'd seen him from a distance before, at a company event in her native Chicago. He'd spoken only to Amanda and the CFO, Alan Bridges, no one else, but there'd been a magnetism about him. She had found it impossible not to look at him, not to study him. It was his strength and charisma, his confidence and intelligence, the ability he had to walk into a room and command it without even bothering to try. Some people were born with that kind of personality, but not many. Salvador da Rocha was a god amongst men. Working with him, even for two weeks, would be a learning curve she would relish.

'You have an impressive CV,' he said, gesturing to his screen once more.

Damn straight. At twenty-six, Harper had worked for some of the biggest names in the corporate world and, except for that awful business with Peter Cavstock, she had covered herself in glory each and every time. For the last two years, she'd been stationed at the Chicago office of da Rocha Industries, working for the head of North American operations.

'Thank you,' she said with a dip of her head.

'Why did you join da Rocha Industries?' he asked, fixing her with a level stare.

She bit back a desire to ask why it mattered. Wasn't it more important that she did work for him? That she was regarded as indispensable to one of his busiest executives?

'It was an excellent opportunity,' she supplied, the answer revealing very little.

'What do you enjoy about your current role?'

'Enjoyment is beside the point,' she said after a beat. 'It's a job.'

'You don't enjoy what you do?'

'I didn't say that,' she said quietly. 'But I'm not turning up each day looking to be entertained. Whether I enjoy my job or not, I still do it to an excellent standard, always. Every day.'

He pressed his chin to his fingers, steepling them once more. His face was fascinating. She found her eyes clinging to his sharp features longer than was necessary or wise, admiring the chiselled cut of his cheekbones, his jaw, the strength of his patrician nose and the effect his five o'clock shadow had on his overall appearance, giving him a 'devil may care' attitude that was, frankly, quite beautiful. 'Do you like working with Jack?'

She frowned, bringing her errant thoughts back to the present situation. 'Yes,' she said, quickly. 'But I've worked with plenty of people I didn't like. I'm a professional, Mr da Rocha. I come to work to get the job done, and don't leave until I'm finished. Does that satisfy you?'

He studied her for so long, with such intensity, she had a new-found sympathy for bugs under the microscope. Finally, he spoke again, his Brazilian accent every bit as mesmerising as his face.

'Amanda tells me you have some conditions of your own.'

Harper had no doubt Amanda had informed him of those conditions, but Salvador was evaluating her, trying to get a read on her confidence to negotiate for herself.

She fixed him with a direct stare. 'Yes.'

'They are?'

'I need half an hour a day to myself. During those thirty minutes, I will be completely unavailable.'

Their eyes were locked in a stare that was laced with challenge on both sides. Who would blink first?

'It's an unusual request,' he said.

'To have some time to myself?'

'Such a specific amount of time.'

She compressed her lips, not willing to be drawn on that. 'Mr da Rocha, I have no doubt I can do this job. I would love to work alongside you, and I'm confident I can take care of things in Amanda's absence. I want the money, yes, but more than that, I want the experience. Jobs like this don't come along every day.'

His eyes flashed gold then copper.

'But I will walk away if you don't agree to this condition.'

She'd surprised him. It was evident in the way his mouth stretched, his brows lifting when they met hers.

'I don't like it,' he said after a beat.

She was unflinching, but beneath the desk, away from his view, she kept her fingers crossed. She couldn't budge on this point. Every day, she called her mother in the nursing home and read to her. The doctors weren't sure how much of it her mother understood, but Harper knew it meant the world to her mum, and she had no intention of disappearing into thin air.

'Shall I wait outside while you consider it?' she asked,

standing to her full height. She wasn't tall, nor was she short, but she was well aware she had a body that drew the attention of the opposite sex, with curves in what her mother would have called 'all the right places'. It made Harper uncomfortable. While her mother had been adored and feted for her looks, Harper had never welcomed that kind of attention. She pulled her dark-brown hair over one shoulder, then winced, because it was a gesture that spoke of nerves—something she'd trained herself never to show.

His eyes flickered over her body and, despite the fact Harper usually hated it when men looked at her, now the lightest goose bumps lifted her skin, which she preferred to attribute to the sea breeze that brushed in through the ocean-side window, bringing with it a hint of salt in the air.

'That won't be necessary,' he said, finally, echoing her movement and standing, eyes latched to hers so she was overly conscious of the beating of her heart. 'If Amanda put you forward for this role, I'm sure you'll be fine.'

Fine.

Talk about being damned with faint praise, she thought to herself.

Mentally, she came up with a list of substitutions for 'fine'—acceptable, average, bearable, okay—and found that, on further analysis, none of them offered any particularly gratifying appraisal.

'I work long hours,' he explained unnecessarily. 'I will not hesitate to call you when I need something.'

'As you've said,' she agreed with a small nod.

'While you need to be available to me almost the entire day, I expect my privacy to be respected.'

'Don't speak unless spoken to?' she couldn't help responding, with an arched brow and a cynical smile.

'Crude, but accurate.'

Crude or rude, she thought, dipping her head forward to conceal her expression. 'I have no problems with that,' she agreed.

'Then we have a deal, Ms Lawson.'

'Oh, you should call me Harper,' she said, as she moved towards the door. He was right behind her, his stride long, his body so close she could feel warmth emanating off him.

Ridiculous, she chided herself. She wasn't usually prone to that kind of fantasy! He reached past her to open the door, and Harper stepped through it, grateful for some clean air-space.

'We are not friends, Ms Lawson. When these two weeks are over, we will never see one another again. I see no need to refer to you by your first name, nor for you to use mine.'

It was a direct smack-down. A warning: *don't get familiar, don't get comfortable*.

'Very well, Mr da Rocha,' she responded. 'Would you care to point me in the direction of my office?'

Ten minutes later, she was ensconced in a stunning office with panoramic views of the ocean, state-of-the-art computers and screens, and only one small problem: Salvador's office was directly next door, separated by a large glass window, so she could see him, and he could see her, the whole time.

There were blinds, she noted, but only on his side, so he could choose when he wanted to close them or open them, leaving the situation entirely in his hands.

A power dynamic she didn't particularly like, but wasn't willing to challenge—not for the sake of two weeks.

'Amanda has brought you up to speed?'

'Yes, sir.'

'Good. This pile is most urgent. Start on that right away.'

He moved towards the door of her office.

'The chef provides meals at seven in the morning, one in the afternoon, a snack at four and dinner at eight, but naturally the kitchen is stocked and you are welcome to help yourself to anything you require. I eat alone. A room has been made up for you—the housekeeper, Catarina, will take you to it later today. Catarina is your point of contact for anything domestic. Did Amanda leave you with a list of my contacts?'

'Of course.'

'Good.' His frown deepened. 'I don't tolerate mistakes, Ms Lawson. Keep your head in the game and I'm sure the next two weeks will go just fine.'

Adequate, reasonable, acceptable, she thought with a flicker of her lashes.

He left the office, the slight hint of a threat still hanging in the air, so she stared at her computer screen with a sinking feeling in her gut, but only for a moment.

Harper rallied, reminding herself that she wasn't a wallflower; she wasn't someone passive to whom life just happened. She grabbed bulls by their horns to make things work in her favour, and that was exactly what she intended to do right now.

So much depended on the next two weeks. While her annual salary was excellent, by the time she paid her mortgage and her mother's medical expenses, she wasn't exactly flush. The idea of earning this kind of money, of being able to build a small nest egg just in case, was ultra-appealing.

Maybe even a college fund? a little voice in the back of her mind pushed, but Harper quickly silenced such a silly thought. College had been a pipe dream. One she'd given up on a long time ago. She'd had to, and she hadn't regretted that for a single moment, she reminded herself forcefully. Not when she considered that she'd been able to provide for her mum by going straight out into the workforce.

* * *

It wasn't Harper Lawson's fault—none of it was.

Not her fault that, twenty-seven years ago, Amanda Carey had a daughter. Nor that, a year ago, that daughter had become engaged, was getting married in two weeks and 'needed' her mother to be there with her. It was not Harper Lawson's fault that Amanda had taken her first proper leave in eight years, and that Salvador had had to grapple with how he'd come completely to depend on the other woman's calm organisation of his life.

And it was definitely not Harper Lawson's fault that she had eyes the colour of the ocean on a stormy afternoon, eyes the exact same shade as another woman Salvador had once known. Eyes he'd seen fill with delighted excitement and crushing devastation in the course of a few short months. Eyes he'd watch go from sparkling like emeralds to dull like slate over the course of two years. Eyes he would never see again, now that she was gone.

He stood, prowling from behind his desk towards the windows that overlooked the ocean, wishing that he could summon a storm cloud or two to go with his mood.

He didn't like change.

He didn't like people—new people, particularly.

And there was something in Harper Lawson's manner that was particularly unnerving, but he couldn't put his finger on it. Beyond her eyes, there was no other resemblance to Anna-Maria. Anna-Maria had had short blonde hair that hung in soft waves around her face. She'd been tall and statuesque, until chemotherapy had made her so thin he'd thought she might break just by breathing—she very nearly had.

His face tightened into a grimace.

He tried not to think of Anna-Maria, or the baby they'd made and lost, and the way Anna-Maria had given her life for their child, delaying necessary cancer treatment so the baby would have the best chance of living. He tried not to think about the years of friendship with Anna-Maria that had been part of his life—the way they'd played together as children, written to one another as teenagers and then, one drunken night, had taken their relationship to the next level, changing all the parameters of his world.

He tried not to think about any of it, but every now and again it all came back to him, and he almost doubled over from grief. Not just at losing them, but at the fact he hadn't been able to halt death. He hadn't been able to destroy cancer. He'd thrown all his money at it, convinced modern medicine would hold the answer, but he'd been arrogant and stupid.

Their daughter had died, and then Anna-Maria had followed just months later. At twenty-nine, he'd buried his wife, one of his oldest friends. A year later, Salvador was still remembering how to put one foot in front of the other, which made the timing of Amanda's absence even more vexing.

None of this was Harper Lawson's fault, but she was here when he didn't want her to be and, worse, he knew he'd be depending on her just as he had Amanda.

Still, it was only two weeks. He could live with that. In fourteen days, Amanda would be back, Harper would be gone and his life returned to normal, just as he liked it.

CHAPTER TWO

HARPER'S EYES WERE stinging but she had no intention of being the first to leave the office. Not when there was still a mountain of work to do and she was conscious of Salvador just beyond the glass window, working with apparently indefatigable energy, looking as bright and intent as he had when they'd met much earlier that day.

Had it seriously only been today?

She dropped her pen on the desk and leaned back in her chair, surrendering for a moment to a wave of fatigue, closing her eyes and inhaling, letting tiredness wash over as she counted to ten, then opened her eyes and refocused on the screen. The numbers blurred.

She pressed her fingers to her eyes, massaging the lids gently.

'You can go.'

Neither of them had spoken in so long, she'd almost forgotten what he sounded like. But now his voice, accented and fascinating, washed over her from the direction of the door. She swivelled in her chair, heart leaping to her throat. He didn't look *quite* as fresh as the morning, she thought with an instinctive frown. He'd unbuttoned his shirt at the collar, flicked open to reveal the thick column of his neck, and his sleeves were pushed up to the elbows, showing tanned forearms covered in a light sprinkling of hair. For some reason, the sight of that made her mouth go dry and her tongue feel too thick.

Awareness of him on any level was a disaster.

He was her boss, just as Peter had been. Alarm bells blared; she listened to them.

Swallowing hard, she turned back to her screen. 'I'll leave soon.'

'You're exhausted.' He sounded disappointed, which raised her hackles.

'Well, it's after twelve,' she pointed out, stretching her neck from side to side.

'If this is too much for you...'

She ground her teeth together. 'It's not.' She clicked a few things on her computer then put it into sleep mode. 'Out of interest, what time does Amanda generally work until?' She stood, gathering her things as she spoke.

'Amanda has been doing the job for eight years.'

'I'll take that to mean she usually leaves her desk much earlier.'

'Again, if it's too much for you...'

'That's not what I'm saying,' she repeated firmly. 'But how does that sentence end, anyway? Do you have an alternative to me? Someone else you can fly over to take on this role?'

She was being crotchety but so what? She was tired and he was expecting *way* too much.

She'd clearly hit a nerve, going by the way his brows knit together and his eyes, so expressive and beautiful, darkened for a moment.

'Did the housekeeper show you to a guest room?'

'I didn't find the housekeeper,' Harper said crisply, resisting the urge to point out that she'd been working all day.

More disapproval. 'Then I'll have to show you.'

'Just tell me where to go and I'm sure I can find it.'

'It's a big house.'

'And I'm a smart woman. Which way?'

He compressed his lips. 'Come on. I will take you.'

Well, this was definitely not going to be a bed of roses for either of them. She told herself he wasn't being antagonistic specifically to her, that he was just an unpleasant, reclusive billionaire, but it was hard not to take it a little personally. She'd worked with some royal pains in the butt in her time, but none quite so outright rude as this guy.

Then again, having a bank balance like his probably eroded the need for civility.

Maybe that was why he had to pay his staff so generously.

She followed him through the house. The panoramic view of the beaches, visible from all windows, was blacked out by night now, revealing the silhouette of ancient trees and sparkly stars in the sky. As they turned a corner, the moon, high and full, cast a silver pathway across the ocean so Harper's breath caught in her throat at the loveliness of it.

Hearing the noise, he turned, frowning, his face a silent question.

'It's so beautiful,' she said, then felt stupid and gauche at such an idealistic comment. But it *was* beautiful.

He didn't respond, which only made her feel worse. Fortunately, their walk was coming to an end. He reached a double set of doors and opened one, pushing it inwards without going inside.

'It's all set up for your stay. There's an office in here too.'

The suite was as luxurious as she'd expect to find in any five-star hotel. She cast her eyes over the large bed, sofa, huge flat-screen TV and French doors, which she presumed led to a balcony.

'Thank you.' Her eyes drifted back to the bed. She couldn't

wait to climb into it and find the oblivion of sleep. But first, a hot shower.

She turned back to Salvador, still standing on the other side of the door. She couldn't understand why, but she was glad for it, glad that he was outside, because there was something so masculine about his presence.

'Good night, Ms Lawson.'

He pulled the door closed and she expelled a breath she hadn't realised she'd been holding, glad to be alone, finally, for almost the first time all day. And what a day! Her head was swimming but, damn it, she wasn't just going to meet his expectations, she was going to blow them out of the water. True, the work today had been immense. She'd summarised complex financial reports, responded to myriad emails from all over the world and scheduled a diary that was bursting at the seams. Her head was swimming.

But she'd achieved everything she'd wanted to, and a sense of pride flooded her veins. She concentrated on her breathing, a stillness meditation, as she unbuttoned her blouse and thought hungrily of the shower and that soft-looking queen-size bed.

It wasn't her fault that she'd forgotten her handbag. He'd basically pushed her out of the office in his insistence to show her to her room, but nonetheless he was cursing Ms Lawson as he scooped up the bag and strode through his home with it tucked under his arm.

It's so beautiful.

He recalled her softly voiced admiration at the moon and the beach as he'd come round the corner and the view had hit him square between the eyes. She was right, he grudgingly admitted–, it was beautiful—breath-taking in fact—

but it had been a long time since he'd allowed himself to see the view, much less admire it.

At the doors to her room, he knocked twice then waited. Immediately after his second knock, he heard her voice call something, which he took to be an invitation, so pushed the door open, striding in with the intention of placing the bag on the coffee table near the sofa, but he froze two steps into the space.

Ms Lawson was midway through stripping out of her clothes. She'd removed her blouse and pencil skirt but not her silk camisole or lace thong, or, God help him, her heels.

Salvador da Rocha was not a man who was surprised easily but in that moment he lost all command of himself. He could only stare at her, at the curves that had been completely hidden by her outfit, at her creamy soft skin, her delicate breasts and nipples hardened into nubs by the gentle sea air she'd welcomed into the room by throwing open the doors. That same breeze pulled against her camisole now, so it showed the flatness of her stomach, her rounded hips. Her legs were long and curved, perfectly proportioned.

She made a small gasping sound and he lifted his eyes to her face, to lips that were full, pink and parted, her tongue darting out to swipe over her lower lip, her cheeks rosy, her eyes sparkling and filled with electricity. Or was that his blood? Sparks zinged through him and he heard a storm in his ears, in his brain, pushing all thought from his head.

'Mr da Rocha,' she said, but in a strange, strangled voice that showed she was as removed from her senses as he was.

'You…' … *Left your bag,* he finished internally, but he couldn't speak the words, couldn't form them with his tongue. She turned a little away from him, so now the curve of her bottom was visible, and he swallowed a curse because he'd never seen anything quite so perfect as that pert, rounded rear. His hands immediately tingled with the need to feel it fill his palms, to roll his hands over her, to slide his fingers into the elastic of her thong and glide it down her legs until she was naked. He imagined the warmth of her skin, the smoothness, and he groaned, a visceral, aching noise that showed how lost he was.

It had been a long time since he'd been intimate with a woman. A long time since he'd seen the unclothed form of one.

And now he was staring at his near-naked assistant like some randy schoolboy. It was a sobering thought, pushing his mind back into gear, even when his body was still growing hard, his blood pounding through his veins like a tsunami.

'Why the hell did you tell me to come in?' he demanded angrily.

'I *didn't*!' She gaped. 'You… I…heard a knock…'

'And called out—'

'I squawked,' she said with obvious anger. 'I was in this state!' Her hands gestured unhelpfully to her body, reminding them both that she was undressed. As if he needed the reminder. 'I was trying to say "don't come in".'

'But you didn't say that.'

'No, I was flustered.' Her eyes dropped away, her jaw moving as she ground her teeth together.

He thought back, trying to remember what he'd heard, and realised her story could be plausible. Not in the mood to admit his own mistake, or to apologise, he clung to his irritation like a life raft. 'Well, don't you know how to lock a dammed door?' he muttered, lifting the bag higher. 'You forgot this.'

She recoiled physically, as though he'd slapped her, and he felt instant regret at his angry words. None of this was her fault—not that he'd stalked into her room to find her in a state of undress, or that she was so incredibly, sinfully beautiful. And definitely not that he'd sworn he'd never want another woman. His throat constricted, making breathing difficult, and finally, belatedly, he did what he should have done from the first moment he'd crossed the threshold and seen her like this: he turned his back.

'I didn't think I'd need to lock the door to my own room,' she responded with a voice that was almost ice-like, except for a fine quiver at the end. He suspected he'd done the impossible on day one and upset the assistant Amanda has assured him would be unflappable. Then again, he was pretty sure he was breaking a hell of a lot of HR guidelines right now.

He placed the bag on a table near the door and moved back, spine straight, shoulders tense.

'I thought you called for me to come in,' he said.

'I didn't.' Her cheeks were still flushed, her body on display, he saw, when he chanced a quick glance over his shoulder. The effect was immediate. His cock jerked in his pants and his chest swelled as he inhaled a breath that might as well have been filled with flames for how much it overheated him.

Before Anna-Maria, he'd dated women. He'd slept with women. He'd lived like a normal, red-blooded man with a billion-dollar empire at his fingertips and had had his choice of company any night of the week. He'd made love to women without compunction, without emotion, but Anna-Maria had changed him. Rather, her shock pregnancy had. For the first time in his life, he'd been faced with the consequences of his lifestyle—a careless one-night stand with one of his oldest friends who'd ended up carrying his baby because he'd failed to use a condom. She'd been on the pill, and they'd both been clean, but that hadn't made it okay.

It had also brought him face to face with the ghost of his own past—of his father's neglect and abandonment, of his father's mistreatment of his mother. He'd been reborn that day into a different man. For almost two years, he'd been celibate, the price he considered it his duty to pay, his atonement for what had happened to Anna-Maria, even when he knew he hadn't caused her cancer.

'I had no idea you'd be changing so quickly.' His voice was raspy. God, but she was beautiful. 'You only came back here a few moments ago.'

'Yes, well, it's late and I'm tired,' she snapped, her words husky, almost as though she was close to tears. That had him turning to face her once more, studying her for signs of distress, but she kept her features schooled into a mask of icy disapproval. 'Naturally, I'm getting ready for bed.'

She had a very valid point, yet it was entirely the wrong thing to have said, because it reminded them both of the bed that was only metres away. His eyes shifted to it, imagining her against the sheets, her hair spread out across the pillows, and his pulse kicked up a notch.

'You should go,' she said barely audibly and, when he looked back at Ms Lawson, she was swallowing so hard her throat was shifting visibly.

'Yes,' he agreed without moving a muscle. It was as though his feet were glued to the ground.

'Mr da Rocha…' She groaned, her nipples so taut they were pulling at the camisole. His eyes dropped to her breasts and his gut rolled with the sheer force of his desire.

'Salvador!' His name was a plea, a desperate, anguished plea, and that alone finally got through to him. She was begging him to leave and he was standing there, staring at her like an idiot.

'I'm sorry,' he said with sincerity and shock. What the hell had just happened to him? As if finally regaining control of his senses, he forced his feet to move, one after the other, until he was out of her damned suite of rooms and away from the temptation of her beautiful, sensual body.

* * *

But it wasn't so easy to put Harper Lawson from his mind. Having ignored his sexual nature for far too long, it had been dragged back to life with an epic bang. A cold shower didn't help, nor did work. When he eventually gave in and went to bed, she filled his head and mind, then his dreams, so he woke harder than granite, so hard it was almost painful to move. And all he wanted to do was reach for her, lift that silk camisole and run his hands over her naked skin, cup her breasts and feel their weight in the palms of his hands. Drag her body against his and kiss her until she was trembling, her pale flesh pink from his stubble, signs of his possession, of his need for her.

He showered again, head pressed against the tiles, eyes closed, trying to focus on work, on anything other than his new assistant, but failing.

So it was with some trepidation that he entered his office the next morning and only exhaled when he realised she wasn't there yet.

Good.

He moved quickly, shutting the blinds to separate their workspaces, needing to see more of her like he needed a hole in the head.

Harper knew he was there, behind the curtains, because he'd had multiple online meetings and his voice had carried. It was deep, sensual and capable of making her knees tremble even through a wall of glass and hidden behind a curtain.

Holy heck.

What was happening?

Last night had been surreal and strange and, while she knew she should be flooded by indignant rage, she wasn't. He shouldn't have barged in, and he surely shouldn't have stayed staring at her like he'd never before seen a woman in his life. He'd been completely transfixed, his expression something she'd never forget.

He'd looked at her as if she was the most desirable woman on the face of the earth. He'd looked at her as if he'd wanted to eat her up then and there, and she couldn't get that out of her mind. She couldn't forget the way he'd stared, the way his breath had snagged between his teeth, hissing into the room. She couldn't forget the way her own body—traitorous, treacherous body—had responded to him, her breasts tingling, desperate to be touched, moist heat building between her legs, her heart in overdrive, her mouth not working properly, her lips full and heavy, aching to be kissed.

It had been a moment of madness for both of them, a strange removal of sense and sanity, the replacement of those things with a primal, physical response that defied logic.

With a pulse that was still none too steady, she flicked up the cuff of her shirt to reveal a tiny tattoo on her inner wrist, a black heart, a reminder to herself that she was her own first love, that she alone was enough. She'd got it after Peter. She still shuddered to think of what a fool she'd been to be taken in by his suave seduction. True, she'd been entirely innocent, with no experience whatsoever in the romance stakes, but she wasn't devoid of all sense, so how come she'd let him make her think she was falling for him? The tattoo was supposed to serve as a reminder that she couldn't trust anyone else with her heart.

Salvador wasn't a contender for that anyway, but it was important to remember her commitment to remaining single. To remember that no man was worth her time—even really, really hot ones.

CHAPTER THREE

'COME WITH ME.'

The words, his voice, pierced her shield of concentration. Harper blinked, disorientated at first, pulling herself, comprehending, out of the documents she'd spent hours reading and back into the office with the beautiful views of the sea. Except there were no views now, because it was night, and she hadn't realised. The office was dark, except for the ultra-bright screen of her computer. It felt like being woken from a long afternoon nap after jet lag, not knowing where she was or when it was.

'Ms Lawson?' His impatience conveyed itself in the tone of his words so she pushed back her chair quickly, moving towards the door, but as she got closer she heard it again— the same hiss of air from between his teeth. And suddenly it all came rushing back to her. The way he'd looked at her. The way his gaze had *felt*. That might seem ridiculous but his gaze had run over her body and had the same effect as if he'd reached out and trailed a finger over her skin.

'I'm here,' she said, voice croaky from misuse.

He flicked on the lights, which should have made things better but instead made them so much worse, because she realised how close they were standing. She stared up at him and the same sense of disorientation wrapped around her, so it was almost impossible to remember where she was and why she was there. For a moment, the briefest moment, she was just a woman, and he a man, and nothing else had any importance.

His mouth tightened, forming a grim line, but a muscle moved in his jaw. He was feeling what she was, fighting it—this strange, drugging wave of attraction threatening to sweep them both up if they weren't careful.

'You wanted me?' she asked, then cringed inwardly at the unintended *double entendre*.

'I have to talk to you. I also have to eat. Have you eaten?'

Eaten? She frowned. 'Hmm, no.' Not since breakfast, in fact, when she'd grabbed a croissant and coffee and scurried into her office, breathing a huge sigh of relief to have avoided Salvador so successfully.

'Fine. Come with me then.' His eyes pierced hers for a moment longer than was necessary before he turned on his heel and stalked out of her office, into the larger shared space and beyond it to the corridor that led to the rest of the house. She fell into step behind him, glad he didn't wait, glad he didn't look at her, because it gave her some precious, vital moments to pull herself the heck together and remember she was a calm, successful professional in her own right.

The lighting in the house was cosy and ambient, creating a warm, golden glow. He walked down a corridor Harper hadn't seen before, then onto a terrace set with a table and a single chair, an image that struck Harper right in her centre, filling her with a tangle of emotions.

It just seemed so *lonely*. This man, this house, were so solitary and isolated. Even the house's position, in the middle of a private island surrounded by mountains, rainforest then miles of beaches, made it almost impossible to reach. Everything about his life seemed designed to push people away. Why?

'Ms Lawson will be joining me,' he said, and Harper

blinked as the efficient, kind-seeming housekeeper Catarina bustled onto the terrace. She nodded, flicked a small smile in Harper's direction then set to work, placing a second seat at the table and, a moment later, returning with extra cutlery and napkins.

'Dinner won't be long,' Catarina explained to them both, before leaving the terrace.

Harper swallowed. It was ridiculous to feel that the walls were closing in on her when there were no walls out here, yet she felt an oppressive sense of something: emotion; awareness of her own attraction to him; fear of doing something really stupid and showing him how she felt...

It was a balmy, warm night and the air hummed with something like magic. The forest whooshed quietly, the ocean rolled towards them, the moon cut a gleaming path across the dark water, the stars shone and the air was heavy with the fragrance of the island: salt, sand, night-flowering jasmine... It was a wonderful, heady scent, quite unique to this part of the planet, and so, so far removed from the long winter she'd left behind in Chicago.

'Sit down.'

It was impossible to pretend to herself that she didn't find his command even sexier, but Harper couldn't dignify that very primitive response with acknowledgement, and could certainly not leave his tone unchallenged.

'Are you going to order me around all night, sir?' she asked with a saccharine beating of her lashes, moving to the chair and pressing her hand to the back of it.

His eyes flicked to hers, hovering there, momentarily showing surprise, perhaps even uncertainty, before they shuttered any emotion from her view and he was once again impenetrable, impossible to read.

'Please sit down,' he amended with a casual shrug, so she

bit back a smile and did as he'd said, pulling the chair back and taking her seat. But the table had been designed for *one*. Adding a second chair was one thing, but it didn't create more leg room beneath it, so the moment he took his seat their ankles and knees brushed. Despite her good intentions, Harper flushed to the roots of her hair, her lips parting as they had last night, heavy with the need to be kissed.

Crap.

Did he feel it too? Or had last night been an aberration, a completely out-of-character moment of distraction that would never be repeated? For Harper, the way he'd looked at her had stirred something deep in her soul, embers of a flame she'd thought extinguished and which, now that it had roared to life, she had no idea how to bank down again.

She crossed one leg over the other, so she took up less physical space, but it was as though his bigger legs, spread wide, exuded a warmth all of their own. So, even though they no longer touched, she felt a static charge brushing her limbs, making it impossible to be aware of anything but him.

'What did you want to talk about?'

'Your work.'

Harper's heart dropped to her toes. 'Is there a problem?'

His frown was reflective. 'Should there be?'

'I— No.' She shook her head and a clump of silky dark hair brushed over one shoulder. She sucked in a deep breath, remembering who she was, what she'd achieved, why she'd sailed to the top of every office she'd ever worked in, and forced a bright smile to her face. Harper had her mother's megawatt-smile lips that were generous and wide, sculpted as if by angels, revealing straight, white teeth. A dimple was gouged in each of her cheeks. It was the kind of smile that invited trust and confidence.

'Go on,' she urged, folding her hands in her lap so she didn't fidget.

'Are you finding everything you need?'

Her brows drew closer together. 'Yes.'

'Because you haven't asked for anything.'

'No.' Her frown deepened. 'Isn't that…wouldn't you prefer that?'

'So long as you are finding what you need, and not fudging your way through things.'

She lifted her eyes heavenwards before she could stop herself, earning a look from him that did funny things to her tummy. His expression darkened, showing disapproval or exasperation—she couldn't tell—but there was something else. Something deep lay within the embers of his irises, something that made her smile drop and her heart go mad.

It was a look that spoke of speculation, of interest. Of the same desire that was thumping through her body, running rampant, begging to be indulged.

She reached for her water glass; it was empty. But a moment later Catarina appeared, brandishing a tray which she perched on the edge of the table so she could remove items, one by one: two wine glasses filled with red liquid, and a platter that overflowed with olives, bread, cheese, oil and some little croquettes.

'That smells delicious,' Harper complimented her honestly. Her stomach gave a rumble of agreement and she laughed awkwardly, pressing a hand to it, so it was the most natural thing in the world for Salvador's eyes to drop lower, skating over the curves he'd stared at the night before, to what he could see of her flat stomach beneath the table.

Harper's mouth went dry, her brain turning to mush. She stared at him helplessly, swimming against the current, trying desperately to hold onto common sense in the face of the most intense physical awareness she'd ever known. With Peter, it had been a slow burn. They'd worked together. He'd been smart and suave, and she'd trusted him. She'd *liked* him. But it had never felt as though every part of her had been struck by lightning. She'd never known anything quite like this before.

'Mr da Rocha,' she murmured, but the words came out breathy, made husky by her desire, so she scrunched up her eyes and tried again. But closing her eyes made her so much more aware of her surroundings: the sound of the forest, the night birds, the rolling, crashing waves, all so elemental and filled with passion; the smell of the tangy night air, the flowers. The island was so wonderfully fragrant and sensual that Harper's skin lifted with goose bumps, the hairs on the back of her neck standing on end.

'Last night,' he said after a beat, and she opened her eyes and stared at him, swallowing past a lump that had formed in her throat, 'Should not have happened.'

He was right, but it still hurt to hear him say that. 'What happened?' she asked unevenly.

His look was disparaging. 'I didn't intend to find you like that.'

Her eyes widened. 'I know.'

'I should have left immediately.'

'It's fine,' she said with a shake of her head. Her body warmed in agreement. She reached for an olive—she was starving—lifting it to her lips and popping it in her mouth. A droplet of oil escaped, so she chased it down her chin with a finger, then stopped when his eyes followed the action with such intensity that she felt he was touching her.

'You live in Chicago.' It was an abrupt change of conversation and, though it hadn't been a question, she nodded anyway.

'All my life,' she said after a moment, her voice uneven.

She reached for the napkin Catarina had brought, wiping her chin, then moved some bread to her plate, breaking it up with her fingers.

'Do you like it?'

'Yes, I suppose so.' She looked around, her lips tugging downwards a little. 'Though it's nothing compared to this.'

He didn't respond.

'This place is…it's so elemental. Here, you could be the last person on earth and there would be more than enough to sustain you.'

He was staring at her as if he could see inside her very soul, but he wasn't replying, so she sighed softly. It was one thing for him to ask questions, but conversation wasn't really possible if he didn't respond to her.

'Do *you* like it?' she asked when he was still just staring at her.

'Like what?'

'Living here.'

His eyes narrowed. 'I haven't thought about it.'

She bit into some bread. 'That's not an answer,' she said after a moment.

'No?'

'No. Even if you haven't thought about it, you could do so now. Think aloud. Ruminate.'

His smile was the last thing she'd expected. In just a flash it was there, like lightning out over the ocean, and then it was gone. But the memory of it danced on her eyelids, and she thought she would say or do almost anything to see that smile again.

'Ruminate?' he repeated, one thick dark brow lifted.

'Sure.'

He looked out to sea, to the streak of milky light cast by the moon. 'I like the privacy.'

She nodded slowly. 'It doesn't get lonely?'

His eyes shifted back to her face, his expression contemplative, so she waited, hands clasped in her lap, breath held, because she really wanted to hear what he had to say. Instead, he reached for his wine and took a sip.

'Mr da Rocha?' she prompted, and his eyes flew back to hers. Some sixth sense told her that he liked her calling him that—liked hearing her use his full name.

'I have staff,' he muttered after a moment. 'I am rarely truly alone.'

And yet, she shivered. There was something in the coldness of his response that made her chest hurt.

'I bet the surfing is amazing.'

'Do you surf?'

She nodded.

'I cannot imagine much opportunity for that in Chicago.'

'No,' she agreed with a smile. 'I take a week off and head to the west coast every summer. I learned as a young girl, and never got over the feeling of being propelled forward by waves. The rush, the power, the connection to the ocean...'

She didn't tell him that it was her father who'd taught her to surf, on the rare weeks he'd remembered he was in fact a father and had flown back into Harper's life. That it was one of the few things he'd given her, that she'd kept as a part of her soul and that, whenever she took a board into the ocean, she felt connected to her dad. A dad who'd deserted her, who didn't deserve a place in her heart, but had burrowed in there nonetheless.

'The waves here are large. I would not recommend you try it.'

'Well, with only a few hours spare in the day, there's not exactly time,' she responded tartly, before remembering she was sitting opposite her boss and that a mite more respect might be called for. She grimaced, lifting her hands. 'I'm sorry.'

She hesitated, then leaned closer so she could study his face better. 'Sir.' His eyes narrowed, his pupils dilated, and she was sure his cheeks had darkened. Her insides stirred and heat built between her legs, so she had to move to un-cross then re-cross them. Only his legs were there, beneath the table, and the action brushed them together. The effect was electric. Sparks flew into the air and up into the night sky, like fireworks.

'What for?' His response was gruff, almost a bark.

'Sometimes, I can't help speaking my mind.'

'I don't dislike that quality.'

'Careful,' she said with a half-smile. 'You might not al-ways like what I have to say.'

'Then I'll find a way to punish you,' he drawled, and she startled, because his meaning was impossibly clear, impos-sibly sensual, and utterly, disastrously desirable.

Her lips parted and his eyes fell to her mouth. This time, she couldn't contain the little moan that escaped, just a whis-pered sound of attraction. It was all too much.

'I'll be good,' she said quietly, looking down at the table, the dangerous game they were playing tying her stomach into knots.

'Are you good, Ms Lawson?'

She bit down into her lip. 'Oh, yes.'

'Always?'

She didn't tell him about the time she'd been bad. The time she'd screwed up, monumentally, by giving into something not entirely dissimilar to this and going to bed with her boss. Of course, she hadn't known he was married! She'd thought they were falling in love, that the feelings were mutual. But she seriously doubted Peter was capable of love—not for his wife, not for Harper either. She'd learned her lesson. Or had she? Because right now, if Salvador da Rocha snapped his fingers, Harper would go to him in a heartbeat.

What kind of fool did that make her?

'I'm not sure I believe you.'

'Are you calling me a liar, sir?' she asked, and though it wasn't intentional she shifted her legs a little, so now her toe brushed his calf. She had to stop this. It was getting way out of hand.

They had two weeks together, and this was only the second day.

What was going on?

Harper didn't usually do casual flirtation. She didn't do this kind of sexually charged banter. Not anymore. The relationship with Peter had killed her confidence and destroyed her faith in her own judgement.

His fingers reached for his wine glass, lifting it to his mouth slowly, thoughtfully, then taking a sip. She echoed his movements, tasting her own wine, savouring the flavour while simultaneously recognising she should *not* be adding alcohol into the mix.

'What do you do for fun?' His question was perhaps an attempt to draw the conversation away from the incendiary volley they'd been sharing. Or perhaps he was expecting her to respond with something that would throw fuel on the fire, by responding with an answer that was sensual and provocative.

Harper was drowning. She stared at Salvador, and felt all of her usual reserve and caution drifting away, so she dug her nails into her palm in an attempt to remember who she was and why this was a very, very bad idea.

'I work,' she said, glad that the words emerged reasonably level.

'For fun?'

'Is there something wrong with that? I would have thought it's a hobby we share.'

He frowned, took another sip of wine and Harper exhaled, because things between them were less charged; the provocative verbal game of cat and mouse had moved on. She could relax a little.

Except, with a man like Salvador, she suspected she would be wise never to let her guard down. It wasn't him, but the way she felt about him meant she needed to be permanently cautious.

'I do not consider work fun.'

'Yet you do so much of it?'

He looked beyond her to a point over her shoulder. 'It's habit, I suppose.'

That didn't sound quite right. She was sure there was more to it, but if there was, he clearly wasn't in the mood to expand. She had a little more bread and some more wine, but was relieved when a few minutes later Catarina returned, this time brandishing two plates, each filled with crunchy spiced potatoes, some sautéed greens and what looked to be two excellent pieces of steak.

The smell was immediately mouth-watering and Harper realised she wasn't just hungry, she was famished. She pushed her bread plate to the side to make room, smiling up at Catarina as the woman manoeuvred the plates into position, unaware of the way Salvador's eyes clung to her face, taking in every detail of her smile. Catarina left and Harper's smile dropped, her eyes moving to the meal instead.

'You are a very beautiful young woman.'

She startled, her heart racing. 'Mr da Rocha...'

He held up a hand, but then returned it to the table, reaching for his cutlery.

'You don't...' What could she say? She shook her head,

frustrated, hemmed in by her own experiences, her job for this man and a desire that was beating through her like a drum.

'I'm simply observing a fact,' he said, cutting into his steak with apparently no idea how his words had affected her.

'It's not a fact,' she said unevenly. 'When it comes to beauty, there is no such thing.'

'I disagree. Some people, like you, are objectively beautiful.'

It was too much. 'You can't…say that.'

'Did I offend you?'

She shook her head and, for some reason she couldn't fathom, felt the warning sting of tears behind her eyes. She cut her steak quickly, furiously, completely thrown off-balance.

'I was simply observing something about you, in the same way I might say your hair is brown or your nails short.' He lifted his shoulders. 'It was not an invitation to my bed, Ms Lawson. You can relax.'

Relax—after he'd so casually mentioned an invitation to his bed? Did he have any idea how riotous her pulse was? How desperately breathless she felt?

'Stop it,' she said after a moment, shaking her head.

'Stop what?'

'Whatever you're doing. You're…flirting with me, or teasing me, or possibly even toying with me. This working relationship will be much better if you don't do any of those things.'

He leaned back in his chair, studying her, dissecting her, reading her like a book, she feared. 'You don't like to be flirted with?'

'Not by my boss.'

He tilted his head to the side a little, silent for several moments, moments in which she knew he was seeing too much. 'Speaking from experience?'

Damn it! Her harsh intake of breath would undoubtedly give her away. 'I'm not going to answer that.'

'You already did,' he said quietly. 'Not your current boss, I presume?'

The colour drained from her face. 'It's none of your business.'

'So I presume a previous employer. Perhaps the reason you left Stanley Moore Graham after only seven months?'

She let out a shuddering breath. Damn him and his perceptiveness, his quick deductions.

'Your reference from the company was excellent, so it cannot have been a professional problem.'

'I said stop it,' she ground out, her appetite failing her now. She placed her cutlery down neatly and took another sip of wine.

'I'm simply trying to understand you.'

'Why?' she said forcefully, her feelings so wild, she couldn't make sense of any of them. 'Why does any of this matter?'

'I like to know the people who work for me.'

'Now who's lying?' she muttered under her breath.

'Explain.'

Her eyes widened. She hadn't meant him to hear! Cheeks flaming, she glared up at him.

'No.'

He lifted his brows.

'No, *sir*.' She added the title mockingly, but that didn't matter. Even now, when they were sparring, it had the same effect as before, so she knew that it was playing into some kind of fantasy of his, just as it was for Harper. The idea of being made love to by this man, dominated, commanded...

Please, sir...

She closed her eyes on the fantasies that were filling her

mind, unwanted, totally unwelcome and definitely unhelpful in the midst of their current conversation.

'Did he break your heart, Ms Lawson?'

She finished her wine in several gulps and replaced the glass a little more heavily than she'd intended.

'That's none of your damned business,' she responded, scraping back her chair. 'Now I see why you always eat alone—you're a terrible dinner companion, Mr da Rocha.' She side-stepped her chair. 'Goodnight.'

CHAPTER FOUR

FOR THE SECOND night in a row, Salvador felt as though a bomb had detonated in the middle of his life. He felt that everything was completely out of control, and he hated that.

But what the hell kind of game had he been playing at? She was right. He'd been flirting with her. Teasing her. Wanting her to flirt back. For no other reason than she did something to him that he liked, something he'd ignored for far too long.

She was stunning, sexy and whip-smart too—he'd checked her work carefully these first two days, not trusting her not to make mistakes. After all, he didn't really know anything about her. But not only had she been faultless, she'd gently corrected other people's errors and she'd reorganised spreadsheets he'd been working from for years, making them easier to read at a glance. She was obviously a phenomenal intellect, a power house, and so far able to keep pace with him without losing her mind.

So why had he teased her?

If he wanted to get laid, he could go to Rio for the night and find a woman, any woman, to take to bed. That would be a hell of a lot simpler than this dangerous, complicated flirtation.

Except, Salvador wasn't in the market for a lover. Losing Anna-Maria and the baby had left Salvador with a kind of emotional paralysis. He knew he was better alone.

Whether he desired Harper Lawson or not, giving into his stupid, masculine impulses would be a shortcut to disaster.

He couldn't do it.

He needed to be strong for the next twelve nights. That was all—twelve nights—and then things would be back to normal. Amanda would be in the office next to his and Ms Lawson far, far away in Chicago, with her whip-smart brain and sensual smile charming someone else.

He groaned as the thought of her mouth filled his mind, as he remembered the way she'd smiled and, even more dangerously, eaten that olive. The plump flesh had been pushed between her lips, her eyes closing briefly as she'd savoured the flavour, and then that glistening droplet squeezing from the corner of her mouth so that he'd wanted to lean forward and lick it with his own tongue, lick her, all over.

Christ.

With the feeling he was fighting a losing battle, he scraped back his chair and left the table, not returning to the house, but taking the well-worn path down the hill towards the beach, in that moment needing to lose himself in the wildness of the island.

She'd been hoping the curtains between their offices would be closed again, but no such luck. So, when Harper arrived at her desk carrying a coffee and croissant the following morning, it was to see Salvador already at work, dressed in what she was coming to realise was his uniform: a button-down shirt with the sleeves rolled up, a pair of trousers and socks but no shoes. That small detail did something funny to her heart.

She blinked as he lifted his head, pretending she hadn't seen him, moving to her own desk quickly and flicking the computer to life with fingers that trembled a little. It was impossible not to be aware of him, though, not to feel him as though he were pulsing through the glass. She made a sound of irritation under her breath while waiting for her computer to load, sipping her coffee, then mentally cursing as her eyes strayed to his office of their own volition, definitely without her consent.

This was impossible! How could she treat him normally when she was aware of every little thing he did? She dove into her work, piling through emails first, pulling her hair over one shoulder and toying with it as she read and triaged, responding as needed before moving onto the next.

She was glad to be busy, because eventually the work distracted her, just enough to forget about the man next door—the desire she felt for him, the fact she was so turned on by him, that he'd told her last night she was beautiful, so matter-of-factly, as though he'd simply been remarking on the weather.

But Harper wasn't charmed by that kind of compliment. She'd heard it said to her mother too many times, and always by men who'd broken her heart, so she'd learned from a young age that being admired for looks didn't really equate to much in the end.

She leaned back in her chair and lifted her coffee to sip it, before realising with disappointment that her cup was empty. On autopilot, she stood and moved to the door right as Salvador stepped through, his head bent over a stack of papers he was reading, so she quickly shelved any idea of this meeting being more than a coincidence.

Nonetheless, it brought them both together for the first time since she'd basically stormed out on him last night.

'Mr da Rocha,' she murmured, using her best professional, ice-queen voice, then kept walking towards the coffee machine set up on a bar in the communal area of their office.

'Ms Lawson.' He frowned, looking at her as if from a long way away. Whatever he'd been reading was clearly engrossing.

'I'm just getting a coffee,' she explained unnecessarily, then could have kicked herself for prolonging the encounter. It was as if she couldn't help herself.

'Good idea.' He put the documents down by his side and walked with her to the bar. It was way too small a space for both of them to occupy, given they were sharing it with a cloud of awareness she couldn't shake. Silence fell, an awkward silence, charged and heavy with words unspoken.

'After you.' She gestured to the machine.

'It was your idea,' he said with a lift of his shoulders. 'You go first.'

'No, I—'

'Ms Lawson, we're both too busy to stand here arguing over who gets to use the damned machine first. Make your coffee.'

She flinched, unprepared for the growl in his voice, the tone of his words or the effect they had on her. He was frustrated. Her eyes flew wide as she stared at him, comprehension dawning. It wasn't about the coffee. This was something more—the same drugging need that made it impossible for Harper to sleep or think was overtaking him. Wasn't it? Was it? She could have screamed with annoyance, because she truly didn't know. She suspected so, but everything was so murky. Perhaps it was just her own feelings making it impossible to see his clearly?

She fed a pod into the machine and waited for the liquid to spool out, not daring to look anywhere near his direction. But that didn't matter. She could feel him. She could hear him. Each exhalation wrapped around her, breathed through her, as tantalising and distracting as the rolling waves of the ocean and the salty sea breeze that was gently brushing through the open windows. Birds sang outside, breaking through her fog, or perhaps adding to the magic of what she was feeling.

'All done,' she said, snatching the cup quickly from the machine and turning to leave. Only she turned too fast, without looking properly, and bumped right into Salvador-bloody-da-Rocha's impressive wall of abdominals.

She groaned and pressed a palm to her forehead. *Seriously?*

'I'm so sorry,' she muttered, sounding angry rather than apologetic. After all, he'd been standing too close, he'd been… No. It had been her fault. She'd been so desperate to escape him, before she said or did something really stupid, and instead she'd done this.

She lifted a hand, pressed it to the dark stain spreading across his chest and felt the moment he breathed in, hard and fast, the second her fingers pressed to his shirt. His reaction was unmistakable, the power of that single breath sapping her willpower, her knowledge of what was right and necessary.

'Mr da Rocha,' she pleaded, looking up at him even as he lifted a hand and curved his fingers around her wrist, holding her hand right where it was.

'Yes, Ms Lawson?' he volleyed, his voice steady but slightly off-pitch. She swallowed, her mouth suddenly filled with dust.

'I…' She stalled, unsure what she'd been about to say. 'If you tell me where your room is, I'll go get you a clean shirt. I— That was so clumsy of me.'

'You were running away.'

Her eyes widened at his perceptive, frank assessment.

'Yes.' She couldn't deny it. Her eyes fluttered shut. His grip on her wrist tightened then relaxed, his thumb padding over her sensitive flesh so she was awash with awareness.

'It's smart of you.'

Neither moved. They were so close. If she inched forward just a little, their bodies would be touching. With his eyes still on hers, his hand holding her wrist where it was, he lifted his other to the top button of his shirt and flicked it, effortlessly parting one side of fabric from the other, then the next button and the next, revealing mahogany skin and a sprinkling of dark hair that arrowed towards his trousers.

Oh, good Lord.

Even with one hand holding hers he was able to unbutton the whole shirt and shrug out of one side of it, but as he reached the other he had to let go of her wrist.

It was a turning point. The moment she could have stepped backwards, stung, and quickly left the room. Instead, she stayed where she was, looking up at him, helpless, flooded with desire and desperate to see more of him. She'd dreamed of him for the last two nights, sensual, high-fantasy dreams that had been filled with what she imagined his naked form looked like. But now she had a chance to colour her vision better and she wasn't going to squander it.

Swallowing, she held her ground as he removed the shirt completely and placed it on the counter to his right, where the coffee machine was.

Her eyes followed the action, then returned to his chest, drinking in the sight of him, the beauty of his sculpted chest, his masculine frame and his leanly muscled arms. He smelled woody and spiced, and her stomach churned, the fragrance drawing her in almost as completely as the sight of him.

'You're beautiful,' she said simply, repeating his observation of her from the night before.

His lips quirked into a half-smile then dropped, a look of frustration crossing his face.

'Ms Lawson—'

'I wonder if you shouldn't call me Harper?'

He closed his eyes, as if to push away that very idea.

She swayed forward, unable to stop herself, even when her sensible, rational brain was shouting at her to stop, to remember the awful danger that could come from this. To remember the pain of her past, the embarrassment, the professional limbo she'd found herself in, having had an affair with her married boss.

But this was different. For one thing, Salvador wasn't married. For another, she wasn't so naïve and innocent any more. She'd grown a lot since her affair with Peter. She no longer expected any other person to hold the key to her happiness, and certainly not Salvador. She would be on his island for two weeks. It no longer seemed possible to be here and fight this. So what was the alternative? To quit? To leave him completely in the lurch? Or to stay and accept that something was going to happen, something that was bigger than them, completely out of their control?

'This is not...' he began with a shake of his head, fixing her with a dark stare, a plea in his own eyes. But a plea for what? Did he wish this weren't happening? Or was he asking her to initiate something? Did he feel that, as her boss, he couldn't be the one to act first? Then again, he'd stripped out of his shirt right in front of her.

She licked her lower lip, breath unsteady, eyes finding his.

'Mr da Rocha,' she said, low and huskily. 'I don't know what's happening between us, but it's obvious that neither of us is immune to this...chemistry.' She was pleased to have been able to pluck the perfect word from thin air. After all, what else explained the literal reaction they shared every time they were close to one another?

'And what are you suggesting?'

'That we stop fighting it,' she said quietly, moving closer

then, surprising herself with how daring she was being, and how little she cared about going out on a limb like this. She lifted a hand, tentatively touching his chest. There it was—that hiss of breath between his teeth, the sign that he was losing his vice-like grip on any ability to control things.

'That we maybe even give into it.' She blinked up at him, letting her fingers trail his chest now, side to side, swirling circles, feeling his flesh shift beneath her enquiry.

'You work for me,' he pointed out in a voice that was strained by the effort of staying right where he was.

'Yes,' she agreed simply.

'Company policy—'

'Yes. But don't you own the company?'

He frowned. 'That doesn't give me a free hand to disregard Human Resources.'

He was giving her a way out. She should stop this—surely she wasn't stupid enough to make this mistake again? But it was different. What she'd felt for Peter was nothing compared to the desire ravaging her system whenever Salvador was near.

'I saw the way you looked at me,' she whispered. 'That night and ever since.'

'How do I look at you?' he asked, the plea back in his eyes.

Her lips lifted at one side. 'Like you're wondering if I'm wearing a camisole beneath my blouse. Like you're wondering if I'm wearing a lace thong. Like you want to remove both from my body.'

He tilted his head back, staring at the ceiling. 'You are playing with fire.'

'Aren't we both?'

He dropped his head so that he was facing her once more. 'But you've already been burned.' He lifted a finger, running it over her cheek. She flinched, the words cutting through the desire that had made everything else seem so far away, as if her past was a part of a whole other person's life.

'What?'

He dropped his finger to her chin, then lower to her décolletage, frowning as his finger moved almost against his will to the valley between her breasts and the pearl button there.

'But you're right.'

She swallowed.

'I have been looking at you and thinking, exactly as you said. It is like you read my mind.' Her button came undone easily. She was trembling, completely awash with so many conflicting emotions that the desire he was stirring easily blotted out anything else.

He moved to the next button, and the next, until her shirt parted, as his had earlier. Rather than removing it, he pulled her silk camisole from the waist of her skirt so his hands could touch her bare waist then move higher, his eyes on hers, challenging her, waiting for her to stop him. He moved slowly, so she had ample opportunity to do exactly that, but in truth she wanted him to hurry up, to reach her breasts, to touch them— as she'd been desperate for him to do since the other night when he'd stared at her like a starving man led to a buffet.

She thrust her chest forward and he laughed softly, but it was a laugh devoid of humour, a laugh of surprise, fear and surrender. Then he finally cupped her breasts, feeling their weight in his palms, palms that were rougher than she'd thought they would be—coarse, as if he spent a lot of time outdoors. She didn't care. She liked the contrast of soft and smooth to hard and demanding.

She groaned, tilting back her head, her dark hair forming a curtain down her back, her body quivering at the demanding touch. He felt every inch of her: the underside of her breasts, their curved roundedness and mostly her nipples, which he ran his fingers over at first and then circled, pulled, plucked one by one, then in unison, gently then hard until her knees almost gave way beneath her and the heat between her legs built to an unbearable crescendo. If he was to touch her there, she knew she'd come. Straight away, no further fore-play needed. She was on fire, absolutely exploding with it.

'Mr da Rocha...' She groaned, aware in the tiniest part of her brain that was capable of speech how strange it was to address him so formally even as he gripped her breasts like this. But, hell, there was also something incredibly hot about it. God, how she needed him.

'I want you,' she said boldly. 'I need you.'

She knew he felt the same. He was standing close enough to feel the evidence of that desire pressed hard against her belly. He could take her here and she wouldn't care. Just so long as she got to feel him inside her. It had been too long since she'd been with a man—since Peter, that snake, her only lover—and suddenly she was desperate to erase him from her body, to take that privilege from him of having been the only man she'd made love to.

It was a fever pitch of need that overcame her, so she wasn't aware of the way Salvador had straightened and was staring down at her, as if from a long way away or as if awakening from a dream.

He dropped his hands quickly, as if the flames inside her had leapt through the air and burned him—burned him and pained him.

'You need to leave.' The words were crisp, his voice rum-bling as it rolled into the room. Harper stared at him, not understanding. It didn't make sense. Nothing made sense. She was still trembling with desire, playing with one hand behind her back because her mind wouldn't cooperate. She had no idea what he meant.

'You need to leave,' he enunciated more clearly.

Her pulse was jerky for another reason now. Something strange was happening to her, a wave of nausea, anger and self-directed fury. She stared at him, trying to work out what had happened.

'This cannot, will not, happen. Get the hell out of my office now, Harper.' He glared at her with so much anger that she trembled. 'Now.' And then, closing his eyes, he dragged a hand through his hair. 'Please.'

It was the last word that got through to her. Something else was going on, something serious. Something she didn't understand. With legs that were barely strong enough to support her, she turned and ran, not bothering to button up her shirt, simply clutching it together and hoping like hell she didn't run into any household staff on the way.

She didn't—*thank heavens for small mercies*. In the sanctuary of her suite, she slammed the door shut and pressed her back against it while waiting to catch her breath and hoping, desperately, to erase the last stupid minutes from her life.

CHAPTER FIVE

GROWING UP IN the suburbs of Rio de Janeiro had given Salvador a handy vocabulary of curse words and he employed each and every one now as he took the steps to the beach two at a time, running as if a demon were at his back.

He ran to escape—but there was no escape from what had just happened, from what would have happened if he hadn't finally grabbed hold of himself. There was no escaping what he wanted, despite having come to his senses—some of them. But she'd been right there, so tantalisingly close, so perfect, so angelically beautiful and, heaven help him, he'd wanted to reach out and take her then and there against the glass walls of his office.

The image of that dragged a powerful groan from his chest. He ran until he reached the sand, hot and white, shimmering in the mid-afternoon sun. He stopped running, letting the heat flame his feet, the pain a worthy punishment for the dangerous game he'd willingly entered into and very nearly lost control of. *Hell.*

At the water's edge, he stopped just long enough to remove his trousers so he could stride into the water, the feeling of it a balm against his skin, a necessary dousing of passion. He didn't care about anything then, only this—only a need to come back to himself, to remember his life, his wife, the promise he'd made to himself when she'd died.

He pushed out deep into the ocean, his stride powerful, his legs kicking him away from his home until finally he could no longer stand. He turned onto his back a moment, staring up at the sky, wondering how many times he'd done this while his wife and friend had lain dying, withering into nothingness inside his home. He'd floated in the ocean like this and cursed the heavens, fate, had wished he could save her, begged to switch places with her, offered himself to God, as if it would have made a difference.

Nothing had.

Day by day, she'd grown weaker. He'd watched, held her hand. Had made her empty promises, offering platitudes they both knew to be fake, such as 'You'll be okay...you'll beat this'. Her survival had become his personal quest, the most important thing to him—in those last few months, even more important than the business he'd built almost from scratch. He'd relied on Amanda then, on her professionalism and intellect, her compassion and understanding.

He floated in the water for a long time, staring up at the sky, remembering his wife, the baby they'd lost and the pain of that moment.

Ever since she'd died, he'd been here, single, alone... But not lonely, when Anna-Maria's ghost was everywhere. So too the ghost of his own failure to save them both—his wife and their daughter.

Finally, when he'd ordered his thoughts and remembered his priorities, he swam to shore, his arms just as powerful on the way back, his purpose clear in his mind.

None of this was Harper Lawson's fault and he owed her one hell of an apology.

Harper heard Salvador return but didn't look up. She couldn't. She was still mortified by what had happened, by how brazen she'd been. Only…she hadn't really been, had she? He was the one who'd removed his shirt. But only after *she'd* run her hands all over his chest, practically begging him to take it further.

She closed her eyes on a bitter wave of regret, wondering what the hell had come over her, needing to understand how she'd been so possessed, so utterly mad. They'd both played their part. They'd both wanted… She was sure of it. Yes, she could remember the way he'd been. He'd wanted her too—just not enough.

'Ms Lawson?' His voice had her startling in her seat, the flames she'd thought embarrassment had extinguished kicking into gear.

'Yes?' She didn't look up from her work. He crossed the office, smelling of the ocean. He'd changed—he wore a different shirt with no coffee stain, and a different pair of trousers too. His hair was wet, slicked back from his face. He'd been swimming, she guessed. Yes, there was sand at his temple, a smudge, wiped there without his realisation. Her fingertips ached to reach up and brush it away.

'Can we talk?' He stood beside her, arms crossed, imposing and so handsome.

She lifted her shoulders in a small shrug. 'I suppose we should.'

He reached past her and flicked off her screen, demanding her full attention, so she turned slowly in her chair, lifting her face to his.

'I owe you an explanation.' He said the words with a frown, as though he was surprised to find himself in a position of owing anyone anything.

'Okay.' She bit down on her lip, waiting for him to continue.

'You are a very attractive woman,' he said slowly after a

beat, his brows close together. 'And it's obvious that I'm interested in you. What did you call it? Chemistry? Yes, we have chemistry,' he muttered, with something like disgust.

Harper frowned.

'Do you know anything about me, Ms Lawson?'

She pulled a face, considering that. 'I know you own the company,' she responded tartly, earning a look of impatience from Salvador.

'Do you know about my wife?' The words were wrenched from him, but she didn't hear his pain, only his mention of a wife. Suddenly it was history repeating itself, the moment of realisation that she'd been with another woman's husband. She made an awful noise, like an animal in pain, and lifted her hand to her lips, eyes immediately filling with tears.

'I didn't know! Oh, my God, I didn't know. I... Where is she?'

His lips were pressed together, his skin pale, and was it any wonder? She'd basically seduced a married man! Okay, he'd gone along with it, but she'd been so completely blown away by their shared desire that she hadn't stopped to think! Beyond the fact he didn't wear a wedding ring, she'd made no effort to ascertain his marital status. How could she have been so stupid, so bloody foolish? But *surely* she would have heard that Salvador da Rocha was married? Nothing made sense.

'She died.' The words were spoken quietly, and her heart was racing so fast, so loud in her own ears, that at first she barely heard what he'd said. But slowly the penny dropped, the horror of that admission cutting through to Harper, who lifted her gaze to his face and saw the anguish there, the pain, and realised it was all so much worse. 'A little over a year ago,' he continued, though she hadn't asked. And then, for good measure, 'Cancer.'

'Oh, Salvador,' she mumbled. It was no time for the formality of his surname. 'I'm so sorry. I had no idea.'

His Adam's apple bobbed as he swallowed, emotions obviously rolling through him.

'So you can see why I'm not in the mood to get involved with another woman, can't you?'

It was so sad, and such a shock, she found it impossible to know how to respond at first, so she simply nodded slowly while letting his words sink in.

He'd been married.

He'd loved someone enough to marry. And then she'd died.

'I don't— How come I've never heard your wife mentioned.'

His lips were a grim slash in his handsome face, his skin paler than usual. 'Our relationship was not publicised. She preferred it that way.' His eyes assumed a faraway look for a moment, as though he was reliving a long-ago pain. 'Still, it's no huge secret. I presumed gossip might have reached your ears.'

She shook her head sadly. It was all so awful, so tragic. Suddenly, Salvador wasn't just a rude jackass, but a guy who might have been perfectly nice once upon a time, until life came and messed it all up. She stood, because she could no longer sit, and moved close to him because it felt as though that was where she had to be.

'Salvador,' she repeated, though what else could she say? She searched for something, anything, and finally heard herself whisper, 'Thank you for explaining.'

He left her office without another word.

Something about his confession changed everything. Harper had gone from feeling as though she had to fight what was happening between them to understanding why she needed to respect his decision to stay single, while no longer seeing a reason to avoid him.

She was interested in him. Interested in what made him the success he was, in what made him tick.

And it had nothing to do with sex.

Well, that was what Harper told herself as she walked out onto the terrace a little past eight that night to find Salvador sitting at the table alone, holding a single glass of red wine, no meal there yet.

'Hello.' Her voice was soft, but he turned immediately. Almost as though he'd been waiting for her.

His eyes flicked over her, there was a ghost of a smile and then, 'I eat alone, remember?'

'You live alone,' she corrected quietly, moving to the seat she'd occupied the night before. 'That doesn't mean you have to spend every minute of the day without company, does it?'

His eyes met hers and held, locked in a silent challenge, each waiting for the other to back down, then finally, reluctantly, he gestured to the seat opposite.

'If you wish.'

She did wish. She couldn't say why, but it just *felt* right and, despite everything she'd sworn to herself since things with Peter had ended so disastrously, she followed those instincts now.

Maybe it was the line he'd drawn in the sand, making any relationship off-limits. Maybe that meant she could relax her guard a little because nothing would happen? Despite the tension that still hummed between them, they'd cleared the air, acknowledged what was holding him back—what would continue to hold him back—which meant they could just be together like normal people. Two weeks was a long time to go without any kind of conversation, anyway.

Harper took the seat opposite and barely flinched this time when their legs brushed beneath the table.

'Have you been swimming today?' she asked, because they needed to start a conversation somewhere.

His eyes flickered, then a short nod. 'Yes.'

She looked towards the night-cloaked beaches. 'Which way?'

He hesitated for so long, she thought he simply might be going to ignore the question, but then finally he dipped his head. 'The best beach for swimming is a small cove to the west.' He pointed that way. 'There is a path over there that leads to the stairs.'

'If there's time tomorrow, I might go down. Just to take a look.'

He was silent. Disapproving? After all, this wasn't a holiday, and nothing had changed since that first morning when he'd told her he expected her to be at his beck and call almost all day and night.

'I'll take my laptop, obviously.'

His throat shifted as he swallowed, then Catarina appeared, abruptly ending their conversation.

'Good evening, miss.' Catarina smiled warmly, simply, and Harper felt something like gladness. He didn't quite live alone. True, these people with whom he surrounded himself with were staff, but they were still people. At least there was some interaction.

'Hi, how are you?' Harper returned the smile as the older woman rearranged some things on the table.

'Very well, thank you, miss.' Harper was almost sure she saw the older woman wink as she turned to leave. A few minutes later, she returned with two glasses of wine, as she had the night before, and a platter of the same sort of delicious morsels.

'I'm glad you came out here,' Salvador said after a few moments of silence.

Harper's chest whooshed. 'Oh?'

'I was going to come and find you after dinner, to talk to you. About work,' he added quickly.

Beneath the table, she balled her hands, a nervous reaction. 'If you're worried that what happened between us is going to affect my work, it won't. I promise.'

He studied her face and her heart sank.

'You're not seriously thinking this is going to be a problem?' She had visions of being packed off the island, sent home, no more working for this dynamic self-made billionaire, no incredibly generous bonus, no more once-in-a-lifetime experience on this stunning private island. She had to think fast. 'It meant nothing, Mr da Rocha. It was just a moment, for God's sake.'

His expression was impossible to read and that was the most unnerving thing of all. In their office space earlier, she'd felt more connected to him than she'd known possible. She'd felt as though he could have a thought and she would hear it, but now he was like a stranger, so cold and formal across the table, so careful not to touch her at all.

'I appreciate that,' he agreed with a dip of his head.

'But you're going to fire me anyway?'

He reached for his wine, took a sip, then returned the glass to the table. 'Apart from the fact that would be breaking about a dozen employment laws, I have no reason to fire you, Ms Lawson. I judge people only on relevant metrics and your work is exceptional. That's all that matters to me.'

'Oh.' A warm flood of pleasure ran through her. 'Is it?'

'Looking for compliments?' he asked, his expression lightly mocking, so her stomach rolled.

Before she could demur, he continued regardless. 'You

are efficient, intelligent, calm and capable. I can see why Amanda insisted you take over for her.'

Harper's smile glowed with all the warmth of her soul. 'I was so glad she suggested it. I've been in my role for two years and there are times…' She stopped talking, as if belatedly realising she was speaking to the owner of the company.

'Yes?'

It was hard to believe he'd report her for expressing a hint of very normal dissatisfaction, having just praised her so fulsomely. Still, she chose her words with tact and care. 'I know what I'm doing,' she said with a shrug. 'The first three months were thrilling. Learning new things always is. Now, the office runs like clockwork and I could do my work mostly in my sleep. I relished the idea of this challenge.'

'I'm a challenge?' he prompted with a twist of his lips.

'I'm not going to lie to you. Amanda did tell me it would be the hardest two weeks of my life.'

His laugh was soft and short but the sound was like music to Harper's ears. Deep and throaty. She wanted to hear more of it.

'Are you looking for a new job?'

The question surprised her. 'No.'

'Even though you're bored?'

'The money's too good,' she said with a shrug. 'Better than any other executive assistant salaries in Chicago.'

'You'd earn more in New York.'

'Cost of living would go up too, though. Besides, I live in Chicago. I'm not looking to move.'

'It's not a huge move. Or there's the west coast,' he pointed out. 'Get a job in a tech giant?'

'Are you trying to get me to quit?' she asked, only half-joking.

His frown was reflective. 'No. I was…' Catarina appeared

again then, bustling to clear their bread plates and make space for the impending main course. 'I was offering suggestions based on what I thought might suit you better.'

'Thank you,' she said, recognising a fellow problem-solver. But he didn't have all the information: her problems weren't so easy to solve. 'But I have a life in Chicago. Family.' She didn't want to go into specifics; she never did. 'I can't leave.'

He studied her for so long, she felt the familiar ratcheting up of tension, the desire they'd been fighting swarming her anew so her throat was dry and she could hardly swallow.

'Perhaps another job in the company?'

'I have one of the most senior executive assistant roles.' She shrugged. 'But thanks. I'll keep my eyes open.'

'Did you ever consider another career?'

She almost flinched. The question was far too close to home. For a flash of time, she imagined how her life might have turned out if her mum hadn't got sick. She saw college life, the degree she'd been accepted to do, the career she might have had, sitting on the other side of the desk, making the decisions rather than just greasing the wheels to allow those decisions to work. But it wasn't possible.

'No.' A flat denial was easier than explaining the truth. She looked away out to the ocean, straining to hear the waves. 'What was it you wanted to talk to me about?'

'I have to go on a trip, leaving the day after tomorrow. I'll send you an email with the details. Amanda usually coordinates with my flight crew to manage the jet. Did she leave you notes about travel?'

She had left notes, copious notes, but had assured Harper they weren't likely to be needed. She'd said Salvador only had one trip on the horizon and that was over a month away.

'I have the notes,' was all Harper said. 'Where will you be travelling to?'

'We,' he corrected with a frown, as though that was the last thing he wanted. Her gut twisted at the idea of more travel and, yes, there was a small part of her that was excited about the thought of travelling *with* Salvador. Cursing her juvenile reaction, she focussed on the business side only.

'To Zakynthos, Venice then Prague.'

She blinked. 'Is that all?'

'It will be a quick trip. Two, three days at the most.'

'Three cities in two days?' She tried not to acknowledge her disappointment. This wouldn't be a holiday.

He nodded. 'I need to view some properties.'

That sparked her interest. 'You can't just tour virtually?'

'I've done that.' He nodded. 'But I believe in the importance of feel. Going somewhere, seeing it in person, smelling the air, hearing the noises, watching locals—these things help me decide if something is a good investment.'

'What kind of properties?'

Catarina returned with dinner—rice, chicken and vegetables. It smelled delicious.

He regarded her a moment. 'It's a chain of hotels.'

'Oh, nothing major, then,' she responded with a hint of a smile.

An answering smile twisted her tummy into knots.

'You can make the arrangements?'

'Of course.' This was probably the task most like any she'd done in her other roles. 'Email me any specifics and I'll handle it.'

Harper Lawson was someone who kept her cards close to her chest by force of habit, he suspected. Whenever she began to speak freely, she stopped herself, changed subject and spoke a little more slowly, as if hearing what she was about to say before she said it.

She was careful with what she said, but her face was so expressive, her eyes so telling, that he understood far more than she probably would have wanted.

He'd seen sadness, for instance, when she'd spoken of her family. And desperation, when she'd briefly mentioned her salary, her need for a high-paying job. There was also her pragmatic assessment of the prospects of New York—it had all been an equation of income and outgoings, no thought of the beauty and pace of that city, of how she might enjoy living somewhere new. It had been the same with the west coast. Despite the fact a move there would take her to the beaches she obviously loved so much, she hadn't shown even a flicker of remorse about it not being right—because of her family in Chicago, which caused her sadness.

There was also the way she'd shut him down when he'd asked about alternative careers. *No.* Then a swift change of subject, refocusing on the business at hand. Which made him believe that in fact there had been something else she'd wanted to do at some point, and yet she hadn't pursued it.

He had gleaned all this from a few minutes' conversation and, though it was none of his business, he found himself wondering about her later that night as he worked propped up in bed, coffee on the bedside table, laptop on his thighs.

It had been the kind of day he'd rather forget.

But it had also been a day filled with memories that he kept looking at, indulging in, even when he should know better. The way she'd felt, pressed up against him. The feel of her breath against his cheek, her parted lips, her breasts... God, her breasts. The way her nipples had hardened beneath his touch, her head thrown back, her silky hair smelling like citrus blossoms, making him ache for her on every level.

It had been way too long, that was all. He'd been celibate

for almost two years. Since that one night with Anna-Maria, when they'd conceived Sofia.

Their teeny, tiny little daughter.

His gut tightened when he remembered that little face, those shallow breaths, the downy skin and fluffy hair, black like his.

His heart squeezed so hard and tight, the pain so intense he almost felt as though he might die from it. But he wouldn't. He knew that from experience. It was not a new pain, but rather a part of him, stitched into his being every day, with every breath, every memory of that baby, his wife, the lives he'd failed to save.

He'd known pain before. Had known his father's rejection, his mother's sudden death. But nothing had prepared him for the ache that had spread through him when he'd held his baby, his fragile, weak baby, and had been forced to accept that there was nothing he could do.

How did one survive such grief?

He was surviving, but he was changed for ever, unable to live as he had before, with a future he considered his own. He was simply going through the motions of life now—he had no right to expect pleasure, to seek joy of his own. He didn't want that. Numbness was the closest thing to salvation he experienced and he refused to let it go.

CHAPTER SIX

SINCE ARRIVING ON Ilha do Sonhos, Harper had come to appreciate that there was something quite unique about the place. Looking east from Salvador's kitchen was the most exquisite sunrise she'd ever seen, filled with pink and purple that turned to orange as it lightened. In the evenings, from the western courtyard where they'd shared dinner twice now, the sunsets were beyond compare. It was the first time she'd been somewhere that showcased such stunning bookends to the day, the natural phenomena a show she couldn't bear to miss. And it had only been a few days!

There was something about marking the beginning and end of the day in a form of ritualistic light-worship that seemed important to Harper and which was grounding and breath-taking. As her fourth day drew to a close, she studied the pile of work on her desk, knowing she'd need to return to it later that night, but that a short break wouldn't make a huge difference. Stretching her arms over her head, she stood, leaving her office and hovering in the shared space a moment before moving to Salvador's door and knocking once.

He lifted his head, eyes piercing hers, so her heart skipped a beat and the smile she forced felt unnatural.

'I'm going to take a break. Do you need anything?'

His eyes lingered for a moment too long on her face before dropping to her lips then looking away. There was consternation on his features, his lips compressed so her heart kicked up a gear, because she understood.

Whatever he'd said, no matter what they'd agreed, he still wanted her.

The air between them sparked a little. 'No.' A gruff response. 'Thank you.'

It was an attempt to soften his initial answer but it didn't really work. She turned and left quickly before she could do something she'd regret.

She knew the beaches around the island had big waves, because Salvador had told her so, and because she heard them day and night, the pounding of water to coastline reassuring and rhythmic. But the path she followed from the house brought her to a cove that was rounded in shape and perfectly still. A natural wave break had been formed by the shape of the land here, so it was the perfect spot to swim calmly and enjoy the serene ocean.

Harper didn't have time to swim and it was enough to dip her toes in the water and feel the cool balm. She walked to the edge, sighing as she felt the ocean, and closed her eyes. She remembered being a little girl at the beach with her dad, a couple of years after her parents had divorced, her dad so strong and big, his laugh the nicest thing she'd ever heard as he'd hoisted a little Harper onto his shoulders and carried her into the ocean. Her toes had dangled into the sea, pleasantly cool like this, and she'd giggled because it had tickled a little. The deeper her father had gone, the more she'd laughed, until the water was at his shoulder height. She'd been so happy to see him, to have the full force of his attention for a change.

'Ready?' he'd called up to her as a wave came close to his face so he had to turn away.

'I don't know, Daddy.'

'You can do it, Harp Seal.'

She'd loved that nickname, though she hadn't heard it for a long time. Not since he'd left.

'I don't know.'

But she'd wanted to impress her dad, maybe even win him back. So she'd ignored her fear and ground her teeth.

'Okay, I'm ready!'

He'd placed his palms beneath her feet, forming a platform, and then ducked his head forward so she was diving into the water—deep, cold, salty heaven. She'd faced her fears in the hope of showing her dad how brave she could be, but he'd left again anyway, disappearing from her life and leaving only disjointed, unsatisfying memories.

Twenty years later, on a different beach, Harper turned her back on the ocean, sighed softly and made her way back to the house.

He checked the itinerary as a matter of course, but it was perfect. She'd booked a room for each of them in the hotels he'd specified, and had managed to schedule his existing commitments into the new time zones, ensuring his normal work schedule wouldn't be affected by the travel. He noted she'd blocked out half-hour times for herself as well, per their agreement, and not for the first time he wondered about that.

Why half an hour? What did she do with that time? She'd been so adamant about it. It wasn't for food—she ate at her desk. Did she nap in the middle of the day? Possible, but unlikely. She didn't seem like someone who'd nap. Then again, a restorative sleep had been proven beneficial for concentration, and she was certainly incredibly focussed. Or did she disappear to read a book?

He didn't know, but he wanted to, almost as much as he wanted to see her naked, to touch her, to feel her... He dropped his head to his hands on a laugh that was totally devoid of humour.

He'd found himself in some kind of hell and there was nothing he could do about it.

Harper had been brought to the island by helicopter, and they left the same way, but this was an entirely different experience because Salvador took the controls. Harper sat in the back, rather than in the empty seat beside him—he didn't offer that seat to her and she was glad. Even the view she had from there was pantie-melting hot.

He was so in control of such a complex instrument panel. So had the pilot on the way over been, and it hadn't affected Harper like this, but now was different. This was Salvador, the man who ran a multi-billion-dollar empire, who seemed able to turn his hand to anything. She sat back in the seat, trying to look out of the window rather than staring at him, at the tanned forearms that were exposed by his shirt as he moved levers and held the flight controls. It was just so incredibly, intoxicatingly masculine...

He landed the helicopter at a private airstrip on the outskirts of Rio de Janeiro—Christ the Redeemer had guided the way—and his private jet sat waiting on the tarmac.

'Are you going to fly this too?' she couldn't help asking as a swarm of staff approached the helicopter, removing luggage, checking controls, greeting Salvador.

Harper had arranged all this, per Amanda's checklist, but she still hadn't quite known what to expect. The reality was actually quite unnerving.

'No. On the plane, I work,' he said, the words holding a warning, as though she'd come along just to try to distract him.

Fine by me, she thought waspishly, falling into step beside him. But as they approached the steps at the bottom of the plane he paused to allow her to precede him, his hand reaching out and touching her lightly in the small of her back to urge her forward. It was a nothing gesture, only it didn't *feel* like nothing. Sparks flew from her back all through her body and ignited the blood in her veins as though it were lava. She couldn't help her sharp intake of breath, nor the way her eyes skidded to his. He kept his gaze resolutely averted, so she saw only his profile, but his jaw was clenched—she knew he felt it too.

Whatever feelings inside Salvador had unknowingly given her were usurped by a sense of awe. She'd naturally expected to be impressed by a private jet and yet she hadn't thought it would be quite as opulent as this—from the grey leather seats, each wide enough to outdo a first-class seat in a commercial jet, to the arrangement of them. It was like a trendy bar rather than a plane, the seats facing one another, low coffee tables between them. There was a partition behind this seating area and Harper moved past it, too curious to be polite and wait to be shown.

The next room was a boardroom with a large table and a big screen on the wall at one end. It would easily accommodate up to twenty people. The sense of awe grew as she moved further down the plane, and then something else overtook it completely.

Bedrooms—two of them—each with a huge double bed and *en suite* bathroom.

Her pulse was thready and she spun guiltily, but Salvador was right there. He must have been following her and she hadn't realised. Now they bumped into one another and his hands came out and caught her arms, his expression exasperated and impatient, even when he held on far longer than was necessary to steady her.

She looked up into his face and everything evaporated—common sense, thought, his confession about his late wife, the certainty that they couldn't, shouldn't act on whatever feelings they had. There was only desire now.

But for Salvador this was clearly not the case. He dropped his hands quickly and stepped backwards, irritation in the depths of his eyes. 'The flight is about fourteen hours. You should choose a room.' He gestured towards both of them. 'I'll work from the front of the plane for now.'

'Which room is yours?'

'Generally I use this one.' He nodded to the left.

'Then I'll take the other,' she said. It was right across the aisle from his. *Oh, great*. That wouldn't be a problem *at all*, she thought sarcastically.

'Fine. The staff will bring your luggage through and take your order. If you need anything, let them know.'

'Is that code for "don't bother me"?' she asked before she could consider the wisdom of being quite so pushy.

He smothered a sigh. 'No, Harper. It's not.' She felt like a silly school girl. Biting into her lower lip, she refused to drop her gaze, though, nor to show him how chastened he'd made her feel. 'Have a nice flight.'

The expectation being that he didn't want to see her for the duration, she thought with a little internal harrumph. No shared dinners on board—well, fine. She had stacks of work to catch up on, and her usual video call to her mother as well.

She hadn't been planning to reply but there wasn't the chance anyway. Salvador turned and left before she could open her mouth to say, 'Thank you very much.'

Just knowing she was on board was his undoing. This was getting out of hand. Salvador da Rocha was famed for his control, his willpower, his ruthless determination, but in the last few days he'd come face to face with a slip of a woman who seemed to have the power to undo all of that—just by bloody existing within his airspace!

He shouldn't have brought her, he realised halfway into the flight. She could have run things from the ground on the island, and he could have got some damned respite from her. Maybe he should send her home immediately.

And pigs might fly, he thought with a grimace.

For, as desperately inconvenient as he found the distraction of Harper Lawson's presence, he suspected her absence would be even more of a concentration-killer. He stretched the fingers of his right hand wide, remembering the sparks he'd felt when he'd done something as innocuous as touch her back to board the flight. Even that simple contact had made him feel alive with the power of a thousand watts.

This wasn't going away. He couldn't ignore her: he couldn't ignore the way she made him feel.

But it wasn't really Harper, he consoled himself quickly. It was the fact she was there: a beautiful, intelligent, interesting woman right beneath his nose who'd declared them to have chemistry; who'd made it obvious she was attracted to him; who'd fall into his bed if he allowed it… God. The willpower required to make that not happen!

But what if it did?

What if he gave into this?

A year after burying his wife, one of his oldest friends—what kind of sick son of a bitch did that make him? Only, their marriage hadn't been quite normal. They hadn't married for love, but rather because Anna-Maria had fallen pregnant. Salvador had been determined not to be like his deadbeat father, refusing to acknowledge his own child, choosing instead to pay off the mother, to silence her. He would never have done that. He'd wanted to be a family, the kind of family he'd never known.

It hadn't been a normal marriage for Salvador but his guilt at not being able to love Anna-Maria in the way she'd deserved as a wife—even as she'd lain dying—was a constant source of pain to him. To move on, and with someone so very fit, healthy and *alive,* would feel like a betrayal of the worst possible kind.

He groaned, pressing his head back against the seat of the plane, scrunching up his eyes and doing his very best not to think of Harper, even as memories and fantasies weaved through his mind like ribbons in a stream.

After the heat of Brazil, Zakynthos was surprisingly cool. Harper had only been away from Chicago for a few days but her body had grown accustomed to the balmy, tropical temperatures. She liked it, she realised. Liked the way the warmth soaked into her skin, her heart, the sea breeze making her feel alive and elemental.

But Zakynthos was stunning, and not just because she was seeing it through the lens of a billionaire's lifestyle. Though that didn't hurt, she thought wryly as she stepped into the back of a large black Range Rover with darkly tinted windows. There was a driver and, though Salvador offered Harper the front seat, she demurred, preferring to sit on her own in the back than feel obliged to make small talk with the driver. Besides, she was staff, and it felt somehow more appropriate. So Salvador took the front seat, his arm resting casually along the side of the door, his fingers drumming a slow, rhythmic beat on the luxury interior. She studied him in the side mirror, which gave her a perfect view of his face, but every now and again his gaze would flick to the mirror, their eyes would meet and it was as though she was being electric-shocked.

Yet she didn't look away.

She couldn't. Not wouldn't—couldn't. It felt physically impossible, despite the stunning scenery of the island that she was aware of in her peripheral vision. Primarily, there was only Salvador and her. Not even the driver entered her thoughts.

After a fifteen-minute drive, the car pulled up onto a sweeping driveway of white gravel, with elegant palms forming lines on either side. At the front of the white-walled hotel, a bougainvillea grew opportunistically, its bright, papery, purple flowers scrambling over every available surface, offering a stark, beautiful contrast to the crisp colour of the walls and the sparkling turquoise ocean beyond.

Everything about the hotel screamed understated luxury, from the grand entrance to the staff waiting by the door dressed in black suits with gold cuffs. They greeted Salvador as though he were royalty, and Harper hovered a little behind, turning to look at the view and inhale, searching for salt and tropical sweetness in the air. While this was beautiful, it was nothing to Ilha do Sonhos, she realised with a thud in the middle of her chest. She'd found heaven on earth, and now even somewhere like this couldn't really compete.

'Ms Lawson?'

Salvador's voice made her spine tingle. She turned to him slowly as a gentle breeze caught at her hair so she had to lift a hand to it, to pull it back over one shoulder. He watched her, frowning, then gestured towards the door, impatient, short and something else. Resigned? Her heart quickened and she took a step towards him with the strangest feeling that she was moving headlong into a fate beyond her control.

CHAPTER SEVEN

IT WAS CLEAR that Salvador had no intention of enjoying a single thing about being in Greece. They toured the hotel—he wore a suit, and avoided doing anything so frivolous as even touching the water of the pool. It was a stunning facility. The rooms were clearly luxurious and decadent while still retaining a local character—wide doors, carved windows open to the water and brightly coloured interiors, such as the bed in Harper's room that was a cheery turquoise and the chair by the window which was a glossy yellow.

The floors were tiled, big, terracotta squares that were cool beneath the feet. Rugs had been added for comfort in some areas. It was sublime. Harper's room had the most amazing view, but she knew from having arranged Salvador's accommodation that his suite included a small infinity pool. She could only imagine what the outlook would be from there in the evening. How would the sunsets here compare to those of the Ilha do Sonhos?

Her lips pulled to the side and she realised, with heat rising in her cheeks, that Salvador was looking at her, waiting for her to respond.

Furious with herself for having missed something, she forced her concentration back to the tour. 'I'm sorry. What was that?'

'Is something the matter, Ms Lawson?' he asked, curtly, so

her embarrassment grew, particularly as they weren't alone—the manager of the hotel was standing nearby, pretending not to hear the interchange.

'No,' she whispered back with a hint of anger. 'I'm fine.'

'Then perhaps you wouldn't mind paying attention? I didn't bring you along to stare off into space.'

She could have slapped him. Anger sizzled in her veins, all the stronger because of her general sense of frustration and thwarted need.

'Yes, sir,' she replied through gritted teeth, pleased when the volley hit its mark. His own cheekbones slashed with a hint of colour, his chest moving as he sucked in a breath then turned away from her.

'Go on,' he commanded the manager, who was running through the latest occupancy figures. Harper made a show of removing her phone, loading up a document and taking notes for the rest of the tour—particularly useful as it gave her an excuse to avoid Salvador's eyes. But, as they returned to the foyer of the hotel, the manager—whose name Harper had uncharacteristically missed—turned to them both, his gaze lingering a little longer on Harper's flushed face.

'The bar is an excellent place to cool down,' he said, with a smile that lasted a second too long, his body a little close to Harper's.

'We have work to do,' came Salvador's clipped reply.

Such was Harper's simmering rage, and now resentment at being spoken for, that she pushed an over-sweet smile onto her face and waved it in Salvador's general direction. 'But afterwards a drink would be lovely. What do you recommend?'

'The hotel has a speciality cocktail; you cannot leave Zakynthos without trying it.'

'Well, that sounds like important research,' she cooed, pleased to feel the glowering presence of Salvador at her side.

'But, as this is not a vacation, this is not the time.'

'Later.' Harper increased the wattage on her smile. This time, when Salvador put his hand in the small of her back, it wasn't as light or gentle as earlier, but the effect was the same, or perhaps stronger. Sparks, flames, fire, fury sizzled inside her body, turning her into a fantastic mess of lava and lust.

He guided her towards the bank of lifts. 'I can walk,' she muttered. He didn't remove his hand and she was glad. The feeling of his fingers splayed wide and possessively was so much more than a simple direction. This was something more—something primal and virile, something that showed his emotion.

The lift doors opened and she stepped in, pulling away from his hand and pressing her back, tingling and warm, against the lift wall. Because if he touched her for a second longer she knew she'd ignite.

'What the hell is going on with you?' she snapped. 'You were so rude to that guy.'

'Because I wasn't batting my eyelids and begging him to buy me a drink?' Salvador responded, staring at her across the expanse of the lift.

'I was just being nice because you'd been such a jerk!'

'A jerk!' he repeated, nostrils flaring. 'I was business-like and professional. There is nothing wrong with that.'

Harper rolled her eyes. 'And how about the way you spoke to me?' she demanded. 'I have done everything you've asked of me, worked day and night non-stop since I came into your life—'

'I told you, that's the job!' he responded with a raised voice.

'Yes, yes, you told me,' she said, mortified to feel the warning sting of tears in the back of her eyes. She refused to give into them and bit into her lower lip until the sensation passed. 'But I have done it, without complaint, and the first moment my attention wandered for even a moment you acted as if I've made some fatal error. You deliberately embarrassed me in front of him!'

Salvador stared at her, darkly complex emotions chasing themselves across his face. Harper made a noise of frustration and then relief when the doors opened to her floor and she could step out.

But Salvador was right behind her, his stride long. 'You're not on this floor,' she reminded him through gritted teeth.

'We're not done!'

'Oh, yes, we are. I have nothing else to say to you right now.'

'Your mind did wander,' he said, not heeding her warning. 'You were distracted.'

'And you were rude about it,' she replied, not looking at him.

'What should I have done?'

'There are a million ways you could have brought me back into the conversation without making it seem as though I'm some incompetent—'

'That wasn't my intention.'

'Wasn't it?' she shouted, then squeezed her eyes shut as emotions rolled through her again. 'You've been acting like I've done something wrong, like you're angry with me. And maybe you are, but if you're angry it's because of what happened between us. And that's not my fault.'

He was close now, so close. She swiped her key card over the door but it didn't work. Her fingers were shaking. She tried again and the light flashed red. Harper cursed silently.

'Allow me.' His voice was gruff, hoarse, those same dark emotions she'd seen on his face evident in his tone now.

'I can do it,' she snapped, pulling her hand away from his.

'Damn it, Harper, for crying out loud, this isn't a big deal.'

'It is to me.'

'You're overreacting.'

She whirled around to face him but, just as on the plane, he was right behind her and this time there was a door at her back, so she was all but trapped between Salvador's rock-hard chest and the door's firmness at her spine.

'Don't tell me I'm overreacting,' she said unevenly. 'You made me feel... You treated me...' She glared up at him but, close like this, it was almost impossible to hold onto her anger. She needed it, like a shield to keep her safe. 'You're a jerk,' she repeated.

'Yes.' His eyes narrowed, his pupils huge in his golden eyes. She swallowed, staring up at him, unable to look away, barely able to breathe. 'I know.'

'So how about you try not to be?'

'And then what happens?' he asked darkly, leaning closer. 'What if I tell you I think you're the smartest person I've ever known?' She gasped. 'What if I tell you I'm blown away by your attention to detail, your planning, your reporting?'

Her heart thumped hard into her rib cage, his praise like warm treacle on her flesh. Of their own volition, her hands lifted to his shirt, pressing to the starched fabric there, the fabric that had seemed so incongruous by the pool, when they'd been surrounded by happy holiday makers, but which now felt like the best thing ever.

'Are you?'

'Yes.' The word was a whip in the air between them. 'I think my admiration is very obvious.'

She snorted. 'Yes, of course, how silly of me not to realise when all you do is berate—'

He pressed a finger to her lips. 'Once. And it won't happen again.' Their eyes met and something passed between them. 'I'm sorry. I was…'

'Frustrated,' she mumbled against his finger, eyes blinking up at his. When he didn't remove his finger, she pursed her lips, kissing it, and when he still didn't pull away opened her mouth to take the tip between her lips just a little way. Nerves were flooding her, because it was so out of character to act like this, and at the same time it felt so *right* and *normal*, as though she had no choice but to act on the feelings that were pulling her towards him.

Salvador groaned, dropping his head forward.

'Yes,' he said unevenly after a moment. It took her a second to realise he was agreeing that he had indeed been frustrated.

He pulled his finger out of her mouth, but not far. He let it rest on her shoulder and slowly, as if a magnetic force were drawing Salvador down and he was desperately fighting it, his head dropped lower and lower, hers tilting upwards until their lips met. It was like a thousand lightning bolts had speared the earth around them.

Harper felt it all through her body, in the air, in the way Salvador shuddered, the kiss shifting tectonic plates and everything in between.

His mouth was firm and insistent, just as she would have expected, his trademark confidence meaning he kissed arrogantly, demandingly, and it was incredible. She surrendered to the kiss, her lips parting beneath his, her hands bunching in his shirt, the power of that connection burning her to the tips of her toes. His tongue flicked hers hungrily and she kissed him back, tangling their tongues, her hands moving from his shirt to the back of his neck, fingers curling in the hair at his nape, her breasts crushed to his chest where her hands had been, her thighs pressed to his.

His body pushed forward so the door was hard at her back,

and she was aware of every inch of his muscular frame. The hardness of his groin made her breathless with need, stars of desire filling her eyes, every bit as bright as the night sky on Ilha do Sonhos.

She kissed his name into his mouth, delighting in the way it tasted, in the feel of his hands on her body as he kissed her senseless and breathless.

And then he stopped, pulling away from her, his eyes glittering when they met hers, his expression hard, shocked and possibly even afraid.

He swore under his breath, staring at her, breath uneven, and she stared back, the world tilting off its axis and everything moving beyond her control.

'Do you see why I cannot say nice things to you, Harper?' he demanded, his hands impersonal now as he straightened her clothes, tucking her shirt back into her skirt.

Hurt, she pushed his hands away, face pale. 'I can do it.'

Taking his lead from her, he took a step backwards, hands on hips. 'Nothing good can come from this. I wish you wouldn't—'

'Don't blame me, don't you dare,' she said. 'None of this is my fault.'

'Isn't it?' he responded, and she had no idea what that meant.

'What did I do wrong, then?' she demanded angrily.

'You came into my life.'

'Gee, thanks.' She blinked down the hallway, her face pale. 'Do you really feel that way? Do you want me to leave? Because I will. I'll go back to Chicago if you'd prefer.'

'What I would prefer is never to have met you.'

She frowned, wondering at the soreness in her chest, the ache that was spreading through her whole body.

'Forget what I said earlier,' she muttered, spinning away

from him and trying her key card once more. She could have cried tears of relief when it worked and the door sprang open. 'You're not a jerk. You're an A-grade asshole and I can't wait to see the back of you.'

She'd never been more satisfied to slam a door in her life.

He'd overreacted.

Royally.

She was right—he'd acted like an asshole.

But if he hadn't stopped what had been happening between them, he would have stripped her naked and taken her right there in the corridor of the hotel. He wracked his brain, staring out at the stunning view from his hotel room, trying to remember what life had been like before Anna-Maria. He'd had lovers—lots of lovers—but had he ever felt an almost demonic need to possess a woman? Had he ever been driven so wild?

His features were grim, his body tense.

If he had, he'd forgotten over time, because the way he'd responded to Harper in the corridor outside her room had felt like a first to Salvador. And a last. It had to be the last. He couldn't keep succumbing to temptation just because she was there, just because he wanted her with the might of a thousand gods.

Every incendiary touch just reminded him of how he'd failed Anna-Maria. Failed to respond to her, to want her beyond that first night. Even to love her as she'd deserved to be loved—not as an old friend, but as a lover and wife. And, the worst failure of all, he hadn't been able to save her or their daughter.

With a groan, he dove into the water of his pool, holding his breath under water, willing himself to push Harper from his mind just as easily as he cut through the pool and emerged on the other side. Would that it could be so easy.

* * *

Venice was not much better. Another stunning hotel, this one on the Grand Canal and with no pretensions to 'rustic charm'. It was the very last word in glamorous luxury, from the enormous marble keystone tiles to the golden chandeliers and curving timber staircase that sat grandly in the entrance foyer. At this hotel, their rooms were side by side—which would have made it harder to ignore him except for the fact they'd barely spoken two words since that kiss in Zakynthos. They'd exchanged emails as necessary, and Harper had tagged along to his meetings, nodding her agreement when he'd asked her to do various tasks, but that had been the extent of it. The flight had been conducted in silence—Harper had gone to her bedroom to work, stony as she'd passed him.

At least, she'd looked stony, but her insides had been quivering and melting, the memories of their kiss driving her almost crazy. Even sleep offered no respite: he was there, his hands on her body, his lips on hers, the kiss so perfect, so hot and demanding, so satisfying. She'd known how perfect it would be for him to come into her room…but she couldn't think like that.

This was a disaster. Harper had become so caught up in how she wanted him that she had forgotten how committed she was to avoiding entanglements. There was nothing simple and uncomplicated about Salvador. He was an emotional wreck, someone she needed to avoid like the plague.

They'd arrived in Venice mid-morning and toured the hotel first, then headed into a meeting with one of the representatives from the consortium selling the chain of hotels. Harper's head was swimming after those three hours—the figures discussed, the terms agreed to; it was all so much, such big business. She hadn't really appreciated how much of this Salvador conducted personally, but of course it was his company, and he was known for taking a hand in all his dealings.

The flame of curiosity burned a little brighter in her chest, because her desire to learn about him hadn't abated, but she wouldn't give him the satisfaction of asking questions.

When the meeting was over and she was walking alone through the hallway, her heels making a reassuring clackety-clack sound on the floor, he caught up with her.

'Ms Lawson.' The way he said her name was a command to stop walking, but she didn't. 'Harper.' The second was said more sharply but she gasped, because the only other time he'd used her first name had been with his mouth pressed to hers. She spun to face him, eyes flashing anger.

'What?'

'What?' he repeated, brows raised.

'I'm sorry,' she said with sarcasm. 'What would you like, sir?'

A muscle jerked in his jaw. 'Have dinner with me.'

'But you eat alone,' she reminded him tartly.

He crossed his arms over his chest. 'Have dinner with me tonight.'

In Venice, of all places. 'Is this work? Are you ordering me to?'

'Ordering you?' he repeated incredulously. 'No, I'm not ordering you to. I'm...asking.'

She was dumbfounded. How dared he? He was blowing hot and cold with her, her not knowing what he wanted from one day to the next, and she wasn't going to be jerked around by him any more.

'Oh, good,' she murmured. 'Then my answer is no. Thank you,' she added for good measure, flashing a false smile before turning and stalking away. There was no door to slam this time but she still felt damned satisfied by her hasty retreat.

He watched her walk away with a strange feeling in the pit of his gut and an anger that was completely self-directed. Why the hell had he done that? After having drawn a line between them in Greece, why invite her for dinner? Because he was a fool and needed to learn his lessons many time over? He made a disgruntled sound of impatience, aware that his body was poised to follow Harper even when he knew it was the last thing he should do. He hated the silence that existed between them, that was why. He hated being near her and not talking. Not hearing *her* talk. But silence was still better than the alternative, so why not let sleeping dogs lie?

It was as though a fever overtook him every time they were together, and he hated it.

What he needed was to make it through this trip without making another Harper Lawson related mistake, and get back to the relative safety of Ilha do Sonhos.

He was still staring at Harper, without realising it, as she approached the lifts. Perhaps he was willing her to look back at him because, as the doors opened, she angled her head, their eyes met and Salvador had the strangest feeling that he was dropping into a deep ravine with nothing to grab hold of and no one to help him.

He turned and stalked away before he could do something really stupid and go after her again.

CHAPTER EIGHT

'THERE HAS TO be a mistake.' Harper spoke in her best, calmest voice as she looked at the clerk across the shiny marble desk. 'I booked two rooms. See?'

'Yes, madam.' The clerk had turned beet-red. 'And I can only apologise again, most sincerely, for this mistake. For some reason, the computer system took one of the rooms from your booking and allocated it to another guest.'

'Well, we require two rooms,' she said, refusing to think about the man standing behind her, listening to this conversation. 'One for Mr da Rocha and one for me.'

'I understand, madam, and again,] I apologise, but we have only the one room available. I can make some calls to different hotels in the city, to see if there is availability, but with the festival Prague is very heavily booked.'

She ground her teeth together. 'Festival?'

'Prague Majales,' he said with a nod. 'I can thoroughly recommend you walk through the town to enjoy it.'

'I'm not really in a festival mood,' Harper said wearily.

'I am sorry.' The clerk's gaze encompassed Harper and Salvador. 'Allow me to make a suggestion.'

'Go right ahead.' Salvador's voice dripped with ice and Harper shivered. She hadn't dared look at him since 'Room Gate' had begun, but now she lifted a gaze and saw an expression that would have turned a dragon to stone.

'The concierge will take your bags to the available room. Go make yourselves comfortable while I arrange some refreshments, with the hotel's compliments. In the meantime, I will endeavour to find a solution—at our expense—in a nearby hotel. Will this be acceptable?'

'It doesn't sound like there's much more you can do,' Harper muttered.

'Thank you, madam, sir.' The clerk either missed the tone or chose to ignore it, handing two key cards across the counter with a cheery smile. 'Enjoy your stay in Prague!'

Harper glared at him before turning away, her worst nightmares unfolding. 'There has to be another room. As soon as he finds it, I'll go.'

Salvador sent her a look that was both weary and, for some reason, bemused. 'Ask yourself if it sounded as though he was going to break a sweat trying to find something else for us,' Salvador commented, and when Harper looked over her shoulder she saw the clerk had already moved on to the next guest, busily drawing lines on a map of Prague.

She turned back to Salvador and her mood deteriorated. 'This isn't funny.'

He sobered. 'I know.'

Mollified, she moved to the lift, waiting as far away from Salvador as she could. The lift took a few minutes to arrive and, by the time it did, she and Salvador had been joined by six or seven other people who crowded in with them, pushing them together at the back of the lift. Harper stood like a stone, completely still.

At one point, Salvador's hand brushed hers and she almost jumped out of her skin, jerking into the woman beside her, who gave Harper a look of irritation. Harper stayed where she was anyway, close to the woman's shoulder, rather than risk another incendiary touch with Salvador.

For all she felt like one touch could light her bones on fire, she just had to remember the way he'd pushed her away in Venice and her desire was extinguished. She wasn't going to be made a fool of. She'd let Peter do that to her, and Harper wasn't going to make that mistake again.

'This is us,' Salvador said when the lift reached the eighth floor. He waited for Harper to step through the other guests, then followed. She looked up and down the hallway, picked the right direction then strode off, a step in front of him, determined to keep things business-like. In all likelihood, the room would be more than large enough to accommodate them both comfortably, as her rooms in Greece and Italy had been. This was a storm in a teacup. Far from ideal, but also not the end of the world.

She swiped the key card, pushed open the door and groaned.

The room was a decent enough size, she supposed, as befitted a hotel of this standard, but there was only one bed in the middle of the room—albeit a king. There wasn't even a sofa she could crawl onto, just two arm chairs near a window that overlooked the ancient city, with the afternoon sun making the wide, curving river sparkle. Oh, well. She could sleep in a chair.

'It will be fine,' Salvador said through gritted teeth. 'Absolutely fine. If you'll excuse me, I'm going to take a shower.'

A shower? She frowned. She supposed they'd been travelling for a few hours, but since when...? Unless he meant a cold shower? She pressed a hand to her forehead, trying to get rid of the idea of Salvador in the hotel bathroom washing away his desire for her—as if he wanted her *that* much. But...she did. She felt an overwhelming need for him despite their fight, despite everything. So what if he felt it too? And he was determined to fight it, even if that meant enduring icy showers?

She'd never know for sure, and it wasn't her place to know. Harper had a mountain of work to catch up on so, rather than imagine Salvador lathering his body in the shower, hot or cold, she opened her laptop and began to read emails. She flicked various ones to Salvador or the appropriate staff member, until she got through at least twenty of the things, then went over the financial reports he'd sent across for Harper to check.

This was the kind of work she loved—meticulous, complicated and important. She lost herself in concentration, so didn't hear the door to the bathroom opening until, a moment later, Salvador strolled across the room to the window dressed in only a low-slung towel, and the movement caught her eye. The sight of him arrested her gaze, making it impossible to look back at her screen.

'Our suitcases aren't here yet,' he said simply, but there was nothing simple about it, and his voice showed his displeasure.

Her tongue tingled with an unwelcome inclination to lick the last remaining water droplets from his toned body. She scowled instead.

'This hotel isn't really up to the same standard as the others, is it?'

'It's got the most potential,' he said with a lift of his shoulders that did nothing to help Harper's overheated mind for two reasons. His muscled chest shifted, his shoulders, biceps—everything—gleaming from the shower, but it also put the towel in grave peril. She wasn't sure how good he was with knots—he didn't seem like Boy Scout material—so she wasn't sure how securely he'd anchored the towel in place. She suspected a few more shrugs and it might drop.

Holy crap.

'This is going to be fine,' he muttered.

Harper closed the lid of her laptop with a snap. 'I'll go back down to Reception and see if there's any news on a room. And then I'll work from the foyer.' She stood, conscious of how close they were in this room, breathing the same air, always within touching distance. Her eyes swept shut because this was *not* going to be fine.

Salvador was a trillionaire. Surely he could *pay* someone to vacate their room?

'We have a meeting at three.'

'I'll sort this out,' she said with a small nod, but her voice was soft, lacking confidence, because the desk clerk had seemed pretty adamant first time round.

He didn't argue. Harper collected her work bag and key card then slid from the room, breathing out when she reached the hallway. As the lift doors opened, the concierge arrived with their suitcases.

With a groan, she stepped into the lift and jabbed her finger against the button, waiting desperately to be whisked away to something more like normality.

At a quarter to three, Harper returned to the room, which she couldn't think of as 'theirs', because that implied too much and it hurt to imagine it. Salvador was standing looking out of the window, so for a moment she had a view of his back, strong and confident, and his powerful body, before he turned, hands in pockets, and offered a tight smile.

She volleyed back something similar. Awkward silence fell.

'I presume you weren't able to find another room?'

'No.' Her lips pulled to the side. 'Anything within a two-mile radius is booked up for the festival. I'm sorry,' she felt obliged to say.

'It was their error. There's nothing you could have done to prevent it.'

But frustration gnawed at her. 'I find it hard to imagine this happening to Amanda,' she said with a small shift of her shoulders, closing the door behind her reluctantly, because it boxed them into this tiny space. She stayed where she was, in the small entrance foyer, because it was as physically far from Salvador as she could get.

'It's beyond your control. Don't worry about it. It's one night. I'm sure we'll survive.'

Was he?

She nodded unevenly, placing her laptop bag back on the bed. 'We're meeting on the roof terrace,' she reminded him.

Salvador's nod was thoughtful; Harper's heart stammered. She had to find a way to get through this. 'Excuse me.' She bolted left, into the bathroom, slamming the door and flicking on the taps so she could wash her hands with ice-cold water and stop panicking. This was going to be a disaster.

Hold on to your anger, she thought. *Remember everything that's happened between the two of you. Remember Peter. Your dad. All the men who've let you down. Don't let Salvador have that power over you!*

Her head hurt. She reached for a glass, filled it with some water from a bottle and drained it, then took in her reflection.

It had been a long day and she was a mess. Using her fingers, she combed her hair over one shoulder and pinched her cheeks, but that was the best she could do without her cosmetics, still stowed in a bag in the hotel room.

A moment later, she emerged, eyes not meeting Salvador's as she reached for her handbag and removed her lipstick, moving to the mirror above the desk and carefully applying a fresh coat. It was amazing what a difference it made. She clicked the lid back in place, turned to locate her bag and found Salvador staring at her, a fulminating frown on his handsome features that spiked her blood pressure all over again. She stared and couldn't move. It was as though she was trapped by his gaze.

'We should go,' he said finally, voice hoarse.

She nodded, but neither of them moved. It took her a moment to galvanise herself against the waves of awareness bouncing off the walls.

'I'm ready.'

Neither moved. Salvador was backlit by the afternoon sun, and he looked god-like in stature, glowing with gold. She frowned as her feet finally stepped, but in the wrong direction, towards him, across the carpet. She stopped, feeling like an idiot. He was like a gravitational well; she found it almost impossible to pull away from him.

'This isn't a big deal.'

She frowned, not understanding what he meant.

'It's just one night.'

'Oh.' She nodded, turning to look at the bed, swallowing. 'I'll take the floor.'

'Don't be stupid, Mr da Rocha. The bed is more than big enough for both of us. We can be adult about this.'

His expression showed cynicism and a healthy degree of doubt on that score.

'Nothing's going to happen,' Harper repeated.

'Are you trying to convince me or yourself?'

She grimaced. 'Nothing's going to happen.' Her heart stitched strangely. 'We really should go. Now.'

It felt as though the building were on fire. She had to escape. Grabbing her bag, she turned and finally moved in the right direction: towards the door, out of the room and into a space that wasn't completely overpowered by Salvador.

She checked her watch again, frowning. The meeting had gone on longer than she'd anticipated. The allotted two hours had bled towards three, the manager prone to waffling and wanting to apologise again and again for the mix up with rooms—which had worn thin after the first time, let alone after at least ten attempts at explaining the problem with their computer system.

Salvador, who clearly didn't suffer fools gladly, had been in no mood to tolerate the excuses.

As time passed, Harper knew she'd have to excuse herself: something she hated doing because it seemed inattentive and unprofessional but she was due to call her mother soon and there was no way she could delay.

As the manager moved towards the banquet rooms to show off the new parquetry, Harper reached out, touching Salvador's arm lightly to arrest his attention. It worked a little too well. He stopped as though he'd been electrified so she quickly dropped her hand.

She felt nervous! Harper, who'd tamed Goliaths for breakfast, was terrified of disappointing this man, of having him think badly of her. She ground her teeth, irritated by her own weakness, refusing to give into it. This was about her mother, and there was nothing that would come between Harper and her commitments there.

'I have a personal matter to attend to,' she said stiltedly. 'I have to go.'

'Go?' He frowned. 'Is this about the room?'

'What? No. I don't mean "go", as in leave Prague.' She shook her head. 'I have to go upstairs to the room. To make a call.' Her stomach twisted. 'It's important.'

He nodded thoughtfully. 'Your thirty minutes?'

She expelled a soft breath. 'It's prearranged. I can't re-schedule it at this late notice. I'm sorry.'

'Don't apologise. Meet me in the bar afterwards to dis-cuss the meeting.' His eyes flicked to the manager, who was waiting by an open door. 'I'll be done by then.'

Harper's smile was automatic. She could see that Salvador was growing impatient, and she suspected he was about to rapidly draw this tour to a close, but she couldn't stick around to enjoy watching that. Her mum was waiting.

He was more than tempted to go up to their room. Curious as all hell, in fact, to know just what she did in these thirty minutes. He now knew that it was a scheduled thing with another party, and it couldn't easily be rescheduled, but be-yond that he was in the dark—not a place Salvador da Rocha generally liked to be.

He sipped his coffee, eyes fixed on the door of the bar, waiting, watchful, his whole body tense and on alert in a state of adrenaline preparing to flow.

She walked in about fifteen minutes past the time her half-hour appointment would have ended, and something clutched in his gut low and fierce, a taste filling his mouth that he couldn't explain. Beneath the table, his hands formed balls on his thighs and his eyes clung to her as she looked around the bar, lips pressed together, eyes hooded, figure hidden in a boxy linen dress.

But he'd seen her. He'd touched her. It didn't matter what she wore; he saw her as she'd been in his office and he yearned for her.

Fire spread through his veins as he remembered the way it had felt to kiss her in Greece. The way her body had been so soft and pliant against him, her slender curves addictive, so he'd wanted to strip her naked right then and there and take her.

It had been a tempest, a storm, a raging desire, and he'd thanked whatever powers there meant that he'd been able to bring it to a close. But he was only a man, a mortal, and resisting Harper would take a superhuman effort, more strength than he possessed.

He closed his eyes for a moment and thought of Anna-Maria, thought of their baby, thought of the pain that had come from opening his heart, from opening *himself*, and he knew he couldn't weaken with Harper.

But then she looked in his direction. Their eyes met and he was sinking, without control, without consent, deep into that abyss again…but now he was no longer sure he wanted to escape.

He stood as she approached the table, the old-fashioned courtesy somehow in keeping with his character. Her heart did a funny little pop. She hovered at the seat opposite without taking it.

'How was your appointment?' he asked casually, too casually. She understood the curiosity he felt. It was natural.

Harper hesitated. She never spoke about her mother, especially not to colleagues. Revealing the vulnerability made her feel weak, or as though people might treat her differently. She liked to be seen as strong and in charge. But Salvador's voice, his eyes, everything about him, made her want to tell him the truth.

'It went well,' she said eventually, a little unevenly. The truth was, it hadn't gone well. Her mother had barely been lucid. Those days were the hardest. Harper offered a tight smile and then belatedly folded herself into the seat opposite. A waiter appeared brandishing a drinks menu. Harper ordered a coffee, taking her lead from Salvador. This was business, not a date, despite the convivial setting. 'How was the rest of your meeting?' she asked, pulling her laptop from her bag. 'Did you like the parquetry?'

He laughed, and she sat bolt-upright, the sound as welcome now as it had been the first time she'd heard it.

'Excellent parquetry,' he confirmed. 'Definitely worth buying the hotel for.'

'If not their reservation system.'

'That I could do without.'

'If these hotels are all part of the same chain, why aren't their systems the same?'

'They've been bought over the years and slowly homogenised, but this was the last to be acquired, and therefore the last to be modernised.'

'So that's a job for you.'

He dipped his head.

'Are you going to buy them?'

He scanned her face. 'What do you think I should do?'

Harper considered that, her pulse racing. 'I think you should.'

'Why? Two of them run at a loss.'

'That's true,' she agreed, leaning forward, all of the tension forgotten as she warmed to her theme, excited to have a chance to say what she'd been thinking for days when she hadn't been thinking obsessively about Salvador. 'But there's a huge amount of wastage. I checked their linen costs, for example, and they're astronomical. They're still running on a policy of laundering all towels and sheets daily. Most hotels, as a concession to the environment, offer guests incentives to reuse towels and skip housekeeping services.'

His eyes narrowed, and he remained very still, but Harper

didn't notice. She was too enlivened by the chance to share what she'd been looking at.

'I ran the figures,' she continued. 'You'd save twelve per cent of operating costs if you implemented a similar scheme. That's in comparison to competing hotels in the same cities,' she explained.

'What else?'

'Food and beverage. All of the hotels offer round-the-clock room service, but between eleven at night and, say, six in the morning, it's running at a huge loss.'

'They're five-star hotels. Guests expect to be catered to at any time of day.'

'That's true,' she agreed eagerly. 'But again, I checked. There are six items that are most commonly ordered between those hours. The kitchen could run a limited overnight menu, as lots of hotels do, and cut overnight staffing costs by more than half, without affecting guest satisfaction. A more substantial minibar offering would also meet late-night cravings, and as you know the profit margin for minibars is huge.'

'You enjoy this.' It was a statement, not a question.

'Yes.' It was like being jolted out of a dream. Harper blinked and looked around them, realising that she was talking to one of the most successful businessmen in the world, as if he wouldn't already know how to maximise profits. 'Anyway,' she said with a shrug. 'I'm sure I'm not telling you anything you haven't already realised.'

He was silent, watchful, and she was glad when her coffee arrived because it gave her something to do with her hands. Salvador turned to the waiter. 'We'll take a couple of menus, thanks.'

'Yes, sir.'

'Oh.' Harper's cheeks flushed. 'I'm not— I don't think—'

'I'm hungry,' he said with a steely look in his eyes. 'You

must be as well. Besides, it makes sense to sample the hotel food.'

But consternation flooded Harper. She couldn't do this. It was all too complicated, with too many layers of competing wants, needs and dangers.

'I—'

'It's just dinner.'

'But it's not,' she said with an exasperated shake of her head. 'Let's at least call a spade a spade.'

'We've eaten together before.'

'That was before.'

'Before what?'

'Greece.'

His expression barely shifted but she saw the tightness around his eyes and felt the air between them hum. The waiter appeared with menus, but even that didn't break the tension.

'Thank you,' Harper murmured, barely lifting her eyes from Salvador's face.

When they were alone again, he put his hand on the table top, extending his fingers then squeezing them into a fist before relaxing them again. He looked as though he wanted to say something, or maybe as though he desperately didn't, so she waited, wondering, and finally he spoke.

'My wife died a year ago,' he said quietly. 'But I can't stop feeling guilty for wanting you like this.' It was so honest—so wrenchingly honest. She felt his grief and wanted to wrap her arms around him, to tell him everything would be okay, even when she didn't know if it would be. She settled for reaching over and putting her hand on his in a spontaneous gesture of comfort. It felt so important, so right.

'I'm very sorry for your loss, Mr da Rocha.'

He lifted a single dark brow.

'Salvador,' she supplied with a frown. Then, because she

was a glutton for punishment, 'You must have loved her very much.'

'I'd known her for a long time,' he said after a pause. 'We were friends,= as children. She moved to Italy as a teenager, but we wrote to each other.'

She nodded slowly. And then they'd fallen in love. It was so…romantic. Jealousy was unmistakable. She wished she didn't feel it, but it was clawing through her.

Salvador stared directly at her, almost through her. Harper shivered. There was so much emotion, so much pain, in the man. She didn't know what to say or how to comfort him, except by sharing some of her own pain to show that he wasn't completely alone.

'My mother is in a nursing home,' she said slowly, the words not ones she formed often. When was the last time she'd spoken about this to anyone besides Amanda?

'She had a stroke seven years ago. It left her partially paralysed. Then, two years after that, a series of strokes left her with brain damage.' Harper's voice quivered a little. She couldn't meet Salvador's eyes. 'Her condition is unpredictable.' She lifted her shoulders. 'Some days, she seems to recognise my voice, to know who I am. Other times, like today, there are no lights on.'

Harper shook her head. 'My mother was one of the most fiercely intelligent women you've ever met. Funny, charismatic and so utterly beautiful. She was like a fairy or a ballerina, something out of a story book. I used to love watching her get ready for shows—she was an actress,' Harper explained. 'I grew up back stage in the theatres, watching her perform.' A cloud crossed her features then, darkening the lights from within her own eyes. 'It's very difficult to see her like this.'

'You call her every day?' he prompted.

She nodded, unable to speak.

'For thirty minutes?'

Harper swallowed. 'I read to her. Scripts, books she used to love…anything. I just want to offer her some comfort, Salvador. Some hint of the woman she used to be.'

'What's her prognosis?'

She appreciated the question, because it was practical and it gave her a chance to blink away her tears and focus on the black-and-white medical situation. 'No one knows. She could live for decades like this, with the right care.'

His eyes honed in on hers. 'But that care is expensive.'

'Yes.' Her smile was wistful. 'Very.'

'You pay for it? There's no husband—insurance?'

'No and no.'

'Your father?'

She shook her head. 'Long gone. And, while mum was pretty successful, she was diagnosed with diabetes a little while after I was born, and it cost a fortune to buy her insulin and other meds, so her savings are pretty non-existent.' Harper grimaced. 'She managed to put a little away for me, over the years. For college.'

Salvador watched without speaking.

'Then she had her stroke and the hospital bills mounted up…'

'You used your tuition savings for hospital fees?'

She nodded. 'Of course.' There was determined pride in that answer, and she tilted her chin at him with a hint of defiance. 'What else could I have done?'

'Nothing,' he agreed after a pause, but the admiration was difficult to miss. 'What did you intend to study?'

'Pre-law.' Another pause, as she took a moment to wonder why she was being so forthcoming. But, much like their physical connection, it was difficult for Harper to control this. There was magic weaving around them, making her want to confide in Salvador, almost to bare her soul to him.

'Had you applied anywhere?'

Heat flushed her cheeks as she nodded.

'And been accepted?'

She nodded again.

'Where?'

'Georgetown. I got a scholarship place, but I couldn't leave mum.'

Sympathy softened Salvador's eyes and he flipped his hand to capture hers, the hand she hadn't realised she was still holding, his eyes locked on Harper's, a challenge in their depths.

'Have you thought about applying for a position through the company?'

She shook her head. 'I missed my opportunity, Salvador. I dealt with that a long time ago. This is what I do now, and I'm very, very good at it.'

He linked their fingers, and her pulse went haywire. What was he doing? Did he know how this was making her feel? Her stomach was in knots, looping like crazy.

'Anyway,' she said awkwardly. 'I don't know why I told you all that. I guess I suppose I just wanted you to know that… I understand…grief and loss and life not turning out how you wanted it to.'

'Thank you.'

It was a funny thing to say and she smiled softly, then went to pull her hand away, but he didn't release his grip and Harper didn't fight. She surrendered to the contact, sighing a little, inching forward in her seat so their knees brushed beneath the table. Neither moved away.

The waiter came to take their orders. Harper's heart was in her throat. Everything felt strange and uncertain, but the same hand at her back that seemed like that of fate or something more was pushing her now, so she heard herself say in a voice that was croaky and uneven, 'I…would be happy to eat in the room.'

Salvador's eyes flared. 'To trial room service?' he said quietly, one side of his lips lifting in a half-smile. 'That does make sense.'

'Yes,' she agreed, because it absolutely did.

CHAPTER NINE

HE DROPPED HER hand when they stood and left the hotel bar, but once they were in the lift their hands brushed and his fingers sought hers lightly…seeking reassurance? Or looking to give it to her, more likely, because Salvador wasn't the kind of man who'd need reassurance.

Except Harper felt the magnitude of this.

Whatever 'this' was.

It was new territory for both of them, and she barely wanted to exhale in case the sound of her breath knocked them off-course. Now it wasn't enough to consider Salvador's concerns, but her own as well, because she'd been running for years from the mistake with Peter, and she didn't want to make another one. She worked for Salvador, not just for this fortnight but back in Chicago, and she needed to be sure this wouldn't become public knowledge. She needed to know it wouldn't change anything for her.

'Salvador?' She turned to face him and her stomach dropped to her toes because he was so devastatingly beautiful. When she looked at him, nothing mattered. She'd lose her job. She'd quit. She'd sacrifice almost anything for this one night with him.

But there was her mother to consider, and everything she'd worked for.

'You were right, the other day,' she whispered. The lift

doors pinged open and another couple stepped in. Harper went to pull her hand free but again Salvador held onto it, his eyes meeting hers, charged with an electrical current. She sucked in a breath, tipping towards something, unable to think clearly.

She didn't speak until they reached their floor and they stepped into the corridor, walking side by side towards the room. Salvador swiped his key, the door clicked open and Harper stepped inside, her pulse raging in her eardrums.

'What was I right about?' he asked, unbuttoning his shirt at the collar to reveal his neck. She tried to move her mouth but found it almost impossible.

She pulled her hair over one shoulder, toying with the ends. 'My last job, I was involved with someone. My boss.' She dropped her hands in front of her, wringing her fingers together. 'It was a very, very bad decision.' She blinked into his eyes. It felt a little like looking at a solar eclipse.

He moved closer, lifting her chin. 'What happened with him?'

She chewed on her lower lip. She didn't really want to bring Peter into this situation. He was part of her past, a part she didn't like to think about often, except as to the lessons she'd learned from it all. 'It was a stupid mistake.'

He waited silently.

'We spent a lot of time together. I liked him. He asked me out on a date, and I knew I should have said no, but it was all so hard—stuff with Mum—and I was lonely. I agreed, reluctantly at first. But it was so good to have someone to talk to, even though, looking back, he did most of the talking.' She shrugged. 'I liked not being alone.' Her voice cracked. 'But it was all a lie. I was totally naïve and inexperienced, Salvador.' She groaned. 'I wish I'd been able to see what kind of man he was—or that not wanting to be alone wasn't a good enough reason to sleep with him.'

'When you say totally inexperienced, do you mean that literally?'

Harper's throat shifted as she swallowed, suddenly self-conscious. 'Caring for Mum, the worry, it took all my time. I never had a chance to meet anyone.'

Salvador's expression changed slightly. 'Did he know?'

'That he'd be my first? Yes. He got off on it, I'm pretty sure. If only I'd known he was married,' she said witheringly. 'He promised me the world but all the while he was going home to his pregnant wife every night.' Bitterness tinged her words. 'Thank God I found out about her after just a few weeks. I can't bear to think how long he would have strung me along for.'

Salvador cursed, wrapping his arms around her waist, drawing her against his body. 'Any man who can behave like that isn't worth an ounce of your time.' He ran his thumb over the base of her spine. 'Did he fire you?'

'God, no, I quit. The same afternoon I found out about his wife. I couldn't bear to be in the same building as him, let alone the same office. I hated him, Salvador. Whatever my feelings had been beforehand, they were unmistakably filled with hatred then.'

'Good. I'm glad. And now?'

'I still hate him,' she admitted. 'Not with quite the same passion, but that's only because I realise he's probably a serial offender. He lied too easily…it was all too smooth. There's no way I was his first affair.'

'More than likely.'

'After that, I swore I'd never get involved with someone I worked with. Come to think of it, I didn't really see me getting involved with anyone.'

He nodded slowly. 'We don't have to do this.'

'Don't we?' she prompted with a small sound, something like a sob, shaking her head a little, because this felt as inevitable to Harper now as it had back on the island that first day in their shared office space.

'I don't want to hurt you, Harper. I don't want to be like him.'

She loved hearing him say her name, even in a sentence that was so full of doubt and concern.

'You won't and you're not. You never could be.' She knew that deep in her heart.

'I haven't slept with a woman in a long time. Years.' The revelation caught her off-guard. She knew he'd been celibate since his wife had passed, but before that? He lifted a hand to her cheek, running his thumb over the soft flesh there. 'I don't want you to read more into this than is there. I don't want to make you promises. I don't want you to think—'

'I don't think anything,' she said quietly.

'Having sex with you is more than I thought I'd let happen. It can't go beyond this.'

She ignored the strange sensation in the middle of her chest, letting his words permeate her soul. He was being honest—something Peter had never had the courage to do. Salvador wasn't pretending this was a prelude to any great future. It was just sex.

'I don't—I can't make sense of what's happening between us,' she said after a beat, being completely honest. 'But I know I'll always regret it if I walk away before letting this play out. Does that make sense?'

He groaned. 'I hate that I can't control this.' Their eyes met and held. 'But, hell, I don't want to control it either. Does that make sense?'

All the sense in the world. She blinked up at him, nod-

ding once, and then he kissed her, slowly, tentatively. It was
as if he were signing on the dotted line, a deal with the devil,
making a pact that he knew he'd regret later but couldn't resist in this moment. And then, as she kissed him back, any
pretence of being gentle was thrown by the wayside, the kiss
becoming urgent, desperate, so animalistic and wild, his big,
strong body practically swallowing hers as he wrapped his
arms around her and pulled her to his chest. His fast-beating heart hammered against hers, which beat with the same
frantic answering rhythm, pounding against her ribs franti-
cally and with force.

His hands found the hem of her dress, lifting it fast as
though he couldn't wait to remove it, as though he needed
to see her naked more than he'd ever needed anything. She
sucked in a breath, but it was hard because he was kissing
her, and she didn't want to break that contact. They were a
tangle of tongues and lips, arms, hands and legs, moving
with the same purpose, desperate to connect flesh to flesh,
to feel and explore.

The dam had burst, the power of a thousand rivers exploding into the room as they stumbled back to the bed,
clothes dropping, hands searching, touching, needing, wanting, kissing. His body was over hers, naked except for his
boxer shorts, and her hands roamed his back, her nails dragging over his bronzed skin, her lips finding his collar bone,
kissing him, tasting him, drowning in a wave of desire, desperate to be fulfilled.

His arousal was so hard against her, reminding her of his
hunger, of his need, of the fact he hadn't been with a woman
in years. Suddenly, the rush of knowing that she'd be his first
filled her with something other than desire and adrenaline,
with something more, despite the limitations of what they
were doing. And yet, how could she not read a little some-

thing into this? It wasn't that either of them wanted a relationship, but that didn't make this meaningless.

Everything had meaning and the fact they'd been thrown together and had chosen one another was shaping parts of her she'd forgotten existed.

She'd only ever been with Peter, and the sex had been okay. Not earth-shattering, not amazing, but pleasant enough most of the time. But this was different. From the first moment she'd met Salvador, there'd been a chemistry there that had threatened to burn Harper alive.

His hand guided her legs apart and she jumped, so unused to being touched there she didn't know how to respond except to cry out. His eyes flew to hers, checking on her, making sure she was okay, and then he kissed her once more, making it impossible to think of anything but this connection, the rightness of what they shared.

'Salvador.' She bit down on her lip, unsure what she wanted to say, just knowing this was more perfect than she could express. 'I need—'

'I know.' His hand moved between her legs, touching her there, feeling her moist core, and she bucked against his hand, so drenched with desire she was already at a precipice. Pulling up onto his elbow, he watched her, his hand moving slowly at first, enquiring, as his eyes probed her face—reading her, watching what made her moan, what drove her wild, getting to know her until, within minutes, he was playing her body so expertly it was as though he'd been practising for this his whole life.

She couldn't control herself. Pleasure exploded through her, her release swift and complete. She wrapped her legs around him and pushed up, needing to kiss him to somehow process the pleasure she was feeling, to wean herself off the high, to cope with the waves that were ravaging her body and shocking her with their intensity.

If she stopped and thought about it, the last few days had been like a wild kind of foreplay. She'd wanted him from almost the first moment they'd met, and bit by bit they'd danced around the subject, probing, promising, even while insisting it wasn't what either of them wanted. And now there was this, the most catastrophic explosion of desire she'd ever known—and it was only just beginning.

Her hands ran down his torso, feeling the ridges of his abdomen, the muscled form, until she brushed the thatch of hair at the base of his arousal and he stilled. She felt his body tremble and, emboldened, moved her hands to clasp his length, squeezing him gently so she heard that sound she'd come to love: the sharp hiss of breath that told her he was at a tipping point.

'Harper.' Her name was a warning, one she didn't heed.

His tip had a hint of pearly liquid already and power soared through her, the knowledge that she'd driven him to this point, that he wanted her so badly.

'Stop.' He groaned, even as he moved within her grip, encouraging her to keep going. 'I'm going to come if you keep touching me like that.'

'Is that a bad thing?' She purred.

'I want to feel you.'

Her heart stammered. 'I want that too.'

He moved then, pulling out of her grip, moving closer and then freezing, pulling up to stare into her eyes, his skin pale beneath his swarthy complexion.

'What?' Her heart sank. *Please, please, don't put an end to this,* she silently pleaded.

'I don't have any condoms.'

The words didn't quite make sense to Harper at first; she was in such a fog of sexual pleasure and euphoria.

'What?'

'Nothing. I have nothing. Why would I?' he said with a gruff laugh that was lacking amusement. 'This was definitely not on my radar.'

She swore. 'I don't either. Same reason.'

They stared at each other, totally bemused and utterly frustrated. He groaned, dropping his head to her shoulder, his breath rough. Harper's pulse was thready, her need growing by the second. She moved her hands back to his length, feeling him convulse, feeling his strength and his power. She desperately wanted to feel him inside her, but at the same time she wanted to drive him to the point of explosion with her hands, because she could do that right now, she could make him feel a thousand things.

'Don't fight me,' she instructed, moving one hand and then the other over his tip, down his length, feeling him, worshiping him. His head stayed where it was in the crook of her neck, his desperation at fever pitch, his breath so warm against her skin, his need so absolute that he surrendered to this finally, to her, to whatever they were to each other.

His breath grew rushed, his voice deep, then he groaned, swore and pulled up to stare at her, but she didn't release him. She moved her hands faster, until he was coming over her bare chest and she was crying out, because it was so illicit and animalistic, so completely full of abandon, that it was the sexiest thing she'd ever felt.

He dropped his head to hers, kissing her, breathing her in, the smell of him in the air, of pleasure and satisfaction, and then he pulled up, staring at her as if he needed to commit this exact image to memory, for all time.

She wasn't self-conscious. Not even a little. She felt exultant, euphoric, and the way he was looking at her only cemented that.

'Come with me.' He reached for her and she put her hands in his, allowing him to pull her to sitting then scoop her up and carry her, cradled against his chest, into the bathroom. It wasn't overly large, but it accommodated both of them easily enough, so he carried her into the shower cubicle and placed her onto the tiled floor, flicking the switches and waiting until warm water began to flow. He stared at her again, drinking her in, studying her, and then shook his head with an expression that was almost impossible to fathom.

'Will you promise me to stay here?'

Something lodged in her throat. 'Where are you going?'

'To find a pharmacy. Or a vending machine. Any kind of prophylactic. I will ask at the bar if I have to,' he ground out, so she laughed.

'I'm sure there'll be a shop somewhere.'

'Stay here.' He hesitated for the briefest moment then leaned in, kissing her hard and fast before pulling away and turning his back. He left the bathroom without closing the door, so a moment later she caught a glimpse of him stalking past, fully dressed and looking more or less completely normal. But Harper had seen him lose his mind and now, she overlaid his passion, his powerful, sensual nature, with the visage he showed to the world and she knew there was so much more to him, so much he would show her.

She washed herself slowly, luxuriating in the way her body was so sensitive all over, in the way it felt to brush a loofah over her breasts, her thighs, her stomach. She groaned as her hand came close to her sex and she remembered how easily he'd undone her, how skilfully he'd mastered her body, and she tilted her head back and pressed it against the tiles as memories overcame her. She stood there for a long time, the water deluging her, reaching for the taps just as the front door opened and Salvador returned.

Her heart fluttered and her insides squeezed. He lifted a brown paper bag, a half-grin making his face so wonderfully sexy that she smiled back fully, properly. She stepped out of the shower as he moved into the bathroom, reaching for a bath sheet, wrapping her in the fluffy fabric and towelling her down slowly from her very wet hair to her shoulders, her breasts, her abdomen, kneeling in front of her to dry between her legs, her calves, her ankles and her feet. She submitted to it, but it was a form of torture to feel him so close yet not have him buried inside her yet—more foreplay after days and days of wanting but knowing him to be off-limits.

She shivered, so he lifted his face from where he knelt. 'Cold?'

She shook her head.

His smile was knowing, but Harper couldn't have realised what he was about to do. Her experience was limited, and Peter had never once kissed her most intimate flesh; he'd never even shown any interest in that. But Salvador leaned forward from where he knelt, pressing his lips to her inner thigh first so she gasped, then moving to the hair at the top of her legs, parting her seam with his tongue and skilfully finding the part of her that was so receptive to his touch.

He flicked her and tasted her, sucking her, probing her until she was quivering with desire and moaning into the tiled bathroom, her frantic cries bouncing off the walls. Harper didn't care how noisy she was, though; she was barely aware of anything: time, space, place or person. She was only a conduit for euphoria now.

He gripped her hips, swivelling her at the same time he shifted his position so she was facing the mirror. It gave her something to lean against and she propped her hands on the marble counter as it became almost impossible to stand. It also gave her a perfect view of this debauched scene in the bathroom mirror—his dark head intently focussed on her femininity, her flushed cheeks, fevered eyes, pert nipples and quivering, goose-bump-covered skin. She looked wanton and ravaged, and she loved it.

She moved one hand to his head, running her fingers through his hair, something bursting inside her at the joy of that—at the freedom to touch him finally, to delight in him like this.

'Salvador...' She groaned, almost unable to bear this a moment longer. He understood. His fingers dug into her buttocks and then he sucked her flesh a little harder, flicked and she died against his mouth. Her knees were so weak she almost crumpled to the floor, so his hands at her rear became an essential part of her support. She pressed her own hand into the marble counter, crying out, almost devastated by the strength of her orgasm.

Before had been mind-blowing; this was reality-ending. She moved her hand to his shoulder and dug her nails into his flesh, as if to convey how close she was to ceasing to exist. He waited, mouth moving to the flat flesh of her belly and planting a kiss there. Then he stood, eyes hooked to hers for a moment before he lifted her once more, carrying her out of the bathroom.

She didn't protest. She really didn't think she could walk anyway.

He dumped her on the bed, staring down at her again, his breath ragged, his eyes devouring her.

'You're over-dressed,' she said simply.

He grunted his agreement. 'What are you going to do about it?'

It was a challenge and a dare, and she grinned. What was

that expression—something about a goose and gander? She stood shakily, glad when he put a hand out and caught her behind the back, drawing her to him, kissing the flesh in the curve of her neck and making it impossible to think, much less act. But she needed to act, she needed to peel his clothes from his body piece by piece.

Her fingers undid the buttons, just as she had in the office that time, but now there was no fear he'd pull away, no sense that she'd gone too far. She dropped his shirt on the ground then, with eyes holding his, she knelt down in front of him, just as he'd done with her a moment ago. Her head tilted up as she undid his belt first, then his trousers, pushing them down his legs as he stepped out of them. She stayed there, looking all the way up his naked body to his eyes at first, and to the flush of his cheeks, before turning her attention to his rock-hard arousal, smiling a little as she leaned closer and tentatively ran her tongue over the tip.

He swore, the curse filling the hotel room, his hips bucking at the contact.

'Harper, no.'

'Why not?' She purred.

'You know why not. I want to feel you.'

'And you will.' She ran her tongue around his circumference. 'But first I want to taste you.'

Another curse, this one on a rough exhalation like a surrender, and then she opened her mouth and took him all the way to the back of her throat, revelling in the power of this—in the way he jerked in her mouth, in the way she could already taste him, in the way he was so incredibly big and powerful so that her insides were jumping at the prospect of accommodating him, of squeezing around his length.

She moved her mouth, wishing there was a mirror here for him to see, wishing she could watch this. There was something so incredibly sexy about feeling him in her mouth, about the way he filled her. She trembled against his body and then he caught her beneath her arms, lifting her until their eyes were almost level, his expression taut, stern, as though he was holding on for dear life.

'I want you,' he said simply. 'It's been a very long time. I can't wait any more.'

She understood. She felt a ripple of excitement as they reached for the bag in unison. He got there first, ripping it open and pulling a foil square from a box, sheathing himself quickly for someone who was out of practice.

And now, at that moment of change, of intimacy, Harper felt a rush of nervousness, because this was more than just sex. It was more to both of them because of what they'd each come through. She stared up at him but he smiled, a tight smile, showing the pain he felt at waiting, and she smiled back because she'd made her peace with this. She knew what they were and what they could never be because of how he still felt about his wife. All she wanted was to have this moment, this single night.

He kissed her at the same time as moving forward so she fell backwards on the bed with him on top of her, so heavy and strong, so hard. His thigh moved between her legs, his knee wedging her apart so his tip could press to her sex, and she whimpered, desire flushing through her body.

'Tell me if this hurts,' he ground out, and then she got why he warned her. Because, though he'd felt big in her mouth, when he began to press inside her she realised that he was really quite huge, stretching her so that she froze a moment and he did likewise, staring down at her. 'Okay?'

She nodded, because she was. Once she got used to it, she was fine. Hungry for him, in fact hungry for more. For all of him.

'Please,' she said simply, lifting her hips, begging, inviting, needing.

He groaned as he sank all of him into her, hitched right to his base, and she cried out, the shocking feeling of how completely he possessed her overwriting everything and anything she'd thought she knew about sex. She might as well still have been a virgin. No man had ever touched her like this.

A sheen of tears filmed her eyes and she blinked furiously, desperate for him not to see or notice, not to worry that this meant something more to her than it was supposed to. It didn't. It was just such good, hot sex. She'd had no idea…

And it became even more mind-blowing once he started to move, thrusting in and out, slowly at first, letting her get used to this and him. Then finally, with all the force of his pent-up desire and long-ignored needs, he pushed into her hard and fast so her body banged against the bed and she cried out with each desperate, hungry thrust. Her own desire pushed to fever pitch, to breaking point, and she called his name into the room, dragging her nails into his back and digging in when her orgasm obliterated her soul in one fierce, agonising moment.

She could hardly breathe, barely see. She lay there, quivering, overcome, totally overpowered. Salvador watched her, satisfaction in his features, pleasure and heat, and then he began to move—with no mercy. He was enjoying this too much. Hell, so was she, and her expectations had been lowered by how long he'd been celibate.

What a fool she'd been to underestimate Salvador! He brought his A-game to whatever he did, and right now that was pleasuring Harper.

He grunted and then pulled out of her completely, pressing his hands to the bed on either side, his breath as forced as if he'd just run a marathon.

'What is it?' she asked, lifting a hand, pressing it to his chest. His heart punched her from the inside.

'Come here.' The command in his tone was as hot now as it had been the first time they'd met and he'd bossed her around. She bit down on her lip to hold back her smile and let him pull her from the bed, going with him as he moved her across the room to a mirror—of course there was a mirror in here—standing in the corner.

'I want to see this. I want you to see it.'

Standing behind her, he moved one hand to her sex and another to her breasts, playing her with the same skill as he'd shown earlier. But this time she was watching how he commanded her, how his hands moved over her, tweaking her nipples, separating her sex. At her back, she felt his arousal, wet from her own desire, nuzzled between her bottom, so on instinct alone she pressed back against him, needing everything he could give her, all that he was, needing him with a passion that she'd never known possible.

He separated her legs and, with their eyes locked in the mirror, he took her and she cried out, tilting her head back, her crown hitting his clavicle, sensations overpowering her as his hands roamed her body, tormenting her.

Finally she had to look, to see, to witness what he was doing to her. She lifted her head bravely, stared in the mirror and almost wept for how beautiful this was. There was something so right about this, about the way they came together, the way they fitted and pleasured each other, about the way they experienced desire and lust as one. Then, finally, release in lockstep, each spilling over the edge, their frantic cries in unison as they tumbled headlong into the kind of pleasure reserved for gods in books of magic and myth.

Harper wasn't sure she'd ever feel human again—she didn't know if she wanted to.

CHAPTER TEN

SALVADOR WAS COMPLETELY DISCOMBOBULATED, his body separated from his mind, from his thoughts and dreams. He frowned. There was a weight on his arm he didn't understand; his eyes searched the dim light for clues as to his whereabouts, while his body surged with a rush of something he barely recognised. And then it all came back to him.

The last few hours. The bar. Their conversation. The room. Her mouth on him. His mouth on her. His possession of her. Her reciprocation. Her total abandonment to this, as if she'd known he'd needed to feel completely animal and wild when he had sex with a woman for the first time since Anna-Maria. As if she'd known everything he needed, everything he was.

The weight on his arm was her head. He turned, looking at her, something strange twisting low in his abdomen.

Guilt.

He'd expected this. He'd known it would come, but it didn't make the pain any less compelling.

It was made even worse by the fact it wasn't all just guilt about Anna-Maria and Sofia. There was so much more. He didn't love Harper. But if he closed his eyes and imagined loving her, imagined needing her then imagined losing her—as he had so many people in his life—he couldn't breathe. He couldn't go through that again.

And you told her that, he reminded himself forcibly. *You made it clear that last night was just about sex.* She wouldn't be weaving any dreams about a future with him. It was what it was: a one-night stand.

One night?

His body revolted in response to that. Why end it now? They'd be travelling back to the island together and she'd see out the rest of her contract, which gave them one more week. If he could make sure she understood, continued to understand, that he would never want more than the kind of passion they'd enjoyed last night, why not make the most of it? They were adults, capable of understanding the difference between lust and love.

It was as if a huge weight was being lifted off his chest. Loyalty, guilt and trauma, and the darkness of those emotions, had made him celibate, but also fear. Fear of caring for someone again, of opening himself up to them and losing them. Anna-Maria had been one of his oldest, dearest friends. He'd lost his wife but he grieved a friend and the baby they'd made together.

He never wanted to feel anything like that again.

But sex was sex—wonderful, hypnotic, drugging sex. So long as he could make sure they remembered that, they could enjoy this.

And, with that in mind, he rolled onto his side, his mouth claiming Harper's as she slept, kissing her awake. Her smile against his lips was all the reassurance he needed that she welcomed his attention, that she wanted him again. Thank God because, after the years he'd gone without, he was a starving man and she the most delicious thing he'd ever tasted.

The hotel in Prague was the least impressive but the city was undeniably Harper's favourite of the three they'd visited, and not just because of how they'd spent the night. As they traversed the bridge, side by side but not holding hands—because that would have been romantic and, whatever they were, it wasn't romantic—she paused to look over the edge, sighing a little. Ancient statues stood sentry along it. 'I would love to have seen this at night,' she said, imagining how dramatic the scenery would be when all lit up.

'We were a little busy.'

She grinned, shooting him a sidelong glance. 'No complaints here.'

'We can stay another night.' The offer was obviously made spontaneously. She saw the surprise in his eyes, but then the certainty as he nodded. 'Yes, let's stay.'

Her eyes widened. 'You're sure?'

'Why not?'

Great question. Why not? She gnawed on her lip, the hint of a misgiving forming at the back of her mind, but she couldn't make sense of it. She had no idea what could be bothering her, in fact, given how perfect last night had been, so she ignored the voice, chalking it up to indecision because everything was different and new.

'Okay. What about work?'

'We can work from the hotel.'

'From that tiny room?'

He lifted his shoulders. 'Or we can do other things.'

She laughed softly. 'Uh-uh…' She waggled her finger. 'I had fun last night, but…'

When their eyes met, it felt as though she was being speared by lightning. That strange misgiving was back.

'But,' she continued, 'I don't want any special treatment. I'm working for you, just like before. Got it?'

'I might find it a little harder to concentrate.'

She poked out her tongue. 'You'll manage.'

'I might make it a little harder for you to concentrate.'
She grinned. 'We'll see.'

Later, back in the hotel, he showed her exactly what he'd meant by that, making it almost impossible for Harper to focus on anything for longer than ten minutes between his trailing fingers, wandering lips and the fact he'd stripped down to boxer shorts alone.

'This is impossible,' she said on a laugh in the late afternoon, closing her laptop and flipping onto the bed to look at him properly.

'Yes.'

'I thought you were a workaholic.'

'I'd forgotten how much I like sex.'

Something jarred in the back of her brain, but there was a salient reminder too. She imprinted the words in her mind because she knew she'd need them later. He liked sex. Not her. Not even sex with her, though obviously he did enjoy that. But she had no reason to suspect she was any more entertaining to him than a woman picked up off the streets or in any random bar might have been. He'd been alone a long time, and she'd been there. Yes, they had chemistry, but maybe he would have felt that with any woman within a yard of his age.

This wasn't special.

She wasn't special.

'I was thinking…' he reached across her for his phone '… that we should eat out tonight.'

She frowned, her heart racing despite the direction her thoughts had just been taking. 'Oh?'

'You said you wanted to see the city.'

'Yes,' she agreed, slightly breathlessly.

He kissed her quickly. 'Then let's.'

She groaned. 'You're a terrible influence.'

He lifted a brow. 'Do you mind?'

'I'll make you a deal,' Harper said, thinking quickly, knowing that it was fundamentally important to her in the circumstances to uphold her end of the bargain. She'd come here to work and she wasn't going to let a fling with her boss derail that.

'Go on.'

'I need to finish reading this report.' She gestured to her closed up laptop. 'Let me do that and then you can have me for the night.'

'I like the sound of that.'

So did Harper, but she kept her expression stern until she had his solemn agreement. Salvador was clearly a man of his word because he dressed without speaking and then moved to the door of the hotel room.

'Where are you going?'

'Out, so you can concentrate.' He winked. 'And so I'm not tempted.'

The problem was, with Salvador gone, she was almost *more* distracted. His smell was everywhere, as was the memory of his touch and the way they'd kissed and made love. She only had to look across the room in a moment of distraction to conjure the image they'd made in the mirror and her heart was bubbling with feelings that were powerful and sort of frightening. So she focussed on her work, instinctively understanding that so much was at stake for her if she didn't remember her professionalism in the midst of all this.

Work first, Salvador second.

But Salvador *was* her work. His name, his very soul, was in every document she read, every email, every business transaction that was bursting with his confidence and *passion*. So much passion! How had she missed that? She'd thought him arrogant and rude, a total jackass, but it wasn't that at all. He was just overflowing with feelings, and he'd had no way of processing them.

Her heart panged because, in another life, Harper would have loved nothing more than to help him. To be with him as he made sense of his loss, to comfort and even love him back to life, to being able to enjoy life, but that wasn't reality. It was never going to happen—not for her, or for him. They weren't those people.

With a sigh, she re-dedicated herself to her report and managed to make it to the end. Some time before six, as she was starting to feel a little bored and lonely, the door opened and Salvador strode in carrying several good quality bags, the sort used by upscale boutiques.

'You've been busy,' she murmured with obvious curiosity.

'Yes.'

'Shopping?' It wasn't an activity she would have thought he'd enjoy.

He placed the bags at the foot of the bed and, not a moment later, there was a knock on the door. He strode towards it, opened it just long enough to retrieve a bottle of ice-cold champagne and two glasses from the hotel staff member then closed it swiftly with his foot.

'Take a look.' He gestured to the bags as his hand moved over the champagne top, after placing the glasses down to enable him to remove the foil and unfurl the cork with a muted pop as he caught it fully in his palm. A little liquid frothed over but he had the glasses ready to splash it in.

Curiosity got the better of Harper and she moved to the end of the bed, opening the closest bag and pulling out a dress of red silk all the way to the floor. Her eyes lifted to Salvador's, her expression unchanged despite the lava pouring into her veins.

'I don't know if it's your style,' she murmured, draping the dress over the end of the bed and moving to the next bag. Shoes and a clutch bag. The next contained lingerie that made her cheeks sting.

'You really have been busy.'

He lifted his shoulders. 'I found it impossible to concentrate on anything *but* you and, as you made yourself unavailable to me, this was the next best option.' He moved to the final bag. 'I enjoyed choosing these,' he said, voice gruff. 'I enjoyed, even more, imagining you wearing them.'

'And removing them?'

'That thought didn't cross my mind,' he lied badly, pulling her towards him and kissing her slowly. But it didn't matter that it was slow—the fireworks in her bloodstream exploded with all the speed of a Gulfstream jet.

Harper, who'd learned to be in control of almost all situations, felt ridiculously nervous as she surveyed her image in the hotel mirror. Salvador had gone downstairs to wait, giving her privacy and space to get ready, which she'd appreciated. As lovely as the city was, and as eager as she was to explore it, she was even keener to keep exploring Salvador. If he'd stayed in the hotel room much longer, she'd have asked him to get a refund on the dress, shoes and all and order in.

Perhaps pre-empting that, he'd showered and changed into a dark suit with a crisp blue shirt, leaving Harper to get ready, the smell of his cologne in the air making her body tingle with anticipation.

It wasn't helped by the sensation of the silk lingerie he'd chosen. It was so fine and luxurious, so incredibly soft against her body. She ran her hands over the mix of lace and fabric and wondered why she'd never bought anything like this for herself.

Because it was so sexy.

The kind of thing a man would buy for his lover.

Only, it didn't have to be. Feeling sexy wasn't just for people in relationships, or people who were having sex. She liked the way this felt. She loved it. And she loved the way it looked.

With a smile, she turned away from the mirror and removed the dress from the edge of the bed. More silky, satin-like material. The dress was a thing of beauty. It had long sleeves and wrapped around her torso, tying at the waist and falling to her ankles, so it was somehow elegant and incredibly sensual all at once. Maybe the sensuality came from knowing she was dressing for Salvador in a dress he'd chosen and would later peel off her body. It showed off her slender waist and the curves of her breasts and hips, and the long, draping sleeves meant she'd be warm enough.

The shoes were a perfect fit—how in the world had he managed that? She could barely remember her own shoe size. She felt like Cinderella, dressing for the ball.

Her eyes travelled to the mirror and her hand lifted to her hair, which she'd parted in the middle and pulled into a low bun at the back of her nape. It was a sophisticated style for a sophisticated dress and the result was breath-taking. It had become second nature for Harper to play down her looks, because more than anything she wanted to be recognised for what she was capable of. But she felt a thrill of pleasure to see herself like this, to know that Salvador had chosen this dress for her because he'd wanted to see her in it. It was sensual and somehow one of the most heart-warming things Harper had ever felt.

Turning away quickly, cheeks warm, she grabbed the essentials from her sensible leather handbag and transferred them to the sparkly clutch Salvador had bought: lipstick, phone, credit card, room key.

Feeling more and more like Cinderella, she left the room with her fingers crossed that this would be every bit as magical as Cinderella's ball. Only there'd be no falling in love with Prince Charming, she reminded herself as she approached the lift.

Much like Cinderella's expectations, this would be a one-time thing—a treat to herself, a slice out of time, before she got back to real life and her normal self.

Except, Harper wasn't sure she could slip back to normality. She wasn't the same woman she'd been in Chicago. So much had changed since then! Even having the confidence to show Salvador that she was interested had been a big step for Harper. Everything that had happened between them had changed something inside her. She'd grown and she liked how she'd changed. She felt as though a door had opened up, showing her a world in which she might have more faith in herself to reach out and grab life with both hands.

When it came to adventure, she'd never been afraid. She'd tried it all—bungee-jumping, sky-diving, rock climbing, abseiling—and she'd loved it all. The high of surfing the biggest waves in the world, with the real threat of being pummelled by the ocean, was like nothing she'd ever known.

But when it came to people, to relationships, to trust and even love, she'd been so cautious. She'd learned to be. Seeing her mother's hurt, and then feeling that first-hand courtesy of Peter on her first foray into the world of relationships, well, had only confirmed what she'd feared all along: that hearts were made for breaking.

So maybe she still didn't want to think about love and giving her heart to anyone else, but there was a lot of middle ground between being determinedly single and getting mar-

ried. Such as dating. Such as having sex. Such as dressing up
and going out with the intention of meeting a guy and keeping things light and low key. It was something she'd avoided
assiduously but suddenly she could see the advantage to it.
She liked this. She wanted more of it.

With someone else…? A little voice in the back of her mind
had her crashing back to reality. Her red lips parted in surprise and, just like that, her pleasant realisation-bubble burst.

She was having fun *with Salvador.* She liked sleeping *with
Salvador.* What if none of this was as good with anyone else?

She stepped into the lift, smiled weakly at an elderly couple already in the space and turned to face the front. Her reflection greeted her there, reminding her of how beautifully
Salvador had chosen for her. She blinked away, self-conscious. This was not how she generally presented herself to
the world. But Salvador made her feel…

It was Salvador, she realised with a little clutch in her
heart. Maybe she hadn't changed at all, but rather Salvador
had brought out qualities in her she'd never acknowledged
before. Would she still feel this way in Chicago? She'd find
out in a little over a week, she supposed.

Salvador had said he'd wait in the bar but he hadn't really enjoyed the experience of waiting. He was strangely energised,
restless, unable to sit still properly or to focus. He had ordered
a Scotch, taken a single sip then pushed it across the table
and sat with one ankle crossed over the other knee, eyes on
the door to the bar, just like the day before, so he'd see her
the moment she walked in. Only the bar was much busier
at night, filled with hotel guests, from children to people in
their dotage and everyone in between milling around, laughing, drinking and talking happily. So he didn't have as clear a
line to the entrance as he'd have liked. But he forced himself

to sit still, to wait, watching, outwardly showing no hint of the adrenaline that was pumping his body like white water.

The door opened as a crowd moved past his table. He saw a flash of red. His gut tightened. He leaned forward, breath held. Dark hair… Yes, it was her. He drummed his fingers into his thigh impatiently. Was it her?

The crowd shifted slightly, so he saw properly and felt as though he'd been punched hard in the gut. Her beauty took his breath away, but it was more than that. It was her confidence. She held herself like a woman who *knew* she looked incredible. She looked perfect.

Her eyes skimmed the bar and, though he was staring at her, he was aware on his periphery of the way heads turned towards her. The same magnetic beauty he was appreciating was noticed by others in the bar. He stood, unfolding his body with slow intent, the action catching her eyes so their gazes locked.

Neither smiled. Electricity arced through the air. He felt it singe his fingertips, his toes, his chest. She lifted a hand to her ear, tucking an imaginary piece of hair back—was she nervous?—then began to walk towards him. The silk caressed her body like a second skin, falling like a waterfall over her hips and shimmering with each step she took so he had to hold back a groan. How the hell was he going to get through this night?

The dress had seemed like such a great idea at the time. Now he realised he'd bought himself several hours of torture.

'I borrowed your dress,' she said with an impish smile as she approached the table, and he laughed, because it was an excellent ice-breaker. The tension that had been making his head pulse dissipated. He put a hand on one of her hips and leaned forward, kissing her cheek, wondering at the strange throb in the middle of his chest.

'It looks better on you than it did on me. Keep it.'

She grinned in return.

'Would you like a drink?'

She looked around the bar, her lips twitching downwards as she considered that. He realised it wasn't a frown but just how she looked when she was in contemplation. 'It's crowded. Besides, we've seen this bar. I'd rather explore somewhere new.' She turned back to face him. 'Is that okay?'

The last little question did something strange to him. He couldn't explain the rush of emotions he felt—vulnerability for her, to ask him that, and annoyance that she thought she had to. Was it because he was her boss? Or because she was so unsure of herself with men?

'Of course it's okay,' he responded, not sure if he did a great job of keeping the irritation from his voice.

'We can stay, if you want,' she said, brows slightly furrowed. 'I know you probably want to suss out the hotel a bit more.'

He shook his head, pulling her closer to him, knowing that there was one way he could get things back on an even keel and restore that beautiful confidence he'd seen when she'd first walked in. 'I want what you want,' he said simply. 'So just say the word.'

Her eyes ran over his face, as if she wasn't sure she could believe him, but then she smiled, so he smiled, because it was impossible not to.

'Then let's get out of here.'

His car was waiting—a limousine with a glass panel between the front and the back. It was plush and lovely, but Harper was nervous again. It wasn't being with Salvador; it was being with Salvador like *this*, on a date. And it didn't matter that they weren't in a relationship and that there was a very definite expiration date on this—tonight was still a date, with all the trimmings, and she really had no idea how to behave.

She didn't realise she was fidgeting with her fingers in her lap until he reached over and put a hand over them. The smile he offered was clearly meant to be reassuring but it only made her feel…something else. Unsettled. Uncertain.

She was overthinking this. And it was going to ruin the experience. She needed to get back in the moment, simply enjoy this one night. Relish being Cinderella, knowing that there would be no 'happily ever after' with her Prince Charming but that it could still be happy right now, happy tonight.

'Where are we going?' she asked as his hand pulled away from hers back to his own lap.

'A rooftop bar, for a drink,' he said. 'Then dinner.'

Her heart stammered and she settled back in the seat. She bit down on her lip, biting back a smile. 'That sounds perfect.'

The bar was exquisite—small, intimate and obviously exclusive. Salvador da Rocha naturally had no problem opening doors and, within a minute of arriving, they were welcomed inside and shown to a low-set table pressed against a window with views of the old city that were second to none. The bridge that had fascinated Harper, and so many millions of tourists ever year, was just across the city, so she could enjoy the vista of people promenading over it, the warm, golden lights making it seem so ancient and magical.

'Have you been to this bar before?'

He shook his head.

'How did you know it would be so nice?'

'A friend of mine owns the building. He recommended it.'

That sparked a thousand questions inside Harper. What were his friends like? Had they supported Salvador in the last year? She knew he was reclusive, sticking mainly to the island, but had his friends come to visit? And had Salvador told whichever friend had recommended this bar about her? If so, what had he said?

She was glad when a waiter appeared with their drinks—a glass of champagne for her and a beer for Salvador. She was thirsty, her mouth dry, her body all tingly. She took a sip, the bubbles icy and enthusiastic.

'And the restaurant we're going to next?'

'Same friend.'

'He's from Prague?'

'He lives here now.'

'Did you see him at all, while you were here?'

'No.'

'Not this afternoon?'

'He's not really the kind of guy you take lingerie shopping,' Salvador pointed out with a wry half-smile.

Her nipples tingled against the silk of her bra and she reached for her champagne, taking a sip quickly. But Salvador's eyes had fallen to her breasts, to the obvious physical response, his smile not so much wry now as resigned.

Her heart leaped into her throat.

'You're not really the kind of guy I'd imagine lingerie shopping either,' she said with a lift of her shoulders.

'There's a first time for everything.'

Her heart stammered. Was that true? Was this really the first time he'd bought lingerie for a woman? Of course not. She focussed on the table between them, trying to steady her breath.

'Usually I have an assistant who can arrange all sorts of things for me,' he said with a hint of amusement in his voice. But there was something underneath it, a tension. She felt it even when he was trying so hard to cover it up. 'But that would have ruined the surprise a little.'

Of course. Amanda would ordinarily have been dispatched to buy things for his girlfriends, and then his wife. To research the best bars and restaurants in whatever city Salvador happened to be in and grease the wheels for him. But, because he was now sleeping with his assistant, he'd had to be a little innovative.

Harper felt the ground shift beneath her, the reality of what she'd allowed to happen slamming into her like a freight train all of a sudden. Everything had seemed so simple, predetermined almost, but the reality was she was walking the exact same path she'd walked with Peter.

It was different in many ways, but the same in one very important particular: she was sleeping with her boss.

The last time had been excruciating. But not because of the relationship, she reminded herself quickly. It wasn't the fact they'd been seeing each other that had caused Harper to quit without notice. It was the fact he'd drafted her into the role of mistress without so much as giving her a single clue that he was married. In fact, he'd gone out of his way to conceal it, never once mentioning the family he'd had across the river.

If she'd been so easily fooled by Peter, with whom she'd worked closely for *months,* what might she be missing about Salvador?

'Are you okay?' He reached across, hand on hers.

'Yep, just fine,' she lied, smiling over-brightly, reaching for her drink and taking a generous gulp. 'What a lovely view,' she remarked, the words sounding close enough to genuine as she forced herself to settle back into her seat and look as though she was truly relaxed.

CHAPTER ELEVEN

BUT THE TENSION stayed with her all through their drink and as the car drove them across town to a restaurant that had so many potted plants out the front, it felt a little like walking through a jungle to get inside. Elegant jazz music played, with a pianist in the corner, and a waiter greeted them as soon as they entered. Whereas the night had started with delicious anticipation and pleasure, Harper was aware now of the risks coming at her from every angle.

'Mr da Rocha, we've been expecting you. This way, please.'

Salvador reached down and weaved their fingers together, holding her hand as he led her through the restaurant, to another 'best' table by a window that had a view of the greenery outside.

Salvador held out a seat for Harper and, as she took it, his hands brushed her shoulders, and she shivered. It felt so good to be touched by him, so right, but there was an answering darkness, knowing how temporary this was and, she had started to fear, how much more this meant to her than him—and how much more high stakes it was for her. After all, what was the worst that could happen to Salvador if anyone found out about their affair?

There'd be no consequences, no professional splash-back, no water-cooler gossip, no knowing looks when a promotion was announced. *Oh, God.*

'Your friend,' she blurted out, when they were alone.

He arched a brow. 'Which friend?'

'The one who helped you organise this.' She gestured to the restaurant. The waiter returned with menus, asking what drinks they'd like.

Harper frowned. 'Oh, um, a white wine, I suppose?'

Salvador ordered a bottle after the briefest glance at the wine list, then turned back to Harper. 'Go on?'

'When you asked him to arrange this, you didn't mention me, did you?'

He lifted a brow. 'Mention you?'

'By name.' She realised how silly it sounded, and made an exasperated noise. 'I'm sorry. I know that sounds paranoid. It's just... I just can't risk anyone ever finding out that we...'

His expression had grown very serious and grave, his eyes holding hers with an intensity that made it hard to focus.

'You think I told my friend I'd slept with my assistant?'

'Well, not Amanda,' she said with a small smile, but Salvador didn't return it. He was silent, so Harper sighed softly. 'I just thought you might have said...something. I don't know.'

'I didn't explain why I needed the information and he didn't ask.' Salvador's nostrils flared and it was so like him, so arrogant and self-assured, that amusement rippled through her, lightening her mood.

'Okay.'

But Salvador wasn't prepared to let it go. 'Why do you ask?'

She pulled her lips to the side. 'It's just—after Peter,' she said with a shake of her head.

'People found out about the two of you?'

Heat flushed her cheeks. She hated the idea of Salvador knowing about her indiscretion and, worse, her stupidity.

'No. He made sure of that.' The words were tinged with bitterness. 'Because we worked together, he said it would be far better if we kept the relationship secret. I agreed whole-heartedly. I'd worked damned hard to get where I was and I didn't want the charge of having slept my way into the job.'

Salvador's eyes narrowed and his lips tightened, and she wondered if he found the idea of imagining her in bed with another man as unpalatable as she found it whenever the sub-ject of his wife came up.

'You never considered reporting him to HR, though? You could have done so confidentially.'

'Believe me, there's no such thing. Besides, what would I have reported him for?' she said with a shrug. 'The relation-ship was consensual. He didn't pressure me. He didn't make me feel obligated to sleep with him.'

'You loved him?'

She frowned. She'd thought maybe she had, once upon a time, but since then she'd grown up and seen the relationship properly. 'I was impressed by him,' she said after a beat. 'He was very smart. I like smart.'

Salvador was quiet, his eyes difficult to read. They sipped their drinks in silence.

'And since him you've been single,' he said thoughtfully.

'Yes.'

'Why?'

She looked over his shoulder, trying to put that into words. 'I guess… I just haven't met anyone I was interested in. I work long hours. I like my job. I don't really go out anywhere like bars or clubs.'

'But you have friends?'

She nodded. 'I'm just not looking for a relationship.'

He frowned.

'Is there something wrong with that?'

'No…' He hesitated, though, so she knew he was puzzling over her circumstances and wasn't likely to let it go unless Harper gave him a little more information.

'My mum was devastated when Dad left,' she said in a low voice. 'She dated lots of guys. Lots and lots. And lots. Always looking for the man who was going to make everything better. And her heart was broken. Again and again and again. I was only a kid, but it was up to me to pick her up off the floor, to try to help her feel better. I hated—hated—how she would give these men such power over her. Like her worth was determined by whichever man she was dating at the time. It's not like I made a conscious decision to stay single, but I knew I couldn't ever live like she did. I didn't ever want to give so much of myself to another person that I risked getting lost, if that makes sense.'

'Perfectly.'

Their eyes met and the air between them crackled and hummed with mutual understanding.

'But you've been married,' she pointed out. 'So I'm sure your perspective is a little different.'

His lips pulled to one side then he drank from his wine.

'What was she like?' The question wasn't planned, but Harper didn't regret asking it. After their conversation, she felt that he'd opened a door to their past, to the spirit of total honesty.

'Anna-Maria was a wonderful person.' The words came out reluctantly. He clearly didn't want to talk about his late wife. Could she blame him? It had only been a year, or a little over. Not long enough to have healed.

'You must miss her.'

A muscle jerked in Salvador's jaw as he gripped his glass tight enough for his knuckles to show white.

'How long were you married?'

'Six months.' This time, he made it quite obvious he wasn't going to be drawn deeper into conversation.

The waiter reappeared to take their orders. Harper chose something at random, not having properly looked at the menu.

'Amanda spoke very highly of you.' Salvador changed the subject when they were alone once more. 'It seemed that she knew a lot about you.'

Harper's smile was genuine. 'She's one of my mum's oldest friends. I've known her since I was a baby—apparently. I don't remember that part, but I do remember her from when I was a girl and she'd come to visit. She'd always bring me little gifts from wherever she was working at the time. She was so glamorous, always overseas on assignment.'

Salvador nodded.

'My mum was the polar opposite—very beautiful and glamorous but a total scatterbrain. She was artistic and creative, so I never lacked for stories and fun, but sometimes dinner didn't get cooked until midnight, or not at all, and I rarely had the right school clothes.' Harper shrugged. 'Whereas Amanda was so organised. Her life seemed to run like clockwork. I was in awe of her efficiency.'

'So she's always been that way?'

'Always,' Harper confirmed with a nod. 'It was Amanda who recommended I apply for the position at da Rocha Industries in Chicago after I quit my last job. She didn't ask questions, but she understood I needed help, and put my CV forward to HR. I was so grateful to her.'

'You needn't be. Your work speaks for itself, Harper. I'm very impressed by you.'

It was just about the best compliment Harper could ever be paid.

She tucked it away into a fold of her brain for later examination and enjoyment. Some memories needed to be clung to, and this, she suspected, was one of them.

Prague was a truly beautiful city—the people, the history, the culture and the architecture. After finishing their dinner, which was sublimely delicious, Salvador and Harper walked across the Charles Street bridge—not holding hands, like the other couples doing an evening promenade, but with Salvador's hand lightly on the small of Harper's back, keeping her close, making her pulse simmer. It was somehow even more intimate and possessive, as though he wanted her welded to his side. He was hard, strong and firm and she fit there so perfectly. Heat flamed inside her body; she had enjoyed their night out but now, more than anything, she wanted to get back to the hotel, to their shared room and that perfect bed they'd enjoyed rumpling so much.

In the small hours of the morning, Salvador shifted a little onto his side so he could see Harper in the light cast by the full moon. She was asleep, sound asleep, and, oh, so beautiful. She'd been stunning tonight in that dress, with her hair, make-up and those heels, but he stared at her like this and felt something shift in his belly, something in his chest that he'd never felt before. It was an ache and a need that he shied away from, because he knew instinctively it was more than he should feel for her. That he was starting to want more than either of them had agreed to.

She was beautiful and she was fascinating, but that was even worse, because true danger lay in the kind of desire he felt—a desire that went beyond the physical.

Harper Lawson was the kind of woman a man could fall head over heels in love with.

Salvador had never been in love. Much like Harper, he'd had his own front-row seat to a cautionary tale of love and had always sought to avoid that. Things with Anna-Maria had been different. He'd loved his wife as one of his oldest friends, but that wasn't the same thing as headlong, romantic love. Their one night together wouldn't have happened if they hadn't been out together, drinking, dancing, laughing and if Salvador hadn't been so carefree with who he took to bed.

The next day, he'd woken up and remembered who Anna-Maria was to him, and wished he could have undone the last twelve hours of his life. It hadn't helped that she'd felt the opposite—that she'd loved him. He'd broken her heart that day, not knowing of course that she'd conceived their baby.

Everything with Harper, though, was different. She was sparky. So sparky that they couldn't help but surge when they were together. She was dangerous. This whole relationship was fraught with risks he couldn't define; he needed to remember that, to keep a grip on reality, to remain in control and not to hesitate to end it when the time came. It was the only thing that would make sense of all of this—to stay focussed on who he was and what he wanted, and that wasn't to get involved with a woman like Harper.

He couldn't. When he let his mind wander and imagined a world in which he opened himself up to this, to being with Harper without any idea of when—or if—it might end, he could see only the flip side. Only the darkness that came from trusting and loving, only the pain. She'd known enough of that, and so had he. Salvador knew he had to be strong for both of them.

Arriving back on Ilha do Sonhos was a strange moment for Harper. She'd committed so much of this scenery to her memory, because it was one of the most beautiful places she'd ever been, but now she saw it differently. It wasn't that the island had changed, but Harper had. She was different from the woman who'd flown out of here.

Something had shifted inside her, and a curiosity had been born that was almost insatiable. This was no longer a collection of trees and mountains leading to some of the most pristine beachfront Harper had ever seen: these were Salvador's trees and mountains, his home, his refuge, the place he'd chosen to live and love, the place where he'd known such awful loss.

To be here, to breathe the air, to see this scenery, was to place herself in his shoes and share a part of his life with him.

It was terrifying and all so *real*.

But Harper didn't want to think about that. There was one week left of her contract, one week left with Salvador, and she didn't intend to ruin it by overthinking anything.

She'd work hard—even harder than she had been doing—to prove to herself and him that nothing had changed for her professionally. And in the evenings...

Her heart rate kicked up a gear. In the evenings, she'd be his, as completely as she had been in Prague. Having opened the floodgates, there was no way to stem this tide. It was overpowering and relentless.

He landed the helicopter with expert skill, unhooked his headset then turned to face her, a frown on his lips that she wanted to lean forward and kiss away.

'We should talk, before we go inside.'

Harper lifted a brow.

'Our relationship...' His frown deepened and he paused, weighing his next words with care. Despite the happiness Harper had just been enjoying, something inside her stilled now and she held her breath, waiting, uncertain, and hating that uncertainty. Hating that he might say something devastating, like he wanted to go back to the way things had been before. Pride wouldn't allow her to argue with him, even though that was the last thing she wanted.

'Yeah?' she pushed when he didn't speak for ages.

'Like you, I'm a private person,' he said eventually. 'I consider my personal life to my business alone.'

She waited, still not able to breathe properly.

'I would prefer the staff here not to suspect anything has changed between us.'

'Oh.' Relief surged inside Harper. 'That would be my preference too.'

His eyes scanned hers, as if looking for reassurance.

'It's not anyone else's business,' he muttered. 'But people talk, and I've had enough of that. After—' He hesitated. 'She died...' His voice cracked a little and tears formed in Harper's eyes because her heart was breaking for him. Sympathy squeezed inside her. He'd loved his wife so much. Anna-Maria must have been a very special person indeed. 'I felt as though everyone was speaking about it. About me. I did not enjoy that.'

'No,' Harper agreed softly. She reached over, putting a hand on his thigh, thrilled that she was able to do so without overthinking it, without worrying he might brush her hand away or frown. Instead, he reached down and squeezed her hand in his.

'So, we'll leave things as they were before,' he said with a nod. 'You have your room. If you agree, I can come to you there...'

'I'll think about it,' she said and then rolled her eyes, flipping her hand over and catching his. She lifted it to her lips and held it to her mouth, eyes sweeping shut a moment as she trapped this memory in the depths of her mind for later examination. It felt like the calm before the storm, the pause before they returned to something far more like normal life.

It was nothing like normal, nothing like before. She worked in the office beside Salvador's, but her every thought was of him. Even worse was knowing he was in the same boat. She only had to lift her eyes to look towards the glass that separated their offices and their eyes would meet. When she forced herself to focus for a period of time, she felt him watching her. It was electrifying and addictive.

The first day passed like some form of torture, both avoiding the other except for essential conversations pertaining to business and the hours moving slowly, oh, so slowly, until finally the day was over.

Harper stood, rubbing a hand over her neck and switching off her computer and sliding her laptop into a bag so she could do a little more in her room later. But for now she needed a break from the reality of being close to Salvador and not touching him, of wanting but knowing she couldn't have.

He was focussed on his screen when she approached his door, but the second she knocked he flicked a glance at her and her heart skipped.

'I'm done for the day, Mr da Rocha,' she said with the hint of a wink.

'Thank you, Ms Lawson.' Then, after a beat, 'Do you have dinner plans?'

She lifted a brow. 'It's a private island. Did you think I might swim to Rio to see a movie or something?'

He scowled. It was a lot of fun teasing him.

'No need to be sarcastic.'

'But it's fun,' she murmured.

'I can think of better ways to have fun.'

'Oh?'

'Later.' He grunted, returning his gaze to his screen, focussing as though his life depended on it.

Later couldn't come soon enough.

Salvador didn't keep Harper waiting long. She just had time to get back to her room and shower, to change into a pair of linen shorts and a tee shirt and he was there, with that brief knock and entrance, like the first time when he'd caught her in a state of undress.

'Hi,' she said breathlessly, moving across the floor quickly and straight into his arms.

He wrapped her in an embrace, kissing her hungrily, desperately, as though they'd been separated for weeks, not a single day. She could have sobbed for how great it felt to be right back here, in his arms, close to his fast-beating heart.

'I was thinking of going for a walk to the beach,' he said, breaking the kiss to pull away and look down at her. 'Join me?'

Her heart fluttered. It was different—more than she'd expected—and she agreed without hesitation. 'I'd like that.' Damn it, her voice sounded a little unsteady. She cleared her throat quickly and gave Salvador her best easy-going smile, as if it was no skin off her nose either way.

'Are you going to go dressed like that?' She gestured to his business shirt and trousers, so Salvador frowned.

'I suppose not.'

Harper skimmed his body. 'Need help getting changed?'

He laughed gruffly. 'I think I can manage.'

She pouted. 'But many hands make light work…' She reached for his shirt, lifting it out of his trousers just enough to be able to connect fingertips to bare flesh. She felt his skin bunch in response and a rush of power flooded her.

'You're impossible.' He kissed her on the tip of her nose. 'I'll meet you downstairs on the terrace.'

She tried not to be too disappointed. After all, he'd still suggested the beach, and they had the whole night ahead of them.

The whole night, and six more nights after that.

And then? a little voice probed. She ignored it. There was no sense getting ahead of herself. They had the week: that had to be enough.

In his room, Salvador moved slowly. He stripped out of his work clothes and dressed in some shorts and a shirt. As he approached the door, his eyes gravitated to the small, framed photo he kept on the shelf. The only family photo they'd taken: Anna-Maria, Sofia and him.

His gut churned and the hollow feeling, that was as much a part of him as his brain and blood, felt enormous and cavernous. He stopped dead in the room, staring at the photo with a visceral pain tearing through him. He was the sole survivor. When they'd taken that photo, they'd been full of hope. Sofia had been weak—the doctors had been very honest—but Salvador hadn't yet known that there were things in life his money could not buy or could not fix. That there were no guarantees.

Anna-Maria looked like herself before she'd started treatment, lost her hair and so much weight. It was a snapshot of a time before his life had gone to pieces. He moved to the picture and pressed a finger to it, guilt, pain and remorse swirling through him, so he couldn't believe that he was about to enjoy an evening of unbidden pleasures with someone as vital as Harper Lawson.

It was a betrayal in every way. Guilt cut him, but he wrapped it up into a little box and kept it buried deep inside. There would be time to feel those emotions later, time to regret and repent. For the next week, he intended to enjoy Harper, somehow understanding that being with her was essential to give him back his own sense of life, his own vitality. He needed her, he realised. Even when he didn't want to, he needed her desperately, and he wasn't strong enough to fight it—not yet, anyway.

CHAPTER TWELVE

'I COULD STAY like this for ever!' she called over the gentle hush of the water lapping against the side of her head, the feel of it around her body like silk. It took her a moment to hear what she'd said, and the implication of those words, and she flushed to the roots of her hair. She hoped he hadn't heard and, if he had, that he didn't read anything into it.

Kicking to her feet, she stood on the sandy floor of the ocean, looking round to where Salvador had last been. He was closer now, right beside her, his expression difficult to read.

'How about the rest of the week?' he asked with a small smile that seemed relaxed enough, so he obviously hadn't interpreted her benign statement as a plea to stay longer.

Which it hadn't been. Never mind that time was passing way too fast, that they'd been back from Prague for four days now and, every minute, Harper was conscious of how close they were coming to the end of her time on the island.

'Hmm.' She pretended to consider that. 'Okay, deal.'

'Do you have any time off when you return to Chicago?'

Reality thudded against her, the prospects of the flight and return to her normal job things she didn't particularly want to contemplate. She swished her fingertips through the beautiful crystal water. 'I fly in on a Saturday night, so I'll have a day. Why?'

'It's been a busy fortnight. Perhaps you should take some leave.'

She threw him a look. 'I don't want special favours, re-member?'

He lifted his hands in a gesture of surrender. 'I meant the work you've been doing here. Long days...'

'I'm used to long days.'

'Not this long.'

'No,' she agreed, moving to him so she could latch her hands behind his waist. She liked touching him. No, she loved it. Being this close to him was a form of nirvana. 'But I'll be fine. I like to be busy.' She suspected she'd *need* to be busy when she got back, if she had any hope of pushing Salvador from her mind.

'Tell me about your job.' It was a command and, like all of Salvador's commands, it sent a shiver down her spine, a wave of desire that was always inspired by his confidence and strength.

'You've seen my CV, right?' she teased.

'I know your position and title, but I mean, what do you do on a day-to-day basis?'

'Standard executive assistant duties,' she said, feeling less enthusiastic about talking than about feeling the sensuality of the moment with the water, the late-afternoon sun and his body—naked except for a pair of board shorts that she could easily dispose of...

But he was insistent. 'Such as?'

'Complex diary management, travel plans; I sit in on meetings, triage emails—a lot of the stuff I've been doing this week with you, but less of it.'

'Do you read and evaluate reports?'

'No.' Her lips twisted. 'At least, not as part of my job.'

His eyes narrowed almost imperceptibly. 'You do it because you enjoy it?'

'The reports are there. I see them. And I think it's good

for me to be informed about what we're doing, so I can spot any errors.'

'I'll bet,' he said, but his jaw was clenched, his expression showing frustration. She blinked up at him, lifting a hand and brushing some wet hair back from his face.

'What is it, Salvador?'

She wondered if she'd ever stop feeling that thrill when she said his name. It felt somehow elicit.

'You're wasting yourself in a job like that.'

Her heart sped up. 'I told you, I like what I do. I'm good at it.'

'Obviously. But you could be good at anything you pursued.'

'We've discussed this. You know why I'm doing this.'

'For the money.'

'That's why most people work. Probably hard for someone like you to understand.'

'Someone like me?'

'I just mean it's been a long time since you've had to think about paying rent or the fact that hospitals cost a fortune.'

'Having money doesn't make me a moron.'

She smiled at that. 'No.'

'What if I were to give you money?' He asked the question completely deadpan, eyes hooked to hers, so she had no idea if he could read every expression that flooded her mind. He was so astute, and she feared she was like an open book to him.

'You *are* giving me money,' she said slightly unevenly, as she tried to regulate her breathing. 'The bonus I get for taking this role is huge.'

His face bore an expression of impatience. 'You've earned that.'

'Exactly.'

'I'm talking about a gift.'

'You're talking about money you wouldn't have thought to offer were it not for the fact we've been sleeping together.'

'You don't know that.'

'Oh, come on, Salvador! Of course I do.' Exasperation coloured the tone of her voice. 'You wouldn't even know about my mum if it weren't for the fact we became intimate. It's bad enough that we've…been…that this has happened… But if you were to give me money as well?' The colour drained from her face. 'I couldn't live with myself.'

'It would be a gift. No strings attached.'

She fought her wave of anger. It would be so easy for him to do as he was suggesting and transfer a large sum of money to her. He wouldn't even notice the difference in his bank balance. The offer he was making wasn't a big deal—to him. But to Harper it was insulting and hurtful, and she couldn't even understand why she was having such a strong reaction to it, only that she knew she didn't want his money.

'The time we've spent together has been a gift,' she said slowly, earnestly. 'I don't need—or want—anything else from you.'

She knew the matter wasn't over but at least he appeared to let it go for now. 'Except the dress?' he murmured in a voice that was completely different now, light and seductive as he drew her closer to him. 'We've already discussed the fact it's not my size.'

'Okay, I'll keep the dress,' she said, as if under duress. 'If you insist.'

The only problem with the dress was that he couldn't imagine her wearing it to anything other than a date, and suddenly the idea of Harper dating some other man made Salvador's skin crawl. It was an inevitability and, hell, it was none of his business, but he couldn't get the idea of her with some creep out of his head.

* * *

It was all he could think of the next day when he should have been reading contracts his lawyers had sent over for the purchase of the hotels. There was a lot to consider, a lot of liability to wade through, and he should have been focussed one hundred per cent on the words in front of him. Instead, he saw Harper in his mind, and then, when he lifted his head for a moment, right in front of him.

If she was having the same issues, she was doing a much better job of concealing them. Her focus looked genuine. She stared at the screen, moving her fingers over the keys, frowning then typing some more, reaching for the phone, talking to someone with a smile on her face that made his gut twist and roll.

He cursed mentally and returned his gaze to the papers, reading the terms several times without taking them in.

This was impossible.

He moved to the curtains and closed them, boxing himself into his office, but unfortunately not pushing Harper even part way from his mind. Or the fact they had two more nights together.

'This is delicious,' Harper murmured, barely able to taste the lobster the chef had prepared. It was their second-last night together and the knowledge of that kept rushing through her like a drum, over and over. *Two more nights. Two more nights.* In Prague, when she'd thought they might just have one night together, it had seemed like enough. A one-night stand, as heaps of people experimented with.

But, the more time she spent with Salvador, the greedier she was for him, the hungrier for more time, laughs, conversation, sex and everything. She loved being with him, here on this island or travelling. She just loved…this.

Her eyes stung a little and she had the mortifying realisation that she was close to tears…so close. She stabbed a piece of lobster in the creamy sauce and lifted it to her lips, forcing a smile as she finished chewing.

'Tell me about this, Salvador,' she said, command in her voice for a change.

He put down his fork, relaxing in the chair, apparently not surfing any of the emotional currents she was; his expression was perfectly normal. 'The lobster? I know only that it was once in the ocean.'

She pouted. 'I mean, this…' She gestured to the house, then the island and the silhouette of the rainforest that led to the beach. 'How does a man your age come to be so successful?'

'That's a matter of public record. I invested wisely.'

She reached for her wine glass, taking a sip, glad they were talking, because it distracted her mind from the inevitability of her departure, and more than anything she needed to be distracted.

'But with what? I know you're "self-made", because that's part of the company's bio,' she said without thinking, then realised it showed she'd researched him a little. 'It was part of my job application,' she supplied quickly. 'I had to demonstrate knowledge of da Rocha Industries.'

'And here I thought you'd had a burning passion for me all this time,' he responded with a smile. There was silence except for the pleasant song of night birds swooping through the trees, making merry, and then Salvador's deep voice. 'I owe it all to my mother, actually.'

Harper lifted a brow, curious about that. 'In what way?'

'She taught me to manage money well. She also had excellent instincts,' he continued. 'We would discuss investments even when I was just a boy.'

'She came from money?'

He shook his head, eyes glittered with so much pride it blew Harper away when his gaze met hers. 'No. Quite the opposite. My mother was dirt-poor. She worked as a cleaner at a hotel in Rio. The man she conceived me with was in town for a few weeks—on holiday,' Salvador said with a voice mute of emotion. 'She fell in love. He saw an opportunity to have some fun while his wife was at home in Sydney, raising their children.'

Harper's lips parted. It was so like her own experience, she felt an immediate rush of sympathy for his mother. 'I'm very sorry for her. That's an awful feeling.'

'Like you, she had no idea he was married. He didn't choose to enlighten her, and was gone before she realised she was pregnant.'

'Awful.' Harper shook her head sadly.

'She was able to get his number through the hotel records.'

'And?'

Salvador ran a finger down the side of his beer glass, eyes fixed on the drink rather than Harper. 'When she told him about me, he denied that I could possibly be his. He accused her of trying to ruin his life, his marriage, and in order to ensure her silence he offered her a reasonably obscene amount of money in exchange for the signing of a non-disclosure.'

Harper gaped. 'You're kidding! And she loved him?'

'Up until that moment, she thought she did. She hadn't seen what he was truly like. He was a spoiled, entitled son of a very successful Sydney real-estate mogul. He grew up with money at his fingertips and thought he could use it to pay people off.' Salvador shook his head angrily.

'What did your mother do?'

'Took his money.' Salvador's expression showed pride. 'She grew up tough. She knew he'd never change his mind—

he'd never be a father to me, and besides she didn't want him in my life after that. She took the money, signed the damned agreement and she worked her fingers to the bone to make a success of her life. She continued to work as a housekeeper until I was born, by which point she'd bought a couple of apartments that earned her a rental income so she could stay home with me. It snowballed from there.'

'She sounds like an amazing woman.'

'She was.'

'She's gone?'

He sipped his drink. 'She died when I was in my early twenties.'

She reached out and put her hand over his, feeling the reliable hum of connection that came whenever they touched. 'Did you ever reach out to your father?'

'He's not my father.'

She dipped her head in silent concession to that.

'I had no interest in knowing him. Any man who can treat a woman like that…' He shook his head. 'What could I possibly want from him?'

Harper agreed completely, but still she marvelled at Salvador's restraint. 'You must have wanted to…'

'He was never a part of my life. Besides a little DNA, I am nothing to do with him. It is because of his choices, though, that I married.'

Harper's heart stitched painfully. 'Oh?' It was the best she could manage. The existence of his late wife was a matter of fact, and Harper knew it wasn't right to feel jealous of Anna-Maria—but how could she not?

'When Anna-Maria fell pregnant, I had only one choice: to offer to marry her. Unlike the man my mother loved, I wanted to be an active father. To know and love my child every day of their life. I also wanted to support my baby's mother.'

She stared at him as if from a thousand miles away. 'I'm sorry. Did you just say…?'

'Anna-Maria was pregnant.' He spoke quietly, as if repeating words learned by rote. 'We only slept together that once. The pregnancy was a complete surprise.'

Harper could hardly breathe. She'd been so curious about his wife, his marriage, his life before she'd known him, but she hadn't expected any of this. They'd only slept together once…even after they'd married? Her heart rabbited into her chest and she leaned forward unconsciously.

'I offered to marry her immediately. I wanted to raise my child. It was important to me—more important than to most, I suspect—because of the abandonment of the man my mother had dated. But it was more than that. Anna-Maria and I had grown up together. We *knew* each other, loved each other as old, close friends. Marriage made sense.'

Harper nodded sympathetically, her throat too thick to allow the formation of words. He'd loved her…as a friend. She was trying to put the pieces together, to understand.

'She agreed, obviously?'

'Not at first. She hated the idea of feeling that she'd "trapped" me. She knew about my dad, knew why I reacted as I did.'

'I can understand that.' Harper sipped her wine. 'So what happened?'

'I convinced her,' he said. 'Quite quickly. We married a few months later—before Sofia was born.'

She could imagine how persuasive Salvador would be once he set his mind to something. 'What happened to Sofia, Salvador?' She was almost afraid to ask.

He clenched his jaw, leaning back in his chair and looking in the direction of the ocean. The moon was behind a cloud tonight.

'When Anna-Maria went for her three-month scan, they found a mass—she had cancer. The doctors wanted her to have an abortion, to begin treatment immediately—it would have been the only hope for her survival.'

Harper gasped. It was all too sad. 'I can't even imagine how hard that must have been.'

'She refused.' Salvador's voice was like a vice. Harper wanted to tell him they could stop talking about this, but at the same time she felt he needed to say these words, and she owed it to him to listen. 'There was no way she was going to lose our baby.'

'Of course,' Harper murmured.

'No.' Salvador's eyes glittered. 'Not *of course*. I told her we could try again, once she was all better. I told her we could have ten more babies, that she had to survive this, but Anna-Maria refused. She said that when she was gone it would give her comfort to know I had our daughter. And God, Harper, how I admired her strength. She sacrificed *everything* for Sofia. Everything.'

Harper's chest hurt. She felt so much affection for Anna-Maria then, for her goodness and kindness, her loving heart.

'When she was at seven months' gestation, the doctors said it was time to induce labour. The baby was big enough— they'd put her on oxygen and begin treatment immediately. By then, Anna-Maria's cancer was spreading rapidly. She'd felt her baby move, and she wanted to be here for our little girl, as much as I wanted her to be.'

Harper sobbed. She couldn't help it. Salvador didn't seem to notice. He was in the past, reliving memories that must have been truly traumatic.

'When Sofia was born, she was utterly perfect but so tiny. Like a little quail, all dainty and bony. She lived for a week.' He said the last words so matter-of-factly, and that was more devastating than if he'd broken down into floods of tears. 'Anna-Maria got to hold our baby, to love her, but that was all. Just three months later, Anna-Maria died.'

He turned to face Harper then, piercing her with the desperation in his eyes.

'They're buried together, here on the island. This was where Anna-Maria was happiest.'

Harper's chest hurt. She couldn't bear it. Standing, she moved over to Salvador and sat in his lap, clutching his face with her hands as tears streamed down her cheeks. She ached for him, for all he'd gone through and for the pain he'd felt. She didn't know how a person could ever recover from that.

And then, it hit her. He hadn't recovered. He was broken, completely destroyed by the loss of his wife and daughter, by the blows fate had dealt him. That was why he walled himself away on this island, why he wouldn't get involved with anyone else. It wasn't just love for his late wife, it was the fear of losing someone he cared about all over again. Even his father's rejection must have shaped his view on life, on people and the unreliable nature of affection.

She knew then why this mattered so much to her. Why she cared so much.

She loved him.

She loved Salvador da Rocha, and the fact he'd turned his heart to stone through sheer willpower alone would have a lasting impact on Harper's life.

'I wish I could fix this for you,' she said quietly, pressing her forehead to his, needing him to hear that. She wished with all her heart that she knew how to make him whole again… She dropped a hand to his chest, pressing it to his heart, wishing that with touch alone she could do just that.

His response was to tilt his face and capture her lips with his, to kiss her as though he was in free fall and she his only touchstone, and she let him, because they both needed this. They needed each other and the connection that came from making love.

Salvador shifted, as though waking from a dream, but he hadn't been asleep. Rather, he'd been possessed. He'd had a need to take Harper here on the terrace, where any member of staff could have walked out and witnessed them. The urgency had driven his hands, his body, to push aside her underpants beneath her dress, unzip his fly and push into her, taking her, because it was the only way to blot the grief from his mind, to feel human again, rather than a spectre of the losses that had shaped him for years now.

He blinked up at Harper, seeing the way her face was illuminated by the soft lighting of the terrace, her eyes still shimmering with unspent tears, and he felt a piece of him break apart—a piece he'd never get back.

This time with Harper had been beyond words, but it had to end. He was losing himself in her, losing himself *to* her, and the risks were simply too great.

CHAPTER THIRTEEN

THE SUN ROSE in a spectacular show of colour, streaks of orange, pink and purple bursting into the sky. The trees beyond the house were the deepest green, their early-morning noises evocative of newness and renewal. Harper blinked out at the view, her heart skipping a beat because she loved this place, almost as much as she loved the man beside her.

Only Salvador wasn't beside her, she realised, reaching out and feeling the empty bed sheets, which were cool to the touch. He'd been gone a while.

Her heart made another strange twist, a jerk in her chest, but she told herself not to panic.

She was feeling uneasy because it was her last full day here. One more night and she'd fly back to the mainland, and then onto Chicago, and all this would be a distant memory. A whole host of them, in fact, memories she would hold close to her heart for ever.

But what if you didn't go?

She paused midway through pushing out of bed and stared at the wall opposite which was creamy white with a huge painting of a floral arrangement in the style of the Dutch masters.

What was the alternative to going? Staying with Salvador? Her heart was pummelling her now, racing hard and fast. She *couldn't* just stay here with him. She had no idea how he'd feel about that. He'd never once expressed any interest in having her stay longer. He hadn't suggested it, hadn't asked—they'd both acknowledged her impending leaving date time and time again.

And did Harper really want to stay? What would happen then? Wouldn't it just be kicking the can down the road to remain on the island for another few nights, a week, two weeks, however long they agreed they needed before they'd be ready for her to leave? The problem with that was that Harper didn't think she'd ever be ready to leave him. She pressed the back of her hand to her mouth, smothering a sharp cry drawn from the very pit of her stomach.

If she asked to stay, it would be because she wanted to stay for ever. And if he said no she would never recover.

But what if he says yes?

She groaned, tears of frustration and uncertainty blinking on her lashes. She loved him, and the thought of rejection was terrifying, but wouldn't she always regret not having that conversation? If she were to return to Chicago and go on with her life—as half a person, really, because she'd left so much of herself here with Salvador—she'd always wonder what might have been, if only she'd been brave enough to speak up about how she felt.

And what if he does say yes?

And so she'd stay, and her heart would belong to him, more fully than her mother's heart had ever belonged to anyone, more than Harper had ever given herself to Peter. Wasn't there a terrifying risk in that? A risk of pain and hurt of a level capable of ripping her to shreds… And yet, there was no alternative.

Harper was a risk-taker by nature, an adrenaline junkie who knew that the sheer moments of fear one experienced when jumping out of a plane or off the side of a bridge were nothing to the feeling of having done it—and survived.

She would survive this. Whatever happened, she'd be okay,

but she had to take the leap, to know she'd at least reached for what she wanted with both hands, even if it didn't work out.

'There you are,' she murmured half an hour later, when she walked onto the terrace to find Salvador sitting with a cup of black coffee and a tablet in front of him with the newspaper on it.

He turned slowly, as if reading something he couldn't quite tear his eyes away from, but there was something in the gesture that didn't quite ring true for Harper. He was avoiding her. Or steeling himself to see her?

The sun was higher now, the sky blue with just a few streaks of morning colour remaining. She moved to the seat opposite but didn't sit down, instead pressing her hands to the back of it and eyeing him a little warily, her stomach in knots as she geared herself up for the most important conversation of her life.

'You left early.'

He made a noise of agreement, eyes piercing hers. If she was wary, he was even more so, but it was an insight into his emotions that only lasted a moment. He controlled his features far more easily than Harper, shielding his feelings from her, his face a mask of impassive politeness.

Her heart dropped to her toes. It was a feeling she was familiar with—the fear before the jump. The doubt, the very natural questioning of one's wisdom.

'I couldn't sleep and didn't want to wake you.'

'I wouldn't have minded being woken,' she murmured, a half-smile flickering across her lips. She suspected this wasn't going to go well when we he frowned in response.

He was sitting where he had been last night, when he'd told her about his wife, his daughter and his father, so much loss, rejection and pain. But, whereas last night he'd opened up to her and she'd seen so deep inside his soul, now he was like a boulder, immovable and strong—and impenetrable too, she feared.

'Would you like some coffee?' He gestured to the pot. There was no second cup but either of them could have retrieved one easily. While Harper would have loved something to do with her hands, she couldn't have eaten or drunk anything. Her nerves were rioting, her insides completely tangled.

'I'm fine,' she demurred, wondering when she'd ever felt less fine. It was unusual to be out here. Generally, they both went into the office first thing. But this morning, their last full day together on the island, even the air seemed changed.

She closed her eyes, just as she did when psyching herself into a jump. 'Can we talk?'

She could barely look at him.

'Aren't we talking?'

This was going to go down like a lead balloon. But when she remembered the last two weeks—the way he'd pushed her away even as he'd drawn her closer, when he'd tried so hard to fight what was happening between them—she saw this as yet another last-ditch attempt by him to exert some kind of control over what was happening between them.

'About us.' She forced herself to meet and hold his gaze even when she felt as though she could pass out from the anxiety of having this conversation. No, not of having the conversation, but of what could go wrong.

'Us?'

Her heart skidded to a stop. It was only by reminding herself that he had form for this—for running away from their relationship when things got real—that she was able to push on and be brave.

'Yes, us. You and me, and what's been happening between us.'

He stared at her without reacting. She gripped the chair

back more tightly, so tightly that her fingers burned and her knuckles showed white.

'This was always meant to be temporary,' she said, mentally approaching the edge of the plane, looking out at the vastness of open air, then down to the ground, her stomach looping as she imagined the feeling of pushing both feet from the security of the flight deck.

'You leave tomorrow,' he pointed out, voice unmoving.

'Yes. I think we both took some kind of assurance from the end date we've been moving towards. It saved us from having to have any conversations about what we wanted, about when and how and why this would end.'

A slight frown shifted his lips.

'Haven't we discussed that?'

She ignored the question. He was pushing hard. She should have expected it. Even knowing *why* he was like this didn't soften the feelings of hurt. She inhaled and exhaled, her breath a little shaky.

'I think that what we have is really good, Salvador.' She cleared her throat, eyes stinging, but she refused to give in to tears. 'I don't want it to end yet.'

She saw his response. Something shifted in the depths of his eyes, and his throat moved as he swallowed, but he didn't speak. Not at first. He was pulling his thoughts together, sifting through what he felt and wanted, and what he wanted to say.

'You're leaving in the morning,' he pointed out again with the appearance of calm.

'But what if I didn't?' she asked with more urgency, because he was making this so damned hard. If he was going to reject her, she wanted to just rip the plaster off now. She came round to him, putting a hand on his shoulder to draw his attention up to her face. He hesitated and then looked into her eyes. She shivered, because he was holding onto his will-power with the strength of a thousand men.

'What if you didn't what, Harper?'

'Leave. Tomorrow.' She moistened her lower lip then continued, even as she was pretty sure what was going to happen. 'What if I stayed here with you?'

He stood abruptly, placing his coffee on the table, the sudden movement an indication that he *was* feeling something in response to this conversation.

'For how long?' he asked, the words reverberating with barely contained anger.

She closed her eyes against the wave of pain. 'I don't know.' It was an honest response. 'For as long as it felt right.' Harper knew for her that would be for the rest of her life, but she was too scared to admit as much now.

'But that's the problem,' he said slowly, eyes like stone when they met hers, none of the golden light shining for her. 'This doesn't feel right to me. It's everything I swore I didn't want.'

'Which is what?' she asked, trying to ignore her own pain and sadness to concentrate on the logic of his statement. 'Utterly alone?'

He compressed his lips. 'You knew this about me.'

'Yes,' she agreed unevenly. 'But then there was Prague.' She frowned, shaking her head. 'That's not right. It was before Prague. It was the first moment we met. You felt it too, I know you did, and it only got more and more obvious the more time we spent together.'

'Felt what?'

She reached across and pressed her hand to his heart. 'This connection.' She blinked up at him, so much hope in her face.

'Desire?' he countered. 'Is it any wonder? I've been celibate for two years. Since that one damned night with Anna-

Maria. And then you arrived, so willing, and naturally I responded. Don't mistake sex for anything more.'

She gasped. He'd said something like this before, but now it cut her deep to her soul. She tried to hold onto her certainty that he was pushing her away because he couldn't cope with the things he felt, the emotions coursing through his veins. But at some point she had to hear his words and realise that, whatever reason he had for issuing them, he was a grown man capable of conveying what he wanted to convey. And, right now, that was a huge, 'no thanks' to Harper's suggestion.

She pulled her hand away, spinning so she could regain her breath and mind and control the tears that were making her throat sting.

'Just to be clear,' she said unevenly—because she knew she'd need to recall this later when she was wondering if there was more she could have said or done, if maybe she'd misunderstood him. 'You're saying that what we shared was nothing special. That, if any other woman you were halfway attracted to had been here on Ilha do Sonhos with you, you'd have slept with them, because it's been so long since you've had sex. That's what I was to you?'

She couldn't look at him. She couldn't turn, so didn't see the way his features tightened, the way he recoiled a little at her words.

'It was sex,' he said finally. 'Great sex. But I was clear with you all along, and no amount of sex is going to change who I am.'

Sex. Just sex. *Great sex,* she thought with an angry tilt of her lips, tears sparkling on her lashes.

'Okay,' she said after a pause. 'Good to know.'

Harper could have changed her flight—she had the ability to make all the arrangements herself—but leaving work, even one day early, was something her pride wouldn't allow her to do. So she sat at her desk and went through the long list of things she'd wanted to check before Amanda's return the following day, ensuring she left clear notes of what she'd done and why, explaining anything that was still to be resolved.

It was painstaking work, because her mind was in shards, and because Salvador sat in the office next door, near but so far. Because he could see her and she refused to allow him to know how much she was hurting, so she worked without a break, without looking up from her computer screen. But as the day drew on and she recognised the end was in sight, that she'd almost got through the long list of jobs on her list, she knew she couldn't stay on this island a moment longer than was professionally necessary.

She was meant to fly out the following morning, but there was no point in remaining for one extra night. With a huge lump in her throat, she opened the travel-booking browser and put in a request for a change of flight—from Rio that evening with the same helicopter pilot booked to return her who'd flown her over to the island. Once she had the confirmation email, she knew it was the right decision.

He didn't want her to stay.

He didn't see any value in what they'd shared beyond great sex. One more night wasn't going to change anything.

She ploughed through her work, completing everything, tidying her desk, aware that Salvador could be watching her at all times, so being very careful to keep her expression neutral before she moved to the area that joined their offices.

She thought about leaving without saying goodbye, without explanation. Technically, she'd completed her contract, what she'd been hired to do. But, while he'd been comfortable reducing their relationship to something simple and one-dimensional, Harper knew that what they'd shared deserved more from her.

Changing direction, she moved to his door and knocked

once. He took a few seconds to stop what he was doing and look up. She ground her teeth and didn't enter his office— too much his space, with his masculine fragrance. She realised that she'd never been in his bedroom, and wondered why she hadn't questioned that. It was yet another example of Salvador keeping a part of himself separate from her, walled off, showing her she didn't mean enough to get all of him.

Whereas she would have given him her soul.

'I just wanted to let you know that I'm leaving in an hour.'

Whatever response he would have made, he concealed too quickly for her to comprehend. Silence prickled her skin, stretching for several moments before he nodded once. 'That's fine.'

She glared at him. 'I wasn't asking for your permission.'

More silence, throbbing now—angry, hurt. She hated that she felt like this. She hated that she'd let another man do this to her. Digging her nails into her palm, she knew she had to hold on to her temper, her rage and her hurt, until she was off the island. Her pride wouldn't allow her to show how badly he'd affected her.

'What do you want me to say, Harper?' he said, his mouth a grim line. 'That I'm sorry? I am. I didn't mean for you to get hurt. I truly thought you understood me, and what I could offer. We both knew you would leave and that would be the end of it.'

She looked away from him, turning her face to profile. He was like a different person. She didn't recognise this Salvador, but maybe that was her mistake. He was renowned for his toughness and strength. She'd even heard him described as ruthless before, but Harper had discounted that once she'd come to know him. But maybe she hadn't really known him at all. Maybe she'd been wrong about him all along, just as with Peter. She was a naïve, trusting fool.

The bottom seemed to be falling out of her world. She had to get the hell out of there.

'I don't think I understood you before, but I do now,' she said with a quiet strength that would form the backbone of Salvador's nightmares for many nights to follow. She took a moment to settle her rioting emotions, so she could speak without a wobbling voice. 'I've left detailed instructions for Amanda. There shouldn't be any issues, but naturally she can call me with whatever she needs.' She hesitated for a beat. 'Goodbye.'

'Goodbye' had such finality.

Goodbye was an ending. A permanent sunset. Not a reprieve, not a temporary farewell.

Just as he wanted, he reminded himself, watching the clock on his computer counting down the hour, knowing he wouldn't be able to breathe properly until he'd heard the helicopter leave and knew she was gone.

Every minute until then was filled with indecision, an uncharacteristic doubt permeating every cell in his body.

How could he let her go?

How could he let her stay?

He felt as if he'd been felled at the knees. After forty-five minutes, he gave up staring at the time and closed his laptop, instead moving to the expansive windows of his office, staring out at the view of the hills, the forest, the dazzling ocean in the distance and far beyond that Rio... Salvador's eyes hunted reprieve and peace, when there was none available to him.

What he needed was to obliterate his senses. Not to think, not to feel, not to imagine Harper packing her bag, tidying her room, boarding a helicopter and preparing to leave.

With a gruff sound, he pushed the chair against his desk

and stalked out of his office. There was only one place he could be right now, and it sure as hell wasn't here.

She'd half-expected, hoped, he'd come after her. There was no way he'd let her walk away like this. Not after what they'd shared. Not after what they'd meant to each other.

And they *did* mean something to each other; she knew they did. She hadn't imagined their connection. This was real and it was true, but one person couldn't love another enough to make a relationship work. Taking one last look back at the house, high up on the hill away from civilisation and the coastline, Harper boarded the helicopter. It was identical to the one that had brought her here two weeks ago, when she'd been filled with a rush of adrenaline at the challenge that lay ahead. She couldn't have known that being here would fundamentally change who she was inside.

The sun was setting as Harper lifted off the island, the colours stunning, striking, as the morning had been. So she thought about that—the way these displays book-ended life here on the island—and tears that she'd been fighting all day finally began to fall down her cheeks. Were they book-ends? Or signs of perennial hope? The sun would set and night would follow, dark and long, but always there'd be morning, a glow streaking across the sky offering a renewal. Was it always the case that day followed night? Hope followed darkness? Or could some nights be so long and so permeating that there was no escape from them, even when morning came?

Harper was about to find out.

CHAPTER FOURTEEN

THE WAVES CRASHED down on Salvador, hard and angrily, just as he'd wanted, here on the southern tip of the island where the ocean buffeted it hard. He'd wanted to drown out everything, but especially the sound of the helicopter leaving. But at the same time his ears were subconsciously straining to hear it, so he turned and saw it as it left the pad, lifting up with blades flapping, taking its sole passenger, Harper, away from Ilha do Sonhos, away from Salvador, away for ever.

It was what he'd wanted. What he'd known was necessary.

A wave pummelled him and Salvador was glad. After all he'd been through, all he'd lost, it was in that moment he truly felt he'd hit rock bottom.

Salvador took an extra interest in Harper's department after that. It was an obsession that he fully recognised was a little sick. After all, she'd offered to stay here with him, where he could have had his fill of her, held her, laughed with her, watched her working and walked with her. But he'd sent her away, unequivocally shutting down any prospect of a relationship, of a future, of anything beyond what they'd shared.

It was sex.

He shuddered, remembering the way Harper had recoiled and the light in her eyes had dimmed, the pain of his brutal appraisal rocking her to her core.

He'd sent her away when she would have stayed, so it made no sense that now he pored over reports from her department, looking for signs of her handiwork and seeing very little. Frustration twisted through him. Why was she being so under-utilised within the company? She'd gone toe to toe with Salvador, working at his pace, totally his equal in every way. There was so much more she could be doing than juggling someone's diary.

Okay, he knew her job was more complicated than that, but it was obvious that she'd settled for a job she could do standing on her head because it paid well.

Her financial needs had him sitting up straighter. When she'd spoken of her mother, he'd felt the fierceness of her love. But, apart from a mother who lay in a nursing home, who did Harper have?

Salvador had been so focussed on his own solitary life that he hadn't stopped to think about Harper. About how she'd also lost the people she loved.

And now Salvador had added to that burden. He was someone else who'd hurt her and left her. Someone else who'd done the wrong thing by her, taking what he wanted while it had suited him then pushing her away because he didn't want to fight for something that might end up destroying him.

He swore, standing, dragging frantic hands through his hair, needing to escape Harper properly but knowing he couldn't. In the three weeks since she'd left, he'd travelled widely and she'd followed him. She was a fixture in his mind all the time.

How could he ever escape her? And did he really want to?

Harper had it down pat now. At first, she'd struggled big time. But after three weeks she knew how to go through the motions adequately enough to fool everyone into thinking she was okay. The trick was to perfectly emulate how she'd been before.

She caught the same train, she wore the same clothes, packed the same lunch, made the same meaningless conversations, walked the same way, called or went to see her mum at the same time as usual. She held the act together just until she walked in her front door each night and could finally give into her state of grief.

It wasn't that her heart was broken. That was too simple. Her heart was in a permanent state of breakage, each breath hurting it more and more, each memory like a fresh blade to her flesh, so she was in literal pain all day, all night—all the time. She couldn't exist without thinking of Salvador, without missing him, and that had become a part of her, stitched into her being. But after three weeks she'd learned to fake it adequately enough so that she could walk through her day without anyone else knowing that she'd gone to Ilha do Sonhos and come back into a living nightmare.

It was the middle of the night when he woke, disturbed by fragments of dreams that shook him up and threw him into a strange, warped past so he couldn't quite piece together what was real and what was a memory.

His mother was there, in a white linen dress, her long, dark hair coiled in a bun at her nape, a caipirinha in her hand and a smile on her face as the sun dipped towards the blanket of the ocean, dragging night in its wake.

'Ilha do Sonhos—Isle of Dreams. Don't you think it's appropriate, *mei filho*?'

Salvador was a twenty-year-old again, arrogant and full of determination to make his mark, to prove to his father, who he never intended to meet, what a mistake he'd made in not wanting Salvador.

'It's a beautiful place.'

'But the dreams.' Her smile was mystical. 'Here, on this island, I feel like anything is possible. Don't you see it? Don't you feel it?'

'I feel warm.' He shrugged.

'No, Salvador. You're not doing it properly. Close your eyes.'

He refused at first, but his mother insisted.

'See?' she asked, her voice lyrical and light.

'No.'

'There's magic here. It's in the air as you breathe, it's in the forest and the waves. And it's in the setting of the sun and the stirring of the new day. This island is a gift. Never forget that.'

'It's an island.' He laughed.

'But here, it's a reminder that all things are possible. Look around us now. Look at this. How can you see this beauty and doubt the truth of that?'

Back in his bedroom now, sheets tangled as evidence of a disrupted night's sleep, his heart was racing. That had just been one fragment of his dream, though. Anna-Maria had been there too, as she'd been towards the end, on the last visit they'd made to Sofia's grave. She'd been so beautiful and ethereal, as though she'd been halfway to assuming an angel's form.

'You have to live for us, Salvador.' She took his hand in hers, fingers so fine he wanted to cry. 'There is no meaning to her death, or mine, unless you give it to us. I don't mean by naming a library after me, or building a statue here in this garden,' she teased, then paused to cough, because she was faint of breath all the time.

Salvador waited patiently, not asking if she was okay, be-cause she hated that. Instead, he pressed a hand reassuringly to her back, wincing as he felt her spine through the fabric of her clothes, knowing she had a very limited number of breaths left to draw—this woman who'd once been a girl he'd run with until their lungs had burned and their cheeks had been flame-red, who'd once been as vital and real as the nights were dark.

'Every day, you have to do something for me. Live your life in a way I would be proud of. Make decisions that prove you're alive, because I won't be. And she never really got to be.' A tear slid down Anna-Maria's cheek and Salvador wanted the world to open up and swallow him into the pits of its lava-filled belly. 'You owe it to us.'

He wiped his forehead now, which was covered in perspiration, then pushed back the sheets, planting both feet over the edge of the bed and leaning forward, elbows braced on his knees and his head cradled in his palms.

Because Harper had been there too.

He dreamed of her as she'd been on that last morning. Not of the words she'd said, but the smile she'd offered when she'd first arrived. It was a smile that had haunted him, over and over, and now he understood, finally, why that was.

Her smile had been like a sunrise. A beautiful, hope-filled, promise-laden, glorious gift, reassuring and bright after the longest night of his life, a grief-soaked slumber from which he thought he'd never stir. Ilha do Sonhos—Isle of Dreams. Magic was everywhere and anything was possible.

He'd already failed the two most important women in his life—his mother and Anna-Maria—by failing to abide by his promises to them.

And now, he'd done exactly the same thing to Harper. Because he had made her a promise, he realised, lifting his face and looking towards the window, surprise changing his features. He'd never told her loved her, but surely he'd shown her with every conversation, with the way he'd tried to push her away but had instead ended up pulling her closer again and again?

He'd made her a thousand little promises every moment that she'd been here and then he'd rejected her because he'd been terrified of what allowing her to stay would mean. How could he have let her stay when that would have meant opening the door to a world that would contain so many risks…? But what was the alternative?

He cursed as he stood, striding across his room with renewed purpose and dressing swiftly.

It wasn't just about a promise to Harper, though. It was about how he felt and what he wanted. It was about pushing through the fear of losing her because every day he had with her would be a gift and he was willing to go through any eventual pain for just one more day, one more kiss. For a little bit of hope and that sunrise smile of hers…if she'd offer it to him again.

'Harper, would you get the boardroom ready?'

Midway through replying to an email, she paused what she was doing to look at her boss, Jack Wotton, as he propped an arm against the door to her office.

'Sure thing. Meeting?'

'Unexpected, but yes.' He looked a little nervous, which was definitely out of character.

'What's the problem?' Harper asked, just wanting to be home. She was tired. Tired of pretending to be fine, tired of pretending she was okay when she absolutely wasn't. It was Friday and she had two days of blissful alone time ahead when she could switch off and stop pretending. When she could wallow in her sadness and loneliness and not have to pretend for anyone else.

'No problem. I hope.' Jack's brow was furrowed.

'Jack?'

'It's Salvador da Rocha. He's coming here. I'm sure everything's just at it should be. I just wish I knew what it was about.'

Harper jerked so hard she whacked her knee into the side of her desk and the breath in her lungs burned as she exhaled.

'When?' The word shot from her lips with panicked urgency.

'Half an hour.'

She looked at her watch. It was almost five. 'Jack, I have an appointment,' she lied, grabbing her bag and placing it on her desk. 'I'll set up the conference room but then I have to go straight away. Do you mind?'

'I'd prefer you stayed and took minutes—'

The very idea made Harper's insides squelch in pain. Seeing Salvador, sharing a room with him…?

She shook her head emphatically, swallowing and reaching for her phone. 'I'll ask David to do it. He owes me a favour.' Then she said reassuringly to Jack, because wild horses wouldn't make her stay in this building a moment longer, 'He's very good, don't worry. Everything will be fine.'

The final reassurance, she added for her own benefit. *Everything will be fine. Everything will be fine.* So long as she got the hell out of there.

But in the end it took longer than expected to set up the meeting room, courtesy of the previous occupants having left coffee cups and old papers lying around. Harper worked as quickly as she could, all the while conscious of the ticking of time and her desperate need to escape. Finally, with only minutes to spare, she finished and zipped into Jack's office.

'I have to go,' she said breathlessly, pulling her bag over her shoulder. 'Good luck.'

'Thanks.' He didn't look up and Harper was glad. She couldn't imagine how pale her face would have looked if he'd given her a moment's thought. She needed to escape: now.

CHAPTER FIFTEEN

SALVADOR HAD NEVER particularly liked the way he was treated when he travelled to his offices. As the head of a billion-dollar company that employed tens of thousands of people worldwide, he understood it a little, but being deified wasn't his idea of a good time, so he avoided this sort of thing as much as possible.

Meetings could be done offsite or online.

But this wasn't really about a meeting, so much as a chance to see Harper on her terms. To *see her*, he thought with a clutch in his chest. Though how the hell he could see her without reaching for her, without kissing her senseless, without blurting out everything he'd realised since she'd left the island, was beyond him.

His hands formed fists at his side as the lift whooshed towards the executive level of his Chicago high-rise. Blessedly, he was alone. He needed the few moments to steel himself for this, for seeing her at her desk, just as she'd been on the island for so much of the time.

What he wasn't prepared for was the doors opening directly into the foyer and Harper standing waiting for a lift. She was looking at the numbers on the top of the panel, so he had a few seconds to study her before her gaze swooped down, a few seconds to see how pale she was, how pinched were her features, how dark were her eyes. And in those few

seconds he died a slow and torturous death, because he understood why she looked like that—he was the cause.

It was because of him.

Unless something else had happened. Something with her
mother? Worry pushed aside his own feelings for a moment,
and then her eyes met his and once more he understood. This
was because of him. Nothing else could explain the jolt of
emotions that flooded her face as comprehension dawned
and she recognised him.

She looked like a terrified animal, haunted and hunted,
and he groaned, pain stabbing his side.

'Harper...' He held up a placating hand but she could only
shake her head, her lips moving without making sound, her
fingers trembling as she lifted one hand to her handbag strap
and yanked on it hard. It was excruciating to see her react
like this, but this was Harper Lawson—she was made of
steel—so she closed her eyes and, when she opened them
again, she looked more like herself. The shock was gone, or
at least concealed behind a look of bored impatience.

'Jack's waiting for you,' she said crisply, gesturing to the
foyer.

Salvador swallowed. The meeting had essentially just been
a ruse to get close to Harper again, but he stepped out of the
lift, noticing the way she moved away from him and took
a circuitous route to the cubicle he'd just occupied, jabbing
the button for the ground-floor lobby impatiently, her face
pale once more, her eyes showing shock. He stared at her and
imagined the doors closing, imagined her disappearing, and
realised he didn't know where she lived and he didn't have
her mobile number. He had only her work email address,
which was a pretty inadequate way to contact someone about
a personal matter.

Just as the doors began to close, he made a split-second

decision and slipped through them, eyes meeting hers, challenging her to say something, his expression carefully contained so she wouldn't know just how terrified he was of the next few moments.

'Mr da Rocha,' she said sternly, but the impression was hampered by the fact her voice trembled slightly. 'Jack is waiting for you. You should go.'

He couldn't relax until the lift doors closed. He figured he had maybe thirty seconds to say what he wanted to say before they reached the ground floor. Harper closed her eyes, blocking him out.

Thirty seconds would never be enough.

'I came here to see you.'

It wasn't the most elegant place to start but it was something.

Her jaw worked overtime as she computed that, swallowing and feeling without emoting anything.

'I should never have spoken to you the way I did on that last day. What we shared was...'

The lift slowed, stopped and the doors pinged open, admitting four more people, talking and laughing until they saw Salvador da Rocha, and then they were silent, awestruck. He glared at them mutinously—did they have any idea what they'd just interrupted? His eyes shifted to Harper but she was looking ahead resolutely, staring at the metallic underbelly of the doors as if she could will the carriage to the ground faster, if only she concentrated hard enough.

The lift reached the foyer without making any additional stops and Harper stepped out in front of him, walking quickly across the tiled entrance. He walked after her, ignoring the looks people sent him, ignoring anyone who came close to thinking they might start a conversation.

She said goodnight to the security guards then pushed

through the swirling glass doors, so he followed in a vacant space behind her. Only once they were in the cold night air—so frigid compared to the island—did Salvador call her name.

Harper didn't turn. The pavement was bustling with people leaving the office, beginning their commutes home. Frustrated, and terrified of losing her now he was so close to her, he reached out, catching her wrist and pulling her to a stop. She didn't fight him. She paused, an island in the midst of the swirling sea of people. But he had to tug on her wrist again to get her to turn to him and, when she did, it felt as if every part of him was cracking apart.

Tears filmed her lashes and she just looked so inconsolably sad, so awfully hurt, that he groaned.

'I'm sorry.' He said the only thing he could think of in that moment, and it was an apology that was dredged from the very bottom of his soul. 'I had no right to talk to you the way I did. Nothing I said that day was true, Harper. You know that. You know that in here.' He pressed a hand to his own heart, remembering how she'd touched him there and he'd felt as though they were connected on a cellular level.

She blinked quickly, trying to look in control, but she couldn't, so she gave up. 'Let me go.'

God, he knew he should. He knew he had no right to hold her like this, to keep her here, but he couldn't risk losing her. 'Will you come with me?' he asked urgently, wiping his thumb over her inner wrist.

'No.'

He was losing her. Maybe he'd already lost her. And didn't he deserve that? Salvador had always excelled at everything he attempted. Being naturally good at things was Salvador's gift in life, so was it any surprise that in trying to push Harper away he'd well and truly succeeded?

'We need to have a conversation,' he said, looking around

and scanning the street. 'Will you at least step this way so we're out of the flow of people?' he asked, nodding towards an alleyway.

She looked from him to the alley and then, with an exasperated sigh, said, 'Jack is waiting for you.'

'To hell with Jack, I came here to see you.'

She ground her teeth. 'Well, nonetheless, Jack's up there, cooling his heels, thinking he's got a meeting with the great Salvador da Rocha, so you should go.'

'I'll go,' he agreed after a beat. 'If you'll give me five minutes.'

She opened her mouth then closed it again and then, with obvious consternation, yanked her wrist free and rubbed it before cutting through the crowds towards the entrance to the alleyway. It was hardly the most romantic of settings— the ground was littered with cigarette butts, dull brick walls were covered with faded graffiti and there was the constant hum of passing strangers. But, whatever else had happened, since seeing Harper again everything Salvador had realised on the island had been confirmed.

And now it felt as though fighting for her, for them, was a matter of life and death. Not in the literal, mortal sense, but in the way that he would have no life if he didn't have Harper. He could exist, but that wasn't the same thing as living, as the last year had so clearly showed. It seemed as good a place as any to start.

'When you came to the island, you brought me back to life, Harper. I hadn't realised how shadowed my existence was, or why there was anything wrong with that, until you came and made me feel whole, more whole than I've ever been. You came and it was like a light had been turned on, a pervasive, beautiful light. And, when you left, the opposite happened: all the lights went out and I am anything but whole now. I miss you so much.'

Her face was impossible to read, but he knew enough to know his words weren't well received.

'Please don't do this,' she whispered, tortured.

'I know that what I said that last day was incredibly hurtful.'

She made a noise that might have been a withering laugh but it lacked all force.

'I didn't understand then how I felt...'

'Then let me enlighten you,' she said quietly, pulling on her handbag again. 'You seem to like playing this sick little game with me—pushing me away, then pulling me back, pushing me away, pulling me back. That was you pushing me away. This is you trying to pull me back. But I'm not playing any more, Salvador. I'm not playing,' she repeated, the last words wobbly, tears falling from her eyes freely now. She dashed them away angrily and he could only stare. Her accusation was both fair and so damaging, because he hated himself then.

'I didn't want to feel this way about you.'

She tilted her face away, looking out of the alley towards the passing hoards.

'And you're right. But it wasn't a game, Harper. I have wanted you from the first moment I saw you, and loved you for almost as long. I wasn't pushing you away to torment you, but because I was fighting how I felt about you from the first day—only my feelings were so strong, I couldn't conquer them. I could make headway, sometimes, but not for long. You were here...' He pressed his fingers to his heart. 'You live here, in me, in my heart, and you always will.'

She jerked her face back to his, eyes frantic as they scanned his face. He thought for a moment he'd got through to her, but then her face paled and she shook her head.

'You're just raising the stakes now. The ultimate attempt to pull me back: you love me. But no one who's in love could say…could say…'

He groaned, hating himself for the words he'd spoken in his office that day.

'It was torture to say it,' he said. 'I was so angry at myself for loving you when I hadn't been able to love her. I felt like every day with you was a betrayal, every feeling I had for you proof of my failure as a husband. None of that excuses my behaviour, but I just want to explain…'

She swallowed, then lifted her phone from her pocket. 'Jack will be waiting,' she said stiffly. He wasn't just losing her, he'd lost her. It was his worst nightmare come to fruition.

'To hell with Jack,' he said again.

'We had a deal.'

He cursed inwardly, because he was trying to win her back, and reneging on their compromise didn't seem like a good way to do that.

'I love you,' he said quietly, eyes boring into hers in the hope she could see the truth of what he was saying. 'I love you with every single fibre of who I am, with all of me. I'm done fighting it, done running from it. I want, for the rest of my life, to fight for us, to run to you, no matter where I am in this world. I am so in love with you, I cannot imagine a life without you in the centre of it. But if I have to, if you don't love me back, you will still always be the centre of who I am. Even if we're not together, I will love you. It's not a choice, Harper, it's who I am now.'

Another tear slid down her cheek. 'This isn't…it's not about if I love you or not,' she said unevenly. 'It's about whether I can be with you again.'

It was hardly anything—barely the cracking open of the door, a tiny ray of light in the midst of so much darkness—but it was *something*.

'It's about whether I can trust you.' She stared up at him. 'You're not the only one who's been hurt before, Salvador. It was *hard* for me to face how I felt about you and hard for me to come to you that morning and ask to stay.'

'I know, I know.' He couldn't help himself. He reached out, lifting his thumb and wiping away one of her tears, but then he kept his hand there, cocooned against the side of her face.

'And I stayed that whole day because it was my job but, in the back of my mind, I kept telling myself you'd come and apologise, that you'd come and see me, that you'd realise you'd reacted badly...'

'I wanted to. God, I wanted to.'

'But you didn't. And, every minute of that day, a part of me broke off and I don't know if you can ever put it back together. I just don't know. You let me go. You were just like my dad, just like Peter. You showed me that I don't have any value, just like they did.' She bit down on her lower lip and he ached for her, for the way she'd been treated and disrespected all her life.

'You are all that I value in this world,' he said angrily—the anger directed at himself. 'How can I show you that? How can I prove myself to you?'

She was silent, staring at him, lost and bereft. He lifted his free hand to her other cheek, holding her face, gently stroking with his thumbs.

'I love you,' he said, quietly. 'And I'm not going anywhere.'

'You live on an island,' she reminded him unevenly. 'Far, far away from here.'

'I want to live wherever you live,' he said with a lift of his shoulders.

'You can't move to Chicago.' She rolled her eyes.

'Why not?'

She stared at him in total confusion. 'I can't— I don't know if you're serious.'

'Harper, I love you. You *know* I love you. That last morning, when you suggested staying, it was because you understood how I felt, how you felt, and what we needed to do. I reacted terribly, and I will never forgive myself for that, but everything we shared before that, that was real. That's who we are.'

'But it's like I said—it's not about love, it's about choice. I did think you loved me,' she admitted carefully. 'But you chose not to be with me. What if you make that choice again? What if you decide in a week's time that, whether you love me or not, you can't be with me? I can't put the pieces of my life back together every time you decide that you're scared of what we feel for each other.'

'I was scared,' he admitted, and it was a lot for someone like Salvador to face that. He was generally fearless but not when it came to his heart. 'I was terrified of what would happen if I lost you too. Then I did lose you. Not to death, but to life and life choices, things that were completely in my control. I woke up every day and had to face how I felt and what I'd done and I know I could never do that again.

'I have no guarantees in life, Harper. I've seen what can happen, what can be taken from us without notice, or in the most awful ways, but only an absolute fool would pass up the happiness we share when we're together out of fear of what might happen. I don't know that we're going to get the great privilege of living together until we're old and grey, with a dozen grandkids scattered at our feet, but hell, I want to do everything I can to try. Don't you?' he pushed, tilting her face towards his. 'Look into your heart and tell me what you *want*.'

She closed her eyes, shielding herself from him, so he bit back a groan. He waited on tenterhooks, so terrified, knowing everything was riding on her answer.

She was silent so long, he thought he was burning up, and then she opened her eyes, frowning so she had a small divot between her brows.

'I want that,' she said finally, with a hint of surprise in her voice.

He wasn't sure he'd understood. 'You want…?'

'I want you. And me. Old and grey. Lots of grandkids and memories—good and bad, the kinds of memories you collect in a rich life that's well lived. I want to start living, Salvador, just like you said: when we're together, I'm alive. Most alive.' And then, sucking in a deep breath, she nodded slightly. 'I love you.'

They were the best words he'd ever heard. He pressed his forehead to hers, needing to fortify himself for what would come next. Because, when they kissed, it was as if all the pieces of heaven exploded and came back together inside them, all the matter in the universe existed just within them for the moment their lips meshed. To anyone walking past, it might have looked like just a couple sharing a passionate, secret embrace, but to Salvador and Harper it was a promise, as real and bonding as any marriage vows ever could be: they were both in this for real, for ever, because it was just exactly where they were meant to be.

On the twenty-ninth floor of the da Rocha Industries tower on Dearborn Street, Jack Wotton tapped his fingers against the dark wood of his desk, a frown on his face. It was not like da Rocha to be late. The man was renowned for his punctuality. He cast a glance at his watch again. Twenty past five. Where could he be?

Standing, he moved to the coffee machine right as his phone began to trill. He reached back for it, perching on the edge of his desk.

'Wotton? It's Salvador.' The man sounded…happy. Laughing… There was the sound of street noise in the background: people walking, cars, then the closing of a car door. 'Something's come up.' His voice sounded louder, because of the absence of street noise now. He was in his own car, Jack guessed.

'Not a problem, sir. Would you like to reschedule?'

There was a different sound, a little like clothing rustling. 'Yes. I'll call Monday.'

Jack pulled a face. 'Was there something specific you wanted to discuss?'

'Just a general touch-base.' Salvador's voice was muffled now, like his mouth was pressed against something. 'Everything's fine. Have a good weekend.'

Just before Jack disconnected the call, he thought he heard a woman's voice laughing and moaning at the same time. He shrugged his shoulders and abandoned the thought of a coffee, deciding instead to grab a beer on the way home. Everything was fine.

EPILOGUE

IN THE END, they chose sunset, the closing of the day, to mark the beginning of the rest of their lives, with a wedding on the edge of the island. The cove was behind them, water coming closer and closer with each minute that passed, with only a small handful of their dearest friends in attendance and Harper's mother listening online.

It was a perfect wedding, but that didn't matter to Harper. A wedding was just a moment, a single day out of a blanket of days that would form the rest of their lives. And not once, since having agreed to marry Salvador almost a year earlier, had she regretted her agreement for even one moment.

He was her other half in every way.

But he was more than that. He was the wind at her back, always pushing her to chase her own dreams, insisting on paying for her mother's medical care so that Harper could finally pursue her dreams of studying, which she did remotely. They lived on the island at first: Salvador had had a state-of-the-art medical facility built for Harper's mother, a place that had brought comfort to an old woman who smiled now, even when she didn't seem to know who or where she was.

Of course, it wasn't just the island, but soon there was the sound of grandchildren, little babies often brought by Harper to visit their nanny. The twins came first, two boys with their father's shock of dark hair and intelligent eyes.

Then two daughters, born only eighteen months apart, and another daughter five years later, a miracle, surprise baby that neither had been expecting but both welcomed and loved with all their hearts.

Sofia was a part of their family, too. They spoke of Anna-Maria and her often, and took the children to the graves each year to mark their birthdays. It was important for them to understand that their family had begun with a different branch, a long time ago. And, though that branch had not survived, it didn't make it any less nor important to them all.

When Harper's mother passed, they were all sad, but also knew that she'd been set free. The grief of losing her mother was made more bearable because she had Salvador and their children to wrap her in their love, to hold her tight and listen to her stories of a time before the strokes, when her mother had been the be all and end all in Harper's life.

By the time the twins started school, they decided it was more practical to leave the island. They moved to New York then, so Harper could take up a position at a prestigious law firm. Within five years, she'd made partner, and two years after that senior partner. There had never been a prouder husband than Salvador.

They were blessed and they knew it—Salvador especially, after the losses he'd endured.

The da Rocha family travelled back to the island frequently for many, many years, so the place became a part of the fabric of their children's lives, and it was naturally where their oldest daughter chose to be married.

As the sun set on that momentous, beautiful day, and Salvador watched his wife with her silver hair and surrounded by their children—now adults—he couldn't help but smile and reflect on how close he'd come to wasting the precious gift that was his life. How close he'd come to letting Harper leave, because he'd been so scared that he might get hurt.

Instead, he'd been given a second chance, to live his life but also to honour the promises he'd made to his mother and Anna-Maria. Every single day of his life had been spent making the absolute most of that precious, second chance, and it always, always would be.

* * * * *

COMING SOON!

We really hope you enjoyed reading this book. If you're looking for more romance be sure to head to the shops when new books are available on

Thursday 3rd August

To see which titles are coming soon, please visit

millsandboon.co.uk/nextmonth

MILLS & BOON

MILLS & BOON®

Coming next month

INNOCENT'S WEDDING DAY WITH THE ITALIAN
Michelle Smart

"Do you, Enzo Alessandro Beresi, take Rebecca Emily Foley to be your wife?"

He looked her in the eye adoringly and without any hesitation said, "I do."

And now it was her turn.

"Do you, Rebecca Emily Foley, take Enzo Alessandro Beresi…"

She breathed in, looked Enzo straight in the eye and, in the strongest voice she could muster, loud enough for the entire congregation to clearly hear, said, "No. I. Do. Not."

Enzo's head jerked back as if she'd slapped him. A half smile froze on his tanned face, which was now drained of colour. His mouth opened but nothing came out.

The only thing that had kept Rebecca together since she'd opened the package that morning was imagining this moment and inflicting an iota of the pain and humiliation racking her on him. There was none of the satisfaction she'd longed for. The speech she'd prepared in her head died in her choked throat.

Unable to look at him a second longer, she wrenched her hands from his and walked back down the aisle, leaving a stunned silence in her wake.

Continue reading
INNOCENT'S WEDDING DAY WITH THE ITALIAN
Michelle Smart

Available next month
www.millsandboon.co.uk

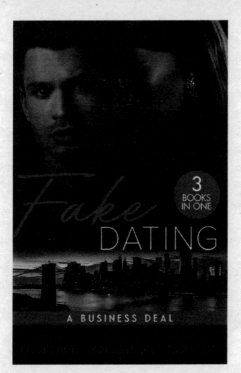

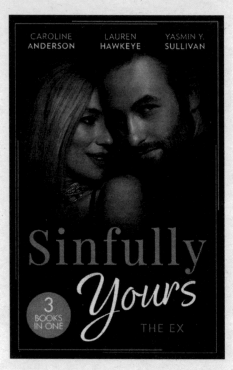

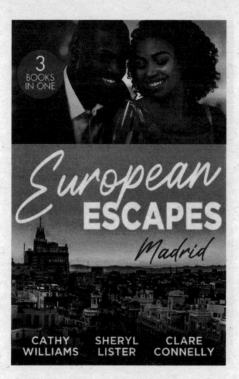

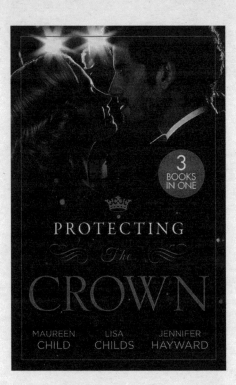

LET'S TALK

Romance

For exclusive extracts, competitions and special offers, find us online:

 MillsandBoon

 @MillsandBoon

 @MillsandBoonUK

 @MillsandBoonUK

Get in touch on 01413 063 232

For all the latest titles coming soon, visit
millsandboon.co.uk/nextmonth

MILLS & BOON

THE HEART OF ROMANCE

A ROMANCE FOR EVERY READER

MODERN
Prepare to be swept off your feet by sophisticated, sexy and seductive heroes, in some of the world's most glamourous and romantic locations, where power and passion collide.

HISTORICAL
Escape with historical heroes from time gone by. Whether your passion is for wicked Regency Rakes, muscled Vikings or rugged Highlanders, awaken the romance of the past.

MEDICAL
Set your pulse racing with dedicated, delectable doctors in the high-pressure world of medicine, where emotions run high and passion, comfort and love are the best medicine.

True Love
Celebrate true love with tender stories of heartfelt romance, from the rush of falling in love to the joy a new baby can bring, and a focus on the emotional heart of a relationship.

Desire
Indulge in secrets and scandal, intense drama and sizzling hot action with heroes who have it all: wealth, status, good looks…everything but the right woman.

HEROES
The excitement of a gripping thriller, with intense romance at its heart. Resourceful, true-to-life women and strong, fearless men face danger and desire - a killer combination!

To see which titles are coming soon, please visit

millsandboon.co.uk/nextmonth